D0962539

STRANGE DAYS

STRANGE DAYS

CONSTANTINE
SINGER

Tom,

I can't ever thank you
enough for being like you are.

It is such an honour to have done

this with you!

Love,

G. P. PUTNAM'S SONS

G. P. PUTNAM'S SONS
an imprint of Penguin Random House LLC
375 Hudson Street
New York, NY 10014

Library of Congress Cataloging-in-Publication Data
Names: Singer, Constantine, author.
Title: Strange days / Constantine Singer.
Description: New York, NY : G. P. Putnam's Sons, [2018]
Summary: "When inexplicable events begin to occur, Los Angeles native Alex Mata uses his special ability of time travel to save the world from alien invasion"—Provided by publisher.
Identifiers: LCCN 2017061063 (print) | LCCN 2018006763 (ebook)
ISBN 9781524740252 (ebook) | ISBN 9781524740245 (hardcover)
Subjects: | CYAC: Science fiction. | Time travel—Fiction.
Extraterrestrial beings—Fiction.
Classification: LCC PZ7.1.S567 (ebook)
LCC PZ7.1.S567 Ne 2018 (print) | DDC [Fic]—dc23
LC record available at https://lccn.loc.gov/2017061063

Printed in the United States of America.
ISBN 9781524740245
1 3 5 7 9 10 8 6 4 2

Design by Dave Kopka. Text set in News Plantin MT Pro.

For my wife, Ariadne, and my daughter, Kizziah.
Also for all my students like Emilio who are
always looking for something good to read.

One

THE TAMALE LADY COMES AROUND THE FRONT OF THE SCHOOL EARLY ON Mondays, so Zeon and Big Schmo are already in line at her cart when I walk up.

Zeon nods when he sees me. Coughs, "T'sup Plugz."

"T'sup." I fall in line behind Schmo, watch as the lady pulls dollars out of people's grips with one hand while grabbing tamales from her thermos box with tongs in her other. She says something in Spanish to a kid in front of me and then she smiles wide enough to show her teeth.

The kid says something back to her and then she says something else and everybody laughs, including the kid, but my Spanish sucks so I don't get the joke.

"You get any of that?" Zeon asks me quietly.

I turn back to him, give him a small shrug. "Yeah."

He smiles like he doesn't believe me. "She just burned him to the ground, Pocho."

Pocho's not my name or anything, it's just a word for people like me who don't know Spanish. Zeon's been translating for me since we were in grade school and he gets tired of it. I move my head a little. "I heard her."

Zeon looks at me weird, but drops it when Fizzin comes up behind us, grabbing my shoulder. "You got me on this, bro?" Fizzin never has any money.

I only have a couple dollars, so I shake my head.

He turns and looks at Zeon, who nods, reaches into his pocket for some bills, and hands them to Fizzin. Zeon's hair whips back when he turns, giving a flash of his ear. His pod doesn't look normal—it's small and matches the color of his skin.

Somebody's playing a guitar nearby, picking at the strings.

"You hear that?"

Nobody says anything. Nobody else seems to notice, so I ignore it too, and point at Zeon's ear. "You got Live-Tech?" I've never seen one in real life, but Tony Baez has been bumping them endlessly on his channel. The size and color-blending are giveaways.

The Tamale Lady looks at us. We tell her what we want and she collects our money before handing us our tamales. We take them and step back across the street into the shade from the big apartment building.

When we're situated, I reach out for Zeon's ear with my free hand so I can pull his hair back.

He lets me, tilting his head so it's easy to see. "Gotta be prepared for Incursions."

Incursions. I can feel my jaw go stiff, so I force myself to open my mouth and take a breath. They've been happening for a while and even though nobody in the government is willing to say they're real, a lot of us are convinced they are. For Beems and Zeon and Schmo and the rest of my crew, it's a faraway thing, like a fight video with kids you don't know—something to talk about, something to joke about—but to me they feel real.

It feels like they're going to be the death of me, but I haven't said that to anybody. I mentioned them to my dad, but he said I should worry more about riding my board in traffic, and that if they were really aliens then the government would've made sure we'd never even heard about them. Still, they scare the shit out of me because the men in my family are cursed and if an Incursion is going to get anybody around here it'll probably be me.

I take another bite of my tamale, but my fear makes it taste bad.

"You believe that shit? You believe that thing'll keep you safe like Jeffrey Sabazios says?" Fizzin asks as he and Schmo fall in on the other side to look. Fizzin reaches out to touch it. "Does it really read your mind?" Then: "Isn't the government getting ready to ban those things?"

Zeon shrugs. "Fuck if I know, man. They're legit cool, though." He slides his screen out of his pocket—it's smaller than most screens, but then it starts to unfold and ends up twice the size of mine. He holds it up in front of us. It brightens from black, scrambles for a moment, then I'm looking at a picture of us looking at his screen.

"Oh shit!" Schmo yells, dancing backward and then jumping back into the circle, pushing Fizzin out of the way. "You did that with your mind? Controlled the screen? You didn't even say anything. That's . . ." He shakes his head. "Do it again."

Zeon's screen brightens again, but this time instead of a picture of us, it's showing something else. "Called your girl, Plugz," he says.

I freeze. He called Mousie. I don't want to talk with Mousie in front of everybody—I don't know what we'd say to each other that wouldn't be weird and embarrassing.

Too late. She's on the screen now. She looks confused. "Who's this?" Her voice isn't going to his earpod—it sounds like it's coming from the screen, so I lean in and shake my head.

I can't stop my mind from playing out all the dumb things I say in front of her when we're alone that she might repeat in front of everybody. "Hey." Lame. "Zeon's got Live-Tech."

"Really?" She's not looking directly at me—she's scanning the heads falling in behind mine. "That's cool."

"Yeah." I reach out behind me, shove Fizzin and Schmo out of the picture. Something rings in my ear, a sustain, like a whispered chord on a distant guitar. I turn to look for the instrument, but there's nothing to see.

"Are you gonna be here?"

Whatever it was, it's gone. I turn back to look at Mousie on Zeon's screen. "Huh?"

"School?"

"What time is it?" I dig into my pocket for my screen.

"Eight."

"No shit." I look down at my tamale. Then: "Yeah. I'll see you at break."

"See you."

Zeon's screen goes blank.

By the time we're ready to walk, we're already ten minutes late, but that's okay. We move slow and eat our tamales as we go. First period is chemistry, and no matter what Mr. Wakefield says, I'm not going to pass it even if I'm there from the beginning of class.

On the way, Fizzin says something about Incursions again. Everybody else laughs, but I can't do more than smile.

Two

EVER SINCE TALK ABOUT INCURSIONS STARTED, MY TÍA JUANA IS THE ONLY person I know who's freaked out by them like me. They haven't happened in America, but she doesn't even like me walking home from school—she thinks it's too dangerous to be outside alone. Her son Alex died before I was born, and because I'm named after him, she takes special care of me.

She messages me right before the end of school saying that she's coming to get me. I can't say my message back to her because I'm in class, so I have to unfold my screen to type her a message telling her she shouldn't because I'm going to hang with Mousie, but she says she's already here.

My hair falls over my face as I look at the screen in my lap, making it hard to see, so I have to readjust myself and my screen. My aunt says for me to meet her down at Beverly so she doesn't get stuck in school traffic.

I text Mousie to tell her that I can't hang, even though I don't want to.

Meet me later? she sends back.

Where?

The lake

The teacher's saying something, she's looking right at me, talking.

I want to text Mousie back, but I can't because the teacher's pinned me with her eyes. I'm supposed to be doing something, but I don't know what, so I lean forward and bring my arm up with my stylus like I'm going to write because that's what everybody else is doing, but there aren't even instructions on my desk's screen and the response window where I'd input my work is grayed out, so I don't know what I'm supposed to do.

"Mr. Mata? Do you have any thoughts?"

"About what?" It comes out with a laugh that I don't mean to do, but I can't stop it.

She sighs, gives me a smile that says she's tired of me. "Why people voted for Eugene Debs even though he was in prison?"

She's still staring at me and now my face is getting hot because I can feel everybody else staring at me, too. I think I sort of know the answer. We were just learning about how he was a socialist who wanted the working people to be in charge of things, and how that was what a lot of people wanted.

But I'm not sure I'm right, so I shrug and shake my head.

"No thoughts?"

"Nah." My screen lights up in my lap. Mousie again.

If I had a Live-Tech pod, I'd be able to message Mousie with my mind and still look like I was working.

My auntie gets me things sometimes. I showed her some stuff about Live-Tech a while ago, but she was totally against it. She doesn't trust things that play with your mind, and like a lot of people she's sure Jeffrey Sabazios is out to get us.

Maybe I'll ask again.

I bring it up when I get in the car. "Jesse's got Live-Tech."

My aunt squints at me. She still has a car that you drive, so she's got her hands on the steering wheel as she pulls away from the curb, moving slow to keep from hitting the other cars picking up kids. "He shouldn't have that," she tells me. "Jeffrey Sabazios's gonna know all his thoughts—even the president says so."

I shrug. "Sabazios says it'll protect him from Incursions."

"That's crazy, mijo." She shakes her head like she's disappointed in my thinking. "He's using the Incursions to get people to give him their *minds*, and your mind is something you should never give up to anyone but God. You think it's coincidence Jeffrey Sabazios 'comes up' "—she makes air quotes with her hand still on the steering wheel—"with his mind-control stuff right when the Incursions begin and that suddenly it's going to save you? Use your brain, Alex. He's conning you. You want to stay safe from the aliens, you stick with me."

This is hopeless. "Maybe, but it means Jesse never needs to worry about getting his screen jacked." The Live-Tech pods and their screens only work for the person they've been mated with. She knows that. "He won't have to worry so much walking alone home from school."

She clucks, shakes her head. "Not about criminals, maybe, but he won't be any safer from an Incursion no matter what Sabazios says." She turns to put her eyes on me. "Sabazios is playing people for fools—trying to earn his money off your fear, scaring people into giving him control of their minds." She bugs her eyes at me. "That's why no serious people are buying his Live-Tech stuff and why President Castle's trying to get it banned." She looks across at me like I'm a baby. "Those are the facts, no matter what you see on your channels."

I reach up to fiddle with my pod. It's new, but it's a little too big for my ear and it hurts after a while, plus the sound pass-thru which they said was going to be 100 percent isn't anywhere near that good. "People are buying it," I say, sounding whiny, which I hate. "Lots of people. It's already everywhere."

"It's not everywhere, and it's not going to be in your ear, mijo."

I don't really hear her, though. There's other noise, sounding like a strummed guitar again. "Do you hear that?"

"Hear what?" she asks, eyes fixed on the road.

"That sound, like a guitar?"

She cocks her head, brushes some of the hair away from her ear, listens, then: "You play that thing too much, now you hear it everywhere. I don't hear anything."

"Yeah." I'm not sure I do, either, anymore.

Three

MY MOM IS CLIPPING HER ROSES IN THE FRONT OF THE HOUSE WHEN MY TÍA drops me off. She smiles when she sees us, walks out the gate to talk. Her smile's not the good smile.

"You didn't need to pick him up, Juana," my mom says when I roll down the window. "He's old enough to walk."

My auntie doesn't smile back. "There was another Incursion today," she says, leaning over me to get closer to my mom. "People are saying they just appeared and took two kids in Peru, right off the street."

My mom rolls her eyes. "How do they know that even happened? It's always in places like that and there's never any video. People are trying to scare each other, that's all."

I see an opportunity. "Live-Tech is supposed to keep people safe from the Incursions."

They both look at me.

Tía Juana pulls herself back into the driver's seat and examines me. "You don't quit, do you? I told you that stuff is the devil's business, Alex. Jeffrey Sabazios is making slaves out of people and you want to just sign right up."

I shrug. My mom hasn't said anything yet, so I look to her. "If the Incursions are real and the Live-Tech does what they say it does, you'd want me to have it."

She looks over at my auntie, then me, then opens my car

door. “Don’t you have enough stuff already, Alex? We just got you that new pod, but now you want something else. You’re never satisfied, are you?”

I shrug again. I should have kept my mouth shut.

My mom steps away from my door. “Go inside. I gotta talk to your aunt.”

I leave them there at the curb, trying not to listen. They’ve never gotten along, but my auntie’s my dad’s only sister and they’re like the only family each other’s got.

Inside the house, things aren’t quiet like they’re supposed to be. There’s a speaker on somewhere, playing music—a guitar solo that goes on and on, a louder, more detailed version of what I was hearing earlier today. I can hear it, except when I try to listen to it, it slips through my ears and disappears—so I can’t name the notes, can’t write them down.

I look through the house to find where it is, but it’s everywhere. I check the TVs and the speaker comms, but they’re not making any noise.

And the solo never grows louder, never quieter, no matter where I am.

It’s like it’s *in* me, so I’m the only one who hears it. I pull my pod and plug my fingers into my ears to see if it helps, but it doesn’t do anything.

I sit down at the dining room table and put my head on my arms and hope it goes away.

“What’s wrong with you?” my mom asks when she comes back inside.

I look up at her. I don’t know what to say and I don’t want to get into it about hearing things, so I just say: “My ears.”

She nods. “Your auntie, she’ll talk them off.” She sets

herself down in the chair on the other side of the table, bumping it into me. "She worries too much, thinks she knows better than everybody."

I hate it when she gets mad about Juana. I never know what to say. "She's just scared about the Incursions."

"She's spoiling you."

I shrug.

"She knows you're failing classes and skipping school and she still buys you stuff, picks you up, drives you places." She shakes her head. "She's not your mom." She points at herself. "I am."

There's nothing to say, and now I'm about to hear about what she went through to have me. I just nod, focus in on the sounds in my head. They're getting slightly louder.

"It took us years of work to have you, Alex—you didn't come easy like your brother did."

Her voice trails off when she mentions my brother, and I speak up to try and head her off. "It wasn't that much—a lot of kids come from IVF and gene therapy these days . . ."

But she's not having it. "It was a lot, Alejandro, a lot for us." She shakes her head. "And your aunt, she doesn't seem to understand that she's going to end up making you soft." She taps the table twice with her fingers. "The fact that she's not getting you that Live-Tech shit only because she listens to paranoid shows about aliens should tell you everything you need to know about your aunt."

"She's not so bad, Mom. And Incursions are real. They're happening, and what if Sabazios is telling the truth—he's superrich—it's not like he's nobody."

My mom sits down across from me. "You really scared about that stuff?"

I shrug. "I don't know." But I can't look at her when I say it.

She sighs, looks at me closely in a way that makes me feel weird. "You're so close to being a man I forget that you're still a little boy on the inside." She sits back, doesn't seem to notice me blushing. "I'm tempted to get you your precious Live-Tech just to piss her off." She taps the pod in her ear. "How much do Live-Tech pods cost?"

The phone tells her that they're $129 and asks if she'd like to order one, for delivery on Thursday.

I look up at her, hopeful. She hesitates. "I'll pay you back."

She rolls her eyes. "With what? You don't have a job."

"I'll find something . . . Do stuff around the house or help dad on his worksites on Saturdays."

"You'd work Saturdays with your dad for how long?"

"Two months."

She looks at me, her eyes narrowing. "Three."

Right now a bunch of Saturdays doesn't feel real, but the fact that I'm suddenly about to get a Live-Tech pod shoves out any sense that I'm giving up too much. "Deal."

She taps her pod. "Order it. Send it to the house."

"Thanks, Mom." I look at the clock above the stove in the kitchen. It's nearly four. I stand up.

"Where you going?"

"I gotta meet someone." I gesture with my chin. "Down at the lake."

She shakes her head. "You're not going anywhere." She points at me and then at my room. "Go do something useful until dinner."

When I text Mousie to tell her that I still can't meet, she doesn't want to let it go, keeps telling me that I should just come anyways. I tell her that it's not a good idea to cross my mom, but she doesn't understand. Eventually she moves on to other stuff, but I can't shake the feeling that she thinks I'm being dumb for staying home. I tell her that I have to go, that I've got stuff to do and that I'll get her later.

She texts back, but I don't even look at it. Instead I pull my song notebook from under my mattress.

I've been playing guitar since I was nine, because my brother Pete played and I wanted to be like him, and after he was gone I kept playing because it feels like I'm with him when I do. I've never played in a band or anything, though, but sometimes me and Beems play together because he's got drums.

I taught myself to read and write music when I was in middle school, when I had thoughts about becoming some sort of rock star, but that was just a kid's dream. I still write lyrics and put them to music on my guitar, but I don't show anybody—not even Beems. It's more about keeping my mind still, connecting with things. Connecting with music itself.

So I mostly play alone in my room.

I open my lyrics book, start to write, thinking about the lie I told to Zeon this morning.

Someday Runaway

In the morning, before the sun,
My mind's awake, born to run.
Haven't slept, and I cannot shake
All this crazy that keeps me lying here

Wide

Awake.

Everybody tells me they got

Ideas for my life, tons, a lot

Ways I should be, things I should do

But they don't know me, no idea, haven't

Got a

Clue.

DUMB!

The word blasts into my brain, blowing the song apart and I have to stop. I put the pen down, take a breath, then start reworking the first verses so they're less singsongy, then turn to the chorus:

I'm here, in front of you but you don't see

Me, staring at my face, seeing who you want me

To be.

I hide my eyes, show you lies, pretend I'm the prize

But I'm dying inside, and my mind, it cries:

Start again without

Start again without

Start again without

Start again without the lies.
Start again without the lies.

I pick up my guitar and start again, but the song's dumb, so eventually I close the book and play other people's music instead.

It drowns out the music I've been hearing in my brain.

Beems hits me up but I ignore my pod, watch his photo come up on my screen. I don't stop playing. It's cool like that with Beems and me. We don't always have to stay on things with each other—we've come up together since preschool.

Eventually, I put down the guitar and tap my pod to check his message: **U down for doing something**

I message him back, tell him I can't—maybe tomorrow.

Tomorrow. Stairs after school.

Four

IT'S JUST BEEMS AND ME HANGING OUT ON THE OLD STAIRS BY MY HOUSE. The city's been through since the last time, painted everything over again. They've left us fresh surfaces.

Beems jerks his head at the wall next to us. He's smiling. He can't hear the strumming that's been in my head all day. When I try and listen it gets worse.

"You hear guitars?"

He shakes his head.

I try to shut it out, think of other things, but today it's louder than my thoughts. Hasn't stopped.

I drop my board and it clatters on the concrete, rolls into the wall next to me. The noise temporarily obscures the guitars.

I pull a paint pen from my bag and shake it: *thack thack thack thack.*

I go to write my name, PLUGZER, on the wall, but the noise makes my name come out wrong, a terrible song in my head. Beems watches me, tapping a marker against his leg.

He sees me screw up, so he laughs. I can barely hear him, but I know.

I want to shake, spin, jump, do something, pound my head, break my ears, but instead I try and stay still to watch as Beems pinches the pen cap between his lips. It sticks out like a lizard tongue as he tosses up a perfect BEEMS.

"Balance," he says around the cap, his words barely penetrating. "You gotta keep it balanced."

I want to trash his tag, but it's a masterpiece just like everything he does. Beems's real name is Julio and he's been Genius Boy since we were both in preschool. He doesn't go to Belmont like the rest of us. He goes to County Arts.

I shake my pen again. *Thack thack thack thack.* The noise becomes a drumbeat.

I toss up a PLUGZER on another section of the stairs. I look up at Julio when it's done and he nods. It's better.

"Where's Mousie?" he asks.

"Watching her niece."

I unfold my screen to check the time. It's nearly six and if I don't get home my mom is going to blow it up.

I stand up, the guitars fade, then rise with me.

"Watch out, scared boy."

I turn to see who's talking and accidentally kick my board. It crashes all the way down the stairs, skidding onto the street below.

Julio looks up at me. "You okay?"

"Who said that?" I start to ask, but I don't finish. I swallow the end of the sentence and try to play it off. The voice didn't actually sound like a person's voice at all and anyways it's just Beems and me here.

"Huh?"

I don't answer him.

"It's about time." The voice is hollow, like a ghost or a dream and even though it's loud—louder than the guitars—I don't feel it in my ears. She's everywhere and nowhere at the same time. *"Be ready to run, scared boy. Strange days are here and you're gonna run away."*

"Shut up," I whisper before I can help it. I don't even look at Beems after I say it. "I need to get home." I hate the fear in my voice.

"Been waiting for you, scared boy, gonna get you ready to run!" The voice is right there, talking in both ears, moving from one side to the other, drowning out even the guitars.

I shake my head hard to try and get her out.

"Shut up shut up!"

Beems stands. He's staring.

The voice pushes at me. *"Beems won't help you, Plugz. It's all been seen and done. He's going to try and get you. Trap you, but he can't stop what's already been seen, boy. You're gonna run away, runaway!"*

I back up the stairs and turn toward home.

"What about your board, man?" Julio reaches out to steady me, but I can't shake what the voice said. I push his hand away and run.

"Run away!" the voice yells, but her words aren't coming in through my ears.

"Shut up!" I yell it in every direction while I run so she'll know I'm yelling at her. "Shut up shut up shut up!"

Silence. I wait for her to say something, but everything is quiet. Even the guitars are scared of her. When I reach the gate to my house, I stand and wait some more.

Nothing.

Eventually I go inside.

I'm scared, sure, but I don't wonder what's happening anymore. Hearing the voice makes it pretty clear.

I'm going to be just like my uncle Chuy.

Five

MY MOM AND ME STILL SET A PLACE AT DINNER FOR MY BROTHER PETE EVEN though he's been dead for six years. The army death guys came in the middle of my eleventh birthday party. I thought my parents had them come because I wanted to join the army like Pete, but they hadn't. We just weren't expecting them because Pete wasn't at war anymore. He was stationed in Texas.

A car crash on a freeway near El Paso.

Mom and I wash his plate every night. When people eat dinner with us, we all sit closer together instead of giving them Pete's spot.

I'd do anything to go back in time and talk to him again, but having his setting at the table helps a little. It makes it feel like he's late, not gone.

I know my dad doesn't like the reminder every day. The men in our family don't talk about death if we can help it. Not that there's many of us left to talk about it—it's really just me and him who are still alive. My dad says Mata men are cursed. So far none of us has lived past the age of forty-eight.

My grandfather died of a heart attack at forty-five. His brother, my uncle Arturo, was hit by a car at thirty-eight. My cousin Alex—Tía Juana's son, who I'm named after—drowned at twenty-six. Pete died at nineteen. My uncle Chuy died on the streets at thirty-two. My dad won't talk about it unless he's been drinking, but when he does he says it's been like that for generations.

My dad is forty-seven.

I'm *always* sure I'm gonna die. Sometimes I think it doesn't matter what I do, so I do whatever. Other times, I get too scared to do anything. It's part of why I don't think much about school.

Lately, I've been convinced I'll be killed in an Incursion, but now I have a new idea.

My uncle Chuy died before I was born. Pete told me about him, said he was schizophrenic. He heard voices that he talked to. They told him to do things.

Just like me.

He'd been living on one of the little islands where the river flows through Frogtown, and when the water rose, it was so fast that he couldn't get out. People had told him not to stay down there in the rainy season, but he wouldn't listen to real people . . . only the voices in his head.

I go down to the river sometimes to listen to the water and watch the birds. When I do I think of him living in the trees and reeds that rise up like a jungle from the high spots on the bed where the water only runs when it rains. There are still people out there now, homeless people, sick people like Chuy. I feel bad watching them out there, knowing what could happen to them, but it's not my place to say anything.

At dinner, the guitars are loud again, but the voice is quiet, so I work up the nerve to ask about him. "When did Uncle Chuy start hearing things?" I put it out there like the weather while scraping rice onto my fork with my tortilla.

My dad looks at me like I asked about his bowel movements.

"Are you going to be a part of the groundbreaking for the

new gym?" My mom. Irrelevant questions are her favorite tool when things get uncomfortable.

I shake my head. Then I shrug when she looks disappointed. I turn and watch my dad instead as I chew. He's looking away from me.

He does that when he's mad.

"Did he tell anybody when it started?" I don't usually press an issue when my dad does the looking-away thing, but this is important.

"When I saw the notice in the school blast, I thought maybe I could go, because we had some good times in that gym back in the day . . ." Mom tries again.

The guitars seem to know I'm asking about them. They're grinding now, metal heavy, sounding like Slayer.

"Dad?" My voice cracks with fear and I hate myself.

He drops the fork onto his plate and the noise makes me jump even though I watched it fall.

"*Jumpy!*" The voice is loud and almost not there at the same time. Like she's talking in clouds. Like skywriting.

"We are not going to talk about my brother." My dad's voice is even, calm, and scary.

"*Don't let scary dad scare you, boy. Bad things are coming. Worse than the curse. Bad things scarier than him.*" And then she laughs. I cringe.

My dad thinks I'm cringing because of him.

"Dad . . ."

He shakes his head.

Mom steps in: "They said they were going to pull up the time capsule from when the gym was built. Have they opened it yet?"

I look at her. She widens her eyes at me. "I can ask questions or I can tell you what I think about you being so disrespectful." She looks at me hard and shakes her head slowly. "You want me to tell you what I think?"

I don't. When she says what she thinks, it takes forever and I have to look her in the eye the whole time or she starts over. With Dad, it's easier. It's just silence.

I sigh. "I don't know about any time capsule."

"The one that was buried in the old gym. Your grandmother, she put things in it when she was in high school."

I shrug and go back to eating. "I didn't know about it."

Somebody knocks at the door. I look up. My dad gestures at me with his chin: Answer it.

It's Beems, holding my board. "You alright, man?"

The Skywriting Voice starts in. *"Bad things coming, Alex. Julio's gonna try and stop you, and you're gonna have to run."*

I nod and begin to close the door. He pushes against it a little. "You know you can talk to me, right?" He raises his eyebrows. "We tell each other things."

I nod. A year ago, he told me he was gay. I'm the only person from the neighborhood who knows about it. He still talks about girls when we hang out with the rest of the crew. He isn't that open about it at his school, either, even though he's far from the only gay kid there. "Yeah. I know."

He pushes against the door again, but I push harder on my side. I can't talk to him. Not about this. "I gotta go."

I put the rest of my weight against the door. We come to a stalemate, and then he pulls his hand away. "What the hell is wrong with you?"

I shake my head. I'm afraid I'm going to lose it if I say

something, so I close the door the rest of the way. I stand there for a moment, getting myself together, holding my board.

The guitars are like an ocean now, waves.

"Who was that?" Mom calls from the dining room.

"Julio," I manage.

"Why didn't you invite the boy in?"

"Just wait for what's in the time capsule, scared boy."

I walk back to the table without answering, because I can't think of anything to say.

Six

THE GUITARS KEPT ME UP ALL NIGHT, SCREECHING, WAILING. SOMETIMES it sounded like just one and other times it was like an orchestra.

I wasn't going to sleep anyway. The Voice was talking, too, calling me *scared boy*, telling me that *bad things* were coming, and that *it all connects.* Kept telling me she was *in the Silly Juice.*

I wanted to shut it all out, but I couldn't play guitar because my parents were asleep, so I spent the night watching videos. Gaming, fails, dashcams, fights. I even went back and watched old ones from when I was little, but eventually I started watching stuff about Incursions. The one in Peru that my auntie was talking about, it turns out that there's this grainy video that shows something. It's the first time anything's been caught on camera, but it doesn't look like much—just a big black smudge that pops up and then disappears. The comments all say it's a hoax, but I don't know about that.

It could be real.

Tony Baez dropped another video in the middle of me reading the comments, so I got to watch it as viewer number seventeen.

It was a sketch about a kid whose parents won't buy him a real Live-Tech so he gets a "Lif-Rekt" at the swap meet for three dollars. When he puts it on, his girlfriend leaves him, his mom dies, he's expelled from school, and then he gets taken by an alien during an Incursion.

It was funny, but it didn't help my mood.

I fell asleep at some point, though, because when I woke up this morning, my head was quieter, guitars like a breeze through palm trees, and the Voice was gone. I sat in my room playing my own guitar and waited for her to come back. I waited for it like you wait for bad news, but it never came.

Even without her, my mind is full of Incursions and *Silly Juice* and *Bad Things*.

On the way to school I skate the path around Echo Park Lake. The wild parrots are eating the fruit from a floss tree, so I stop and watch. They're loud as hell and their noise somehow makes me brave enough to try and coax the Voice out, like picking a scab, but it doesn't show.

I stop when I realize I'm muttering to myself like a crazy person, and I go fast down the path to get away from my embarrassment.

Mousie's waiting for me outside her building. We've only been talking for a few weeks, and she's cool but she's barely turning fifteen and she already wants me to escort her at her quinceañera, but that's not for another six months. I said yes, but I don't know if we'll still be a thing then. Looking at her and thinking about it makes me anxious, but I smile and lean back as I walk up to her.

She looks at me shyly from behind her hair and then steps into my arms, presses herself against me. I lean in for a kiss.

Even touching her doesn't wake up the Voice, and I start to feel a little bit of hope.

We walk slowly the rest of the way to school, our feet matching the rhythm of the guitars that have come back into my mind. She talks about how much she hates having to take care of her niece, and I carry my board and her books. I watch her while she talks. We don't have that much to say to each other—it's mostly me listening to her, and then her asking me questions about my life that I don't have answers to. I did tell her that I write music, which I've never told any other girl, but I think it was a mistake because then she wanted to hear some and read my lyrics. I told her I'd show her someday, but it would feel so embarrassing to see her reading it that I don't think I'll ever do it.

She finishes talking about her niece and stuff, and we're quiet as we walk for a minute. I can tell she's waiting for me to say something, but the only things on my mind are guitars and voices. I want to tell her about them, but I don't know how without sounding crazy.

Eventually, as we're walking up the last little hill to school, I ask: "Do you ever think about things you can't see?" There are kids all around us and I'm not sure I want to talk about what I'm hearing, but it's right there inside me and I can't help it.

Mousie looks at me. She's confused.

I shift her books a little while I think about what I'm trying to say. "That maybe there's things beyond life and what we see and stuff? Things that sometimes people . . ."

Mousie looks up at me, slows her pace a little. "Like aliens?" She looks at me wide-eyed. "Like the Incursions?"

I shrug. Maybe. I don't know. "Like things . . ." I shrug.

Like voices that talk to you and invisible guitars and stuff. I shake my head. I don't even know why I'm asking. "Yeah."

We walk the rest of the way quiet.

Mousie blows up my pod all morning, but I don't even know what to say, so I don't reply. If she's mad, I'll tell her I got my screen taken by a teacher.

I'm thinking about that when Dean Wagner calls me out of second period. I'm not worried, because he's always been out for me. I review possible infractions while I walk the hall. I'm not holding anything today, so that's not a concern, and I've slapped up the empty rooms on the third floor a few times, but it's not my regular tag so I don't know how he'd pin it on me. Truth is, I don't do much that's bad, so I'm not sure what he thinks he's found.

"Alex Mata," I tell the old lady who runs the dean's office when I reach the counter. She looks like everybody's nasty abuela—the one who doesn't love you. "Wagner called for me."

She scowls and I stare back. Just when I'm winning, the Skywriting Voice returns:

"Plugzie's busted and there's nothing he can do. Seen time's fixed and done, boy. Get ready, Plugzer, cuz you're gonna want to take a picture of that picture."

I flinch and the old lady thinks she won.

What picture? I shake my head.

"Sit down," the old lady says. "Dean Wagner will come get you when he's ready."

The guitars ramp up again—they seem to increase with the beat of my heart. I breathe deep to try and calm down, but my breath hitches before I can get it all the way in and I start feeling panicked.

The guitars rage, amplification, infiltration in my brain.

Insane.

I'm starting to sweat, sticky, wet. The guitars. I make myself breathe.

Close my eyes.

The volume drops.

My mind shoots forward to a life on the street, shouting at lampposts, sleeping on cardboard with my foot laced through the wheels of my grocery cart.

I'm going to die like Uncle Chuy.

I barely hear Wagner when he calls my name.

"Mr. Mata?" he repeats. "Come in here, will ya?"

Wagner has me sit across from his desk. He makes a production of sitting down slowly and organizing himself before he says anything to me. He does this with all of us. He thinks it makes us nervous but it doesn't. The familiar part of it relaxes me.

Finally: "How'd you do it?"

I don't know what he's talking about. I shrug.

"Listen, son, I'm not even that mad—I've got respect for good plays and this was a good one, but Dr. Anderson? He's not happy." Dr. Anderson is the ghost principal—his name's on everything, but nobody's ever even seen him.

I still don't know what he's talking about, so I shrug again.

He imitates my shrug. "That's all you got? You had to know it would come right back on you."

I shake my head. Run my hand through my hair. "I don't know what you're talking about."

"Look me in the eye and tell me that, Mata." His voice is hard.

I look up. He's fat. There are folds of skin coming out of his collar that make his head look like a turtle's. Like he could pull the whole thing down into his shirt if he wanted. His eyes are green. The muscles under his cheeks twitch, sending little waves down to his chin. "I really don't know what you're talking about." I don't look away even though the effort makes me sweat.

He sighs. "Don't be stupid." He reaches into a file folder on his desk and pulls out a photograph. Photographs are bad news—they're proof. I try and see what it's of, but I can't because he's holding it too close. I start to feel a little sick.

The Skywriting Voice said there'd be a photograph.

"What's that?" My voice cracks like a little boy's.

"You think you're nervous now, wait 'til you see the picture, Plugzie."

I work to not react. I think with all my mind: SHUTUP!

She doesn't reply, but the guitars do. A hundred of them in my brain, all playing different songs. They make it hard to hear.

Wagner looks at the picture, then at me. He shrugs and slides it over to me upside down. I reach for it but he lays a meaty hand over it and starts to talk. "How'd you get it into the time capsule, Alex?" he asks me softly. "You ruined a public event for a lot of people. A lot of people made time to be here this morning—including a city councilman and a school-board member, by the way—so they could watch as a time capsule that was supposed to have been untouched for fifty goddamned years got opened up and what did they find, instead?" He looks at me like I'm supposed to know what he's talking about. "You got nothing to say?"

My heart sinks. I suddenly have to go to the bathroom. He's never sworn at me before. Whatever he thinks I did, it's bad. I rack my brain to come up with what he could be talking about, but I'm totally lost.

"Well?"

I can't think of other responses, so I shake my head.

"They find that some little punk has dug in and opened it all up ahead of time and put a picture in it so everybody can know how cool he thinks he is."

"What are you talking about?"

He flips the picture over. It's of two people, a guy and a girl, standing on a beach that's piled with thick white sand and rocks. There's water behind them and mountains up the far side of the water.

His hair's cut different, and I don't own the clothes that the guy is dressed in, but he looks exactly like me. I look at the girl he's standing with for a clue. She's blond, a little pretty. She's dressed like Madonna from the eighties. I've never seen her before.

"That's not me." I shake my head. "I don't own those clothes and my hair's never been like that." Once I start talking, I just keep going. "And I've never been to that beach and I've never seen that girl before."

But Wagner's shaking his head before I'm even halfway done. He flips it over. There's something written in the upper right-hand corner.

PLUGZER

I don't know how, but I can't deny it—tags are like signatures and this one's mine. I start shaking my head like it's on a spring or something, because even though it's mine, I never did it. "I didn't—" I start, but then I look back at the picture and I see it.

My throat closes and I feel like I'm on fire.

The guy in the picture has a mole on his jaw and a crooked canine tooth that comes out way too high in the mouth.

Just like me.

"That's me."

"Obviously. How'd you get it in the time capsule?"

I look up at him. "I didn't do it!" I'm whining, shouting, but I don't care. "This is messed up, Mr. Wagner, because that's me, but I've never looked like that or been anywhere like that—and that tag on the back"—I flip it over again—"that's mine, too, but I haven't ever done that one before."

Wagner tells me to shut up.

I ask him if I can keep the picture. He tells me I've got brass balls, but when he gets up to go get my suspension order off the printer, I'm together enough to unfold my screen and take a picture of the picture.

Just like the Voice told me to.

"You're out for three days, Mata." He slides the suspension order to me. "And you're going to do community service to show how sorry you are for messing up the time capsule."

I nod like a dumbass.

"Your mom's been called. She says you can walk home." He picks up the picture and tucks it back into the folder. "Sign."

I sign the order without looking. Wagner watches and then nods. "Get outta here, Mata. Take a few days and we'll meet with you and your folks on Monday. You can come back then if you allocute."

I nod again. I've just agreed to tell the whole story when I come back. I'm lost on how I'm going to do that, though. I don't have a single clue how my picture got into the time capsule.

Seven

MY HEAD IS FULL OF GUITARS WHEN I LEAVE SCHOOL. WHEN THEY FADE enough for me to think, I message Mousie. She's a little mad about me not texting back earlier, but she calms down when I tell her I got suspended. She offers to skip the next couple days to hang with me. I think about it and it sounds good, but I don't know what my parents are going to do so I tell her no.

We keep texting, talking about stupid stuff, but my mind isn't in it. The Voice is quiet again and this time I've got questions for her: She knew about the time capsule and the picture.

I'm listening for her while I walk, the way I used to listen for monsters at night. I'd hear them everywhere even when they weren't there at all.

All I get is guitars.

I think about what would happen if I told Mousie about everything. She would think I was crazy.

I am crazy.

"I'm going schizo." The words catch in my mouth. I'm walking under the freeway and it's so loud around me I can't hear them anyway.

I'm about to try again when there's a noise behind me. Loud and sharp like a gunshot. Without thinking I hit the deck in case there's more, but as I'm going down someone grabs me from behind and pulls me to the side.

I get slammed into the dirt above the sidewalk.

I hit hard. There's dust in my eyes and dirt in my mouth, and I'm just reaching for whoever the hell's on top of me when there's a massive crash that makes the ground shake. Glass breaks, metal crunches.

The weight lifts and I roll onto my back. A driverless car is jammed up against the support pillar I was next to. There's a lady in an old-style driven car scraped up beside it, too. She's still behind the wheel, looking scared.

No doubt the driverless would have killed me if I hadn't been knocked out of the way.

I sit up and shake my head clear, spit the grit from my mouth. I look around for the person who saved me. When I see her, she's already all the way up the embankment. My vision isn't completely clear, but I know who it is.

It's the girl from the picture.

She turns back to look at me and when she sees me watching she blows a kiss before disappearing up beyond the side of the freeway.

I want to go after her, but I stop before I even start because she can't be real.

Crazy people see things. A substitute showed us *A Beautiful Mind* in class one time, and that guy made people up. I haven't wanted to cry in forever, probably since Pete was killed, but I want to cry now. I can feel it in my throat. I swallow hard.

I turn to check on the driver of the car, but she seems alright.

I swipe at my denim jacket, trying to knock some of the dirt off—there's big swipes of brown across one whole side. The Sepultura patch on my sleeve is torn, which sucks because they're my favorite old-school metal band.

I look around for my board. It's in the middle of the road. It's been hit and it's in pieces all over the street.

I guess I'm walking home.

Eight

MY MOM DRIVES FOR METRO. WHEN I WAS LITTLE AND I WAS HOME SICK from school, she would have Pete wait with me at a bus stop for her. I'd get on her bus and ride with her all day and she'd talk to me about the things she passed and the people she met each day. She could have gotten in trouble for that, but she did it anyway.

When she left for work this morning, I wanted more than anything to sit in the seat right behind her and reach my hand through the gap in the screen so I could hold her elbow while I slept like I used to. I felt safe on her bus.

I didn't even ask if I could go with her. She's really mad about the time capsule. She says I ruined something beautiful. I tried to tell her I didn't do it but she called me a liar.

My dad hasn't looked at me since he got home yesterday. All he said was, "You disappoint me." Then he went to my room and collected the TV remote, computer, controllers, and even the old pod I only use for music, and locked them all in the toolbox in the bed of his truck.

He took my pod and screen, too. I panicked when I thought he was going to lock them, because I wanted the picture. He didn't, though. Instead, he set them on restricted. I'll only be able to make and get calls to and from him, Mom, and my aunt.

He didn't take my guitar, which is good, and he doesn't even know about my lyric book. I don't know if I could live without those. Playing guitar keeps my fingers attached to my brain, which keeps me from exploding.

This morning before he left, he told me to scrub the kitchen until it shined.

They forgot to lock up the ancient tablet in Pete's room, though, so instead of cleaning, I've been searching the internet for people who hear music that isn't there. Pete would have known what to do. But he's not here, and there's nobody who can help me.

And nothing I'm learning is making me feel any better.

There's something called Musical Ear Syndrome, but it's for people who are hard of hearing and they hear actual music that isn't there instead of random guitars.

And they don't hear voices that tell them what to do.

I start looking up things like schizophrenia and psychosis, but that just ends up being scarier, even though I don't have many of those symptoms.

It's scary because they're the ones that hear voices.

The only person I can think of to talk to is Julio, but he's at school, and when he gets home my mom'll be home, too. I look at my phone. It's a little after eleven. I could be at County Arts in time for his lunch period.

I email myself the picture and print it off on Pete's ancient printer.

I throw on some clothes, toss my lyrics book in my back-pack, and look for my board. *Damn.*

The mailman's at the gate when I leave. He's an old guy, weird but generally cool. "Hey young mister," he says when he sees me. He always calls me young mister. "You got yourself a letter today." He hands me an envelope, then stuffs the rest of the mail into our box.

It's a regular white envelope. The address is handwritten in big blue block letters:

ALEX MATA
1562 LAVETA TERRACE
LOS ANGELES, CA 90026

There isn't a return address, but I hardly notice because I recognize the handwriting. It's mine.

I mumble thanks to the mailman, who says, "No problemo, young mister," and walks back out the gate.

I don't think I can handle one more weird thing happening.

"Get ready runaway boy." The Skywriting Voice drowns out the guitars momentarily. *"Your ride's about to begin."*

"What ride?" I say the words out loud even though I don't mean to.

"Your wild ride, scared boy. You're about to run away, gotta be brave."

"Shut *up*!" She's so loud in my head there's no way the world doesn't hear her and I can't explain her. "You gotta shut *up*!"

She's quiet again. I think for her, search inside, but she's left my brain for the moment.

My wild ride. I look back at the letter in my hand.

I'm sweating. My fingers slip as I try to open the envelope, but eventually, I manage to pull out the sheet of lined paper inside.

The handwriting on the paper is mine, too. It's terrible because I'm a lefty, and this is it right down to the smears where my sweaty hand ran through the ink. I unfold the paper, but it's hard because my hand's shaking, and it's hard to read because my head is lousy with guitars:

Hey Alex,

This is you. Really. Please listen up, man, your stupid life depends totally on it. Can you please open your ears right now? Listen, I know it's not cool what's all happening, but you need to stop doubting and lift your ugly eyes up so you can see what's happening around you. You're not crazy, man—all this is real. You'll understand when you get to Seattle and I can't even begin to tell you about it now, because you'd think I'm crazy, but you're not.

Yesterday you got suspended from school and you were nearly killed by a driverless. You're hearing guitars in your mind and you just spent the morning on Pete's tablet reading about Musical Ear Syndrome because you think you're going insane. You're going to find Beems and tell him about this, and he's going to call your parents and they're gonna try and 5150 you. It all started a couple days ago when you and

Beems were writing on the stairs. You know what happened and no, you're not crazy. I should know since I am you.

OPEN THE PACKAGE WHEN YOU GET HOME TONIGHT.

Anyway, it's really important that you get out of town. Take the bus to Seattle. Keep this letter. You'll need it when you get there—you'll understand why when you're at the bus stop.

The Incursions are real and it's gonna get worse if we don't stop them.

You're gonna save the world.

Seen time is the only truth.

Alex AKA Plugzer

PS. Even though you won't believe it, there are some things that happen no matter what and when they tell you that of all the ways things could have happened, this is the least bad way, it's really true.

I'm standing there, stupidly holding the letter like it's going to change or something—like it's suddenly not going to describe exactly what's been happening to me. I look at the envelope again and fold it open. Inside there's a paper ticket for a

Greyhound bus from LA to Seattle attached to a small stack of twenty-dollar bills with a paper clip.

"Don't be a scared boy, Plugzer."

"Go away." It comes out halfway between a squeak and a growl.

"You're gonna do what you're gonna do. You'll see it's true."

I'm trying to think about the letter, trying to think about what it says, what it means, how it's real, but every time she talks, my mind shatters and I'm left with only scattered pieces of thoughts.

"Shut. The. Hell. *Up!*"

She laughs at me. *"Oh, Plugzie's mad now, but when you're ready, you'll come find me. You'll dig out the drain under your brain."*

WHAT THE HELL ARE YOU TALKING ABOUT? I don't say it, just think it, but it doesn't matter. She's gone.

Fuck her. I'm done with her. I'm done with all of it—the only person I know I can trust is me.

The letter warned me against going to Beems and I start to rethink my plan but then it occurs to me: If I'm crazy, I wrote the letter because I'm paranoid. I may not remember doing it, but I must have.

Plus, I've got no other play.

Nine

I READ THE LETTER AGAIN THREE TIMES ON THE BUS.

The guitars are like a ringing in my ears, loud, constant, but when I'm not thinking about them, I forget. Until I remember and then they're loud again.

My voice hasn't said anything since I yelled at her and now I have questions.

HEY! I try, but I can tell: She's not with me.

Dig out the drain under your brain.

I'm not sure what she means, but I close my eyes and search hard for her. At first I don't know what I'm looking for, but when I go really still I get a feeling like there's a way through the bottom of my brain, that there's a world underneath. There's a barrier between me and it, a membrane. I can feel myself bouncing against it, searching it for a way in.

There's a hole, small, a drain. A drain in my brain. It's dream-clear to me—not something I can see, but something I know is there—a feeling of a picture—the idea of something solid and real.

And there's something down there, under the drain.

The bus shifts as we get off the freeway, and I open my eyes, feeling alone.

I read about people who went off their medication because they missed the company of their voices and hallucinations;

they said it was easier to think without the drugs. I thought that was ridiculous, but now I'm beginning to get it. Once you've had people in your head, when they're gone it feels like your house after a party—messy and empty and lonely.

I get off the bus at the Cal State LA Station and walk up to campus. Julio's school is on the college campus and his school friends eat in the student union every day, so I stand by the union door like an idiot and wait for him. When he sees me he raises his eyebrows.

"Plugzie?"

"I need to talk to you."

He nods, puts his arm around me. "What's up?"

"I think I'm going crazy and I'm freaking out." My eyes start to burn. *Stupid.* I blot them with the back of my hand and hold my lips tight to keep from making noises.

He pulls me around the corner to a small set of empty tables. "Talk to me."

I clear my throat and start to talk. I begin with the guitars that have been happening since Monday. I tell him about the Skywriting Voice on the stairs and my freak-out, and I keep going through the letter this morning. I show him the letter and he reads it.

I show him the picture. He looks at it, then at me. "That's you?"

"Yeah, but I don't even know that girl and I've never been there."

He puts his hand on my leg, squeezes it. It's weird having him do it because we don't ever touch each other, but the rules have changed and I don't want him to stop.

"Listen, man, I got to get my food or I'm not going to eat. Have you eaten?"

I shake my head. I can't even think about food right now.

He pulls his hand from my knee. "Give me a minute." He's around the corner before I can ask him not to leave.

When he gets back I don't notice until he says my name because I'm deep in my own head, trying to get down the drain. When I get really still and I picture myself folding inward like a flower in reverse, it feels like maybe I can slip down the drainpipe, but something's stopping me.

I think my Voice is down there.

When I come back up to the surface, Julio's looking at me and holding a burrito encouragingly.

I take it to be polite. "Thanks."

We sit and talk about other things while we eat. I realize how hungry I am and it's all I can do to keep from shoving the whole burrito in my mouth at once. Being with Beems, having him listen and just be normal with me makes me feel better than I've felt since it all started.

He's telling me about some drama at his school when I happen to look over his shoulder.

My dad is crossing the quad toward the student union.

He's bent forward, walking like an old man walks, but there's no doubt it's him. Beems sees my expression change and looks where I'm looking.

"You need help, man," he says softly.

"You called my *parents.*" It comes out like a screech. I back off the bench and stumble into the bushes behind me.

"You're scarin' me. You tell me you're hearing things

and that there's some invisible mind-voice telling you what to do—you need help."

"But the letter." I wave it at him.

"*You* wrote it, man!"

He thinks I faked it. I thought I'd faked it, too. Right up until the moment Julio did exactly what it said he would do.

It all falls apart in my head. I don't have any proof of anything. I have a letter I wrote and an envelope that I filled out. I have a bus ticket I could have bought myself.

But the letter told the truth, and for the first time I begin to think that maybe I'm not going crazy. I think hard for something that I can use to prove that it's all real. "The picture of me!" I shout at Beems. "I didn't do that!"

He shrugs and shakes his head in reply. "I don't know what you did or didn't do, man, but you need help."

My dad is closing in. I see him through the glass in the doors. He looks small and old, his face creased up like a paper ball.

For a moment I'm nearly overwhelmed with a need to tell my dad I'm sorry, but it passes and I need to get away.

"Fuck you, Beems." I push backward through the bushes and out onto the walkway that leads up to the gate on the side of the university. Julio and my dad are shouting and running after me, but I've always been faster than Julio, and my dad is out of shape.

It doesn't take long before I can't hear them anymore, but I keep running anyway, out the gate and up the street. My denim jacket is heavy, stiff and hot. Sweat sticks my shirt and backpack to my spine. My jeans chafe against my legs, but I can't stop. I end up on the far side of Lincoln Heights when I just can't go any farther and fall against a retaining wall. My heart feels like it's going to break my ribs and I've got a thirst like I've never had before.

I pull out my screen to check the time. Both my parents have blown up my pod and so has my tía. I have a dozen missed calls and a half dozen messages from each of them. My dad tells me that he's sorry and that he loves me. My mom's long messages are filled with crying, and my auntie just keeps saying to call her. I stop them because I can't listen without crying.

I pull my pod from my ear and disable my screen. I can't stay here, so I start over the hill.

I want to steer clear of main streets, but I don't know the neighborhood. I don't know who's likely to mess with me or which blocks are bad, but at this point I don't really care. Getting taken in an Incursion or killed by some Lincoln Heights bangers couldn't make my day any worse. I begin to fantasize about getting shot.

I picture my funeral as I walk. My mom's crying and my dad's swimming in pain. My auntie keeps moaning about me and her Alex and that she doesn't have anything left to live for. I picture Julio, too, sitting there silently, wishing he hadn't called my parents, thinking that maybe I'd still be alive if he hadn't.

Fuck Julio.

I spend the rest of the walk thinking about all the things that won't happen anymore if I'm crazy and put in a psych ward. My mom took me to Vegas once, just me, when I was young, before Pete died. It was amazing because we went up to the top of the Stratosphere and rode the roller coaster and went to a show with wild acrobats and clowns that blew my eight-year-old mind.

Never again for crazy me.

By the time I make it to Union Station, it's full dark. I'm hungry again and I've got a heat rash on the inside of my legs that burns with each step.

I catch the bus at Hill Street and collapse in the air-conditioning, able to close my eyes for the first time since running away. I try the folding-in thing again. I picture my mind like a piece of flat paper and begin to pull the edges in toward the center, which opens up. I can feel myself beginning to drop down the drain, pulling the paper surface of my mind in over me like a security blanket.

The opening is too small, though. I can't get through, but I can *feel* my voice on the other side.

The bus jolts to a sudden stop, throwing me against the seat in front of me. Pain. I've hit my head hard on the plastic frame of the seat and I'm back in reality.

I've ridden beyond the stop near Mousie's place and I'm going to have to walk back.

I pull the cord.

Ten

MOUSIE LIVES IN THE CONVERTED GARAGE PORTION OF A BIG HOUSE ON Rampart. She's lived there for her whole time in LA with her mom, her dad, her abuela, her brother, his wife, and their baby girl. She says she won't let me see it because she's not supposed to be dating yet and I'm not Salvi and I don't even speak Spanish, but I think it's more about keeping me from seeing how they live.

She's perfectly willing to meet me out front.

The garage is dark when I get there. It's shockingly small, half the size of our living room and dining room. Seven people live inside.

I regret letting Mousie pay for things.

There's a window on the far side. I knock on it. I don't know who's going to wake up, but I'm desperate and I don't have a choice.

A screen lights up inside within seconds of me knocking, and then a face appears. It's a girl a little older than me and she looks pissed. It's probably her brother's girl. Her name is Ana. "Ana, I really need to talk to Mayra."

She just looks at me. "Do you have any idea what time it is?"

I shake my head. "It's late and I'm real sorry, but it's important."

She stares at me through the window and I stare back. I'm not even bothered, because everything has gotten so completely messed up. Finally, she nods and turns away. A minute later, Mousie's at a door that's been cut into the side of the garage, dressed in loose plaid pajamas. Even now she looks good.

"Plugzie?" she asks. "What's going on? You can't come here like this." She glances over her shoulder before closing the door lightly behind her. "You're gonna get me in trouble." When she sees my face her expression changes. I must look really bad, because suddenly, instead of worrying about herself, she's worried about me.

Somebody inside says something in Spanish. She replies, sounding stressed. I think she tells them that she needs to talk to me, that it won't be long.

I step back from the door and she turns and closes it behind her, comes to me, asks me what happened. I do my best to tell her, but it starts to sound really bad—I can't say it without seeming crazy, so instead I just tell her that I ran away from home.

It's a stupid lie, but I can't tell her the truth.

We walk down to the wall in front of the house, sit down. Our skin is touching, but I feel millions of miles away. Every word I say takes the energy of a scream and I'm too tired to keep trying.

Mousie isn't going to be able to help me. I sigh and tell her that I just really wanted to see her. She melts into my arms and pulls me tight. She's warm and I can feel the strength in her small body. She pulls back far enough for me to see her and gives me a little kiss on the lips and then another, slightly longer one.

"Call me, Plugzie." And then: "I really want to . . ." But she trails off. I wait for her to finish her thought. I'm not sure if I want her to say anything at all, but I'll be disappointed if she doesn't say something deep.

She doesn't say anything.

The garage door opens and a man comes out. Mousie gets stiff under my arm and pulls away. The man looks me up and down. He says something in Spanish that I don't totally understand, but I get the point.

I walk back up the street and turn. Her dad has his hand on her shoulder, pulling her up the drive toward their little door.

I'm walking like a cowboy because the heat rash burns with each step.

Eleven

I SPEND THE REST OF THE WALK LOST IN MY THOUGHTS, SO I DON'T SEE THE guy on the bicycle until he's nearly on top of me. He's coming fast down the hill that leads up to my house and he's looking at his screen as he rides. I'm right in his path as he comes around the corner, so I have to jump to the side.

He skids—his wheels slide sideways and the rear one goes over the curb backward—but he gets control before he spins into traffic. His screen doesn't stop. It escapes his hand and falls into the gutter. He comes to a stop facing me, blond hair falling out from under his helmet, dismounts and picks up his screen.

"Damn, you okay?" I ask.

He looks at me, a little surprised, then smiles, checks himself out, turns to look down at his bike before scooting the whole thing back onto the sidewalk. "Yeah, man." He looks down at his screen, then holds it up to show me. "These Live-Tech screens'll survive anything." Then he smiles. "Really sorry I almost hit you, dude. I had a delivery at the top of the hill and got carried away coming down. It's my bad."

I shrug. "T'salright."

He taps his helmet and rights his bike. "You take good care of yourself, man. All sorts of things can happen."

And then he leaves, biking down the street back the way I came from. I watch him go, feeling weird about the whole thing. When he turns the corner down Echo Park Avenue, I start up the hill, still anxious.

The lights are on at my house and the gate is open. My dad's truck is sitting on the driveway next to my mom's rosebushes. I take a deep breath and let it out before I walk to the front door. I search my pockets for my keys, but when I get to the door, I see that I don't need them. The door is open. The TV's blaring in the living room.

"Mom?" I call as I push the door. "I'm home."

There's no answer.

"Dad?"

Nothing.

I look in the living room. There's no one watching TV. Something smells bad, like an unflushed toilet. I wrinkle my nose and sniff again. There's something else, too. Something sour.

I go to call them again, but there's a package on the table next to the door with my name on it.

My letter said that there'd be a package, that I should open it.

I pick it up. It's about the size of a book and it doesn't weigh much. It's the Live-Tech. My mom ordered it before I fucked everything up and it's here now.

I open the package as quietly as I can. I've watched the videos about them already, so I know how it works. All I need to do is put the pod in my ear and it does everything else—even contacts my carrier to make the switch.

In the package the screen is on top, folded tight and small so it's the size of a Post-it. The pod is nestled in packaging under it. It's a bright green–colored lump right now, the top side identified by the Live-Tech logo, and a pentagon with a triangle inside it along with a bunch of starlike dots are etched in black. When I activate it, the logo will disappear and it'll change color to match my skin, making the pod nearly invisible. I lay the screen on the table and pick up the pod. It's attached to a piece of thick paper that says: "KEEP THIS DEACTIVATION CODE WITH YOUR RECORDS," followed by a long series of random words.

I put the paper back in the box and put the pod in my ear, tapping it three times in the middle. It vibrates, then the lump begins to shift and change shape. When it's done, I have to reach up to touch it to make sure it's still in my ear.

It vibrates again. This time it sends a tingling sensation down my neck and arm that makes me shiver slightly. It passes.

Call Mom, I think.

The screen lights and unfolds even though I didn't do or say anything. *Mom* appears along with a picture.

It rings.

My mom's phone rings at the other end of the hall. I walk to the kitchen to find her.

The bad smell gets worse as I enter the kitchen.

At first, I think they're playing a game when I see them both on the floor. My mom is curled up like a baby and my dad is spread out on his stomach like you do when you get a big bed all to yourself. But they're not playing—my dad's shirt is stained red with blood so thick that it's hard to tell where his clothes stop and the pool on the floor starts. My mom's shirt has ridden up on her back to where I can see her bra strap.

My mom's phone is ringing on the counter.

They're not moving. They're not breathing.

I think they're dead.

Adrenaline sends shooting pains down both arms. My fingers burn and tingle.

"MOM!" I'm just bending down to touch her when something moves off to my right. I redirect myself away from whoever's there, turning to size them up as I do.

What I see doesn't make any sense.

It's tall. Dark. Not black or brown, but dark—like a hole. Almost impossible to see. Its head is pointed, shaped like a pin, but I can't tell what part of its head has the face on it—there are bumps and spaces and light spots, but they don't make any sense.

It moves again, but not the way anything should ever move. It's dead silent, a shadow without a body to block the light. The legs are long and there are more than two, but I can't tell how many because it looks like it's wearing a cape that covers it nearly to its feet.

Incursion. This is an Incursion. They are real. That's a bug. An alien. The thoughts all happen as I'm backing away, half squatting.

I've been in enough fights to know what to do. I rise slowly, keeping my knees bent so I can jump if I need to. It's circling back toward the hallway to the front door and I turn, too, keeping my eyes on it.

An arm comes out from under the cape, pushing it aside just a little bit. There are a lot of arms under there, but they aren't paired up. They seem like a collection of options, like if people were utility knives.

The one that comes out ends like a knife blade, and unlike the rest of the bug, which seems to just suck light away, the knife blade is covered with something reflective, slick and wet. When it moves, flecks come off, spattering red on the white of the wall.

Blood.

My dad's body is between us now. There's a gash in his back, and his shirt is bunched up into it. There's another in his thigh.

"Get the fuck away from me!" I shout at the bug, but it doesn't care, it just keeps circling me. "Why don't you just leave me the fuck alone!"

I'm near the knife drawer now. It's closed and I don't know if I can open it, grab a knife, and get ready before it comes at me, but I also don't think I have any other play here. I shift my movement a bit so I'm backing straight up to the drawer.

The bug follows, keeping the space between us the same.

I bring my hand up slow. The bug stays still.

When my hand's on the drawer, I slide it open. The bug's knife hand begins to twitch, and another appendage comes out the other side. This one looks like a crab claw.

I reach into the drawer. My hand is just grasping the handle of a knife when the bug launches itself at me.

I scream, pull the knife from the drawer, and swing it wildly at the bug with my eyes closed.

My knife slashes the air in front of me, but there's nothing there. I open my eyes.

The bug stopped bare inches from the edge of my reach. It's not moving any closer and its head is moving slowly up and down. I can't tell if it has eyes, but it feels like it's looking at something.

I move my hand. The bug's head moves, but then it stops tracking the knife. It seems to refocus on me.

On my head.

On my Live-Tech.

The bug makes a sound, like buttons being pushed, then another that sounds like sandpaper against metal. Together, the noises sound like frustration.

I stand up. It doesn't move. I step forward. It steps back, its arms doing something I don't understand, then the air to my side begins to wave and turn dark.

The bug leaps into the dark air and disappears.

I stand up, look around again. I'm breathing hard and my fingers feel like they're on fire.

Something cracks in my mind. The drain I was trying to open before begins to leak as I look at my dad.

I hear my Skywriting Voice. She breaks through, loud:

"YOU BETTER RUN AWAY, BOY! RUN AWAY."

I look back down at my parents. I hear what she says and part of me wants to run away. I don't want to be here anymore. I don't want to be anywhere. I want this to stop, to go away, to go back.

I'm on my knees now, between them. I reach out for my dad, but when my hands get close to him, I stop. I don't even want to touch him because I'm afraid he'll be cold and I can't handle him being cold.

I force myself. My hand brushes his shoulder. His muscles give and he feels normal and I get a hope that he's not dead, but when I roll him over, it goes away.

His face is gray.

I stand up and step back again. I think about trying to touch my mom, but I can't. I don't want to roll her over. I don't want to see.

"RUN! THEY'RE GONNA SAY YOU DID IT, CRAZY-BOY KILLED HIS FAMILY."

"It was a bug," I tell her. My voice is just a whisper. "A bug killed them."

"THEY WON'T BELIEVE YOU, CRAZY-BOY. TROUBLED-TEEN. NOT GONNA BUY IT SO YOU BETTER RUN!"

"I can't leave them . . ." Then: "I gotta call the police."

"JUST RUN!"

Something shifts in me when she says it this time. A sudden clarity that shatters into blind panic because I know she's right. I stand there for a moment longer, not sure what to do or where to go.

"RUN!"

I stop thinking. I run. I see my dad's key fob in the bowl by the door and grab it on the way out.

I've driven my dad's truck before. We went out to the desert to shoot guns last summer. It was just me and him and we'd never done anything like that just the two of us. My dad hadn't done anything fun like that since Pete died, and it felt like my family was being reborn. We spent two days riding around in the Mojave talking and hiking, shooting and driving.

The memory sticks to my mind and even though I'm running to the truck, what I'm seeing is my dad sitting next to me while I drove on some deserted road up beyond Joshua Tree. He's smiling and trying hard to look relaxed, but I can tell he's stressed about me driving his beloved truck.

It was the best part of the best day of the best trip I've ever taken.

The image crumbles when I unlock the truck. Now all

I can see is what I've just seen inside. Mom. Dad. The bug. The blood.

My parents are dead.

The truck starts, a high-pitched electric whine the only sign it's on, and I press the gate button on the visor. It opens very slowly. Part of me wants to back over it so I can get out faster, but that would make a lot of noise. The guitars are back a little, grinding quietly in my head, but my Voice has gone quiet. I know what to do even without her, though.

I have to get to the bus station.

Twelve

I GRAB MY BACKPACK AND LEAVE MY DAD'S TRUCK ON A WAREHOUSE STREET away from the bus station. I wipe down the steering wheel and the driver's door. It looks easy on TV, but I don't know if I did it right. I'm not a criminal.

Before I leave the truck, I find the key for the toolbox in the back and rescue my old pod and screen. It's not useful for anything but music, but that's what I need right now.

I wish I'd brought my guitar.

"Bye, Dad," I whisper before I turn around. It doesn't feel like enough to say, but I can't think of anything else. All I can see is the look on his face this afternoon when I was running away from him. I always thought my dad was strong, but he looked so weak and sad.

And then he was dead before I could say I'm sorry.

My eyes blur and I have to cough against the lump in my throat.

I'm about to toss the fob onto the driver's seat when the picture on the chain catches my eye. It's a little photo encased in plastic from a photo booth at the Santa Monica Pier. We hadn't gone for any particular reason. Maybe Dad just wanted us all having fun as a family one last time before Pete grew up. I was nine, so Pete must've just turned eighteen. There was a special photo booth there where they'd take the picture for free and then you could buy it, so we went in and took a bunch. The one Mom got for us was the one where Pete and Dad were holding me between them like a hammock and my mom was standing behind us. We were all laughing.

She got three: one for me, one for Pete, and one for Dad. I lost mine somewhere and Pete was buried with his.

I pull the picture off the key chain and drop the fob in the cupholder between the seats. I roll the window down, hoping somebody will steal the truck before the cops find it.

I walk away quickly, fingering the picture in my pocket, then catch my reflection in a window. My denim is streaked with blood. There are spots on my pants, too.

The pants I can't do anything about, but I take off my jacket, examine the patches, the small rips, the soft spots on the sleeves, looking for some way I can tell myself it's okay to keep it, but I know it's not.

"Fuck." I twist it up in my hands, curl it around my fist, and start walking again, feet moving to the rhythm of guitars. At the next bus stop, I drop my denim in the trash can.

"Plugzer's losing everything, today," my voice whispers. *"Not done losing. Not yet."* She's not playful now, not mean. She sounds so sad for me that it's hard not to cry.

There's a payphone on Alameda. I've never used one before, so I don't know how they work, but when I pick up the handset and dial 911, it connects.

An operator answers and asks me to state my emergency.

"I heard noises like a fight . . . at a house . . . It was an Incursion." My mind is racing. I can't even think about how to say what I need to tell her.

"Sir, where is the house?"

"Uh . . ." I try and think of my address, but even that's disappearing under the pressure. "On Laveta Terrace . . . It was a bug!"

"Can you describe what you heard?"

I can't.

Instead of trying to describe it, I hang up and bang my head against the top of the booth to try and clear it. The pain cuts through the noise so I do it again hard. And again. And again.

There's something wet on my cheeks. I'm sure it's blood, but when I wipe it away, it's clear.

Tears.

When I can breathe again, I use one sleeve to wipe my eyes, my nose, my chin. I use the other to wipe down the phone.

Tía Juana. I want to call her, too, but I can't. Not now.

The clock on the wall of the bus station says 4:53 in the morning. Even at this hour the station is full. Kids are asleep on parents in the chairs, homeless guys mill around, and angry-looking dudes stare at each other and at me from their places against the walls.

Everybody looks tired.

The ticket is still in the envelope with the small stack of twenties. I pull it out to look at it more closely. It's for a single passenger going to Seattle from Los Angeles. It's a "standard fare" ticket, whatever that means, and it's for today.

For a bus that leaves in less than an hour.

I try to come up with ways to explain how the bus ticket was prepurchased, mailed with a letter from me, for exactly one hour after I randomly ended up in the bus station. My mind is fuzzy with sleep so instead of explanations, all I end up with is a panicky feeling that makes my chest hurt.

Tell my auntie I didn't do it. I don't know if my Live-Tech will send the message—I have no way of checking because the screen is still on the table by the door. **Tell Juana I didn't do it.** I think it again. Then: **I didn't do it.**

Nothing happens.

Images of my mom and dad cut through my thoughts like razor blades. Every time they flash I feel sick.

Every time I close my eyes, I see black holes that look like the bug.

The look on my dad's face through the door at the student union. Him and Mom dead on the floor.

I make myself sit still in a chair until they call the bus. My seatmate opens her eyes when I sit down. She smiles, but doesn't say anything. I smile back and she shuts her eyes again. I put in my pod and turn up Metallica as loud as it goes before I put my head back and close my own eyes. I'm asleep before the bus pulls from the station.

Thirteen

I DREAM ABOUT MY PARENTS. WE'RE TOGETHER SOMEWHERE THAT ISN'T our house. There's a beach with a beach bar. Thatched huts like you see on TV shows about Florida or Mexico or the Caribbean. My mom is drinking a huge drink that she's standing next to and it's almost as big as she is.

I ask her where Dad is and she shrugs like she doesn't know and doesn't care.

I have his keys and he needs them or something really bad will happen so I go looking for him at school, and then at the grocery store, but I can't find him. I go back to his truck and he's sitting in the driver's seat. In the dream, I know he's dead and he seems to know he's dead, too, because he whispers to me instead of talking and I somehow know that he's whispering because dead people aren't supposed to talk to live people and he doesn't want to get caught.

"*Watch yourself, Alex,*" he tells me. "*Bad things are coming. Strange things. Worse things than what happened to us. We were going to die, scared boy. Nothing to be done for it. Nothing could change it. Worse things for everybody, Alex, unless you stop it. Seen time is the only truth.*"

I ask him what he means and he says, "*You have to save the Earth.*" And then he looks away from me.

"I'm sorry I ran away from you," I whisper back when he's not looking.

He says nothing, still looking away.

"Look at me, Dad?" I beg him. "Please?"

He turns and looks into my eyes. *"You've always been scared boy, mijo, scared of who you are,"* he says, shaking his head. *"Strange days, mijo. Scared boy's going to have to be brave."*

"I'm scared."

My dad nods wisely. *"Scared boy's not too scared. Runaway boy."*

He doesn't talk anymore. His eyes are closed and he's the dead version of himself that I saw on the floor.

When I wake up it's full light outside and my neighbor is looking out the window at fields. Pictures from my dream keep surfacing like dead fish. I pull out my screen and change the playlist.

After a while, I pull out the letter again and reread it.

Even though you won't believe it, there are some things that happen no matter what and when they tell you that of all the ways things could have happened, this is the least bad way, it's really true.

Seen time is the only truth.

My dad said in my dream that nothing could change it. They were going to die.

The letter says this is the best way.

"Bullshit." I say it out loud. Fuck the letter and everything it says.

My seatmate looks at me.

"Sorry."

I spend the rest of the morning staring out the window,

using my music to drown out the guitars, feeling more alone than I've ever felt in my life.

I buy a sandwich in Redding. I feel better after food and I use the Wi-Fi in Subway to look at the news from Los Angeles on my old screen. There's no report on my parents and for a moment I start to think that the cops went to the house and found out they were just fine. Maybe I only imagined the bug. Maybe I just imagined them being dead.

When I open my messenger, there are messages from people asking about whether I'm okay or not. Julio, Mousie, Fizzin, Schmo, everybody.

Everybody except my parents.

I message my dad anyways: **Hey Dad are you ok**

There's no response.

I message again. **Dad**

Nothing.

I message Mom. **Mom? Are you ok?** Then, a few seconds later: **Mom**

They're not messaging me back. They always message back.

It's not that they're not dead, it's just that the cops never went by and nobody's going to miss them until my mom doesn't show up for her route at 5:00 on Sunday morning.

In my mind I see my mom in her driver's seat, talking to me through the gap in the panel that separates her from her passengers. I shake off the image before it forms completely. It's hard to breathe through the lump I get in my throat when I think about it.

They're still lying dead on the floor of the kitchen. I should call the police again but I'd give away where I am. I'm sure they track where calls come from and I'd be calling from Redding at the time the Seattle-bound bus was in town. They'd figure it out.

Sorry, Mom. I think. "Sorry, Dad," I say out loud because somehow it's easier to talk to him since he was a big part of my dream this morning.

While I'm sitting there, a message comes in from my Tía: **Mijo, you ok?**

Eventually: **It wasn't me.** Then: **It was an Incursion.** Then: **I love you.** Then: **I'm scared.**

She responds fast: **What are you talking about?**

I can't answer her so I sign off the Wi-Fi before my head explodes.

It's dark when we get back on the bus and I put my headphones back on. *Mastodon.* Seattle's getting close and I don't know what's going to happen when I get there. I don't know what I'm going to do, but I know I'll do better with it all if I can sleep a little bit.

Fourteen

THE EDGES OF THE HIGHWAY ARE LINED WITH BIG TREES. EVERYTHING LOOKS dark and gloomy because the clouds are low. The concrete is grayer and the cars look dirty. It all feels more serious than LA.

When the bus makes its way into the downtown Seattle station, I don't want to get off. I've gotten to know the Greyhound. I feel safe on it. Even my guitars feel more manageable. Everyone else is already gone before I push past the cleaning crew. The air feels like winter and I'm cold with just my hoodie and no jacket.

There's a Burger King attached to the station and I'm hungry, so I go there.

It's dark inside. I order a Whopper, fries and a Sprite. When my food comes I take the tray to a corner where there aren't many people. I listen to an old man talking on his pod while I eat. He's upset because someone named Lydia wasn't waiting for him when the bus arrived.

I tune him out and try and think about what I'm going to do. I check my screen. Burger King has Wi-Fi. I log on and check the news.

They're there. It's real.

• • •

COUPLE FOUND DEAD IN THEIR ECHO PARK HOME

by: SARAH CAMPBELL, *City Desk*

Police this morning responded to a request for a wellness check on a Los Angeles Metro driver who missed her route time and found both the driver and her husband dead in their home. The driver, whose name is being withheld pending notification of next of kin, has driven for Metro for over twenty years. Her husband, described by a neighbor as a contractor, was not due at work until Monday morning.

The cause of death has not been released, but detectives are classifying the case as a homicide.

Neighbors report hearing shouting late Friday night, but police are not commenting further.

The couple have a teenage son who police are asking for the public's help in locating. He has not been seen since Friday. He is described by family members as being a popular and friendly boy who had recently become troubled.

Juana Perez, the sister of one of the victims, has told us that the son has been in contact with her since the tragedy and that he says he's innocent and that the couple was killed by an alien "Incursion," of the sort being reported on the internet in recent months.

Police dismissed the claim, saying that there is no evidence that Incursions are real and that the weapons used in the attack were of purely "terrestrial origin."

Police are not naming the son as a suspect, saying that they are following several strong leads, but they do consider him a person of interest and are encouraging him to come forward.

• • •

A popular and friendly boy. Recently troubled. Police dismissed the claim.

"You don't need to read that."

I don't look up because I think she's just in my head, but then a shadow falls over me. There's a girl standing over my table. She's black and dark with a thick tight afro cut close to her head.

"What? What do you mean?"

She rolls her eyes like I'm being dense. "I mean you don't need to read that stuff. I'm seriously really sorry about what happened, but I think you know they weren't going to believe you. Reading about it'll just make you feel worse."

I shake my head like she's got the wrong guy or the wrong idea. She waves it off and sits down on the swivel chair across from me, swinging her legs around to one side and crossing them in one smooth gesture. I fight my urge to look at them more closely. Focus on what's important.

"Look." She leans into me. "I wish we could change things, but we can't. Seen time and all that." She smiles and leans forward to pick at my French fries. I start to get ridiculously upset about her stealing a French fry but I'm able to put it all into perspective before I throw a fit.

"What the fuck do you know about what happened? Who are you?"

She sighs, looks seriously at me, a little sad. "I promise that you'll understand everything really soon, but you've got to come with me first." She smiles. She's pretty. "My name's Corina." She steals another fry. "I'm here to pick you up." She reaches into her back pocket. "Here." She pulls out a folded piece of paper. "You wrote this tonight and we sent it back for me to give to you because evidently you were a hot mess when I came to get you."

I don't understand what she just said, but I take the paper she's pushing at me. It's another letter. This one's not in an envelope, it's just folded up. It's short:

> *Hey Alex,*
>
> *This is Corina. She was sent here to get you. She's cool. Go with her.*
>
> *—Plugzer*

It's in my handwriting again. I look up at her and she nods like she understands. "It's a lot to deal with, but it'll all make sense when we get to the compound."

"Compound?" I ask, because even though I want to know how she has a letter from me telling me to go with her when I know for a *fact* that I have never written one—or been to Seattle—plus I don't know her, I can't get the words out.

She sighs. "Just come with me, Alex." She picks up the note and points to the last part. "'She's cool,'" she reads. "'Go with her.'"

"I don't even know you." I shake my head. "Why would I go with you?" I point at the note on the table. "That? That's just . . ." But I don't know what to say, so I lean back instead, look away.

She takes another fry. "You have a better offer, Alex, you should take it." Then she stands up and walks to the exit. She stops at the door, calls back to me: "You coming?"

"You better go, runaway boy. Nowhere else to go."

I scramble up and knock my backpack onto the floor. She rolls her eyes and waits for me.

When I reach the parking lot, she's already getting into a car that looks way too nice for someone who isn't old enough to be driving.

She waves me over.

"Nice car," I say when I get in. I can see the vague definition of the dashboard reflected on the windshield even though it doesn't block the view at all. "This is cool."

Corina smiles and shrugs. "I don't know squat about cars," she says as the car pulls out of the parking space, "but when you work for Sabazios, these are what's available."

Jeffrey Sabazios has been a name in my life for as long as I can remember. He used to be just a big technology guy, but then he developed Live-Tech and some people say he's gone too far with things that read minds. Then he started talking about Incursions and how Live-Tech could protect us, and a lot of people stopped taking him seriously, especially when the president started saying that Live-Tech is bad. But now I have proof that he was right, because of what happened to me. "Live-Tech saved my life."

"I know." Corina nods but she's not really paying attention. I'm about to give up on getting more details, but when the car pulls out into traffic, she taps me on the shoulder. "You can tell him all about it because you'll be working for him, too."

I start to ask more questions but she just shakes her head. "I'll explain when we get to the compound."

We move to a freeway, then a tunnel, then a bridge right on the water, and then another freeway before she pulls us off onto surface streets and winds her way up and down some hills on roads that get smaller and smaller.

I don't know what I was expecting, since she just called it the compound, but we pull through a motorized gate into a driveway that goes in a big circle around a fountain. There's a whole set of buildings on one side of the drive, but they don't look like normal buildings. They're just big bumps that are covered in the same grass and trees that cover the rest of the ground.

"Where are we?" I ask.

"Sabazios's compound."

"You were serious?"

She gets out of the car without replying. I watch as she walks away. She's just wearing jeans and a shirt, but the weather doesn't seem to bother her. I get out, too, try to walk tall like her, but end up tightening my hoodie because I'm cold.

Fifteen

I EXAMINE THE "COMPOUND" A LITTLE MORE CAREFULLY. THERE ARE TWO main sets of hills. They're big and they're covered in trees, so I can't see what's behind them. The one on the left is much taller than the one on the right, and it's got an entrance burrowed into its side that looks like it was cut with an enormous hole punch. The door is round, and as big as three normal doors put together. There's a doorway into the hill on the right, too. This one is average sized, and it's the one Corina's walking to.

She's almost there when she sees I haven't left the car. She turns to wait for me. "Jesus. C'mon."

I jog to catch up.

I haven't showered or changed my clothes in three days. I sniff at my armpit and cringe at how I must've smelled in the car next to Corina.

"You're fine," she tells me when I catch up. "Nobody's getting their noses up in you until you've had a chance to take a shower."

I nod, ready to move on. "This is the door?" I ask as we step up to it. "We're going into the hill?"

"Not a hill," she corrects me. "A house that's built like a hill."

"Jeffrey Sabazios lives in a hill?"

She turns to look at me, her face suddenly serious. "Alex, Jeffrey Sabazios is a vampire. He can't live aboveground."

I don't know if I should laugh or not. It's obviously a joke, but with everything else that's happened . . .

I test out a smile to see if she laughs.

She doesn't.

"You're serious?"

Then she laughs. "No." She gestures up at the hills. "Sabazios is into sustainability and security and he says that this is the best way to live in a large place that doesn't suck up energy, doesn't kill the environment, and is nearly impossible to spy on."

"So he lives in a hill."

"Yes," she says. "He does, and so do I." She opens the door and steps into the hill. "And now, so do you."

I follow her through the door and stop, facing a long hallway that slopes slightly downward. Corina stops, turns to look at me.

There aren't any doors or windows.

The light seems to come directly from the bare white walls. The ground is covered by hardwood, with a thin line of carpet running down the middle.

"This is a long hallway," I comment for lack of anything else to say, buying time to steel myself for moving forward.

"And we call it the Long Hall. Appropriate. Just wait, though," she says, and as she continues walking, things start to change. The walls on either side of us brighten up and then fade into photographs. At first they just look like people doing regular people things, but then one stops me cold. A young guy just a little older than me, wearing desert fatigues, is standing in a parking lot surrounded by lots of other people. There's a bus in the background.

The guy in the photo is my brother Pete.

I know the scene—it was the day he shipped out for the first time, but it's not a picture we took that day—my mom's hands were shaking so bad that none of the pictures came out. He looks happy, and he looks like he's looking right at me.

Like he sees me.

Like he loves me.

"What the . . ." I stop walking to stare at it.

"You get used to it. It's a new use for Live-Tech—connects to your mind just like that pod you've got in your ear but without the contact—like Bluetooth." She motions from my wrist to a photo of a black woman watching us from across a bumpy brick road. "That's my mom. We were at the riverfront in Portland and I was chasing birds. I was like four or something."

I shake my head. "That picture of my brother can't be real."

"The wall reads our memories." She points to Pete. "He's your brother?"

I nod.

She studies me. "Did something happen to him?"

"Yeah."

She shakes her head. "Sorry. That's why this version isn't being sold yet—it's supposed to only grab happy memories, but a lot of times stronger and more complicated memories get picked up."

I don't say anything and I don't move. I just look at Pete.

She looks from Pete to me. "You've been through a lot. I'm really sorry, Alex." She reaches her hand out to me. Her moves are awkward and tentative, like she's approaching a strange dog, but when she touches my arm, I lean into it. It's the first time I've been touched since I said goodbye to Mousie, the first contact since I found my parents.

Maybe it's because of the picture of my brother or just the fact that she's reaching out to me, but I start losing control a little. I shake my head to try and clear it.

Corina starts to walk again. I stare at Pete for a long moment. Seeing him look at me like that makes me feel small, scared, and lonely.

I walk the rest of the distance trying hard not to look at the walls, focusing instead on the guitars.

The Long Hall ends at another door, which opens up onto an outdoor patio cut out of the back side of one of the hills. It's huge—maybe half the size of a soccer field—and it's lined with plants in pots. There's a fire pit on one side that's surrounded by chairs and benches. There's a volleyball net and a workout station, too.

The far edge of the patio has a glass wall that's taller than me by quite a bit. There's a beautiful view of water and hills on the other side of it, with just the tops of the buildings of downtown Seattle visible in the distance. "Is that the ocean?" I ask.

She tells me that it's not, that it's a lake.

She leads me toward a set of glass doors built into a wall on the far side of the patio.

"It's not cold here."

She shakes her head. "We're inside." She points to the glass wall. "No sense in a big outdoor patio in Seattle. Follow the curve—it goes all the way over."

I look where she's pointing. It takes a few seconds for my eyes to see it, but it's true—the glass wall continues up, over, almost impossible to detect.

She opens the double doors. "The common room," she explains.

There's a pool table, Ping-Pong, air hockey, a short row of VR consoles against one wall, and tall shelves with books and games. The other side is dominated by a TV pit surrounded by couches.

Corina gestures to a couch that faces the TV. "Have a seat," she says. "You want a soda?"

I tell her I'm fine and she looks at me like my mom does when she doesn't believe me.

Like my mom *used to* look at me.

I reach into my pocket for the key chain. I don't want to pull it out in front of Corina, but touching it makes me feel better.

I settle onto the couch.

"You going to be okay for a minute?"

I nod.

"I'll be right back." She steps out another door and disappears.

I turn on the TV.

A kids' cartoon I haven't watched in years rises up out of the floor. I think about changing the channel, but instead I just turn the projection base so I'm looking at the faces instead of the backs of the characters. I turn the channel to see what else is on, but stop when it gets to the news. There's nothing about my parents because this is Seattle and that's Los Angeles, but I watch anyway, hoping. Instead they talk about President Castle's push to get Live-Tech regulated. He says we shouldn't have tools that can read our minds because it's not moral, that only God should know our innermost thoughts, but the spokesman for Live-Tech says Castle doesn't like Live-Tech because Sabazios donates to the other party's candidates.

The whole thing makes me think about the Incursion and I switch back to the first channel.

I try and focus, suck in a breath and push it out, but it's no use.

I'm so spun I can't even track a cartoon.

I turn the TV off, wait for the images to descend back into the projector's base, and go inside myself to find my Voice. Ever since the time at my house when she screamed at me to run, it's been easier and easier to get down to where she is.

My Voice is right there on the edge of my regular mind like she's expecting me:

"I'm your secret, scared boy." She doesn't sound like a regular human—her voice is too hollow and ghostly—but even so, right now she feels like a friend, and hearing her fills me with relief.

WAIT! I shout inside. WHO ARE YOU?

"Who am I?" she asks me back. *"I'm your secret. Your girl Sly. Your friend in the Silly Juice."*

I DON'T UNDERSTAND.

"You will, scared boy." She doesn't get any quieter. *"I'm your secret Sly Girl, on the sly, runaway. Don't go telling people about me, boy—snitches and stitches."*

I'M NOT A SNITCH!

Silence. Her calling me a snitch pisses me off and I feel myself slipping back up to the surface against my will. When I return, Corina's there. She's standing over me, holding a pile of clothes and some bathroom stuff. "You alright?"

I'm your secret. I nod. "I think I'm just tired. It's been a weird few days." I can't tell what I do when I'm down under the drain. I might make faces or talk out loud or something—I just don't know.

Snitches and stitches . . .

I'm suddenly nervous I've given something away. "Why?"

She shrugs. "Because I wasn't alright when I got here, and you've had more shit happen to you than I ever have." She hands me a pile of clothes. "Here. The bathroom's down that way on your right."

"Towel?" I ask.

"On the counter. Go get cleaned up and then we'll get you started."

"Started on what?"

"You got a job to do, Alex Mata—just like me." She raises an eyebrow. "So get your ass on it." She smiles and gestures with her chin toward the door she just came through.

Her smile makes me feel better instantly.

I walk out and down a hallway. When I'm through the door I turn back to Corina. She's looking at something on her hand. From here she looks like a little kid who should be watching cartoons with me. When I first saw her, I didn't think about how old she was, but now I can see that she's my age or maybe a little bit older than me.

Sixteen

INSIDE THE SHOWER, I START TO SCRUB.

I've always been a "the water will get it" sort of showerer, focusing on my hair, face, and privates with the soap and letting the water run over the rest of me, but now I feel like I need to scrub off layers of skin all over. My skin is growing red and starting to hurt, but I can't stop scrubbing. Each swipe leaves me feeling slightly better, which makes me want to scrub harder.

I want to scrub off my parents on the kitchen floor. I want to scrub away the bug that killed them. I want to scrub off the idea that I'm never going to be able to go back to my old life. I want to scrub off being wanted for murder.

Everybody thinks I murdered my parents. They all think I'm crazy. I can't scrub that away. All the worries I had before seem so dumb compared to what's happened.

I picture Auntie, suddenly alone. I can't imagine what she thinks right now. Mousie thinks . . .

Mousie. *Mayra.* All of our street names now sound ridiculous. Three days ago, tossing up tags, skating, and playing guitar were the most important things in my life. It's all so stupid.

Things for little kids who don't know any better.

After the shower, I turn my attention to the clothes Corina gave me. There's a pretty good pair of jeans and a black T-shirt, along with some boxer briefs and a pair of socks.

They're all my size, and when I get my shoes back on, I feel okay. I pick up my dirty clothes and my hoodie but I don't know what to do with them except carry them back out in my backpack.

There are people in the commons when I return. Corina's there, but there also three older white guys.

They all look up from their conversation when I enter.

The oldest of the three stands up and offers me his hand. He's over six feet with thick brown hair and gray eyes, big and intense like an owl's. He's thin, but even just looking at him, I can see his strength. He moves like a fighter, smooth and without waste.

I recognize him. I've seen him on the news and being interviewed. It's Jeffrey Sabazios.

"Alex!" He smiles when he says my name, like we're old friends. I take his hand and he grips mine firmly, shaking and not letting go. "I'm glad you're finally here. And I'm so sorry about what happened to your parents."

I nod, but I can't think of what to say.

He doesn't seem to notice that he's still shaking my hand. "I'm Jeff and this is John Bishop." He gestures at the guy next to him who's smiling at me. John Bishop is baby-faced. He's dressed nice, and is burly under his shirt, built like a wrestler, with not enough blond hair to cover his head all the way. "John's my number one guy—he's in charge of all aspects of the project here at the compound."

I let what he just said fly past me because John is already moving in to say hi. "Good to have you on board, Alex. Again, sorry for what you're going through." His voice is surprisingly small and soft for his size.

Sabazios still has my hand, so I can only nod in John Bishop's direction.

"And this"—Jeff continues on to the last guy—"is Richard Beeman, who runs the witness program." Richard is younger—twentysomething.

Witness program? Before I can even wonder what the hell he's talking about, Richard blushes and steps up to me. "It really is good to have you here, Alex." He's got a face that's full of sharp edges, and his brown hair is tucked back into a short ponytail with free wisps that fall into his face when he stands. His smile is warm and reassuring. I smile back without meaning to.

Sabazios is still pumping my hand. "Normally, I don't greet new witnesses on their first day, but Alex"—he nods his head like he's just confirmed something he already knew—"you are a special case—we haven't managed to recruit a one-fifty plus before and I have heard pretty amazing reports about what you'll be able to do."

"Okay," I mumble as he finally drops my hand. *One-fifty plus?* I'm hoping that something will happen that I can understand.

"Alex." Bishop steps in before I can ask what Sabazios means. "I know this is a big ask after everything you've been through, but we don't have a lot of time." He puts a hand on my shoulder and levels his head so he's looking into my eyes. "We're not exaggerating about the fate of the world being in the balance here." He pauses, but doesn't look away. "Do you have it in you to help us? To get right to work?"

I nod. I'm not weak.

He nods back, lets my shoulders go, smiles slightly. "Thank you. Your courage is impressive."

Richard steps in, putting his hand protectively on my shoulder. "I think this is a little much for Alex right now." He turns to me and continues. "We've all been excited to meet you."

"Absolutely right. We're glad to have you here." Jeffrey Sabazios reaches out to shake my hand one more time, and when he lets it go, he nods to Richard, then turns to John Bishop. "There are some things we need to settle before I head to DC."

Bishop nods lightly and follows Jeff as he steps back out onto the patio and disappears toward the way we came in.

Richard still has his hand on my shoulder. "You're probably hungry."

I start to say that I'm fine, but then I realize that he's right. Burger King didn't do it. I am hungry. Really hungry. I nod.

Richard smiles. "Let's go feed you, then."

Seventeen

RICHARD LEADS US OUT ONTO THE PATIO AND THEN THROUGH A SECOND door. We step inside an enormous indoor gym that looks too big to be buried in the hillside you can see from the outside. There's a basketball hoop at either end, painted hardwood in the middle, and a weight room on the other side of a glass wall beyond the far hoop. The gym is lit like daylight, which confuses me until I turn around and see that the entire wall around the door is a single enormous window.

"It's a real window," Corina says when she catches me looking stupidly at it. "You can see out of it, but the wall and the roof of the patio are made from the same stuff and nobody can see in—it just looks like a hill."

Richard is already on the far side of the gym. "This way," he says, and leaves through an open doorway.

I follow him into what looks like it might be a kitchen, but I don't recognize any of the appliances. There's no obvious stove or dishwasher, just a little drink fridge, but there are counters and a sink. Richard settles into a wooden chair at a dinette table that looks a lot like the one we have at home except that there's something that looks like the Live-Tech design in the middle of it: A white pentagon filled with thousands of random gray dots that look like stars. Among the gray dots are three bright red ones that are connected with red lines to make a triangle.

Even with the design, the table's the first almost-familiar thing I've seen in the house, and I want to hug it.

I sit down across from him, Corina on my side, and look around.

The same version of the Live-Tech design from the table is painted on the wall to our right, but huge.

I wait, but they don't make any moves about getting us something to eat. "You said something about food?"

Richard nods. "Go check the box on the counter. Put your hand on the indentation. It'll make you something."

The box he's talking about is one of the things that made me question whether this was a kitchen, because it doesn't look like a kitchen thing. It looks like a cat carrier that somebody covered in aluminum foil. There are holes in the side and a glass panel that covers the main opening. On the side is a hand-shaped dent, so I put my hand in it. The interior lights up and I watch through the glass as a panel opens in the bottom of the box and a plate rises slowly up from somewhere.

Nozzles emerge from the top and sides, begin squirting goo, sculpting it, but they're moving so fast back and forth across the plate that I can't even really see them.

They work so fast, the goo spreads like ripples across the plate, like a muscleman's abs.

I pull my hand away.

The nozzles slip back to where they came from, the plate rises slightly from the bottom. The flap in front moves out of the way, revealing a plate with what looks like two steaming hot pupusas covered in pickled cabbage. I sniff and I can smell the tortillas and cheese and chicharrón.

"The plate won't be hot," Richard advises from behind me. "The food should be something you like."

It is.

The pupusas look exactly like the ones I used to order when we went to Atlacatl for dinner as a family. I've been ordering them since before I could even talk. It was Pete's favorite restaurant when he was a little kid, so we used to go at least once a week. We haven't gone as a family since Pete was killed, but I go on my own sometimes.

Went.

Mousie and me went last week. We ate pupusas just like these.

I wasn't thinking about them when Richard asked if I wanted something to eat, but they really are the most familiar food I can think of.

Richard directs me to a drawer for silverware.

I reach in and grab a Hawaiian Punch from the drink fridge.

I carry it all back to the table in a daze and stare at my plate as I sit down.

"It's cool," Corina tells me. "Go ahead and eat—there's nothing wrong with it."

I nod and cut off a piece with my knife and fork and scrape some of the cabbage onto it.

It tastes perfect. I chew and swallow as best I can while my whole world begins to swim in memories and feelings. I can feel my eyes growing wet and my throat closing but I get it down.

They don't say anything while I eat. I hurry to finish because being watched while I eat makes me feel rude.

When my plate's clean, I set my fork down and look up.

"Are you ready?"

He doesn't specify for what. I nod, shrug, nod. "Yeah."

He reaches into his pocket and pulls out a portable projection square, placing it in the middle of the table. "Alex, I'm going to warn you that this won't be easy, especially considering your last few days."

I try not to show that he's scaring me, but I end up scooting back in my chair a little bit anyway.

"Are you ready?"

"Sure."

He touches the square and the light changes above it in the middle of the table, turns black, spreads out of focus, and then comes clear.

It's a bug. I scramble backward, knocking over my chair, but the bug doesn't move or react. The cape doesn't split, none of the arms come out.

Corina's hand lands on my arm. "It's just a picture. It can't hurt you."

I look over at her, embarrassed. I can feel my face flushing so I turn and make myself look back up at the bug on the table. The bug is black—not like paint but black like empty darkness. It doesn't reflect any light at all, so even though it's within feet of me and spinning slowly, it's hard to understand what I'm seeing. It was almost easier when one was . . .

Trying to picture that bug brings it all back, flashes of skin, blood. The dark. The bug crashes around in my head, a collection of images, each terrifying, none complete.

I look down at the table so they don't see my eyes.

"This is a Locust. The Incursion theorists have taken to

calling them bugs, but Locust is more accurate because they behave a lot like Locusts. Do you know what Locusts do?"

I shake my head without taking my eyes off the table.

"They swarm. Millions of them descend at once on an area, consuming everything edible and then moving on, leaving a wasteland behind them. We have good reason to believe that the 'Incursions,' as people call them, are just the beginning—forward scouts if you will. If we don't act fast, the whole swarm will come."

I nod. I started looking at the thing when he was talking and now I can't take my eyes off it. My fear forces me to know the thing. "What do they want with us?"

"I can show you." He stands up. "I'll be right back." He reaches out to the little box and makes the bug disappear.

When it's gone, I feel like I can breathe again. I turn toward Corina. She's looking right at me. I smile at her and my face flushes a little. She smiles back shyly and looks away.

"How long have you been here?" I ask her eventually, just for something to say.

"About a year," she says, shrugging. "It's home now."

"You said you were from Portland?" I try and picture anything I know about Portland, but I come up blank. "That's Oregon, right?"

She looks at me, her face entirely neutral, gives me the dead-eye, and nods slowly. "Yeah."

Richard comes back before I think of something else to say that isn't completely stupid.

"Sorry," he says. He holds up a thing for me to see. "I forgot this in my office."

I can't make sense of the thing he's holding. It looks like a combination of a pair of binoculars and a gas mask. "What's that?"

He holds it up to admire it. "This is one of my favorite toys, Alex. This is what's called a tunneling telescope." He sets it down next to me, leans in like he's going to tell me a secret. "The Locusts aren't the only aliens out there. We have an ally in our fight, and they've been giving us technological and strategic assistance. The tunneling telescope is one of our ally's inventions, and it works on principles even I barely understand, but I can tell you this: it works."

"Other aliens?" is all I can think of to ask.

"They call themselves the Gentry. You can think of them as sort of a 'parent'"—he makes air quotes—"race to us—they've been taking care of us for a long time from a distance and now they're helping us more directly. Jeff's been working with them for a while."

"So Live-Tech and all his other inventions . . ."

Corina laughs. "Jeff's smart, but he's not that smart."

"Gentry tech, mostly. Live-Tech you're familiar with." He gestures at my ear. I fight the urge to move my hair to hide the pod from him. "Live-Tech creates a bridge between biology and technology—essentially they've found a way of translating instructions directly from our minds without having to use common coding language to communicate—very handy for making things like phones and food fabricators"—he points at the cat carrier—"do what we want without having to tell them."

"So it really is mind . . ." I get halfway through the question when I start to feel dumb again and trail off.

Richard nods. "Yep. The Gentry are a millennium ahead of us when it comes to biological technology—essentially,

Live-Tech bonds with us, gathers specific elements of our thoughts, and translates them into usable information for nonbiological technologies. The food fabricator? When you touched the hand indentation, you created a temporary bond with a Live-Tech sensor. It searched your mind for specific food-related information and then turned it into computer code for the rest of the fabricator to utilize."

"I get it," I say, nodding. "It's like Google Translate between brain and computer."

Corina smiles, looks at me, smiles wider. "That's pretty much it."

I have another question before he goes any further: "How does it stop the . . ." I can't even say the word out loud. "How does it stop them?"

Richard points a finger at me. "Good question. Live-Tech, when it's paired and operational, creates a field effect that can hurt or even kill them." He points at my ear again. "You're living proof that a single pod can protect a single person, but there's also a cumulative effect. If we can get Live-Tech everywhere, attached to everyone, not only would each person be protected individually, but there would be a field effect that would be so strong they won't even be able to come through their portals without frying."

Corina makes a circle with her finger. "That's where we come in. We've got to get Live-Tech attached to every single person on Earth. We won't be safe until we do."

Richard points back at the thing in his hand. "Now you have some direct experience with what we're facing, but I need to show you something so you'll truly understand." He holds the thing up. "Bring it to your face. It'll attach itself, so you'll be able to let go."

I reach for the thing on the table, pull it toward me and pick it up. It's a lot lighter than I expect it to be.

"What you're going to see is frightening, but remember, it's not happening here. You're watching through a telescope and seeing something that's happening very far away, alright?"

I was bringing it up to my face when he started talking, but I stop when he says this. I start lowering it. I don't want this. I can barely deal with what I've already seen and heard.

"Alex." Corina leans in toward me, stops my hand from lowering the telescope any farther. "You need to see this."

I look at her, nod. I bring it the rest of the way up to my face.

My world evaporates. I'm not in the kitchen. I'm not anywhere I recognize. I can't tell up from down. Everything is wrong. "What the hell?!" I feel like I'm losing my balance. I reach out to steady myself, but my hand hits the table even though I can't see it.

"Don't worry. You're still in the kitchen." Richard's voice is coming from somewhere nearby. "You're just looking through the telescope. Tell me what you see."

His voice steadies me. I focus on what's in my view.

There's sky and there's ground, but they're wrong. The sky is dark and thick with yellow and purple clouds that move like water through the air. They're so low and close, I could reach up and dip my hand in. The ground beneath me is smooth like a dinner plate, slightly curved and white as milk.

I look for horizons to orient myself, but the plate I'm standing on is surrounded by other, taller plates that make it hard to see beyond them. "What the hell . . ." I reach out for the table again to make sure it's still there. I take a breath. "I'm standing on something." I look again, more closely, more able to concentrate. They aren't plates, they're the tops of things. "I think it's some kind of building." Pieces begin to fall into place. "Yeah, a building. Where is this?"

I feel Richard press against the telescope. Suddenly my view shifts upward like I'm being launched in a rocket. The world spreads out below me as I fly. The clouds whip past and melt into a bruise-colored swirl that then slips to a quarter-sized spot in a sea of sickly yellow-tinged clouds that belt the entire planet.

I'm not looking at Earth.

There's a huge glowing red star in the sky that looks near enough to touch. "Holy crap."

"You're looking at a planet about twelve light-years from Earth."

"The Locusts live there?" The buildings. I immediately feel dumb for asking.

"Indeed." I feel Richard's hand against the telescope again and I'm suddenly back on the top of the white building. His hand moves again. "Remember, what you're seeing is happening, but you are not actually there. Nothing that you see can hurt you and they have no way of knowing that you're watching, okay?"

"Okay."

"You're perfectly safe."

The way he says it makes me feel like it's not true at all, but before I can even get nervous about it, I'm in a different place. It's a big place, bumpy, hard to understand.

The light is bad, but I suddenly wish it was worse. The room is filled with Locusts. They're huddled in bunches on the floor, the walls, even the ceiling, where they hang like bats.

The whole place seems to quiver with their movement.

He touches the telescope again and I'm somewhere new. There are cages and equipment. It looks like a lab but I don't recognize anything inside it. "Look into a cage."

I float over to the nearest one and look inside. There's a body there. It's attached to a bunch of black, spaghetti-like tubes that seem to be coming right out of her skin. She looks like she's been dead for a while.

She's human, with dark skin and dark hair that are still visible through the mess. "How did she get here?"

"She was taken in an Incursion in Peru a few days ago. The Locusts have the technology to open targeted portals between their world and other places, which allows them to travel huge distances instantly. During these initial Incursions, they're just taking victims back to their planet to run tests."

But I don't hear the last part of his answer because the dead lady opens her eyes and now I'm screaming.

"She's alive!" I pull back as fast as I can, but that just lets me see that there are dozens of cages, just like hers, and they've all got bodies in them.

"For now. Soon they'll have finished their preliminary exams, and then . . ."

"Then what?"

He doesn't say anything for a moment and I think he didn't hear me. I'm just about to repeat myself when he speaks.

"Right now the victims of the Incursions are being used as test subjects. The Locusts are establishing that we have proper nutrient capacity and that there are no elements of our biology that might pose a risk if eaten. They're also testing our endurance and minimum requirements for sustaining life. Once that's done, they're going to perform one more test on her and the others."

"What's that?"

He looks at me, his face serious. "They're going to eat her and the others, and we suspect that they will like our taste. The Locusts are going to use us as food."

"They're gonna farm us," Corina says.

My brain is on overload. I start thinking about the lady and suddenly I'm back hovering over her. She's looking up at me and I swear she can see me. Her lips are moving. She's saying something over and over and over again.

I think she's praying.

I panic. *I want to go home.* Before I finish my thought, my view shifts.

I'm standing in the kitchen of my own house. There's dried blood on the floor where my mom and dad were. There's black powder over everything, clustered like mold along the cabinets, the door handles, and the open knife drawer.

I close my eyes so I won't have to look. The blood and the dirt, the fact that I won't ever see my parents again.

I'll never go home again.

I don't want to see anything else. There isn't anything out there in the whole universe that can make things better for me right now. I want to rip the telescope off my face and throw it to the ground, but as I reach up to rip it off it just falls into my hand.

The sudden change in light and the fresh air on my face make me squint. My eyes are full of tears and squinting sends them down my cheeks.

Richard is staring at me. "Alex? You can talk to me . . ." He says it like he's hurting, too.

I don't want to talk to him about it. Instead, I look at the telescope in my hand and try to get myself under control.

"I'm so sorry about your parents, Alex."

I start to nod, but something finally catches, something that's been bothering me. I look at Richard. "How do you all know about that?"

Richard looks confused.

"How . . ." My emotions are still strangling me. I clear my throat, can't clear the guitars. "How do you all know about what happened to my parents?"

He nods, purses his lips. "I know it's hard not to focus on that right now, but I promise that you'll understand soon."

I stand up, edge toward the door. "Tell me or I'm out."

Richard looks at Corina.

"Show him," she says. Then she turns to me. "This is gonna be weird for you, so prepare yourself."

I don't know what she's talking about, and this is all weird, so I don't know what she means by prepare myself. "Whatever. You need to tell me how you know."

Richard seems to realize that he just stepped in it. He sighs, then: "We know because you're going to tell us, Alex."

I shake my head. "I haven't told you anything."

Richard looks squarely at me, then nods and reaches out to the box on the table.

The air gets cloudy again, not black this time, but a mix of colors. A video begins. It's me. I'm sitting in a chair in a room I don't recognize and I'm wearing the black T-shirt I'm wearing right now. As I try to make sense of that, the me on the recording begins to talk:

"I found them on the kitchen floor when I got home on Friday night—I was going to tell them I needed help and that I was ready to go to the psych ward if that's what they thought I needed. I didn't even see the bug at first, it was totally silent and it looked like a shadow in the doorway or something, but when I went to go to my mom, it moved and then I saw it . . . It showed me its arm, the one with the knife on it . . . It had their blood on it, so it was the only part that showed anything, any light . . ."

I don't wait for the video to end before I turn away.

Being wanted for murder, being crazy, life in prison—those are all normal things, and right now they all seem so much safer than a world where things are unstuck in time and float around, where aliens are going to kill us and other aliens are helping us and people know things that they cannot possibly know.

Richard reaches out for me.

"Let me go." The words are drowned out by the guitars shredding in my head. I try and shout over them, "LET ME GO!"

I push away from him and run through the door we came in, across the patio, and back out through the Long Hall.

Nobody tries to stop me.

I run for blocks, but I don't know where I am or where I'm going. I've left my backpack, which has my money in it along with everything else I own. I've got nothing. I'm in a strange part of a strange city. I've got no wheels of any sort and no way to get any. So I have no money and nowhere to go.

And I'm wanted for murder.

There's a bus stop with a bench down the street and I go sit on it. I have only one friend that I know of right now, and I want to hear her voice.

I close my eyes and slip through the drain to go down deep. She's there.

I NEED HELP.

She responds: "*You already helped yourself, running boy.*"

HOW?

"*You wrote it in the letter.*"

HOW?

"*Read your letter, scared boy—read it like it's from your crew, boy.*"

And then she's gone.

I surface and open my eyes. Corina's car is pulling into the bus stop in front of me. She rolls down the window and holds something out to me. "You told me to bring this." She raises her eyebrows. "Your crew?"

When we were in middle school, we had a tagging crew called BTC. We thought we were really cool. Beems developed a code that we could use to discuss business without anybody knowing what we were doing. It was dumb, but it worked because when teachers or parents found the notes, they only read stupid stuff about girls or classes or just random words. All we did was use the first letter of every third word. We got really good at writing like that and it was sort of a competition to write the most boring note that made sense while hiding the real message, BTC style.

Corina's handing me the letter.

"Where did you get this?"

"I pulled it out of your backpack."

"What the—" But she cuts me off.

"You told me to do it, so don't get extra."

I give up and unfold the note, flattening it against my thigh.

Hey Alex,

This is you. Really. Please listen up, man, your stupid life depends totally on it. Can you please open your ears right now? Listen, I know it's not cool what's all happening, but you need to stop doubting and lift your ugly eyes up so you can see what's happening around you. You're not crazy, man—all this is real

My mind is flighty and it's hard to concentrate, but I see it. First letter of every third word. When I'm done, I look up. Corina's watching me through the rolled-down window from the driver's seat. I catch motion coming up on my left. A bus is coming. She's going to have to move the car, so I get up and open the door.

"To the bus or to the compound? I'll do it either way."

"The compound, I guess."

She nods and pulls out from in front of the bus. "What'd the note say?"

The note hadn't said much, just two words, but they were all I had. Nothing makes sense today, but I figure I probably have my own back even if nobody else does. The message was just:

TRUST CORINA

Eighteen

RICHARD IS WAITING FOR US IN FRONT OF THE DOOR TO THE LONG HALL. "I'm sorry, Alex," he says before I even get across the driveway. "This is hard enough for the other kids who come here whose parents weren't killed—I just . . ." He shrugs and looks at me, waiting to be forgiven.

I nod. "T'salright."

His whole body slumps with relief, and I want to put my hand on his arm to let him know that it's okay. I don't, though. Instead, I shake my head and step into the hallway. I don't want to talk about it anymore because I don't even know what I think.

Once we're back in the kitchen, I'm ready to ask more questions. "How did you do that with the video?"

He gestures at the chair I was sitting in and then sits down across the table. "The simple answer is that you made that video, and then we sent it back in time using a device we got from the Gentry."

I nod. It makes as much sense as anything else. "Richard?"

"Yeah?"

"The bug—the Locust—that killed my parents?"

He nods, encouraging me.

"Why didn't it just take them? Take me? The Incursions . . ." This is hard to talk about. "They took people."

"Why did it try and kill you instead of taking you back to their planet?"

"Yeah."

"Because they know you're a threat, Alex. They know what you can do. That's why we had to get you that Live-Tech pod." He shakes his head. "It took a lot of work on a lot of people's part for you to survive long enough to get here. We had to get your mom to order the Live-Tech, make sure it was delivered in time, make sure you put it on before the Locust got you." He chuckles. "Just getting your mom to order the Live-Tech was nearly impossible—there weren't many futures where she was willing to." He refocuses on me. "It was worth it because we knew what you would be able to do as well as they do." He leans forward. "Getting you here is a major victory for us."

"What are you talking about?"

He nods, leans back again. "The Gentry have shown us a way, Alex, to make sure that things happen the right way *even before they happen—to control the future* so we can keep the Earth safe. This technology is what we used to make sure you got the Live-Tech that saved your life—it's very effective, but it's also very difficult. It's a job that only very specific people can do." He leans in, nods his head like he's pointing at me with it. "People like you."

"So you need me to . . . ?"

"We need you to be an advance spy for us. We need you to witness the future, to make sure it happens the way humanity needs it to. In order to protect ourselves from a full-scale Locust invasion, we have very little time to get Live-Tech into the hands of every person on Earth, which won't be easy, and will require a lot of different people making exactly the decisions we need them to make. As you probably know, Live-Tech gets a lot of pushback—people are afraid of it, the US government thinks it might be dangerous. You see the issues we face. We can ensure victory for Earth, but we urgently need your help to do it."

I'm already shaking my head, but it's mostly just habit. "That's not . . ." I'm about to say it's not possible, but everything happening is impossible, so instead: "How?"

He nods his head. "Time, Alex, is not what you think it is. Einstein called time a *stubborn illusion*, because even though he knew it was different than it appeared to him, even he had trouble wrapping his mind around the truth—and in the end, even he hadn't fully understood what time is or how it works. He thought time—past, present, and future—had all already occurred, and that there was no such thing as free will. But he was wrong." Richard leans back, smiles. "He got the past right—that's fixed and can't be changed, but he didn't understand the role of the present and the future."

He pauses, waiting for me to let him know if I get it. I think I do, even though I don't have any idea where he's headed. I wait for him to continue.

He nods. "Good." Then: "The Gentry know that the future is not fixed—it's an endless field of possibility where every single thing that could happen already exists. The present acts like the shuttle on a weaver's loom, setting the threads in place and locking them in. The present creates the glue that holds the past firmly in place forever."

He looks at me again, his eyebrows raised. There's hair falling forward again over his eyes, but he doesn't seem to notice; he's too into what he's telling me. "Okay," I say.

"Well, the Gentry have developed a tool that allows them to scan all the possible futures and find the exact moments that they want to make happen—the moments we need in order to implement our plan to save ourselves. It's a device that they call the Oracle. The Oracle can see the whole sweep of possibilities, but it can't fix human futures in place—only a human can witness human futures—and not just any human, either, it takes a special sort."

"Special how?" Then: "I'm . . ."

"There are genetic variations that occur naturally in a very few people—fewer than one in a hundred million—people to whom the Gentry can attach a Live-Tech device, which allows them to see the future." He points at me and then Corina. "You both have those variations, and with the proper Live-Tech aides, you can visit the desired future events and lock them in, ensuring our survival." He pushes lightly at my shoulder. "You, Alex. You can save the world."

Part of me wants to nod and be done with it, but I can't. They've made a big mistake. Jeffrey Sabazios, Richard, the rest of them, they're wrong about one thing.

"I'm not special." I say it slow so he'll understand. "I'm not . . ." But I don't know what I'm not because I don't know what they think I *am*.

But Richard just smiles. "Oh, Alex, you are special. Very special. You remember how Jeff called you a one-fifty plus?"

I don't want to let on how curious I am about that, so I don't say anything.

"That means you're not one in a hundred million, you're not even one in a billion. You are a near-perfect genetic match for the Gentry technology that allows people to see the future—you've got one hundred and fifty-three of the genetic markers that facilitate witnessing—more than anybody in our history." He reaches for Corina. "Corina's very good at what she does, but she has less than half the genetic markers you do. She can see and sense many things when she witnesses, but compared to you, she's blindfolded and wearing earplugs. You're going to be the most powerful witness we've ever had. The futures that you witness, they're going to be so clear that they'll be *impossible* to change." He looks at his watch. "Listen, we'll get you up to speed and ready tomorrow, but we need to leave now."

"Where?"

"It's time to meet your team."

Nineteen

THERE ARE PEOPLE IN THE COMMONS WHEN RICHARD AND CORINA BRING me back. I hesitate at the door, not ready for strangers.

Corina nudges me inside, and Richard follows, making it impossible for me to back out again. He's still standing behind me, just in the doorway, when he blasts my name to the room. "Hey, everybody, I'd like to introduce you to Alex."

A black kid with a big messy afro looks up from his book. He smiles at me, nods. "Hey, man." He's got sharp features, and something in his eyes that makes it feel like he can see right through me. "Calvin," he tells me. "Alex?"

I nod. "Yeah."

"Welcome to it, man." He looks up at Richard. "Marcus already gone?"

I feel Richard nodding behind me. "Yeah. We pulled his patch and put him on a flight to Denver this morning."

Calvin nods. I look around to the other people in the room. They're all kids about my age. Corina pulls on my arm a little bit and I turn to her.

"I'm gonna introduce you around—everybody here's cool, so don't stress."

"I'm fine," I tell her.

She smiles. "Sure." She points to the couch where there are two kids watching a soccer game. I don't recognize the teams.

One's a white girl with a long blond ponytail. "That's Maddie."

"Hey," I try. The girl, Maddie, looks up at me and nods before turning her attention back to the game.

The other one, a guy, is big, white, built like a football player. He's been watching me since we came in, but he hasn't turned to face us yet. Instead, he's pretending to watch the game. I don't like him on sight.

"And that's Damon," Corina says.

He turns around slightly and raises his eyebrows at me.

I raise my chin back at him, but he's already turned away.

Corina takes my arm. Her fingers feel cool against my skin. "Nobody can talk to Maddie if there's a game on, and Damon . . ." She pulls at me to follow her over to another kid. "This is Paul—he's our resident teddy bear."

Paul hops up from the couch, bounces once and sticks his hand out to me. He's my height, so medium, but he's white and he's built thick. "She's totally exaggerating—I don't have stuffing."

When he speaks, I immediately figure he's gay. I shake his hand. "I'm Alex."

He tugs my sleeve and steps away toward the hallway with the bathroom. "It's supercool that you're here."

Richard jogs up to us, takes my hand. "Welcome aboard again, Alex." He looks at Paul. "Paul's going to take good care of you."

Paul smiles, wrinkles his nose at me.

"Yeah. Okay."

"Paul, can you get Alex set up to write his letter?" He looks to me. "Get settled and then we've got some notes to write and we need to record that video you saw."

Paul leads me down the hallway. "So LA, huh? I've never been there, but we drove by it once on the way to Comic-Con. Did you ever go to Comic-Con? It's supercool if you're into that sort of stuff. Are you?"

I don't say anything because I'm not ready for a future filled with comic book references I don't get.

"I'm from Arizona—between Phoenix and Tucson. Ranchland hell, eight-five-one-two-three."

I still don't say anything. He's like having a spastic puppy jumping up at me.

I turn around to look back at Corina. She's at a table. Damon's sitting with her. He says something. She laughs. She's already forgotten about me. I look back down at the floor.

Fuck both of them.

"Yeah." Paul waves his arm. "This place is too much. Corina just got you this morning? It's weird now, but you are going to absolutely love it here—witnessing's amazing." He ducks his head down into my sight line so we make eye contact. "We're going to save the world!"

I nod a little and look away. I know I'm being a dick, but I can't stop it. His whole way of talking just agitates me. He can tell, too, which makes me feel even worse.

"Yeah. That's what they told me."

He stops in front of a door, opens it. "Welcome to your tiny shared plain ugly dorm room." He shakes his head. "You'd think a billionaire fronting for aliens would invest a little in making things nice, but . . ."

I make myself smile and look inside. The room's nice but small. Two beds—one against each long wall with four or five feet of space between them—two dressers and a set of desks. One side is obviously occupied—the wall is covered with an American flag and a collection of cowboy hats. The bed isn't made, papers litter the desk. An Ibanez acoustic guitar sits on a stand between the bed and desk.

"You play?" I ask him before I can stop myself.

Paul nods, smiles. "I can pick a tune. You?"

I shrug. "Yeah, I guess."

He's looking at me and I realize I'm staring at his guitar. "You can play it if you want to . . ."

I do want to. Nothing would make me happier right now than losing myself in music, but it feels weird to do it right now, in front of this kid. I make myself look up at the other side of the room. It looks like it's never been touched.

"That side's yours. It's all been cleaned and restocked for you."

The other kid just left. I'm a replacement. I don't know what I'll do if I have to leave—nothing to go back to. My stomach begins to burn and I look away to keep from losing it.

Paul walks past me to my dresser and opens the top drawer. It's filled with clothes. "They just bought you new clothes. Take a look."

I walk up behind him and look at the neat stacks of underwear and socks in the top drawer. Boxers, which is what I wear. The socks are all variations on green and beige, which are the colors I usually pick. I pull open the next drawer and find a selection of T-shirts. There are jeans in the drawer below that and the bottom drawer holds a pile of hoodies in red, gray, and brown.

"They got it right?"

"Yeah."

"We show up here and there's clothes waiting for us and then, a little later, we'll tell them what to get us—give them our shopping list—and they'll send the list back in time so all the clothes are there waiting for us. It'll freak you out if you think about it too much, so I try not to." He shakes his head. "A trip."

I'm trying to listen, but my mind's having trouble keeping up. It takes all my will to make myself pay attention.

Paul's saying, "When I first got here I was sure they'd been spying on me and I told them they got it totally wrong—like I would never have ever considered wearing what they gave me in a million years, but they knew I was lying."

"How?"

He laughs again. "I just told you—*I* told them what to get."

I feel dumb. I hate feeling dumb.

He waves me down. "Don't stress. It takes a while to get used to these things." He suddenly claps his hands together. "You're going to travel in time!"

"Yeah." I don't think I've ever been as excited about anything in life as he sounds about everything. "Yeah, how do we do that?"

"We use this." He lifts up his sleeve to reveal something that looks like a big square Band-Aid on his arm just below his shoulder.

I look at it up close. It's made of the same leathery stuff as my pod. "Is that Live-Tech?" I reach up and touch my ear. The pod's still there, but I'd nearly forgotten about it.

"I wish they'd come up with less dumb-sounding names for things, but, yeah." He cocks his head and looks at me. "Do you want some time to relax? Maybe take a nap? I'm supposed to get you started on writing your letter, but . . ."

The letter.

When he says it, I'm flooded with relief I wasn't even aware I needed. I can write it different. I'm going to be able to save my parents. My chest expands and my jaw slips out of the clench it's been in for the last week. I open and close my mouth a few times, relishing the feeling of freedom. I find the key chain in my pocket. "Nah." I shake my head. "I'm cool. I'm ready."

He studies me for a moment, then shrugs. "Paper's in the center drawer along with pens and envelopes. Just give it to Richard when you're done."

"Alright." I start edging toward the desk and Paul moves toward the door.

"I'll be in the commons if you need something." When he leaves, he closes the door behind him.

I sit down at the desk, taking a pen and paper from the drawer. I don't even know what I want to say this time, just that I need to start the whole damn thing off with a big warning about Mom and Dad being murdered.

I start to write:

> Hey Alex,
>
> This is you. Really. Please listen up, man, your stupid life depends totally on it. Can you please open your ears right now?

It's not what I tried to write at all. It's what the letter already said.

Panic edges in. Sweat. My hands are shaking. I crumple the paper and grab another sheet.

I think through what I'm going to say. I say it out loud as I write:

"Alex, whatever you do, get your parents out of the house tonight or they'll be killed."

But that's not what comes out on paper:

> *Hey Alex,*
>
> *This is you. Really. Please listen up, man, your stupid life depends totally on it. Can you please open your ears right now?*

"What the hell?!" I'm having trouble breathing.

Again.

And again.

I don't know what's happening. They're stopping me somehow. Making it impossible. Making sure my parents stay dead. Making sure I don't save them.

I'm ready to kill, but I don't know who. Somebody needs to give me answers and the only one who's been with me from the beginning is the voice in my head.

I lie down on the empty bed and slip underneath. Even though I'm upset, it happens fast.

HELLO?

She's there. I feel her. She's quiet though, not talking.

WHY WON'T THEY LET ME CHANGE MY LETTER? WHY ARE THEY STOPPING ME FROM SAVING MY PARENTS?

Eventually, she speaks: *"So sorry, scared boy. Runaways can't change what's been witnessed, boy. No scared boy runaway can change it. Seen time and all that."*

DON'T LIE TO ME! YOU'RE SIDING WITH THEM. YOU'RE HELPING THEM.

I'm so angry it's hard to stay under. I'm fighting with everything I've got to keep from breaking back up to the surface in a rage.

"No sides. Sly's got skin in your game. Bones in your game. In your game, Plugzie, and what's done is done. Seen is seen."

NO!

"Your letter didn't lie. Every way ends with dead parents. Other ways end even worse for runaways and the rest. Can't be changed, anyway. Seen time is the only—"

She's still talking when I come back up. I'm not even mad anymore.

I just feel defeated.

I grab my backpack and take out the photograph from the time capsule. Nobody here seems to know about it, so I decide to keep it hidden. I fold it carefully and slide it up into the lining of my pack where I keep my knife, then stick my pack into the bottom drawer of the desk.

I lie back down, my mind tossing back and forth between home and what I saw in the telescope.

The Locusts. The woman in the cage, waiting to be eaten.

There's a knock on the door. I don't say anything.

"Alex?" It's Corina.

"Yeah?"

She's quiet for a moment. "I wanna come in," she says eventually.

"Do what you want."

She opens the door and stands in the doorway. I look at her with my eyebrows raised. She looks at me and raises her own eyebrows. "You're friendly." She comes in and sits on the chair at my desk.

I sigh. I don't even know why I'm being rude to her. "Sorry. This all got me . . ." I wave a hand.

She smiles. I feel it deep in me like she's giving me gold. "It's cool," she tells me, "I don't know how I'd be doing if my parents had been killed on top of how much of a trip this place can be."

"Where are your parents?" I ask.

"It was just my mom," she says. "My dad died in a car crash when I was two. My step-dad left a few years ago." She shrugs. "She's still in Portland with my half siblings, I think." She makes a face. "We don't talk."

"What happened?"

She sucks on her lip for a second, then tells me, "I wasn't always good at handling my business." She shrugs. "I used to run wild, did things that my mom didn't approve of"—she points at herself—"things I don't approve of. My mom, she tried to stop me and I ran away." She looks sad now, distant.

"But you ended up here."

She nods her head and touches her chest. "While I was on the streets, I started to hear things, then a letter and a bus ticket showed up at the house I was staying at." She shrugs, "I didn't have anywhere else to go, so . . ." She pats my knee. "Anyways." She walks to my desk and opens the drawer, pulling out a single sheet of paper, which she tears in half. She doesn't say anything about the crumpled-up letters. She comes back to where I am and hands me the half sheets and a pen. "Take a minute and write out the note I showed you earlier today."

"What?" I look at the paper, then back at her. "The one at Burger King?"

She nods. "We have to send it back." She hands me the other half. "On this one, write your sizes and what clothes you like."

I follow her instructions. The first note slides out of the pen without me thinking, just like the letter did.

The letter. My stomach clenches when I think about it.

It takes me longer to write out my sizes and stuff. "Can't I just take a picture of what's in there?" I ask eventually, pointing at the dresser.

She chuckles. "Richard has a half sheet of paper with your writing on it, so no. You've already sent what you're writing now—no picture."

When I finish, I hand them to her and she folds them in half. She tightens her lips like she's got something unpleasant to say. "Now the video." She says it softly, like she knows it's going to hurt.

It does, but I'm not going to show her. Instead, I point at the door behind her. "I think that's what we used as a background." I get up and grab my desk chair, drag it to the doorway, then close the door and sit in front of it. I look over at Corina, who's not moving. "Ready?"

She bites her lip, wrinkles her nose. "I act like this is all natural, but sometimes the strangeness of sending shit back in time that we've already seen gets to me."

I smile, shake my hair back. I'm weirded out, too, but

I'm also sort of okay right now, too. "Let's shoot this shit." It comes out with more confidence than I mean it to, but she doesn't seem to notice.

She pulls out her screen, arranges herself. "Go."

I open my mouth, start to talk. "I found them on the kitchen floor when I got home on Friday night . . ." It comes out unemotionally and while I'm talking, even though I'm talking about my parents being murdered, I don't feel anything. It doesn't even feel like it's me talking, it's more like I'm just letting the words I heard earlier pass through me into the video so I can have watched them. "I was going to tell them I needed help and that I was ready to go to the psych ward if that's what they thought I needed . . ."

The feelings come crashing back as soon as I finish, though, and I'm suddenly feeling worse than I can remember feeling—empty, lonely, hopeless.

"Alrighty, then." She puts her screen away and grabs the notes. "Let me drop these off to Richard and then we should go to dinner."

I want her to leave. I don't want dinner, I want to close my eyes and disappear. Instead I stand up, move the chair away from the door and lie back down on the bed. "You go." I close my eyes. "I'm not hungry." Even though I'm trying to keep my voice clear, I know I sound as bad as I feel.

My eyes are closed, but I can hear her move, and feel the bed shift as she sits on the edge. She touches my hand. "I bet that was rough, and I'm sorry."

I don't say anything, but I don't move my hand out of the way, either.

"You're not hungry, but you should come hang out." She squeezes my hand. I open my eyes. "You'll feel better."

I don't want to, but I don't want to say no to her, either. I nod, sit up. She shifts out of my way and stands, putting her hand down for me. I don't take it, but I get up, and we go to dinner. Together.

Twenty

IN THE KITCHEN, CORINA GETS IN LINE AT THE CAT CARRIER NEXT TO DAMON. She smiles when she sees him. He smiles back at her.

I look around the room, feeling alone.

I don't want to stand in line at the cat carrier next to Damon and Corina feeling like a charity case, so I sit down next to Maddie, who's already got her plate. It's chicken of some sort.

She offers me a bite of it and I take it to be polite. It's good, I suppose, but it's not my style.

"You're from LA?" she asks me.

I nod. "What about you?"

"Colorado," she says as she scrapes up more chicken. "Aurora—near Denver." She's quiet for a moment and then she turns to examine me. "You down with all this?"

She looks like she's actually asking. I sigh. "I don't know. I'm freaking out a little bit, I think. This's pretty weird."

She nods. "Yeah. It was hard coming here." She drags a finger through her hair to get it out of her face. "Freaked me the fuck out."

"Yeah . . ." I offer, not sure what else to say. "Me too."

She cuts off another small bite of her chicken. "It gets better," she says as she eats it. She chews slowly and I scan the table for other conversations. Nobody's looking back at me.

The line at the cat carrier is down to just the black guy, Calvin. Everybody else is already seated around us. Corina's got a slab of salmon on top of rice.

Damon returns from the cat carrier with a burrito. He looks at me again as he sits down next to Corina. I try not to care, but I do. He says something to her. She laughs and I'm suddenly not hungry at all.

I walk to the cat carrier anyways, just for something to do.

"Mac and cheese," Calvin says as he passes me with his plate. He gestures back at the carrier with his chin. "That thing's bomb."

I laugh. I don't know what I'm looking to eat when I get to the cat carrier. I was thinking burger, but then as I was thinking about it, it disappeared in a flash of Locusts eating people. The carrier pulses and then stops. I open it.

Pizza. The cat carrier *is* bomb.

There's not much talking while we eat, but as soon as we're done, the questions start coming fast and furious at me.

Maddie: "You're into soccer."

It's not a question as much as it's a statement. I shrug and nod. I like soccer alright. Pete was the big soccer fan. He and my dad used to watch games together. They took me down to see the Galaxy play in Carson a couple times, too. Dad stopped watching soccer when Pete died.

"I watch it sometimes."

Paul wants to know how old I am and what music I like. I tell him that I like metal, rap, and oldies, which starts a whole discussion about whether it's possible to like both metal and rap equally. Calvin says it's impossible because anybody who likes metal doesn't have an ear to really appreciate rap, and

Corina says that they're both annoying so it's perfectly possible to be tasteless enough to enjoy them both equally, which makes Calvin laugh and Maddie roll her eyes. Corina asks what sort of oldies and doesn't believe me when I tell her stuff like the Temptations and the Platters. Paul asks whether I could ever listen to country. I tell him to not be ridiculous before I can stop myself. At first he looks hurt, but then he turns to Calvin and says that he can't marry me anymore, which weirds me out for a second, but then I laugh. Maddie says she likes country and that he can marry her and he looks at her like she's got scabies until Maddie promises to love the gay right off of him.

While we're talking about music and stuff like that, I start to really just chill and I'm almost able to forget why we're here.

Until Damon says out of the blue: "I wonder what Marcus is doing right now."

The table goes quiet, then Calvin speaks: "Whatever it is, he's doing it with a mind clear of Locusts, Live-Tech, Gentry, and the end of the world."

Maddie turns, speaks quietly just to me: "When they send us back, they wipe our memories and give us new ones. Marcus doesn't remember shit about this now."

I nod to show her I heard, but I don't know what to feel about that.

"Can't be easy going back like that, but it's better than the alternative." Corina shakes her head. "Can you imagine going home *remembering all this shit, but not being able to say boo about it to anybody*?" She pinches some rice between her thumb and finger and pops it into her mouth. "All this shit wears on me too much. I can't wait for them to wipe it from my mind."

Calvin shrugs. "Yeah, me too. It'd be bad to have this all in my head out there. Nobody to talk to about it."

The conversation splinters again after that. Everybody's talking, but nobody's talking to me.

Which is fine, because I don't want to talk anymore.

I clear my plate. When I try and sneak out, Corina catches my eye. She gives me a shy little wave, which warms me up.

Back in my room, I get ready for bed. I usually sleep in my boxers, but I feel really exposed just wearing my underwear here, so I keep my T-shirt on and crawl under the covers.

As I fall asleep, I think about the people I used to know. I try to get a picture of my mom and dad, but their faces keep changing and I'm suddenly sure I'm going to forget them.

I try to imagine Mousie sitting on her retaining wall, waiting for me to pick her up for school, but I end up with a fuzzy mess of colors and shapes in my head instead.

I do the same with Pete, and then with Julio and my aunt, but they're not clear either.

Tía Juana. She's probably in the apartment, feeling like the world ended. She lost her house when my uncle died, and she had to move into a big apartment building in Boyle Heights that she hates because it's loud and the walls are thin and it's right next to the freeway. That's part of the reason she was always at our house. But she can't do that anymore because our house is . . .

My auntie believes in ghosts.

I get out of bed and grab my backpack, looking for my old screen. Its battery's dead, so I plug it in and turn it on. While it loads, I imagine what I'll find when I get connected. Texts from people, wondering why I did it, where I am. Articles about me being a murderer.

Messages from my Tía begging me to call her. I imagine the conversation, telling her that I didn't do it, describing what happened, telling her about Sabazios and where I am now.

I want to see the article again, the one that quoted her. I want to get a message to the reporter so she knows that I'm innocent.

Maybe she'll publish it and let everyone else know.

The screen comes on finally, but there's no Wi-Fi. Not like there's no open connection; there's no connection at all. There's no emergency service reception, either. It's like we're in a hole.

I move the phone around the room a bit to see if I can get the corner of some service, but there's nothing.

I look at the door, but I'm not dressed and I don't want to talk to anybody here.

There's only one person I want to talk to. I dive to try and find her. I feel her.

HELLO?

She says nothing, and then:

"Goodbye, scared boy."

She sounds sad.

WHAT DO YOU MEAN?

"You're on your own, runaway boy. You're gonna get your patch. Gonna plug the drain in your brain where the Silly Juice and me come through. Don't be scared, boy. I'll be here when you need to run away again."

And then she's gone. I call for her. I wait.

Nothing.

I fall asleep totally alone.

Twenty-One

PAUL SHAKES ME AWAKE IN THE MORNING. AT FIRST I DON'T KNOW WHERE I am or who he is, but by the time I've gotten halfway up it all comes back in a heap that lands on me like a physical weight. Time travel, dead parents, evil aliens who want to eat us, other aliens here to help us.

I lie back down and pull the blankets up.

"Oh, no you don't," Paul says. "You've got to save the Earth today." He grabs my hand and leans back as he pulls me into a reluctant standing position.

"Holy hell," I manage to say, but I'm not sure exactly which part I'm saying it about.

Paul points at the desk, where there's now a bottle of shampoo and some soap. "Go. Shower. Get dressed!"

Everything he says has a smile attached to it like it's a joke that only he gets.

In the shower, I spend the time thinking about people who I don't have anymore, and about Locusts eating the rest of everybody. By the time I'm dried off, I feel horrible.

Paul's sitting in his desk chair playing guitar when I get back to the room.

He stands up and returns the guitar to its stand. "You ready, champ?"

"Yeah." I drop my clothes and shampoo onto the bed.

The crumpled papers from the letter I tried to write are still on the desk. I want to throw them away, make them disappear, but Paul's sitting right where I need to go to get to the desk.

He's looking at me, making me feel weird, just strumming quietly. When I go past him I end up knocking the head of his guitar. I don't mean to, but I don't make much of an effort to avoid it, either.

"Excuse me," he says.

I don't reply, just gather the papers and throw them in the garbage under the desk.

When I turn around, he's standing, the guitar laid across his bed. He's smiling, but his eyes are street hard. "No," he says. He shakes his head. "Uh-uh. Alex, this will not work. We are partners and roommates and I am working very hard to make you feel welcome here. If you've got a problem, say it now."

I go to stare back at him, but my hair is wet and it falls straight in my face and I have to move it away with my hand and somehow having to do it takes the anger out of me and leaves me tired.

"It's nothing," I mutter. "I don't have a problem with you." Then I look at him, my face as calm as I can make it.

He squints at me. Nods his head slowly. "You sure?"

I shrug. "Yeah." Then: "It's just . . ."

He raises an eyebrow.

I don't reply immediately, not even sure what I'm going to say. Eventually: "I got a lot in my head right now."

"Yeah," he says softly. His eyes relax. "I bet you do. Maybe don't take it out on me, though, okay?"

I nod. "Yeah. Okay."

He waits a moment. "Alright, then. We should get breakfast—gliding on an empty stomach sucks."

"Okay." Food sounds alright. "Yeah."

Together, we walk to the kitchen.

It's just us and Calvin there while we eat. "Calvin's always here," Paul says.

Calvin bobs his head. "Good a place as any." He stuffs a spoonful of cereal into his mouth, chews.

I'm just finishing my Pop-Tarts when Richard walks in. "Alex!" he sings as he walks up behind me and puts his hands on my shoulders. "You ready to get started?"

I shrug. "Is there a way I can get a message home first? My aunt . . ."

He shakes his head slowly. "I'm sorry, man. While you're with us, we have to keep total control on the information that goes out." He waves at the stuff around us. "Our only chance for success is by working under the radar until we're ready to go public, so we have to keep the lid screwed on tight." When he sees the look on my face, he stops smiling. "I know how much it would mean to you, though, so we'll figure out a way to let your aunt know you're alright, and that you didn't . . ." He trails off. "Okay?"

I bob my head, feel myself smile a little bit even though I don't mean it.

He pinches my shoulder, looks over at Paul, then down at me. "You've got a big a day ahead, Alex, so we probably should get going." He raises his eyebrows. "You think you're up to it?"

I bob my head again, raise my shoulder under his hand.

"Good man." He laughs. "Let's go."

Paul stands with us. "You're coming, too?" I try to keep my voice level.

He grins. "Sure am. I'm gonna train you." He leans in over the table. "You can call me Morpheus."

I shake my head, try not to smile, but he's goofy as hell and he's actually funny. "I'm not calling you Morpheus."

"Then you shouldn't've taken the red pill."

Richard and Paul take me back to the central patio and then through the door that leads up a set of stairs and into a wide hallway that looks too big and too long to fit inside the hill. Richard opens a door about halfway down and gestures for me to go inside. It's a doctor's office. "Take a seat on the exam table," he tells me. "We've got to get your patch attached."

I sit on the table.

"Do you have your letter?"

I freeze. Even the memory of the panic I felt yesterday when I was trying to write it makes me sweat. I don't respond, hoping that'll be the end of it.

It's not. Richard's whole attitude changes. "You tried to change what it said? For your parents?"

"No." It comes out like a whisper. My cheeks are starting to get hot. I can feel my eyes begin to burn.

Richard speaks softly. "Alex, there's no way to do that."

And that's it. Too much. I make it out of the room and into the hallway before the tears come. I'm so mad that I'm shaking. I don't even notice the door open until Richard's got his hand on me.

"Alex?" His voice cuts through me.

"I'm not writing it."

He nods his head. "You're right. You don't need to do it today. I should've been more sensitive."

I look up. His face is right there, just above me, so close. I want to . . .

I don't.

"I'm not ever writing that fucking letter." I point at him. "Ever."

He backs up, pulls himself out of range, which lets me relax a little. "Alex . . ." But then he trails off. He takes in a breath like he's going to say something else, but instead he just lets it go.

"What?"

He shakes his head. "Nothing you need to be bothered with right now."

"Tell me."

He shakes his head, blows out another breath. "Look, the way these things work is that you got the letter, so somehow, someday, you will write it and it will be the exact letter you received." He holds up his hands to slow my response. "But it doesn't have to be now and it doesn't have to be any time soon, so we don't need to worry about it here and now."

I wipe my sleeve hard across my face, push my eyes in with my thumbs, then shake my head. "I'm not writing it."

He picks his hand off my shoulder. "I understand."

I'm not feeling much of anything anymore, except that I don't want to continue this conversation. I try to talk, but my throat's full. I cough to clear it. "Does the patch hurt?"

Paul smiles, big and goofy. "Nope. And it'll give you superpowers."

Back in the exam room, I sit down on the bed. "How does this all work?"

"All what?" Richard sounds relieved that I'm back to business.

I don't want to say *everything*. "Witnessing, I guess."

Richard smiles like he's truly glad I asked. "Like I mentioned yesterday, once something's done and past, it's locked in, it can't ever be changed, right?"

Even hearing it reminds me of the whole letter thing and makes my stomach hurt. "Okay."

"Well, the same thing happens if we see something that, by our way of experiencing time, *hasn't happened yet*." He gestures at Paul, who's standing above his shoulder. "Normally the future's wide open—picture an infinite field of bubble wrap stretching out in front of us. Every single bubble on that field is a possibility—what could happen—depending on decisions that conscious beings make and on the semi-random events of the physical universe—earthquakes, tornadoes, asteroids, that sort of thing." He looks at me.

I nod so he knows I get it.

"But remember, the present fixes time, we experience it and it becomes unmovable and unchangeable, right? So let's say you get to see a future—one bubble, way over here"—he points at a space between us—"that has some particular event in it. What would that mean?"

I keep thinking I get it, but as soon as I try to close my mind around the ideas, they squirt out the side. "That it's going to happen . . ."

Richard nods. "Yes! Exactly! Seeing that small part of the future ensures that it will happen and all the future bubbles that don't include the events in the bubble you saw are suddenly popped—we say they're collapsed—they're no longer possible. Do you know why?"

I don't. But I don't want to sit there with my mouth open, so I say something even though it's dumb. "Because I saw it?"

"That's it exactly!" He pats me on the knee. "Observation makes reality, Alex. The present is defined by those of us who see and think and remember. "*We*"— he points at me and Paul, himself too—"we are what changes time from the unformed infinite future to the locked-in, immutable past. When we witness the present, we lock things in, and when we witness a piece of future, we lock it in just the same—it's like it becomes part of the fixed past even though it hasn't happened yet as we stubbornly see the illusion of time. No matter what anybody does, as long as you remember it, it can't be changed, not by Locusts or anybody else." He smiles like he's seen a wonder of the world. "Your knowledge of what will happen absolutely makes sure that it does—you're going to make sure that Live-Tech spreads, that President Castle doesn't get a chance to have it regulated, that people trust Jeff enough about Incursions that he can get Live-Tech everywhere it needs to go."

I can't think of anything to say, so I say, "Okay." Then: "How do we know what futures to see?"

Richard looks pleased with my question. "The Gentry's

Oracle device I told you about yesterday? It selects the desired possibilities and it's the thing that guides you on your witness journeys." He points to Paul's arm. "The patch you're going to get is Live-Tech—it's going to act as a bridge between you and the Oracle device, except this time instead of reading your thoughts and telling the machine, it's going to be reading the machine and translating it into thought for you." He waits for me to catch up. I nod, but I don't really get it.

He must see my confusion because he keeps explaining. "The patch is going to take its guidance from the Oracle device and it's going to connect to your mind while also making some slight alterations to your DNA—the end result is that you'll not only be able to glide into the future, but you'll only witness the futures the Oracle chooses for you."

The door opens, making me jump. A woman I haven't seen before comes in. She says hi to Richard and Paul and then tells me her name is Christina and that she's the one who maintains the witness-patches.

She steps over to the wall where a panel slides back. When she turns back around, she's got a square of Live-Tech pod material clutched at the end of a pair of tongs. Just like the Live-Tech pod was before I activated it, this one's streetlight green with the Live-Tech logo etched into it in black line, clutched in the end of a pair of tongs. "You ready, Alex?"

I shrug. "Sure."

She smiles and approaches, but stops when she sees my wrist. "You're gonna have to remove the pod first."

I tell her I forgot the deactivation code. She tells me to repeat after her and then recites a long string of letters and numbers. When I'm done, the pod vibrates twice and falls out of my ear onto the floor. I watch as it turns red, indicating that it's no longer in use.

"Great," she says as Richard bends down to pick it up. "Now we can attach it, and it will connect you to the Oracle and give you the ability to witness."

I look at the patch. It's just a flat square flap of bright green leather. "How . . ." I want to ask the big questions about how all of this is possible, but I don't even know how to put it, so I end up just waving my hand at the patch and looking lost.

"How does this"— she wiggles the patch with the tongs— "make it possible for you to see the future?"

I nod. Richard just told me, but as long as people are talking I don't have to actually put the patch on. It makes me nervous.

"Well, you've got those genetic markers—one hundred and fifty-three of them, right?"

I shrug, nod.

"Well, think of those as being like a keyhole to a door inside you. This patch? It's the key. It's genetically encoded to pair with your specific markers to unlock that door and let you witness."

"What's behind the door?"

"The place where time lives." Richard smiles. "And, Alex, you're going to be very good at witnessing. Most witnesses— their ability is like a two-lane road—they can get there and they can come back, but there's a limit to the amount of traffic—information—that the road can handle—they see and hear things, but the things they witness aren't always clear, which makes them less completely locked in." He gestures at me. "You, on the other hand, with your one hundred and fifty-three markers, you're going to have a ten-lane expressway. Things will be crystal clear for you when you see them. You'll get details that the rest of the team wouldn't even be able to dream of."

"Alright."

"You need to understand." Richard leans into me. "Once you've started witnessing, we have to make sure to keep you safe and protected until the futures you've seen have come to pass . . ." He sees my eyes widen, begins to shake his head. "We're not talking years, Alex, we're talking months." He raises an eyebrow to ask if I'm comfortable with that. I don't say anything, so he continues: "If we know what you saw, that alone won't keep the future fixed. Only the witness's own mind can do that. Once you're done, though, and your patch has been removed, we'll wipe this compound out of your memory, give you some implanted memories that'll feel very real to you, and make sure you have the resources to make up for the lost time." He raises his eyebrows. "Are you still willing?"

"What about . . ." I focus, try to make my voice clear. "I can't go back, though. They want me for murder."

Richard smiles at me. "By the time we send you back, Alex, that won't be an issue, but you just have to trust me, okay?"

The whole idea weirds me out, and even thinking about it makes me anxious, but I've got nowhere else to go. I try and think it through, really turn it into a decision, but it's just for appearances. "Okay. I'm in."

"Good man," Richard says and claps me on the leg before leaning back to make room for Christina.

"Here we go. It'll feel a bit like when you put in your pod." She brings the patch close to my skin. I wince as I feel it touch—it's soft and cool and I get a sensation like an electric shock that vibrates up and down my arm. It sticks to me, pulls at my skin. It doesn't hurt, but it feels weird, like my skin's got Velcro on it and something's being peeled off. I try and keep still but I get an overwhelming urge to shake my arm. I start to think I'm going to explode if I don't move it.

"Done!" Christina says.

I'm about to say something, but then the patch starts to change. The Live-Tech logo fades away and the bright green fades to white before changing again to match my skin. The area of my arm around the patch feels weird, like the patch is wiggling—tickling me from the inside. I try and shake it off, but it grows worse and worse until I get a full-body shiver that starts at my head and goes all the way down to my feet. It keeps happening and just when I think it's going to go on forever and that I'm going to shake myself to death, it stops.

When I look up at Christina, she's smiling. "He won't come off no matter how much you move now, Alex—he's your new partner!" She seems to think this is a really good thing, because she's looking at me—at us—like a priest at a wedding.

Twenty-Two

WE STEP OUT INTO THE HALL. CHRISTINA EXCUSES HERSELF AND DISAPPEARS into another doorway.

Richard asks how I'm feeling.

I'm just about to tell him that I feel fine when I realize that that isn't exactly true.

I don't feel *bad*.

As matter of fact I'm feeling good, but I'm also feeling really weird. I turn around to face him because he's a little behind me, but as I turn, I startle myself because I feel like there's more of me turning than there is of me. It's like my body has extra rooms somewhere—little hidden places that I can't see are taking up space and making me bigger than I'm supposed to be.

"I don't know," I tell him. "A little weird, honestly."

Paul grabs me by the arm, starts to pull me down the hall. "Come with me."

My balance is funny right now, so I stumble a bit as he pulls me. "Where are we going?"

"Glide rooms," he says. "Gonna show you how it works."

Richard follows us down the stairs and into the common room, where Paul drags me to a second hallway that leads off to the opposite side of the dorms.

We stop in front of a door. Next to it is a picture of a *Ghostbusters*-style cartoon Locust holding a knife and fork over the Earth with a big red circle around it and a slash through it. "THE KITCHEN IS CLOSED" is written in block letters underneath.

I gesture at it. "Funny."

Paul shrugs. "Who ya' gonna call?" He motions for me to look through the glass. Corina is inside with Damon. They're both dressed in white bodysuits that have the pentagon and triangle design on the back. Corina seems to be asleep on the bed and Damon's talking into a thin microphone that rises like a weed off an otherwise empty desk.

"Witness chamber," Paul tells me. "They act like an amplifier for the signals that the patch transmits, so they're the only place where we glide—it doesn't work anywhere else." He shrugs. "When we glide, we go one at a time. Corina's under now, and the other person—in this case Damon—dictates what they witnessed while the other person is under."

I watch for a moment. Corina isn't moving at all. She looks dead.

I step away from the window. "Isn't it not okay for others to know what we witness?" I ask him. "How come Damon's doing that with Corina in the room?"

Paul giggles. "You wouldn't hear a nuclear bomb going off when you're under." He tugs at my shirt. "Corina's not even *in* Corina right now. She's somewhere else as someone else some other time—not home right now, please leave a message."

"Paul?"

"Morpheus." He tries to make his voice deep when he says it, but his baby face just makes the whole thing ridiculous.

"Stop that. How does the person who goes second dictate? Isn't the other person awake then?"

It's Richard who answers. "The second witness waits until their partner leaves the room."

"Why don't they just have us go alone?"

Paul smiles. "Because witnessing's like the Force—it has a light side and a dark side. We've got to watch out for each other in there." He turns to face me. "When we're under, our mind isn't in our bodies and if it gets untethered, we're in trouble."

I can't help but be a little irritated that this is the first I'm hearing about this. "What happens if we get untethered?"

Paul looks at Richard and then back through the window at Damon and Corina. "We die."

"We die? We can die in there?"

"Really not a big concern, Alex." Richard points at a thing hanging on the wall above Corina. It looks like a slice of Live-Tech. "Gliding is only dangerous to the witness if they're down too long and the biology gets exhausted, so if somebody's under for more than thirty minutes, all the glide partner has to do is attach that to the witness's neck and it brings them back."

I look at the thing Richard's pointing at. "That'll save us?" I turn to Paul. "Have you ever had to use it?"

"Nope." He turns, smiles, raises his eyebrows at me. "But I'm sure as heck gonna make sure *you* know how."

We walk farther down the corridor and stop at the door to another chamber. "What's with the suits?"

Paul shrugs. "They're part of the job description." He wrinkles his nose. "They help regulate our biology while we're on long glides—that's why they fit so tight. I keep bugging Richard to change them, but he doesn't like my designs." He looks accusingly at Richard, who shrugs. "I'm a pudgy white boy, so these ones make me look like cauliflower."

Paul opens the door and jerks his head. "C'mon."

Inside, he points at the couch. "Lie down. Close your eyes."

I shake my head. "Nah." Then: "I'm good."

Paul rolls his eyes. "Don't be silly." He points at the couch. "Lie down."

Richard steps in from behind me. "It's perfectly safe, Alex, but it's fine if you're not ready." He shrugs, looks pointedly at Paul. "We could do this just as easily tomorrow."

I look at the couch, then at Paul, then at Richard. They don't seem worried. I'm being stupid. I sigh, shrug. "Now's fine." Then: "Don't I need a suit?"

Richard looks at me, smiles. "Suits are necessary when you're down for substantial time. You won't be down that long—at worst you'll be a little short of breath when you come up."

I nod and lie down on the couch, relieved not to have to change into weird clothes for the moment. When I close my eyes, I feel strange again, like I'm bigger on the inside, too, like my mind and my body have extra spaces. It's disorienting, like I walked through the door to my bedroom and ended up in Walmart. "It's bigger in here."

"I know. Now picture yourself in something that moves—I use a mining cart like in Indiana Jones, but it doesn't have to be that. Calvin uses a horse and Corina pictures a train—it can be anything."

There's only one thing that moves that I can imagine using. I picture my board. I can see it in my mind, the grip tape covered in spray stencils that Julio cut for me. "Got it."

"Now get in it, or on it, or over it, or whatever it is that you do with it, and start going downhill."

At first I'm confused, but then I figure it out. I just have to picture it. "Got it."

"Don't open your eyes."

I relax into it, sliding down like I did before, searching for my Voice.

But then things get weird.

Instead of the simple guitars I heard before, now it's like a death metal band with a billion electric guitars playing power chords and noodle solos.

It's so loud that it hurts and I think I start to whimper or something, because suddenly Paul's hand is on me.

"Stay on the path," he says.

I don't know what he means until I think, *Path?* Then I see a path and I'm on it. When I'm on the path, it's like there's walls up on either side of it and all the guitar noise gets muffled.

"Take the first off-ramp you see."

Off-ramp? And then there is one. I tell Paul.

"Take it."

I lean to the right to guide my board onto it. I feel it lock in.

It gets suddenly dark. And then there's a light ahead. It gets brighter and brighter until suddenly:

It's all wrong. The couch is gone. Paul. The glide room. I'm not . . . We're in the Central Hall. It's glaring, nearly blinding from the yellow carpet, the white furniture. There are books on shelves in front of me, red leather bindings—somehow I know they're red, but they don't look red; they look a nearly screaming orange.

There's a grand piano. I play the piano. I've played since I was four. Grandma Bev bought me a keyboard.

I breathe in, but it's not me breathing. It's somebody else. The breath is shallower than I expect. I want more air, but I don't need more. The breath is fine for her.

Us.

I'm not just me right now. I'm mainly someone else. My name is Jordan. I brush hair out of my face. It's not in my face, I just do it as a habit. It makes me feel like a pop star.

"There's one more," my mom says. The sound of her voice is strange, a dream-sound that would scare the shit out of me if I heard it in my life, but to Jordan it's just the way her mom sounds, like all voices sound. "It's from Grandma Bev." She holds out a package to me. It's wrapped in paper that Jordan knows is blue, but to me it looks gray. The pink balloons that dot it look comfortingly normal to the way I see them when I'm me.

Excitement. Jordan has been waiting for this present. Grandma Bev. Jordan pictures her—an older woman, dyed red hair, heavyset but made of love. Jordan's hand quivers as she reaches for the package. She takes it. I feel it pressed against her fingers, the weight of it as her mom lets go.

She brings it back toward us slowly. She's still smiling, but it feels different on the inside. It's work now.

Jordan is sad. Her feelings sit inside her and me both. I'm sad with her. We miss Grandma Bev, want her here.

Know we can't say anything. Mom says she loves her mom, but she worries that Grandma is an ungodly influence on us, the girls. Jordan doesn't bring it up anymore. She's found other ways to communicate with Grandma Bev—secret ways.

The girls: I have sisters, Samantha and Avery. Jordan's feelings cloud over, thinking about it. She never used to lie, keep secrets, but her mom and dad . . .

They wouldn't understand. They'd think she was falling, failing, turning bad.

Girls shouldn't have secrets, not from their mothers.

Girls shouldn't have boyfriends, not unless their fathers approve.

Jordan presses a nail underneath the tape of the package in her lap, serrates it. "I wonder what it is . . ." Our voice sounds as strange in our head as the others do outside.

The speaker comm on the table chimes. Jordan's mom lights up. "That'll be your dad!"

Jordan pauses, but I want Jordan to keep unwrapping. I can feel how much she wants to have something more of Grandma. I feel Jordan's frustration, but she says nothing, her fingernail still pinched between the flaps of the box.

She smiles, but it's not a real one. We think about our lips, our eyes, how high to raise our eyebrows. We're practiced at this. "Hey, Dad!" we say brightly to the face on the screen.

We lie well.

He smiles back at us; his face is lined. His hair is gray. He insists it's regal, stentorian, but Jordan knows the truth. He looks old.

He does. I've always thought so, too. I know the man on the screen.

He's the president of the United States.

"Happy birthday, JJ!" he says.

"Thanks, Dad!" Jordan looks down. "I'm opening Gram's present."

He nods, looks warily at Mom. "What is it?"

Jordan takes the cue, slipping the box out of the wrap. "A new screen . . ." She has a screen. Grandma knows this. It's not a better screen, either. It unfolds to the same size, weighs the same.

It's the same brand. "Wow," she says, opening the box to examine the contents.

New feelings. Disappointment. Something else. Concern. She's worried about her Grams. She presses the power button, watches as the screen brightens.

Icons appear.

It takes her a moment. I see it before she does, but when she does, she works hard to keep her face neutral.

The icons have labels. The labels have a message. "Press me," the first one says. "When no one," the next. "Is watching," the third. "Especially," the next icon continues, "your parents."

Then: "Love Naomi."

It's just a name to me, but the Bible story is thick in Jordan. Naomi, the mother-in-law of Ruth, a woman Ruth would follow anywhere, who helped Ruth navigate her way into a new life with her own people, away from the Moabites from which Ruth had come. Jordan first called her Naomi *after she snuck a disguised copy of Harry Potter into Jordan's reader when she was ten, an invitation to break away from her mom and dad's strict sense of right and wrong.*

Grandma Bev calls Jordan Ruth *sometimes, especially when she's forwarding a letter from Will.*

The last icon says "Press me now."

Jordan's finger hesitates over the icon before she taps it; pressing it commits her to another secret.

Tap.

The icons shuffle and rename themselves. She holds it up to show the family.

"Why do you get two screens when I don't even have one?" Avery asks.

Jordan doesn't roll her eyes. Instead: "You can have my other one, okay?"

And then I'm back in myself and I'm looking through my own eyes at Paul. My mind is racing and I can hardly breathe. When I lift up my hand, it's shaking. I think I might be dying and I look at Paul for help, but he's laughing at me.

"First witness's a bitch."

"What . . ." I have to take a breath and try again before I can even say a sentence. "What the hell was that?"

"Superpowers, man! I told you—you just went into the future in somebody else's mind!" He's squatting down to get his head at my level and he leans in. "So?"

"What?" I ask, not sure what he wants.

"How was it?"

I think about what I saw. I can still see the images and I can recall the voices and smells. It's all way too weird. I shake my head. "The colors . . ."

"What you see is different with every target." He smacks his lips. "I bet for you, it's more than just the colors and stuff. For you it's probably—"

"They're different . . ."

Richard is sitting in the chair at the desk, watching us. "Sensory perception is different for everybody. My blue is going to be different than yours. We both call it blue because that's what we were told to call the color we see, but we aren't seeing it the same way. Electrical impulses from our ears aren't necessarily interpreted the same way by our minds. We have different numbers and qualities of olfactory and taste sensors, too. Different levels of sensitivity at our nerve endings, so when you're in somebody else's mind, every sensation's going to be different."

Paul rolls his eyes. "I wouldn't know from all that. Except for color and sound, for me it's all fuzzy, like I'm watching underwater." Paul looks at me. "But you with your ten-lane highway, you probably see so clear you could count fleas on the family dog."

The experience was so strange to begin with and now, thinking about it afterward, it's like having a strong memory that couldn't have ever happened. Like when the little girl pushes through all the coats in *The Lion, the Witch and the Wardrobe* and finds the snowy forest. In my mind, Jordan Castle's birthday melts and now I'm remembering me watching the Narnia movie with Pete.

"So? Was it clear, like you were actually there?" Paul brings me back to the moment.

Jordan. Being there, in her head, was clear. I think that's what was so weird about it—I was her *and* me at the same time. Her eyes were mine. Ears, nose, all of it. "Yeah." And then: "I was Jordan."

Richard shakes his head. "Leave names out of it." But it barely registers.

"I was a girl," I continue.

I turn to Richard. He looks uncomfortable.

Paul is laughing, though.

I start to say more, but Richard waves me off. "We don't share what happens on the job with anybody, Alex—if the wrong information spreads, it could cause real complications."

"She's been lying to her parents." I think a little more. "She's got a boyfriend," I add helpfully before realizing that I must sound like a total idiot.

"That's good, buddy." Paul pats my knee. "It's all part of being a healthy adolescent."

Twenty-Three

PAUL'S GOT SOMETHING TO DO AND POINTS ME TOWARD THE KITCHEN FOR lunch. Corina and Damon are already at a table when I walk in. They've got empty plates in front of them and they're deep in some conversation, but Corina stops talking when she sees me in the doorway.

"Hey, Alex." She smiles. I think she looks happy to see me. "Got your patch?"

Damon looks up, too. He looks less happy.

I nod, smile a little bit. "Yeah."

"C'mere." She waves me over. I cross from the door so I'm standing next to her. "Let's see it."

"See what?"

"Your patch." She touches my arm just below my sleeve and tugs at the fabric. "Roll it up."

I do. She leaves her hand on my arm. I sneak a look over at Damon while she and I fiddle with my sleeve. He's annoyed.

"It's so strange." Corina touches my patch. Her voice is so soft it's almost a whisper. "Feeling things like they're happening to skin when something touches the patch."

I pay attention to her touch. She's right. Even though I can tell that there's something different about the feel of her finger based on whether it's touching me or the patch, I can still feel both. I nod.

Damon stands up and leans over the table. "Let me see."

He reaches over and pinches my patch, hard.

The pain is awful, like getting kicked in the nuts with a boot. I scream and pull away, but the pain is so intense that I can't even make my legs work. My eyes start to water and he laughs.

"You and your patch—you're both pussies." He walks around to the other side of the table and sheds his jacket onto a chair before walking his plate back to the counter. He doesn't even look in my direction.

Corina's saying something to him, but I can't hear her words. I can't hear anything. I see red. The adrenaline spikes in my fingers and my feet. My sight narrows.

Everything that's gone wrong in the world in the last week floods my mind at once.

He's going to pay.

I'm up and over to him in a flash. Corina calls my name, but I'm not stopping. I can't see anything but him going down. I move to intercept him but he ignores me so I shove him hard from behind. "You messed up, bitch." He stumbles into the counter.

He's got me by six inches in height and he's thicker than me, too, but I don't care. He turns toward me like he's going to say something but I don't give him the chance. He's right in my range, so I box him at the temple and he goes down in a pile. I kick him once, hard, to drive the point home. His shirtsleeve pulls up when he falls and his patch is showing. I reach for it, ready to make him hurt worse than he made me, but then there's new hands on me.

Instinct kicks in and I drop down under the grip of

whoever's got me and send an elbow backward. I land it hard in their stomach and I hear the air go out of them like I popped a balloon.

"Oh shit," Corina shrieks. "What did you do?" I whip around to see what she means.

It's Paul. He's wiggling in pain, his face is red, and it looks like his eyes are about to pop out of his head.

I look back at Damon, but he's still on the floor.

"Damn," Corina says, staring at me. She crosses over to Paul and kneels down next to him. Richard runs in, sees us, pulls a radio from somewhere and mumbles into it like a security guard.

I've just screwed everything up.

I don't know what else to do, so I make a break for it, pushing past Richard, through the gym and out onto the patio. Richard calls my name, but I don't slow down until I'm in the Long Hall, headed for the driveway.

I hear the door on the deck side close behind me and lock. The driveway door is locked, too. I look around, but there's nowhere else to go.

I slide to the floor.

The walls brighten so I look up. There's a picture of Corina driving, and another of Julio and Zeon squaring off on the day they met for the first time in sixth grade. It was one of the most entertaining fights I've ever seen. Zeon took Julio down.

I've got nowhere to go. I close my eyes to dive deep for my Voice. Things are different with the patch—the drain's not there anymore. It's like the patch stopped it up. Instead, there's just the path Paul took me down. I can hear the jackhammer pile of guitars behind the wall but that's it.

HELLO?

Nothing. Just like she said.

When I resurface, Corina's coming up the hall toward me.

"Alex? You okay?"

"Yeah." Then: "You saw. He pinched my patch and called me a pussy," I tell her before she can even ask. I shake my head. "He shouldn't have done that."

She's standing over me now. I look up at her, but her eyes aren't on me—they're on the wall with the picture of her in the car. "That's how I look to you?"

The heat of embarrassment rises in my face, overwhelming what was left of the adrenaline from the fight. I don't answer her. Instead I think of anything else besides her so the picture will change.

"*South Park*?" she asks. I look up again and her picture is gone, replaced by a scene with Kenny from *South Park*. I realize I've been holding my breath. I let it out.

"I like *South Park*."

"Me too," she says. She slides down against the wall across from me. She's wearing a skirt and it's hard not to look at where her foot has kicked it up to her upper thigh. She follows my eyes and shifts her position, making me feel even more awkward.

"Sorry," I mutter, not sure whether I'm sorry for looking at her legs or for thinking about her and making the picture happen or for clocking Damon and knocking Paul down.

She shrugs. "It happens," she says. "Damon plays too much."

"Paul doesn't. He didn't deserve that."

She shakes her head. "Nope. You shouldn't have done that."

"He should've minded his own business." But even while I'm saying it I know it's stupid. "Never mind. I didn't . . ."

"He's alright. You didn't do any permanent damage."

"What about Damon?"

She shrugs. "He'll live and maybe grow up a little bit."

Before I can stop myself I think about her and Damon at dinner the night before. They looked cozy and like they were really into each other. I hear her laugh. She's looking over my head and when I look up, I see the two of them at dinner last night in a big picture on the wall. I want to die and I desperately try and think of anything else.

A picture of Benny, my mom's old Chihuahua.

"Cute dog," she says. "You think me and Damon . . . ?" She laughs. "There are rules here, though, and one of the big ones is that we aren't allowed to 'develop emotional or romantic attachments' with other witnesses."

"So? It's not like everybody follows the rules." I'm obviously totally jealous. My face gets all hot again and I feel myself sweating. "Not that I care," I lie.

"Course you don't." She smiles and shifts her weight so that she frees a leg and kicks me with it. Not hard or anything, just like you do. "But just so you know, Damon is most definitely not my type."

I smile and look down, almost too embarrassed to form words. "Don't matter." Then: "How much trouble am I in?"

She shakes her head. "You and Damon are going to have to work things out and you're going to need to make this up to Paul somehow, but I think that'll probably be the end of it."

"Richard isn't pissed at me?"

She shrugs. "I think he was a little surprised at having

his suburban compound life suddenly go street, but he'll get over it."

"It's hard not to . . ." I shrug. "What was I supposed to do?"

"I feel you, but here at the compound, we're supposed to talk it out." She rolls her eyes. "Even when people deserve a little pain."

Twenty-Four

"LET'S TALK IN MY OFFICE," RICHARD SAYS WHEN HE SEES CORINA WALK me back across the pool deck.

I'm scared. However weird this place is, the thought of being kicked out makes me feel even worse. "Okay," I say.

He smiles gently and gestures toward the gym door with his chin. "It's the first door on the right on the other side of the basketball court." He nods agreeably. "I'll be right there."

I wait for him to show me, but he doesn't.

He just looks at me encouragingly. "I'll be right there, kiddo."

I shrug and walk through the door into the gym. I can feel him and Corina waiting until I'm out of earshot before they start to talk about me.

Richard's office looks like a cross between a man cave and a school principal's office. There's a desk covered with papers and a couple of padded chairs that face it, and the walls are covered with posters—Einstein with his tongue out, Seahawks, Mariners. There's a blown-up photo of a Locust, too, that keeps drawing my eye. Coldplay, AntiSeems, and an enormous Taylor Swift round out the collection.

Richard seems like a nice enough guy, but I can't say we see eye to eye musically.

There's an old-school 2-D TV tucked into a bookshelf

and a strange-looking box thing underneath it that I don't recognize. I'm wondering whether I can get a closer look at it when Richard comes in.

"Hey, man," he says as he comes through the door. He pats me on the shoulder as he passes me on the way to his desk. "That was quite a thing."

"Is Paul okay?"

Richard shakes his head as he sits down. "Paul's fine—you just knocked the wind out of him."

"I didn't mean to . . ."

"I bet." He takes a deep breath. "I'm sure you didn't."

This isn't going the way I want it to. He's not yelling at me or telling me the ways I've screwed up. "Damon started it."

"Yeah . . ." Richard's voice is kind, filled with understanding. "I watched the feed. There's no doubt."

I can hear the enormous *but* hanging off the end of his sentence. "But?"

"But in the end you lost your temper, Alex." He appraises me like a doctor.

I shrug. I don't want to tell him he's right.

"If Damon pinching your patch can set you off that much, what are you going to do when the fate of the world is on your shoulders—you're not going to be useful to anybody, including us."

My heart stops. He's going to kick me out. My world goes black. Images of the street, prison, being insane. "Don't," I whisper. "I won't . . ."

But he waves me off. "You're not getting out that easy. I know you understand that this can't happen again?"

"I do."

He nods. "I trust you. You're going to be on your game for me, right?"

Whatever was sitting on my heart before moves. I can breathe again. "Yessir."

He cocks an eye at me. "Damon's not going anywhere."

"It'll be cool. I won't start anything."

"Or finish anything?"

I shake my head. "But Damon's getting in trouble, too, right?"

He doesn't answer my question. Instead he stands up. "You going to be alright?"

I nod. He offers me his hand. I stand and take it. He surprises me by pulling me in for a hug and I surprise myself by returning it. He lets me hold him for a second and then separates himself. "You're going to be fine," he whispers. "You're safe here."

I want to tell him that I know that, but I can't make the words happen.

When he lets go, I ask him the question that's been floating in the back of my mind since yesterday. "Richard?"

"Yeah?"

"Why didn't I warn myself about my parents? When I wrote the letter?"

He studies me, biting his lip as he thinks. "The Gentry's Oracle device? The one that chooses your targets? It sees all the possibilities, Alex. When we started evaluating you, it saw all the ways your life and the lives of all the people around you could play out."

Too much. "It chose to let my parents be murdered?!"

He leans back against his desk, out of my arms' reach, before he says more. "Alex, your parents were going to die in every future the Oracle saw. As painful as it is to accept, having it happen like this was the least terrible way for everybody, including them."

"Bullshit." The word hurts coming out because my throat is so tight, but even while I'm saying it, I'm remembering what my Voice told me before the patch sent her away.

Remembering what I said to me in my letter.

He sighs, shrugs, shakes his head slowly. "There was no saving them, Alex, and trying to save them could have meant that you wouldn't be here right now and that we would all die an even more horrible death at the hands of the Locusts. Your parents' murders aren't your fault, and what you eventually write will save your life and your freedom and allow you to come here to be with us as part of the team whose work means the human race has a chance to survive."

I nod because I don't want to talk about this anymore. I'm still not writing the letter.

"I'm going to meet with you and Damon this afternoon when you've both cooled off a bit more." He nods. "Right now, go find Paul. Tell him you're sorry."

Paul's in the commons talking with Corina when I come back. She raises her eyebrows at me to see if I'm okay. I smile, pretend that I am.

"I'm gonna let you two talk."

I watch her go up the hallway to the bunks before I turn to Paul, who's looking up at me from the couch.

My hands are sweaty, so I wipe them on my pants.

"I . . ." I start, but I don't know exactly what to say. "I'm sorry I hit you."

He nods, starts untucking his shirt from his pants. "Do you want to see my bruise? It's gonna be a good one."

I don't want to see his bruise. I feel bad enough without seeing anything at all. "Nah. I . . . Look, I am sorry. I didn't know it was you, I thought—I wasn't . . ."

He stops pulling at his shirt. "You're sure you don't want to see it? It's gonna look just like your elbow." He tucks his shirt back. "Seriously, though . . . it did hurt."

"I didn't even know it was you."

He waits a moment, then lets out a breath. "I know." Then: "It's cool. I've had worse knocks that I deserved less."

"Nah, I shouldn't've done it."

He smiles and it gets quiet. I don't know what to do, so I start looking at the door to the dormitory, but I don't know if it's right to leave.

Paul follows my eyes, then looks over at the games along the wall. He gestures with his chin at a motocross VR near the pinball machines. "You wanna race?"

He ends up beating me five times before I win once. I try and tell myself it's because I feel bad for elbowing him, but the fact is that he's just flat-out better at it than I am.

After dinner, back in the room: "We're cool, right?"

He looks at me, shrugs. "Yeah, why? You'd rather I was mad at you?"

"No . . ." But in a way, I would. As is, I just feel bad with nobody to get mad at for it.

"Good." He points at my bed. "Now, lights out, Neo. You gotta witness tomorrow."

Ridiculous. "Why? It's not even eight." I haven't had this conversation since I was in elementary school.

"Why, *Morpheus.*" He raises his eyebrows at me. "Because you're witnessing tomorrow and there's nothing that'll suck your energy like time travel."

"I'm not calling you Morpheus."

He grabs my toothbrush from the shelf above my desk and hands it to me. "G'night, Neo." He's smiling.

"Seriously?"

"Yeah." He stops smiling and nods his head. "Seriously. You need to sleep."

I don't want to give in, but it's not like I have much else I was going to do tonight. And I guess I am pretty tired.

Twenty-Five

PAUL WAKES ME UP WITH A PILLOW TO THE HEAD. "WAKE UP! YOU'RE witnessing today!" When I sit up, he screams and begs me not to hurt him.

If this continues, I'm going to have to elbow him again.

We're the only ones at breakfast.

"Where's Corina?" I ask Paul as innocently as I can.

He starts to shrug but it turns into a full-body leer. "Why do *you* want to know where Corina is?"

I act like I don't care, but I can feel myself turning red. "Just curious."

He wrinkles his nose and winks at me. "Simple curiosity. She's working with Calvin today."

I nod like it doesn't matter. It shouldn't matter. I don't even know her.

Paul chats about this and that through breakfast. Afterward, he leads me back to the commons to the same glide room we were in yesterday.

"Today's the real deal, so you're going to need to suit up." He opens the door. There are two white suits laid out on the couch. "That's yours," Paul says, pointing to one of the suits. "You can change in there." He points at a door.

I take the suit and change, putting my clothes in the cubby

marked with my name. When I come back, Paul hands me a headset. "You'll get your instructions through this. Put it on while I change." He stops in the doorway to the changing room and turns back to me. "And don't laugh when I come back." He touches his chest. "Sensitive."

I smile, but I don't know if he's joking or not and put on the headset. There's no sound that comes through it, but when I put it on, I feel something shift in my head, like I suddenly understand the answer to a problem I didn't know I had. It's disorienting.

I now know all about my target.

Jordan Castle, the president's daughter. I was in Jordan's mind yesterday. She is the eldest daughter of President Vincent Castle and is the poster child for the presidential "More to Life, America" campaign that promotes healthy, values-based decision-making for teens and tweens.

My job will be to witness futures where she grows concerned about Incursions, starts believing that they're real—despite her father's public denial of their existence—and becomes determined to use her platform to make the world aware of the danger the Locusts pose, *and* of how Live-Tech can protect us.

Then there's nothing more and the headset is just an uncomfortable thing on my head.

When Paul comes back, he stands awkwardly in the doorway and I have to bite my cheek hard to keep from laughing. He's visibly chunky in normal clothes, but the suit makes it so much more . . . like cauliflower. "You know what you're doing?" he asks me.

I nod. "Yeah, I think so." I point at the headset. "This thing . . ."

"That thing," he agrees. "You go first. I'll be here to make sure everything goes alright for you." He pats the bed. "Lay your one-fifty-plus self down on the witness couch."

I lie down.

"Alright," Paul says as I stretch out. "Before you go, as a Jedi, there's some rules I'm supposed to make sure my Padawan understands."

The references. "Okay."

"Well, then. The big-time-big rule is that we never ever ever *ever* talk about what we witness with anyone. No one. Nobody. If Sabazios himself asks you, you say: 'No, sir. I will not tell you, sir.' Capisce?"

I don't know what *capisce* means, but I remember what Richard said yesterday after I got my patch. "Yeah, Richard said that."

"Good. Next rule: What we see *cannot* change what we do. If you see something that says 'NEWS FLASH: Underwear Causes Ball Cancer,' you can't tell me to start going commando."

"Okay."

Paul hesitates, wags his fingers in the air. "Three . . . Oh yeah—and this is another big one—no matter what you see—you report it. Doesn't matter what it is—could be a newspaper article on the desk in front of you—a bit of gossip from your wife or husband—don't matter. Report it."

"Gotcha."

"And if you see something really awful—a horrible accident that kills children and nuns or a massive earthquake that swallows Iowa or whatever—you've still got to report it."

I was feeling pretty good about the whole thing, but when he says this, I sit up. "You've seen things like that?"

He raises his eyebrows and sighs. "Can't tell you that. Rule number one. You ready?"

I take some deep breaths. They don't help much. "I guess." I close my eyes. Path. Skateboard. Off-ramp. Darkness. Light.

It's too bright for me from where I'm perched. Everything is a wash of white so intense that the walls themselves seem backlit to me. Not to Jordan, though. The brightness, the paleness, that's all normal to her—I get that now. What's making her uncomfortable is something else entirely.

We're at a table, chrome rimmed with a hard red spotted surface that makes me think of the 1950s. The table's round, big. We're surrounded by people who are laughing, talking, whispering, eating. There's a mess of sound so confusing and unnatural that I want to close my ears, make it go away, but I can't.

I don't have ears here, Jordan does, and these sounds are normal to her.

There's ice cream in front of us. We're out for her birthday with a hand-selected group of people her age from church. We're smiling, even though the whole thing is a charade. We're making eye contact with a girl our age who's sitting next to Jordan. She's blond, too, like Jordan. Her hair is straight, shorter than it should be, so her face looks wide even when it isn't. Her name is Melissa, and we're talking about the More to Life, America Working Conference we went to last month in Des Moines.

More to Life, America is why Jordan's uncomfortable. Melissa talks about it like a true believer. Melissa's excited and every time she smiles, Jordan wants to wince.

Jordan doesn't like More to Life, America. The whole thing was her mom's idea. Her mom and Dr. Halliday, the family pastor.

The only thing she likes about MtLA is The Conference.

The Conference. In Jordan's mind, The Conference is capitalized and written in big bold letters. The Conference changed her life. It was at The Conference where Jordan met Will. Jordan's mind is a whirl of activity—replaying images of her time with Will in Des Moines—arguing in a working group that became a silly game of one-upmanship, talking one-on-one at the lunch table when the rest of the room seemed to disappear.

Copying his name off the contact list, along with his email and phone number, and hiding it from Julia, her chaperone.

Hiding Will.

But Julia knew. Will's working group was changed. Jordan was made to sit elsewhere at lunch.

Grandma Bev helped her contact him afterward. She's been their Friar Tuck ever since.

Will.

Will reads books, has never eaten Korean food, wants to join the marines. Will shares her doubts about MtLA, about church, about God.

Will is someone with whom she can be honest. Her true self.

Will's face is everywhere in Jordan's mind, clouding out Melissa, the melting ice cream in front of her, the fact that she's minutes away from having to make her birthday "speech" to the group—a two-minute sound bite promoting MtLA, and its mission to "help restore traditional family social values through community building and fostering social support networks, which will help adolescents make positive choices and get the help they need to avoid poor decisions, which might result in lifelong damage and trauma."

". . . I still think it would have been a good addition to the MtLA mission." Melissa makes a face like she's missed an opportunity.

"Yeah," Jordan agrees, not knowing what Melissa's talking about.

Linda Castle catches our eye from the table where she's sitting with Denise, her chief of staff. Jordan's mom nods at Jordan, holds up a finger. One minute. Behind us, Jordan can hear the doors opening, the shuffle and clacks of press people and their cameras coming into the ice cream parlor, then the whiz of shutters.

Jordan turns to try and pay attention to what's happening elsewhere at the table. Melissa is the only person she really knows here. The others are kids she's seen before, sat in church youth classes with, but that's it.

None that know her. The feeling in her seems to blend with me. It's familiar enough that it could be my own. The kids around her have a life in common that isn't hers. Jordan thinks about what they would do if they knew about Will, the lies, the charade she lives.

Charlatan. *The word is large in her brain, flashing to draw attention. She winces against it, takes a breath, focuses on what's happening now.*

The tall boy sitting directly across the table is talking loudly now. He's got an easy face, playful. Jordan listens, but she doesn't know what he's talking about. These kids all go to school together. Jordan is homeschooled in her Rapunzel's tower.

Instead of just laughing along, Jordan looks at Melissa for guidance—asks her with our eyes what he's talking about. The part of us that's me can't help but think about how I feel when I have to ask Zeon or Beems what's happening.

Unlike Zeon, Melissa looks thrilled to be asked, which sends the flush of discomfort through Jordan that she gets whenever something reminds her of how different she is. Melissa leans in: "Ms.

Fredericks—she's our math teacher? She's getting married to Mr. Sung." Melissa doesn't tell us who Mr. Sung is.

Neither of us care enough to follow up. We're both camouflaged outsiders, pretending to understand. Instead, Jordan listens.

She likes the boy's voice. Likes . . . but she clamps down on whatever feeling there was before it can even rise to the level of a thought. Instead she looks down at her ice cream, forces herself to take another bite. She watches the spoon rise to her mouth, bracing herself. She does not like half-melted ice cream in the least. It feels bad in her mouth, like cold mayonnaise.

She sucks it off the spoon anyway and her mouth is awash in chocolate-flavored cold-mayonnaise-feeling half-melted ice cream. She smiles through it, then turns the spoon upside down in the bowl and pushes it softly away from herself.

There's a hand on our shoulder. We look up at her mom, smile. "JJ, do you want to say something to your friends for your birthday?"

It's speech time. Jordan stands, begins to talk.

The speech scrolls through Jordan's mind like movie credits. She reads it, the words, the gestures, the smiles, the pauses, but that's not where Jordan's mind is.

Jordan's mind is on the gift from Grandma Bev, the screen. The one that'll help her talk to Will.

When I open my eyes, memories of Jordan's mind are left behind in me like morning dew. "Oh shit."

Paul looks at me.

I shake my head. "Just weird."

He smiles. "Wish you could talk about it?"

I nod, then feel like I've broken some rule by even admitting that. I sit up and step away from the couch.

"Someday," Paul says as he lies down where I just was, "when all this is over, we're going to hold a witness reunion"—he props himself up on one elbow—"and I'm going to make Sabazios pay for it, and all we're going to do is talk about all this stuff we couldn't talk about at the time." He bugs his eyes. "I have things to *tell* you, my boy. Things to tell you."

I think about Jordan Castle's secret boyfriend. "Yeah." I walk around to the dictation station. "I bet."

I dictate everything I can remember into the microphone while Paul goes under. It's eerie having him there—he's completely still, barely breathing. I keep thinking he might be dead, which makes it hard to focus on the dictation.

Untethered. The word begins to chime in my head. I keep picturing Paul's mind wandering around on the glide path, floating past the noisy parts, lost forever while his body starts to decay. I look up a lot at the Live-Tech device on the wall above his head that Paul said would save us. It's not a patch—it looks more like a feather, and I don't understand how I'm supposed to use it. Paul said he'd teach me, but I guess he forgot. I'll have to ask when he wakes up.

If he wakes up.

I finish dictating and wait for him to open his eyes. I stare at him to make sure he's alive. When he finally does, I'm relieved, but it's even more awkward. I don't know how I'm going to wait for some reunion to talk about this shit. I want to talk *now*. Instead I ask about the feather. He laughs and shows me that I just have to hold it against his neck to bring him out of a glide.

I feel a little relief knowing how to use the feather, but all the stuff I really want to talk about is still penned inside me.

Frustrating.

Paul stays in the chamber to dictate and I walk back to the room alone.

At first I have plans for eating lunch and maybe playing some VR games, but instead I lie down on the bed. Paul said witnessing made you tired, but I had no idea. In the moments before I fall asleep, I try and remember what life was like last week, but instead I end up thinking about Jordan Castle.

I've always wondered what it would be like to be someone else, to know how they felt, to know how they knew what to say or do, because I never seem to. Now I'm seeing it. My wish is coming true, but I'm more confused than ever.

I've seen Jordan Castle on Channel 0, which we have to watch every day during advisory period for current events, and she always seemed so sure of what she was saying, like she really believed all that stuff. At the time I never thought much about her except that she seemed unreal, like a grown-up in a kid package. But she's not. She's got secrets and she doesn't say what she means even when she wants to. Just like me.

She hides whole parts of herself from her parents, just like me.

We're a lot alike. She looks like the people around her, sounds like them, but she doesn't feel like them, doesn't know what they're talking about.

Twenty-Six

I WAKE UP WHEN PAUL COMES IN. HE FLOPS DOWN ON HIS BED. I LOOK OVER at him, but his wall full of stuff catches my eye instead. "Where'd you get all that?"

"All what?"

I point at the flag and hats on his wall with my chin. "That." And then: "And the guitar?"

He looks up at the wall. His energy changes. "I had it all with me when I came here."

"Why would you have a flag and a bunch of cowboy hats?"

Paul sighs and sits up, leaning his back against the wall below the flag. "I just did."

"You just did?"

He shrugs a little bit, sits up, and reaches for the guitar, pulling it onto his lap. I suddenly want to play, too. "I didn't come here straight from home and I didn't want to leave any of it behind." He looks up behind his head at the stuff on his wall, strums the guitar. "When I left home, I didn't know what to bring—it was complicated—so I just grabbed the things that felt important." He strums the guitar again, starts simple straight blues progression when he talks. I'm concerned he's going to break out in song, but he doesn't. "The flag was my grandpa's—from when he died, and that hat"—he gestures at the more beat-up of the hats on the wall—"belonged to my uncle and I got it when he died."

Him talking about those things makes me send my hand to my pocket to search for my dad's key chain photo. It's not there and for a moment I panic and it's hard to breathe but then I remember: It's in my hoodie, which is hanging on a hook by the door. I get up and grab it.

"This is all I've got from my family." I look at it. My dad's laughing and Pete's making a face. My mom's got her head tilted back so her eyes nearly disappear in her smile. Ten-year-old me looks happier than I ever remember being.

I hand the photo to Paul. He takes it, examines the picture. While he's looking at it, I start to get tense because I don't know what he's going to say. I imagine him giving me sympathy and it makes me feel irritated, but so does the thought of him treating it like it's nothing.

He looks up at me. His face is serious and sad. I tell myself to relax. He's trying to be nice.

"What do you miss the most about them?"

Which is something I'm totally not ready for. I'm too surprised to lie or pretend I don't know. "They made me feel safe." It's out before I can stop it. It's pure truth.

He nods. When he speaks, it's quiet. "You were really lucky to have that."

I nod back at him and then look up at the hats and flag again, pressing my tongue hard against my front teeth until I'm back in control.

Eventually, I gesture at the stuff on the wall again. "So you brought all that with you here?"

He shrugs. "I didn't know anything about here when I left home. I walked out of my folks' place months before I even knew here existed. I got my letter at the youth services shelter in Phoenix when I stopped in for a shower."

I sit up on my bed. "Why'd you leave home?"

He shrugs again. Strums the guitar once more before picking out a twangy country riff. Then he mutes the strings before looking straight at me. "You're really asking?"

"I . . ." I do want to know, but things are getting heavy and it's making me uncomfortable. "Yeah . . ." I manage. And then: "If you want to tell me."

He stares at me a moment longer. I can feel him judging me. "Alright." He puts the guitar back onto its stand. "I've known who I am for a while—like since I was a kid—and I've never been one to keep things to myself, right?"

I haven't known him long, but that seems about right. I nod.

"Yeah. Well, my folks—they weren't so into the idea of me being gay. They didn't send me to reparative therapy or anything, but they kept telling me that if I gave girls a chance . . . if I just acted like . . ." He shrugs, leans back against the wall. "So we didn't talk about it much. My brother, Danny, he pretended I didn't exist. Anyways, the charade sustained itself until I was in eleventh grade, when me and a boy got caught together at school."

When he says it, I cringe without meaning to. I don't know what his school was like, but I know in mine, there were a lot of kids who wouldn't tolerate that. There's a reason Julio acts like everyone else when he's in the neighborhood. "Caught by who? What'd they do?"

He purses his lips and smiles at me. "They beat us up." He says it like an apology—as if he's sorry for me to have to hear it.

"Jeez, man, I'm sorry." It feels so strange to me to say I'm sorry about what he's telling me, because even when I'm saying it, I'm also remembering all the times I stood by when kids called other kids faggots and threatened to beat their asses for being gay.

I didn't think about it much then, but hearing it now from Paul, I really am sorry about what happened to them.

"So when my folks came to get me at the hospital—" He sees the look on my face and waves it off. "It wasn't that bad. I didn't really need to go. The school insisted for liability reasons. Anyways, when my folks came and the counselor who was waiting with me told them what happened . . ." He shakes his head, twists around a little on the bed before he finishes. "They told me that I needed to get myself under control because otherwise they wouldn't be able to deal with me anymore. Then my mom asked me if I knew how humiliating this was for her."

"Yeah, I bet." I say it before I even think about it—I'm thinking about what Julio's mom would do if she knew—and it just comes out of my mouth and falls there into the space between us. Even before I finish the sentence, I can hear it echo in my head, like it's being fed through a reverb. I want to take it back before he hears it, suck the words right back inside, but I can't. It's too late.

Paul sits perfectly still on the bed. His eyes are hard again. "Fuck you," he says quietly. He stretches out on his bed. "I'm tired. I'm going to sleep."

"Paul, man . . ." But he doesn't look at me. He closes

his eyes. I get up. I'm not begging anybody for forgiveness. "Forget you, then," I tell him as I walk out the door, closing it hard behind me.

I spend the afternoon in the commons watching soccer with Maddie. She knows every player on every team and spends the whole time telling me about them. I can barely track the ball because my mind is still replaying the whole thing with Paul.

I shouldn't have even asked him about shit, but like a dumbass, I opened my mouth.

And then I couldn't just keep it shut, nod my head or something. I had to say something. Even when I said it, I knew it was stupid.

He didn't have to be such a dick about it. I tried to apologize. He's too sensitive.

Paul's not . . . He's . . .

Fuck. I'm trying to feel better, but all the words in my head can't cover the truth: I'm a dumbass.

Every time I replay the whole conversation, my cheeks start to burn.

Maddie talks constantly, playing with her ponytail the whole time. She played soccer, too. Played since she was three. She's giving me her history along with the history of all the players on the teams.

"You could at least *pretend* to give a crap," she says finally.

"Sorry." I shake my head. "I'm trying." Then I stumble for more words. "I got things on my mind."

She nods. I look at her, trying to focus on what she's saying. She's got blue eyes and a face that's edged nicely by the bones in her cheek and jaw. She's really pretty, but it's hard to think about her that way.

Not like Corina.

I run through what I remember of what she was saying, trying to come up with a question to ask that'll show her that I was paying even a little bit of attention. All I can come up with is: "Why'd you stop playing?"

She shakes her head, rolls her eyes. "My coach screwed me."

I don't know how she means it. "Wow."

She bites her lip. "He suspended me from the team in the middle of scouting season."

"Really?" I don't know what else to say.

She nods. "He was an asshole."

I nod. I'm not going to ask what she did. I've learned my lesson.

"Bunch of girls cheated on an English final and he said it was my fault because I'd been in the class before and gave them a copy of the test I'd kept." She shakes her head. "How was I supposed to know their teacher didn't change it every year?" She raises a finger like she's warning me. "Not my fucking fault."

"Oh no."

"Yeah. It was awful." She looks back at the game.

I nod and don't say anything, wishing I'd done the same thing with Paul. My cheeks start to burn again.

When Maddie and I get to the dinner table, Paul's already there talking to Calvin. He doesn't look up when I come in, and I feel the whole weight of this afternoon all over again.

"What's wrong with you?" Corina asks when I sit down.

I want to tell her, but I also don't want to tell her because she'll think I'm such a dick. "Nothing," I try. "I think I'm just tired." I look up at her. "Witnessing . . ."

She nods. "It'll tire you out, that's for damn sure." And I think I've gotten away with it, but then she adds: "But it won't make you look like a puppy died. What happened?"

I sigh. Pick at the pancakes the cat carrier gave me for dinner. The room around us is filled with people talking, and I don't see anybody listening to us just now. "Paul's mad at me about something I said."

"How mad?"

I sigh. "He said 'fuck you.'"

Corina just nods and pulls up a forkful of pasta. Then: "Damn. Paul don't cuss. You probably shouldn't say whatever you said anymore."

Which makes me laugh because it's such dumb advice. "Yeah, alright."

"And you should probably go apologize."

"He doesn't want to hear it."

She shakes her head. "He *didn't* want to hear it. You don't know what he wants now."

I can hear Paul playing guitar from down the hall. My chest tightens but I suck it up and walk into the room like I live there. "Hey."

He looks up at me. "Hey."

I don't want to sit down, because it feels weird, so I just stand in the middle of the room above him, twisting like an idiot just like the last time I apologized to him. "Look, man . . ." But it comes out as a mumble. A little louder: "I was a dick before."

He stops playing and looks up at me. He's perfectly still, then shakes his head slowly. "Alex, I am sure you are a good guy at heart, but I am absolutely not ready to talk about any of this yet."

"I didn't even know what I was saying . . . I didn't . . ." But I can already feel the heat on my neck and my throat is small. It's hard to breathe and if he doesn't give me something soon, then screw him and all of this because I'm not going to dangle—

He holds up a hand. "Just come on in—it's your room, too—and do your thing while I do mine for a while, alright?"

I look away from him, stare up at my big blank wall. "Whatever, man." Then I grab my toothbrush.

When I get back to the room, Paul's gone and so's his guitar.

It takes me a long time to fall asleep, but even so, Paul's still gone when I do.

Paul's already gone when I wake up. He's gliding today, but I'm not. What I said yesterday starts playing in my head before I'm even in a sitting position.

By the time I'm on my feet with my shower stuff, I'm already reliving the part where he told me that he didn't want to talk about it yet.

By the time I'm out of the shower I'm completely spun again. Half of me hates myself and the other half hates everyone else.

At least I won't have to see anybody today—I'm the only one not working. I'm a little sad I won't get to spend more time with Jordan, but really I'm thinking about how good that is when I walk into the kitchen.

"Hey, Alex." Richard's sitting at the table, smiling at me. He lifts his coffee mug at me. "Enjoying your day off?"

"Yeah." I don't look at him and head straight for the cat carrier instead, hoping it'll give me something really good that'll take my mind off of things.

Pop-Tarts, a banana. Nothing exciting, but watching them form, I can't help but know that nothing I was going to eat was going to be all that good today, so old standards are probably the best choice.

Richard's still at the table when I get back. He must see me hesitate because he says, "It's alright. Don't have to talk if you don't want to."

I nod, sit, start to eat. I can see him out of the corner of my eye, reading something on a tablet, sipping his coffee. My eye wanders to the design in the center and then to the big one on the wall.

"What's with the Live-Tech logo thing?"

Richard looks up at me, surprised. "What?"

I point at the design on the table with the uneaten side of my Pop-Tart. "The design. It's all over everything here. What's it mean?"

Richard looks at it, then smiles, sets his tablet down, and reaches out with his hand to trace the edge of the pentagon closest to him. "This?"

I nod. "Yeah, Live-Tech."

Richard chuckles. "Jeff uses a simplified version of this for Live-Tech, but it's much more meaningful than just a corporate logo." He strokes the design again with his finger. "This is a powerful symbol—something the Gentry used to explain things to Jeff when they first contacted him."

"How'd they do that?" He looks confused, so I clarify. "First contact Sabazios?"

"They sent him a patch." Richard takes a sip of coffee, leans back. "The device we use to send letters back and such? Well, since space and time are essentially of the same substance, it's useful for sending small objects over great distances to specific places, as well. Under the guidance of the Oracle device, they could drop a winning lottery ticket into the back pocket of my great-grandfather as he walked across campus in nineteen seventy-five." He looks at me like he's hoping I'm impressed.

I don't really get all of what he's saying, but I'm glad to listen because it's got me thinking about things besides how much my life sucks right now. It also explains how the photo ended up in the time capsule. I nod. "So they sent him a patch? They can't do what the Locusts do?"

Richard shakes his head. "Nope. What the Locusts do is unique. The Gentry have to stick to the limits of their own technology."

I scratch my chin and try to look wise.

"So they sent the patch, Jeff put it on and they've been guiding all this ever since."

"So he's never, like"—I shrug—"seen one or anything? A Gentry?"

Richard shakes his head. "Nope, though we can fairly safely assume they look a bit like us."

"Why?"

He leans forward, raises his eyebrows. "They're the ones who seeded us here."

He looks at me like he's expecting me to fall on the floor in shock, but that's not how I feel. I just wait for him to continue.

"Evidently, there's all sorts of different kinds of life in the universe, but not all of it can communicate. The Gentry, a hundred million years ago when they first made the leap to become an interstellar civilization, found that they were nearly unique—couldn't really talk to anybody else—so they seeded the galaxy with life that they would, eventually, be able to talk to—including life here on Earth."

My mind's blank. I know what he's just said is huge—like life, the universe, and everything huge—but it doesn't even feel like that. It just feels . . . normal. "They made us? Like God?"

"I don't know about that, but they're responsible for much of life on Earth being the way it is."

"Oh." It's all I can think of to say.

He points at the design on the table. "And that's got a lot to do with the insignia." He taps the edge. "It's got a couple different meanings." He drags his finger across the field of gray dots. "The dots can be seen as stars and the red dots can be seen as the homes of species like us—the ones the Gentry created who are working with the Gentry against the Locusts." He traces the triangle. "The triangle is the strongest physical shape." He pushes at the top dot with his finger. "Pressure up here—it's distributed evenly to both sides, which makes it very strong—that's why bridges are made with triangular trusses—so they can bear all the weight on top of them."

Then he puts his finger over one of the red dots. "But if a single vertex of the triangle disconnected, the remaining shape is just an open angle—one of the weakest physical forms in nature. Even a small amount of pressure can break it." He looks up at me. "That's how the Gentry view our alliance—we're a part of the strength of their community, and if we succumb to the Locusts, it will threaten all Gentry life.

"There's another meaning, too," he tells me. "Your work. You can also see this field of gray dots as a field of future possibilities—and the red lines are made up of ones that we need to secure in order to survive." He traces the red triangle with his finger. "Every time you go under, Alex, you add to the red, and only when the lines are complete are we truly safe."

"I'm part of something good?" It sounds cheesy as hell, but it's honestly how I feel.

Richard smiles a really big smile. "Yeah, Alex." His voice cracks. "You are. We all are."

I nod, feel myself getting choked up, too.

I wish I could call my Tía.

"Richard?"

He looks at me.

"You said we'd work on getting word . . ." He doesn't seem to understand what I'm saying. "Like to my aunt?"

He begins to nod, then reaches into his messenger bag and pulls out a sheet of paper. "Write her a message. Tell her that you didn't do it. You can even tell her you'll be coming home when it's safe for you."

I take his paper, and he offers me a pen. I write the note as best I can. When I hand it to him it feels empty, no better than blank paper.

He creases it, folds it in half without reading it, then examines my face. "I know it's not enough, Alex, but it's the most we can do."

I look back down at the design on the table. "I know I can't *talk* to anybody, but maybe you can help me get some news from home?" He looks at me, his lips pressed together.

He sighs. "I guess the local news here isn't going to carry what you want to know, is it?" He slaps his hands together softly and stands up. "Come with me." Then: "Just remember—you can see what's out there, but you won't be able to communicate with anybody, is that clear?"

"Yeah," I say before he can change his mind. I stand up and follow him to his office, where he sits me at his desk. There's a screen I use to search for information on my parents' case.

The first thing I find is that my Tía made a plea on TV for me to come home. Richard is right behind me as I watch. She's up at a podium with some cops who announce that there was a $25,000 reward for information that leads to the arrest and conviction of my parents' killer. Then she stands up and she talks.

She's weak when she comes up. One of the cops has to hold her hand because there's nobody else there to do it.

I feel Richard behind me and I want him to not be there because I don't know how I'm going to handle myself when she starts to talk.

"Little Alex." Her voice isn't her normal voice. It's shaky and she's nearly shouting. "Please come home right now because we love you and we need to talk to you so we can know what happened to your parents. You need to come home, mijo. You need to come home because you're sick and you need help." She's crying now, her words coming out like barks from a dog. The cop who helped her up puts a hand on her shoulder. She tries to shake it off, but ends up just falling against him because she's crying too hard.

Richard doesn't say anything when the video ends. He

just stands up and pats me on the back, squeezes my shoulder. Then he leaves me in his office.

When I'm able to, I search up more things. The *LA Times* has a thing called the Homicide Report. It has all the updates on the case, but there haven't been any recently. It has some comments on the story, so I read them.

The first one is from "Anonymous": *Their family is in my prayers. Whoever did this needs to fry.*

The second one is signed. It's from Julio: *They were good people. Plugzer, if you're reading this, come home. No matter what happened, I got your back.*

"Bullshit." Nobody in LA has my back. They all think I killed my parents and no little note is going to change that.

I need to set things straight.

I go back and find the article that I read at the bus station—the first one that had the quote from my Tía. It was written by a lady named Sarah Campbell. Her email's right there on the page. I know it won't change anything, but I feel like I'll explode if I don't say something.

I stretch to look out into the gym on the other side of Richard's door, but I can't see or hear anybody nearby. I go back and copy down her email on a Post-it note and then open up a proxy server and go to an email service I've never used before and sign up for an account. When I've gotten it set up, I check the gym again—still empty—and then open up an email and put her address in the address bar.

I write the thing fast because I need to get finished before Richard gets back and I'm not really good at writing things anyway, so I probably don't say it right. In the end, it says:

To the Reporter Sarah Campbell

My name is Alejandro Pulido Mata. You wrote an article about my parents being murdered and I want to tell you that I didn't do it. I know you all don't believe me when I say it was an Incursion, but it was. The bug has a hand like a knife and that's what it used to stab my parents before it disappeared. I only survived because I had a Live-Tech and I scared it away.

The Incursions are real and we're all in danger unless you listen to Jeffrey Sabazios. I'm innocent.

Can you tell my auntie Juana that I'm ok? I'm safe and I'm not crazy and I didn't kill anybody.

Don't try and find me. I'm not anywhere people would think to look, and please please please do not publish this or let people know I talked to you—it's not safe yet. I'll write you again when I can.

Tell my aunt that I'm doing good things.

I send it, then stare at the screen awhile longer. Then I close it up.

Richard's nowhere to be found and there's nobody in the commons when I get back. Nobody in the kitchen.

They're all working. I wish I was working, too.

I'm lying on the bed when Paul comes in. He hesitates for a moment when he sees me, then gives me a small tight smile before grabbing his guitar and turning to go.

"Hey." I sit up. "Wait a minute."

He stops, but he doesn't turn around.

"Look man, I . . . There's nothing wrong with you."

He doesn't say anything back, he doesn't move either, he just stands there, perfectly still, holding his guitar by the neck.

His silence makes feelings come up inside me that I have to work to keep from spilling out. "I don't . . ." But then I trail off because I don't know what else to say. "Never mind." I stand up. "You don't have to leave. I'll go."

I have to step past him to get to the door. It's awkward and close and part of me wants to shove him and part of me wants to hug him and all of me just wants this to be over with, but as I reach the door, he opens his mouth:

"You don't think I should hide who I am? You don't think my mom was right to be humiliated?"

I stop, turn, shake my head. "No." Then I look him in the eyes. "No."

He smiles. It's a really nice smile. "Okay, then." He points at my bed with his pick. "Sit."

I look at the bed.

"Yes. There."

I sit.

He hands the guitar across to me. I don't even reach for it at first but then he shakes it at me and I take it. "Play something."

"Like what?"

He shakes his head. "Something that means something to you."

My eyes move over to my backpack, to where my songbook is. "I don't know . . ."

"Then tell me something."

"What?" I can't help myself from fingering an E major and running my thumb down the strings before tapping the harmonics on the twelfth fret.

"Something important. The only way for us to get things back in balance is for you to pour your heart out to me about something."

I don't look at him. I don't want him to see the fear in my face, but he sees it anyway. "I won't be a jerk about it. I'm not out for revenge," he says.

I look up at him. "Serious?"

He stares at me. He's serious.

I sigh. Strum. "Alright."

And then I tell him. I tell him about Pete and I tell him about my mom and dad. I tell him about the look the last time I saw my dad and about Julio, who's always better than me. I tell him about Mousie and about how much I miss my mom.

He's not a jerk about it. Even when I get so I can't speak at all.

We go to dinner, and when we come back to the room, I tell him: "I actually do have some songs I wrote."

He smiles at me. "You going to play me one?"

"I . . ." Fuck it. "Yeah." I go to my backpack and pull out the notebook, open to a page that has the right song. "I wrote this about my ex-girlfriend."

We weren't together that long—I've never had a thing with a girl that lasted more than a month—but she's the only one who ever broke up with me.

"She broke your heart?"

I shake my head. "Nah." Then: "She just . . . she just didn't like me."

I play him the song. I have to read the lyrics as I play, so it's not smooth, and I keep looking at Paul, waiting for him to laugh at me, or for his face to say he thinks it's dumb, but he's quiet, looks focused on what I'm doing.

When I get to the last lines of the song:

Dear Alex, just so you know, I'm out the door, I'm gonna go
Just so you know, it's not me, though. You should never have shown
Me the real you.

He waits a moment, then nods slowly. "That's powerful, man." Then he cocks his head. "You don't really think people would like you if they knew you? The real you?"

I shrug. "I've . . ." I look at him, ready to answer but the moment passes. "I don't know, man. It's just a song."

He drops it.

He plays me a song, too, but it's not by him. Johnny Cash. "Ring of Fire."

Then we talk more.

It's really late when we fall asleep. Working in the morning is going to suck.

When I do lie down on my bed, though, I'm not even worried about tomorrow. Some things are worth being tired for.

Twenty-Seven

WE'RE SITTING ON A COUCH, LEGS PULLED UP UNDER US CRISSCROSS APPLE-*sauce. The air is bright all around us. Her colors are bleached even inside, and with the glare of the sun, everything looks like a faded Polaroid of the world she lives in.*

Jordan is nervous. Excited. Her breath is shallow and I can feel her heart beating fast in her chest. She forces herself to take a deep breath. She hasn't been alone since the party—tutors, church, the "birthday event."

Last night when she got home, she wrote her thank-you note to Grandma Bev—and a longer letter, which she tucked inside for Grandma Bev to pass on to Will, a reply to the one he sent through Grandma Bev last week, in which he asked her to describe the party she would have.

Party.

Jordan couldn't use the word when describing her birthday in the letter. It would have been a lie, and Will only gets the truth from her. He deserves the truth. It wasn't a party. It was her mom, her sisters, Dr. Halliday, Julia, Fran and Tom, Dad on video. In the Central Hall, locked in the tower.

A Rapunzel event. Something her parents did for the daughter they think they have.

The ice cream social last night? She called that her "political cotillion."

"Alrighty, then," she says out loud, bringing the screen up so she can see it. We listen. Her dad is back, returned this morning. He's in the game room next door with Jack, his chief of staff. She can hear them talking, muted by the distance in the hallways between them and her in the solarium. The windows are open, though, and she can hear them more clearly from across the patio.

But they're not interested in her.

She taps the icon her grandmother told her to. Even though the icon is for a common finance application, that's not what opens. SECRYPT. She doesn't recognize the name, but I do. People use it for messages they don't want anybody *seeing.*

Jordan wrinkles her forehead, clicks on the "contacts" box.

There are only two names:

Naomi

Will

Will. Jordan's mind fills with moments. The More to Life, America Working Youth Congress. Will—brown hair cut short, white, built like a football player. He smiles. She laughs. Him touching her hand. A momentary sensation beneath the pit of her stomach, something I don't recognize until I do. She shifts, straightens her legs, resettles, crosses them. Her heart is beating faster than it was even before.

She taps his name. A window opens. There's already a message from Will waiting:

"Rapunzel Rapunzel, let down your hair."

She giggles, taps out a reply. "Climb on up, young prince."

She taps on Naomi. A new window opens. "Ruth cannot thank you enough! How on Earth did you think this up?"

Will's name begins to throb. There's a new message. Jordan's breath catches. She taps his name. "There's video . . ."

Jordan takes a quick look around. Her pod is in, already connected to the screen.

She could . . . She wants to see Will so badly it hurts physically, but just as we're about to connect, the patio door opens from the game room. She sees shapes through the curtains, one tall, one shorter. Her dad and Jack.

"Can't. People around." *Then:* "Sometime soon."

"Soon."

More movement on the patio. She can see their shapes clearly, watches as Jack lights a cigarette. "It's not if, it's when, *Vince," he says. "Every two days, like clockwork—it's just dumb luck none of them have been filmed yet—you think you'd survive an Incursion video if you go out there and deny they're happening? How's that gonna play?"*

Incursions. *Jordan freezes, her finger hovering over the screen. She knows what Incursions are—she sees a lot of the same channels I do—but she didn't think.*

Incursion.

The word sits heavy in Jordan the same way it did in me before.

"We'll capture one before that happens, Jack." Her father always sounds confident, like he has access to the truth, but Jordan knows better—the more confident he sounds, the less he believes. "Operation Roach Hotel is going to work."

"With all due respect, Vince, that's crap—Roach Hotel hasn't captured diddly-squat so far, and they're not sounding hopeful, either."

Jordan's mind races. Secrets are hard to keep in the White House—floors squeak, voices carry. She's got to keep Sam and Avery from learning that Incursions are real.

Incursion. Roaches. Uncatchable, unseeable.

Demons. Abaddon, *destroyers of things. Jordan's mind swims in biblical names and stories—the image of Dr. Halliday, who leads Bible studies, stories of the crimes of man punished. The beginning of end of days. Jordan thinks about these things like a professor, not a believer—a secret she keeps locked away from all but Grandma Bev, who is the one who told her it was okay not to believe.*

Jordan sees a scale in her mind, drops Incursions on the side with the Bible, bringing it to near equality with the side that says "untrue."

ABADDON. The word is huge in her mind, the letter's colors thick and dark like a nightmare.

Jordan's mind fills with pictures when she thinks, in a way that my mind does not. The images make good things better, but they also make scary things even scarier to me.

To her. Jordan's mind fills with enormous roaches crawling out of a wall, engulfing a screaming child, devouring it until it's gone. "It'll play better than the president of the United States citing stuff off conspiracy sites as a legitimate national security threat." Her dad turns, walks closer to the window of the solarium where Jordan is sitting. We freeze, try not to even breathe. "Unless we're willing to declassify what we know, our only real option is to pretend it's not happening."

"That's short-term thinking, Vince. Short-term at best—that could come back and kick you in the ass tomorrow—even later today. What happens when one of those things zaps into a TGI Fridays in Fredericksburg and steals a kid? And what about when it turns out that Sabazios has been right all along? Do you think he's going to stay on the sidelines if you get caught with your pants down?

People may think he's a crackpot now, but if it turns out he's been right about everything and you ignored the problem, he's going to beat the pants off you if he runs next year."

"I don't know that'll happen and neither do you, but if we legitimize this threat too soon by talking about it, we're going to tank the markets and cause panic in the streets." Her dad turns around again, walks back toward the game room, stops, turns again to face Jack, his voice a low growl. "And that's why we've got to crush this Live-Tech thing before it takes hold—not only is it an immoral invasion allowing man to see what only God should know, but if it is *useful against these Incursions we need it to be ours, not his."*

The smell of Jack's cigarette wafts in through the window—the smoke makes Jordan's nose tingle; to her the smell is sweet, closer to bread burning than what cigarette smoke smells like to me—and she breathes deeply to get more of it.

Shame settles in. Smoking is wrong. She shouldn't enjoy the smell.

Jack drops the cigarette. She watches his silhouette through the curtain as he steps on it, grinds it out with his foot. "Don't sit on this too long or you'll go down in history as President Nero, fiddling while the world burns."

They go back inside.

Jordan tries to breathe. Her hand is shaking, her mind filled with blackness and visions of demons.

Her screen flashes. She looks down. Will's name is throbbing again. She taps on it. This time it isn't words, it's a picture.

Of Will. She taps it, clears her throat against the thickness she feels in it and waits as the photo crystallizes on the display.

He's cut his hair—a flattop. In the picture he waves, makes a slow turn around to show off his entire self, then waves again. "Hey, JJ!" scrolls from his mouth when it opens. "Send me one, too!"

Will is preparing to join the marines and he said in his last letter that the recruiter encouraged him to close-crop so he would be used to it when he enlisted. His face looks square to her, sharp at the edges, less kindly than the shaggy farm boy she sees in her mind. She studies it more closely, sees that there's still softness there, hidden in the eyes, the partial smile.

She enlarges the picture so it lifts off the screen and she can examine it from all sides like a Will statue. She takes a quick look around before bringing it to her face, placing a kiss in the air where his lips display.

Then more shame. A flush that heats up our face. She wipes the screen.

She watches the screen fade to black in her lap, her thoughts back on Abaddon, her father. Incursions are real, people are dying, and he is saying nothing.

The child in her vision morphs into Will's face, being devoured by alien bugs, flesh, to bone, to dust.

She can't let that happen.

Paul's sitting at the desk when I come up. He smiles when he sees my eyes. "Any longer and I was going to have to read a book or something."

It gets boring in the glide room when your partner's down. Richard keeps telling us to bring a book if we've got second glide, but me and Paul don't really like reading that much.

"Beat me and you can get first glide and spend your time dictating, I say." We play rock-paper-scissors to decide who goes first, but Paul's completely predictable, so he always loses.

Twenty-Eight

I'M STATIONED WITH PAUL. CALVIN'S STATIONED WITH DAMON. CORINA AND Maddie float, so we each get one day off every week. We need them. Two glides a day and I'm so wiped I can't do anything but eat and fall asleep on the couch.

While we're under, our bodies stop functioning except for essential services. Our consciousness is in the target, and there's nothing more exhausting for human biology than to maintain ties to the consciousness while it's traveling.

I can see why we do it in pairs. It seems like the tie could break easily if we stretched too far, permanently separating body and mind.

We've got to be vigilant or there will be dead witnesses.

I used to sleep six hours each night, but now I'm sleeping ten. Except when I can't sleep at all.

The only other witness who seems to have trouble sleeping is Calvin. He's always in the kitchen, sitting at the table, reading a book. I've gone in to get something for a midnight snack. Calvin and a book. Breakfast? Calvin and a book. Afternoon popcorn? Calvin and a book.

It's three in the morning and I've given up on sleeping. I keep thinking about how Jordan Castle is always pretending at home, but completely open with Will. I don't think I've ever had that with anyone. I was close with Beems, but there were still things I never told him about myself. Parts of my heart feel like the dark side of the moon, and I can't imagine ever letting another person know all of me.

I'm in the kitchen for a snack. I'm not looking for company, but of course, Calvin's already there.

"What'cha reading?" I ask as I step toward the cat carrier.

He looks up at me, then down at his book before holding it out for me to see. In the weeks I've been here, it's been different every time I've asked:

"*Breakfast of Champions.*" "*Choke.*" "*The Wind-Up Bird Chronicle.*" "*Heart of Darkness.*"

This time it's *Tuva or Bust!*

Richard gives them to him. Calvin says there are shelves full of books in his office, but I don't remember seeing them.

"You're always reading."

Calvin shrugs and puts down his book. "Books keep my mind occupied. When I'm not reading, my brain gets sticky so thoughts don't leave." He raises his eyes like he's trying to look at his own brain. "My head gets full up. It's why I can't sleep."

I know exactly what he means, too. My head's just done the same thing, which is why I'm in for a midnight snack. "Maybe I should try that."

Calvin nods, strokes his goatee. He looks like a wise owl when he does it. "I got a book for you, man." He stands up. "Wait here." He walks out of the room before I can say no thanks.

When Calvin comes back, he's holding a book clutched up against his chest like it's a baby. I can't see what it is, and he doesn't give it to me right away. Instead he sits down across from me and looks at it for a minute before handing it over.

"This is the only book I came in with," he tells me as I look at it. It's got a drawing of a big red knife across the cover, but it's barely visible because the cover is so trashed. I'm afraid to even pick it up because it might fall apart. "I was in the system before I came here." He looks at me, raises his eyebrows to see if I get what he means.

"Foster?"

He nods. "Yeah. Been in homes since before I was old enough to know anything. I got moved around a lot, so I didn't get to have much, but this . . ." He points at the book. "This was *mine*. I got it from a book thing at school when I was thirteen—one of those things where they call you up and you get to pick a book and it's yours?"

I nod. I know what he's talking about, but I never had feelings about them.

"I was just starting a new school, a new house, and neither one of them were good places for me, so I sucked up into this book and I lived there instead." He taps the cover, pushes it over to me. "Your turn."

It's called *The Knife of Never Letting Go*, and it's by a guy named Patrick Ness. I look up at him and he's looking at me and the book like we're supposed to understand what he means. He's making me nervous, so I just shake my head a little.

He nods slowly. "It's about this kid named Todd who lives on a planet where all the men and all the animals, they broadcast their thoughts to each other—they call it 'Noise.' His people are killed and he's got to go on the run with nobody but his dog."

I say thanks, then hand it back. It looks like it means a lot to him and I don't want to be responsible, but he shakes his head at me.

"Nah, man. Read it. Keep it." He shrugs and picks up the book he's reading now. "I memorized that shit."

Twenty-Nine

JORDAN IS HUNGRY. THE FEELING IS LARGER THAN MY OWN HUNGER EVER *is, a huge empty spot in her that needs to be filled. She put in a request for a cheeseburger with Andrew, but he's not back with it yet. I'm excited for the cheeseburger, too. I love it when Jordan eats things she likes—things taste better to her. Eating my own meals is becoming a frustrating disappointment, because I can't get her tastes out of my head.*

We have a screen unfolded on her lap, open to a document she's writing. The second MtLA Working Conference is in Las Vegas next week. Jordan will be delivering the opening address.

Jordan hates writing speeches, especially when her heart isn't in the work. Speeches are boring. She'd rather write poems—her heart can find a place in poetry.

Her heart isn't with MtLA, but her heart is with Will and he will be there, so we're doing this. "Over the course of the two months since we last met as a team, there has been an upswelling of support for what we at the More to Life, America Working Conference are aiming to achieve . . ." It's a lie. The word appears in her mind, a big flashing sign: "LIE." There hasn't been an upswelling of support. Nobody seems to care about it at all. It's not like she's upset about that—Jordan doesn't care, either. She pushes past it, continues: "I hear from young people around the nation—dozens each day—hoping that we can help re-create the safe, joyous, values-based childhoods for them and their siblings that they hear about from their grandparents . . ." Too much bull. Her voice cracks and she stumbles over the word grandparents. *"Dammit."*

She stops talking, watches the words and punctuation form on-screen, waits for the auto-complete to populate, offering her stronger choices and better words for the tone she's selected. "The word dammit *may not be your best choice here, Jordan," the screen tells her. "If you're looking for a way to strengthen your statement at this point, consider using verbal cues such as a louder voice or slower cadence."*

"Screw you," Jordan mumbles to the screen.

"Also not appropriate for the tone and manner of speech you've selected. If you're looking for a way to strengthen your statement at this point—"

"Off!" Jordan's shaking now, her voice almost a screech.

"JJ?"

We look up. Her mom is looking at us from the Central Hall. We don't know what she heard.

Breath. Smile. "Hi, Mom."

"I thought I heard some frustrated language coming from over here." She walks toward us, comes to settle next to us on the couch. "Is everything okay?"

Jordan smiles again, tries to look embarrassed. Jordan doesn't think she's ever been okay. "Yeah, I was just frustrated with my . . ." She points at the dark screen on her lap.

"What's the problem?" Linda Castle smiles brightly, looks excited. "Maybe I can help."

Jordan opens her mouth, ready to says something about how she's got it handled, but when she tries to say it, she can't. She takes a breath, then shakes her head. Everything feels black inside.

For a moment, things grow clear to Jordan: She can't do this much longer—live like she's someone she's not. The need to tell her mom the truth starts to feel like a compulsion, unquenched, unbearable.

Truth Will Out.

Jordan knows the quote is from Shakespeare. A momentary memory of reading The Merchant of Venice *with Julia invades, but is instantly crushed by the weight of Jordan's pain. Words: "I can't do this, Mom." We're whispering, trying not to cry. "I don't believe in it."*

I want her to continue. It feels so wrong for her to keep herself hidden, but even as she says it, Jordan knows it's wrong. The judgment, the disappointment, the hurt will all be too much. And Will. In her head Will is fading away.

Without MtLA, they will never see each other, never be able to be together. Living without the hope of Will is worse than lying. "Never mind." She shakes her head, looks over at her mom, eyes shy, vulnerable. "I think I'm just stressed about this and . . ."

The moment passes inside Jordan. The pain lifts when Linda Castle nods sympathetically, returns our smile, though hers looks real. She reaches for us and pulls us in against her side. "I know, JJ." She squeezes us. "We ask a lot of you, more than most families ask of their children, and more, even, than most presidents ask of theirs." She sighs. "But you're no ordinary kid, JJ."

Jordan doesn't answer. Her mind is already on to another subject—another thing that's been weighing her down. "Mom?"

"Yeah?"

"Dad can keep us safe from the Incursions, right?"

Linda Castle stiffens under us. "They aren't real." The lie is as smooth as one of Jordan's.

"Yes they are, Mom." Jordan pulls away and sits up. "I've heard Dad and Jack talking about them."

Her mom sits up, too, looks like she's ready to deny again, but then she falls back, looks down and takes Jordan's hand. "I trust God, JJ."

We nod, our chin against her shoulder. "But what if Jeffrey Sabazios is right and he has the answer already? Why isn't Dad at least looking at Live-Tech instead of trying to get rid of it?"

Linda Castle doesn't say anything for a moment. Jordan's chest tightens; she's gone too far. She pulls her head back, ready to apologize, but before she can: "There are things I don't know, sweetheart, but God seems to trust your dad enough to have made him president." She squeezes our hand. "Maybe you should, too."

Jordan doesn't reply. Doesn't squeeze back. Her mind is filled with images from the illustrated Bible she had as kid. Pictures of Nabal, of Holofernes, of Pharaoh.

Powerful kings who weren't up to God's task.

Andrew comes around the corner with the cheeseburger, hesitates when he sees us with the First Lady, but then strides over and lays the tray on the coffee table in front of us.

"Miss," he says. "Your cheeseburger."

Jordan gives him a tight little smile. "Thank you."

But she doesn't reach for it. She no longer feels like eating, because her mind is occupied with thoughts of Incursions, of Abaddon the destroyer coming, and her father, the president, remaining quiet.

Live-Tech. *The words light up in her head. A flash thought nestled in an image of her dad and Jack on the patio.*

If her dad won't do anything, maybe we can.

On my way back up from Jordan, I notice something—there's another path. It's faint compared to the one I'm on, goes in both directions, one narrow and straight, the other more like the one I take when I glide.

Over lunch, I ask Paul: "What's the other path?"

"Other path?"

"When we go down, sometimes there're two paths . . ."

"Yeah, that," he says between bites of his grilled cheese sandwich. "That's your path. You open up on that one, you'll Zombie yourself."

"Zombie myself?"

"Yeah. Time Zombie." He points the sandwich at me. "You know how whatever we see gets collapsed? If we see our own future, when you get there in real time it becomes like you're just along for the ride. Evidently you can't do anything." He sets the sandwich down. "Can't even *think* normally."

I flash on trying to change my letter—which I still haven't written. Another question I haven't asked: "What's the loud place we go through on the way down?"

He looks at me. "Loud place?"

I don't even know how to describe it, but I try. "On the path, just as I'm going down, I pass this area where everything is suddenly really loud. It's like a million guitars playing on the other side of the wall—it's like what I heard in my head before I got patched . . ." I trail off because I don't even know what I'm saying. "It's like walking past a jungle or something. They're sort of like the ones I was hearing before the patch."

"A jungle of guitars?" he asks, his eyebrows raised.

The words sound silly coming from him, but when I think about the place, the picture I get in my head is from cartoons where people are lost in some tropical place and there're monkeys and birds and stuff yelling. "Yeah, I guess. A jungle of guitars."

"I don't know." He tucks a fry into his mouth. I watch him chew. I can't tell if he's done or just using the fry to make a dramatic pause. "If it changed when you got the patch, then it's got to be related to witnessing somehow." He shrugs. "It's probably some one-fifty-plus superpowery thing. I'm just a forty-two, so I don't get to hear anything."

Irritating. I *want* to know.

Thirty

ON MY TRIP AFTER LUNCH, MY CURIOSITY ABOUT THE JUNGLE OF GUITARS gets the best of me and I stop on my way down. I'm in, but I'm not deep. I can still hear Paul as he's shuffling around the room, waiting for me to go under so he can dictate. When I get to the Jungle, I take a detour.

Going down is a bit like walking through a maze. There are paths and then there are places that are behind the walls. The Jungle is behind the wall. Even though I can hear it clearly, I can't find a way to get there. I focus my energy on the noise and feel it wash over me. It feels nearly familiar, like a dream that's fading after I wake up. I feel like I should be able to name it like it's an old friend, but it doesn't have a name and I don't even remember what the old friend looks like.

I only remember remembering.

I focus my energy on the wall between me and the Jungle. I get flashes of a new path, but I can't see how to get onto it or where it goes.

I sense Paul watching me. I'm taking too long, so I ride down under on my board, speeding toward my target.

Jordan's bedroom. The room is painted a pale pink, which looks nearly the same to Jordan as it would to me. The furniture is all old; some of it dates back a hundred years.

Queens and kings have slept in the bed. When she was little, in the first years they lived in the White House, Jordan wasn't clear on the difference between a real-world king and queen and the fantasy ones. In her mind, Queen Kate, King William, and Cinderella were basically the same thing, and when she learned that royalty had stayed in her room, she insisted on keeping all the same furniture.

She regrets it a bit now. The chairs are stiff. The bed squeaks. The desk is small. They're all heavy, dark wood. She regrets it, but not enough to ask anybody to change it.

She's at the desk. She has a check-in with Julia in her role as English teacher in an hour, and Jordan's supposed to show her what she's completed. Poetry.

Jordan likes poetry. She writes a lot—has a journal for her schoolwork that everybody sees, but has another one, too, that she keeps tucked under a hidden bottom in her jewelry box—an early gift from Grandma Bev. "A girl needs her secrets," the note had said.

Thinking about the note makes her angry. She shouldn't have to keep secrets. She pictures her mother, her father, Julia, Dr. Halliday, all the people who would be horrified to learn her truths.

She thinks about Will, who knows them all already and loves her anyway.

She returns her focus to the notebook in front of her. What she's writing now is for school, which is annoying, but it's a poem, which Jordan enjoys.

It's a place where the Truth Will Out, but only to those who know how to see it.

Since this poem is for school, not just for her, she's writing it in in her "public" journal where she edits as she writes, false starts that hitch up, editing her content to fit what Julia will accept.

How her mom will see it.

The assignment: Poetry in the modernist style. Eliot, Cummings, Dickinson, Yeats. Allusion, compression, fragmentation, imagery, fractured meter.

Music filters in from the Central Hall. The sound swims into Jordan's ears, muffled and strange to me. She doesn't recognize it, assumes it's from Samantha's room—she regularly plays music with the door open when Dad and Mom aren't in the residence.

The music grates on her. Anxiety swells. Jordan is afraid.

Abaddon the Destroyer is here, preparing to end us. The conversation with her mom didn't put her mind at rest. Instead she's more afraid; more sure that her father will not keep the world safe.

More sure that defending us from Abaddon will fall to others more willing than her father.

"Alex!" she calls out into the hall. She's calling one of the Secret Service detail, a big black guy who Jordan likes more than she likes the other ones. It's strange hearing her call my name.

"What's up, Jordan?" Alex pokes his head into the doorway.

Jordan smiles through her fear. "Can you turn off Samantha's music and then bind and gag her for me?"

He wrinkles his face likes he's thinking about it, then: "Don't think that's in my job description, kid." Then more brightly: "But I can teach you how to bind and gag someone properly so you'll be able to better handle your own business in the future?"

She giggles. "Fine. I'll deal with it myself." Feeling safer having talked with him.

He smiles, steps back from the doorway. She watches him go, feeling sad. Alone again.

The poem is half complete in front of us. Jordan's handwriting is uneven. The start of the poem is the loopy girlish cursive she uses for her public work, but as it's continued, it's grown more real, more felt. She's transitioned to her private scrawl, a blocky print that has only been seen by Grandma Bev and Will.

She rips the page neatly out of her journal, begins to rewrite.

She edits as she goes, pushing the pen across the paper in a single smooth motion for each line. The words don't form fully in her mind before she writes—inside, she and I are both reading them as they appear like they're new to us.

Abigail on the Day of Her Becoming

In Carmel, again, it is the tailing end of day.
The sun falls again, rolled behind the fields of grain,
The pigs, slopped, are quiet.
Inside I sit, dine on caked dates, raisins shriveled by
exposure reduced to sweetness and grit,
And wait, as I do,
For the coming demon, and on men.
On Nabal, the husband, The Fool, alit, enflamed,
building rage.
David, the boy, the King, hungry, near, his shield may
Protect us all.
For Abaddon, whose day
has come.

She's filled with Bible stories. My family never spent much time in church, so I don't know anything about it beyond what Jordan's shared with me in her thoughts. To her, the stories are real, almost like family legends. Abigail is married to Nabal. Nabal is rich but bad and Abigail has dealt with it for years, but when Nabal turns his back on King David, whose people are hungry in the desert, she betrays her husband, steals his food, and delivers it to David because she knows it's the right thing to do.

Jordan identifies with Abigail, imagines her looking like Grandma Bev in her wedding pictures. As she's been writing the poem, an idea has solidified in her mind:

Her father is Nabal. She is Abigail. She bides her time, waiting for the right moment to take a stand, to expose herself to them as she really is. She suspects the time is now. Abaddon has risen. He is stealing souls, preparing to destroy the world and Nabal does nothing but rage and watch his sheep and worry that David might have a better weapon.

Jordan, the modern-day Abigail, will tell the truth to the world, about Abaddon and about herself.

She leans back, looks up at the ceiling. The music has stopped, which makes this easier. She leans forward again, puts the pen to paper:

> Nabal, a fool, husband to sheep, which he sees,
> to me who lives life outside his vision. A womb, my
> breasts, my service have disguised me.
> Until now;
> Abaddon is rising.
> The Fool, my husband, the shepherd king, has denied
> Great David, our strength,
> kept his sheep as he shed his honor.
> But Tonight,
> As I secrete the Fool's stores, date cakes, shriveled
> raisins, sheep and grain, a river of sustenance

guided by me across the dead plains of home
to fill,
Sustain,
The glory of David, tool-maker, slayer of monsters
and giants,
His sword, our wisp-hope against Abaddon, destroyer.
I am revealed.
And Carmel has never seen the likes of me.

She stops. We read it. She likes it, feels it's pretty good. It is *good. I think about the songs I've written, and compared to her poem they seem dumb.*

Jordan hesitates. She's worried. It's personal, too revealing. Maybe not something she should share with Julia or her sisters. They may see her truth too soon. Jordan is careful when she pulls the poem from her notebook, folds it twice, sets it aside to be placed in her personal journal.

She will be Abigail, but only when the time is right. For the first time since I've been gliding her, Jordan closes her eyes to pray.

"My God, my creator, if it be your will, let me be your Abigail. Give me a sign and I will go public about Abaddon and I will stop at nothing to get your message out." *Her words are slow, precise, complete in her mind up until this point, when she falters.* "If that is not your will . . ." *She pauses, but she can't stop the thoughts that follow it inside: I'll know you aren't real, or that you don't care. Then:* "Give me a sign."

When I come out, Paul's looking at me funny.

"What?" My hands start to sweat because all I can think of is that he somehow saw me loitering around the Jungle.

"I can't believe you didn't even tell me," he says. He sounds hurt, but I don't know what he's hurt about. Probably not the Jungle, which is a relief.

"Tell you what?"

He cocks his head at me. "Your birthday?"

He seems really concerned. My birthday's not until March 30. "What about it?" There's a clock/calendar above the dictation microphone. I strain my eyes to read it. "Oh."

It's March 28 today. My birthday's in two days. I shrug. "It's no big deal."

He narrows his eyes and examines me. I feel naked in my suit. "Really?"

No. Not really. It's the sixth anniversary of Pete's death and it's my first birthday since my parents were killed. It is a big deal, but I don't want it to be a big deal for anybody but me. It's my big deal. "Yeah. It's not a thing."

He keeps looking at me, but then nods his head, smiles brightly. "Alright. No big deal."

I slide off the couch and he slides on. "Thanks, man. I appreciate it."

He closes his eyes. "No problem." And then he's gone.

I dictate as best I can, but my mind's not on it. I keep seeing my dad's face from when I ran from him at Julio's school. I see my mom on the kitchen floor.

I see Pete from the picture in the Long Hall.

By the time Paul comes back, I've made up my mind. If that other path through the Jungle is mine, then I'm going to take it. Backward.

Tonight, I'm going home.

Thirty-One

I DON'T KNOW HOW I'M GOING TO GET TO THE GLIDE ROOMS WITHOUT PEOPLE seeing me, but I know the first part of the plan is to get Paul to go away. When we get back to the room, I lie down on the bed and tell him that I'm too tired to do anything. He doesn't really believe me, but he gives in. He gets his guitar from the room and leaves me to myself.

When he's safely gone, I peek out into the hallway. It's empty. The glide rooms are on the other side of the commons and I still can't think of a good excuse to be going over there if anybody sees me, so instead I walk into the commons acting like that's where I want to be.

It's empty. I cut across to the glide hall as fast as I can, but just as I'm stepping into the hallway, I hear a door open behind me. I press myself against the wall, trying to stay out of sight of whoever it is that's walked in.

I hold my breath. My heart is thudding hard. Nobody's ever said I shouldn't do this, but there's no doubt I'm not supposed to glide on my own time.

The TV turns on. I peek around the corner to see who it is just as Damon stands up from the couch and turns to walk to the snacks galley.

I flatten myself back against the wall, watch him go.

He doesn't see me.

While his back is turned, I edge farther into the hallway, out of sight, but then something I hear on the TV stops me—they're talking about Jordan.

". . . made her political debut today in Des Moines, Iowa, by leading a two-day working congress tasked with developing the scope and master plan for the White House's More to Life, America values education program."

Des Moines. That's where she met Will. She just met Will yesterday.

Tonight is when she's going to talk to Grandma Bev and reach out to him.

It's happening. "Go Jordan," I whisper to nobody in particular.

Damon is crossing back to the couch, so I slip farther down the hall, to the last room, the one farthest away from the commons, and step inside. I don't turn on the lights, and the room is nearly pitch black except for the square of light from the window on the door. I lie down on the couch without getting into a glide suit. I don't imagine I'll be down long, and it seems better to be a little out of breath than to have to explain an extra used glide suit. I don't know what the penalties for what I'm doing are, but my guess is that they won't be much worse for doing it in jeans.

I close my eyes and dip down past the Jungle of Guitars until I see the second path. My path. I ride onto it. There's a noisy direction in front of me and I'm pretty sure that's my future. I'm a little bit tempted, but I resist. Instead I picture myself turning around. The path I'm facing now is narrow and bright. I slide down along it.

Darkness. Light.

On the floor of the living room. It's dark outside and I'm in my pajamas. They've got Thomas on them. I can see my hands in front of me, holding a plate with half a concha *on it. The concha comes from the panaderia on Sunset and it's my favorite thing in the world. I'm not happy, though. I'm mad.*

At Pete, who's next to me on the floor. We're watching George Lopez *and I don't want to be watching* George Lopez. *I want to watch* Toy Story *again.*

"Pete's piece is bigger than mine."

I look up from my piece of concha to Pete. He's ignoring me. His half is nearly gone and I suddenly feel how urgent the situation is. If I don't get some of Pete's RIGHT NOW, I'm not ever ever going to get any more and it'll be gone and I'll only have my half.

I feel myself taking in a breath to say it again louder.

"Don't!" I think it as hard as I can, but five-year-old me doesn't listen. Doesn't even know I'm here. I'm trapped in my own life. A passenger, just like Paul said.

Time Zombie.

"Mama, Pete's eating it all!" I shriek. "Tell him to give me more. He got more than me."

"Shut. Up," Pete tells me. "I can't hear."

"Mooooommmmmmmmmmmm!" Things are unfair. My eyes start to burn.

I want to make myself stop. I know how this plays out, but there's nothing I can do. I've already done it.

Then Pete's foot catches me in the side, knocking me over. My piece goes flying onto the floor. "You haven't even touched yours, you little brat."

Benny sees the food on the floor. I can get to it before he does but I don't. Instead I watch while mom's little dog grabs it.

My life is over. Nothing is okay. I'm sobbing.

DON'T BE SUCH A LITTLE BRAT!

I think it, but I can't do anything. I'm watching myself and all I can think is how stupid I am. I'm five. Pete's thirteen. He's going to be dead in seven years and I'm going to spend almost all of it as a whiny little brat.

I can't watch any more. I pull back, ride forward. As I ride, I realize I can tell mostly what I'm passing. It's like fast-forwarding on a DVD—flashes of scenes, totally out of context but that I recognize enough to tell me where I am.

A teacher from sixth grade. A stray dog I walked past on my way to get lunch in middle school. My mom and me washing Pete's plate. Xeon laughing in the alley near the park.

Julio giving me a burrito at his school.

I stop. Dark. Light.

"But the letter," I remind him, and I wave it at him.

"You *wrote it, man!"*

"The picture of me!" I shout at Beems. "I didn't do that!"

He shrugs and shakes his head. "I don't know what you did or didn't do, man, but you need help."

My dad is closing in.

DAD!

I see him through the glass in the doors.

I'M SORRY, DAD.

I'M SAVING THE WORLD, DAD.

I feel my body preparing to run. My legs stabilize under me. My body begins to turn. My heart breaks.

NO!!! DON'T GO HOME, DAD! STAY AWAY!! KEEP MOM AWAY!!!

But nothing changes. Nothing stops.

My dad falls out of my field of vision, lost behind me as I push out through the bushes and onto the road.

"Alex!" my dad calls after me as I run.

It's the last thing I hear before I surface.

When I come to, my heart's racing and I'm drenched in sweat. Even so, I keep my eyes closed for a while. I don't want to open them.

For bare moments, I'm able to pretend that everybody's still alive.

But then I can't pretend anymore and I open my eyes. The glide room is completely dark. I don't know how long I was down, so I don't know what time it is. If I glided through dinner, then everybody's going to be in the commons when I come out.

I get off the couch and open the hallway door as quietly as I can, then make my way to the end of the hallway where I can see a little bit better.

I don't see anybody.

A little closer.

Nothing.

I step into the commons just as Corina is coming in from the patio doorway.

"Hey," she says, looking at me. "Where were you?"

My heart thuds in my chest. My fingers tingle, but I don't show anything. Instead, I shrug. "Didn't feel like eating."

She smiles. I like her smile and while she's smiling I almost forget that I've got no way to explain why I'm coming out of the glide hallway.

But she doesn't ask me why I'm there. Instead: "You need to talk about it?"

I shake my head, try to smile back to her. "Nah, just not feeling well. I think I'm gonna go to bed." I start toward the dorm hall.

"Wait up." I stop and she crosses the room to me. When she gets to me, she hugs me, pulls me against her.

I hug her back, breathing deep to get more of her smell, and for a moment I forget I'm covered in sweat. I even forget why I was sad.

When she lets me go, she touches my face. "You ever do want to talk, you know where I am, right?"

I nod. "Yeah, I'm okay." I can only feel her hand on my cheek. Everything else is gone. I've been watching Corina from across tables and stuff, and listening to her, and talking with her, but with it there's been something else, something scary strong and different from anything I've ever felt before with girls I went for. Before, I've always felt in charge, like I was the one making the decisions, but right now I don't even feel fully in control of my own mouth, much less the conversation.

"You sure?"

I flash on Jordan, copying Will's information off the contact list, pursuing him through Grandma Bev. Jordan tells Will things. She lets him see her . . . but the thought crumbles under Corina's questioning eyes. I'm ridiculous. She's smart, I'm fooling myself. I pull away. "I'm gonna go to bed."

She takes her hand back and there's a look on her face when she does it—like she's done something wrong. "Sorry." Then: "You may be sick, but you also look like you need to not be alone in your room right now."

I don't want to be alone in my room, but being here, with her, is asking a lot right now. "I'm good." I try and look up from the floor, but it's harder than I expect. When our eyes do meet: "Thanks."

She smiles without parting her lips, shifts her head to the side. "G'night, then."

I have to look away before I say, "G'night."

When I get to my room, I keep the lights off and sit at my desk chair, lost in the darkness. The whole evening is collected in my mind, glued together with feelings into a ball that sits on my chest. I close my eyes and all I can see are unrelated parts of my day coming together: flashes of Jordan being afraid, me being whiny. Pete.

Corina.

Me.

A thought bubbles up from under the knot of feelings, words I heard in Jordan's mind that I can't stop forming in my own. The knot becomes heavier, makes it hard to get air. I sit up and open my eyes, try to breathe it away, but it won't leave:

I told Corina I was okay. I lie about myself, just like Jordan does.

But Jordan doesn't lie to Will. She has a person who knows her. All of her.

I've never been okay.

With everyone but Will, Jordan feels outside of things even when she's inside them, like a secret agent without a mission who's living under deep cover.

I know what she means. I feel like that, too. Not an agent, though. A baby. An infant in teenage clothes.

I was five when I had that tantrum about the concha with Pete, but I acted like a baby and I'm still a baby.

I'm scared all the time like a baby.

And like a baby I get feelings that I can't explain that I shouldn't have, like the ones I have for Corina, and I don't have a single person left who knows me.

I'm about to turn seventeen and I still cry.

Happy birthday.

Thirty-Two

I DIDN'T EVEN WANT TO WAKE UP THIS MORNING BECAUSE I DIDN'T WANT to have a birthday. Paul didn't mention it at all, which was good. I don't think I could have dealt with a "happy birthday" from him first thing. And nobody else said anything either.

We don't say much through breakfast, and when we get to the glide chamber, he offers to let me go down first. No rock-paper-scissors, no nothing.

"Thanks," I manage before lying down.

Darkness. Light.

It's dark. We're in Jordan's bed, the scrim curtains pulled around between the posts to obscure us. The lights are off, leaving only the tablet's glow, which makes everything look ghostly and sick.

SECRYPT is open, Will's name is throbbing, a camera icon flashes in time with vibrations from the tablet.

Jordan has spent the last forty-five minutes preparing for this moment. Her hair is brushed and clipped back on the left side behind her ear. The blue silk button-up pajama top she's wearing was the end product of a twenty-minute decision, about which she's still not entirely sure. The white thermal top with red piping may have been better. She chose against it because she thought it might look too young, but now, as Will is calling, she's suddenly sure that any *pajama top is going to make her look like a child.*

She should have stayed dressed, but that would've taken

explaining if anybody saw her—it's after midnight, but it's only just after nine in where Will lives in Cle Elum in Washington State. He couldn't call until after church.

"Suck it up," she says to herself, taps the camera. The screen goes dark momentarily, sending a wave of adrenaline through us because we're sure we've just lost the call, but then the darkness resolves into an image, flat at first like an old photograph, then stretching out into three dimensions.

It's Will. He cocks his head slightly to the side, like he's having trouble seeing her. She checks her own image in the bottom. She's shrouded, grainy. It's impossible to tell what she's wearing or what she looks like.

"Hey, Rapunzel." Will's voice sounds clear and present in her pod, like he's there with her, in her head. His voice is deep, a musical rumble.

"Hello, Prince." Then: "Can you see me?"

He smiles. It's goofy, a little lopsided. Shakes his head. "Not really—it's dark . . ."

"Sec." She drops the tablet and leans backward, reaching through the scrim to the bedside table where her light is. She clicks it on—it's blindingly bright, makes us squint against it, washes out all the colors and leaves a flashing imprint on her eyes. She sits up and adjusts the tablet, scanning her picture in the process.

She's clear. She's side-lit, her hair shines in it. The blue was a good choice. "That better?"

He smiles. "Yeah. Yeah, that's better."

"How's Cle Elum today?"

"I'll show you." He stands up, takes the tablet with him. She follows him into a hallway, down a flight of stairs. He narrates as he goes: "Hall—bathroom, brother's room, parents' room, stairs,

living room." He twirls the table in a quick circle. Details are impossible, but there's an overall impression of hominess. "Front door." He opens it, steps out onto a porch. It's nearly dark, but not quite; the sky is a deep brilliant blue and the clouds shine bright white with reflected sunlight from the other side of the mountains that rise from what seems to be next door to his house. "Cle Elum," he says, finally.

"It's beautiful." Then: "The mountains are really that close to you?"

"We're sort of in *them—we're up at like two thousand feet or something." He looks behind him at the mountains and the trees.*

"It's amazing. Is it cold?"

He looks down at himself. He's wearing a T-shirt that says MARINES across the front. No jacket. He shrugs. "Not really. Not today. It gets pretty bad in the winter sometimes, but today is . . ." He looks at her, spiking her with his eyes through the camera. "I wish you were here so I could really show you."

Jordan flips her hair, casting a sudden shadow on the inside of the scrim in front of her.

Panic.

Incursion. *No. Just a shadow, but Abaddon is now large in her consciousness, a bugbeast climbing in her mind. Jordan's mind creates an image, a horrible one, a demon cresting the trees behind Will, large as a mountain, dark as char, smoking, sulfurous. It reaches down, bone fingers, tendons exposed, gibbets of flesh falling as it moves. The hand grabs Will, plucks him, lifts him, crushes him, drops him to his own porch, a mangled mess on camera for her to watch.*

"Why don't you go back inside?" She can't keep the urgency out of her voice.

"Why?" He looks confused. "It's really nice out . . ."

She wants to tell him. We need to tell him. He's at risk and we don't keep secrets from Will. Abaddon is here and if he doesn't know, then he can't be safe.

If nobody knows, nobody can be safe. She nods. There's too much happening in her mind for her to do anything more complicated.

But telling him is a crime. "I wrote a poem."

A flicker in his eyes—something I see but Jordan doesn't. Disappointment. "Really?" he asks, sounding interested. "Can I hear it?"

"Yup." She can't tell him. It's a state secret. But he needs to know. "It's a little weird—I'm not sure what anybody would think of it, but . . ."

"I want to hear it."

She nods. The poem is on her bed stand next to the light. She was ready for this. Hoping he'd be interested. She reaches for it, pushing the scrim aside again, causing a ripple of shadows across the wall above her desk.

She gasps. Abaddon. Incursion.

A shadow. She breathes.

"You alright?" Will asks in her ear. "Did something happen?"

She grabs the poem, sits up, collecting herself along the way. "No, just startled myself with a shadow—thought somebody was coming."

"POTUS and FLOTUS aren't asleep?" he asks brightly. "Would've thought they were early-to-bed types."

She laughs. "They are, indeed." Will doesn't talk much about her family, doesn't ask many questions, unlike a lot of the kids she meets at Bible study or at conferences. Mostly they're interested in what *she is, not* who *she is.*

The image of Abaddon in the forest returns to her. She freezes, then shakes her head, coughs. Tries again: "Why don't you go back inside?"

He doesn't register her request, instead: "Poem me, please."

She takes a breath, unfolds the paper. "You know the story of Abigail and David, right?"

He nods. "Spent as much time in church school as you have."

"Well, I really identify with Abigail—she's cool, you know—smart, bides her time, and then when she's needed to do God's work she rises to the occasion, even though it means betraying her husband and potentially losing everything." She shrugs. "I guess I've always thought that I'd like to do that . . . make up for being docile little Rapunzel when the world needs me or something?"

He nods his head, makes a little chuckling sound. "Like Frodo?"

Jordan hasn't seen or read Lord of the Rings, but she knows who he means. "Yeah." She smiles. "Like Frodo." Then: "Anyways . . ."

She reads him the poem. She reads it slowly so it sounds like it does in her head when she reads it. She watches the screen as she goes, looking for some sign that he understands. She's good at reading things out loud. When it's done, she looks up from the paper, raises her eyebrows. "So?" But she already knows. He didn't get it.

He shakes his head slowly. "Wow." Then: "That's really good. I mean not like high school good, but real person good."

She likes the compliment. Momentarily, we brighten. "You think so?" But it fades fast.

"Absolutely. You should submit it to a contest or something."

"Maybe." He didn't hear the message. He didn't get the warning. I can't tell him. *"I can't wait to see you this weekend."*

He smiles, too. "Me too." His voice is quiet, but powerful enough to interrupt her breath.

She shakes her head. The demon rattles loose inside and she flashes on the crumpled Will again. Too much. National Security Act be damned. "Will?"

"Yeah?"

"I need to tell you something."

"Yeah?"

"It's a secret. I mean . . . a real one, like, important to national security."

He looks less sure, but he nods again. "Okay."

Jordan looks through the scrim of her bed at the shadows beyond. "It's scary."

"What is it?"

She leans in, close to the speaker, whispers: "The Incursions are real." It's out now. Released. Jordan feels no regret.

He looks confused, but then his eyes widen. "What? Really?"

She nods. "Dad has the army trying to catch one of the aliens, but it's not going well. They're sure it's going to happen here soon, and they definitely think it's going to get worse."

"They're real? Like, real-from-another-planet aliens?"

She nods again.

He turns around, looks at the mountains behind him, the growing darkness. Without commenting, he steps back inside, closes and locks the door. "What are they?"

"The government doesn't know. But if people don't know they're real, then they can't protect themselves."

"If nobody knows what they are, what're we supposed to?"

Jordan looks through the scrim toward her door. There's no noise in the Central Hall, but she still whispers when she says, "Dad and Jack think that there might be something to Live-Tech . . ."

He looks surprised. "Really?"

She nods. "Yeah. They aren't sure, but . . ."

He nods absently, looks around, then back at the camera. "Then I guess this is your Abigail moment."

She sighs. He looks scared. She suddenly doubts that she's helped him by saying something. "You can't tell anybody, okay?" Then: "I'll make sure it gets out."

He nods. "Jordan, I . . ." But he doesn't say anything after that. He just looks at her. Then: "You're pretty amazing, you know that?"

"I'm nobody," she tells him. "I'm just glad I have you."

"I can't wait to see you."

"Me neither," Jordan replies. She can't, either.

She feels like she'll explode first.

After our afternoon work, I start to feel bad about not having a birthday, which is dumb because it's what I asked for.

It isn't what I want.

What I want is to have a birthday with my family, but every time I think about my family, all I can see is Pete at thirteen and how whiny and miserable I was. Or my dad at Julio's school.

I go back to our room alone. When Paul comes back, he doesn't even ask about how I'm feeling. He just grabs his guitar, says, "Later, man," and walks out.

When he's gone and the hallway's quiet again, I get up and walk to the common room.

I've been thinking about this for days, but this morning I decided that today was the day because I couldn't bear the idea of sitting alone in my room. There may be nothing down my thread except a past that's only for Zombies, but there's another place I want to see and today is the day.

I'm going to the Jungle.

The commons is empty. I cross to the glide hall.

There are lights on in the first room, so I duck under the window as I walk past, catching only the barest glimpse of Calvin and Damon at work.

They're working late—everybody should be done already. Doesn't matter—nobody else'll be coming back here.

I slip into the last room, closing the door behind me as lightly as I can, and lie down on the couch, closing my eyes.

The Jungle.

I stand at the place on the path where I can hear the Jungle best. I can pull out some individual sounds. There are things that sound like guitars and things that sound like bass and things that sound like mandolins and banjos—for some reason I hear them all as strings.

It sounds like strings, but they're like voices, too. They aren't talkie voices. They're not making words—it's more of a feelings-and-ideas thing, like if you could hear the inside of other people's heads.

I'm pretty sure that when I go under, everything I "see" is something I've pulled from my own mind. I invented the skateboard and the path I'm on, so it seems like I probably built the walls that separate the Jungle from the paths, too.

I just need to "see" something that I can use to knock them down.

I imagine a sledgehammer. I feel its weight in my hands. I lift it over my head and begin to pound against the wall.

It gives. The blackness that makes up the wall leaks out onto the path, rearranging itself to create a fork in the road. One fork goes down deep on the path, and a new path—a narrow one that I can barely see—leads to the Jungle road.

I squeeze and push through. The walls give and I'm on the narrow path. The guitars grow louder. It feels like they're going to break my eardrums but I know they can't—they're inside me and underneath, not anywhere near my ears.

I can see something ahead. It's growing brighter, lighting up the road as I move with flashes of color that make everything glow and then fade back to black.

As I approach the source of the flash, the road gives way.

I'm falling. Then I'm floating.

Things brush against me. My patch begins to hurt and then I feel it move on my arm. I'm suddenly sure that I'm going to lose my connection to my biology but I can't free myself to go back.

"Relax. Welcome to the Jungle, scared boy."

I hear her and feel her at the same moment. She is a cascade of relief. I reach out toward her, but I can't find her. I'm mixed up in a web of colorful musical threads. There are millions of them, billions, trillions, *bazillions.* They are everywhere, tied together, tangling and untangling, going on forever. I can't see where one strand ends or any others begin, they just seem to unfold and go. They feel like the way music is sometimes shown in cartoons—endless wavy banners of notes that grow big, then small, winding and twisting all around.

But they're more than music. More than color.

They are *us.*

They are us. Each strand is somebody. Vibrating, pulsing, moving, screaming.

And the colors. Bright, brilliant, iridescent, incandescent, shimmering, intense, colors like I've never seen, sensed, known.

I'm not physically here in the Jungle, but I can't tell that by how it feels. I have no arms here and no body.

I can feel it. Here, in the Jungle, I am music, too.

WHAT IS THIS PLACE?

"Scared boy's floating in the Silly Juice. But scared boy's not ready to run away."

WHAT'S THE SILLY JUICE? WHY DO I NEED TO RUN AWAY?

"Time comes up, we do our thing, and time goes down again. Silly Juice, it's the splash."

I find myself focusing on a single musical thread floating near me. The strand is thin like spiderweb, but strong like metal. Colors shift, flash, pulse so fast I can't name them before they change.

I'm floating into it.

As I get closer, it expands, grows thicker until it feels bigger than me. Or not. I don't know my size here. I feel it pull on me like it has gravity.

I'm falling onto it. Falling fast. Faster.

I'm afraid.

If I touch it I might stick. I might become stuck to it, trapped in the Silly Juice, the Jungle of Guitars.

I'm falling closer to the spider-silk strand that is, I suddenly know:

Corina.

I'm about to fall into Corina. I don't know what any of this means. I don't know what will happen if we get tangled.

NOOO!

I'm pulled back, away from Corina and the million other strands that I can see, back out from down deep and back into my biology. It happens so fast that I forget how to breathe and I think I'm going to die from strangling.

My eyes fly open and I sit up fast, sucking in air as hard as I can.

I'm still sweating, regretting not stealing a glide suit, when I edge into the common room. Again, I think it's empty when I cross into it, but again it's not.

Corina's coming out of the dorm hall.

"I was just looking for you," she says when she sees me. Then: "What were you doing up in the glide rooms?"

I shrug, try to look sad instead of scared. "Hiding." As naturally as I can, swallowing my concern: "What's up?"

She smiles. "I just wanted to find you . . ."

My heart thumps. "Really?" My feelings get control of me and it comes out like a little boy who's been told he's going to Disneyland instead of like a question. *Stupid baby.*

She giggles, which makes me feel dumber. "Yeah. Come on."

I turn to look back to the glide hall. It's dark behind me and suddenly all I want is to go back there, go back into the Jungle, explore, see more. Be where I won't embarrass myself. "I don't . . ."

"Alex," she says. "I really am starting to worry about you."

I shrug and shake my head. "There's nothing to worry about." But I don't even believe me when I say it.

"Course not." She rolls her eyes, but then she looks at me,

face friendly. "I do like a boy who can't hide his feelings—even if he won't admit he's got them." She reaches out a hand for me. "C'mon."

I don't take her hand immediately because I'm still back with what she just said to me, still trying to rehear it, write it down in my mind so I can take it apart, word for word, later when I'm alone. Right now I don't know if I'm feeling things because she said she likes boys like me, or if I'm feeling embarrassed because I can't control my emotions. Or both.

I make myself reach out to her. It's never been hard like this for me to be around a girl, but right now, with her, it almost hurts and all I can think about is how I'm going to do something stupid, say something wrong.

When our hands meet, I stop worrying, though. Her fingers are warm, dry, and the sensation of her touch is stronger than my resistance.

She lets go of my hand at the patio door. We walk together silently. Our arms brush.

When we get to the door to the gym, she starts to giggle again. When she opens it, I see why.

Everybody's there.

They're all collected around a drum kit that Calvin's sitting at. Richard's at a piano and Paul's got his guitar. Maddie is wearing one of Paul's cowboy hats and standing at a microphone. There's another microphone in front of Paul.

Somebody's found some hay bales somewhere and stacked them around. There's red-and-blue-checked streamers hanging from the basket hoops. The whole room looks like it was decorated by a cut-rate prom committee.

John Bishop is standing to the side with his arms crossed

across his chest and when they all see me, Paul counts off and Corina runs to the microphone where Maddie hands her a hat.

"What the hell . . ." is all I manage to get out before the song starts.

Paul sings it full country, staring right at me.

We've all been where you've been before
Life seems over, everybody's slammin' their doors
No one's coming to save you—no one notices or cares
And when things look their worst, you end up here.

Maddie and Corina are dancing, wearing Paul's cowboy hats. I can't do anything but stand and watch. It's all so stupid and ridiculous, but it's . . .

So now you're here, things are queer—
roommates and aliens—saving the human race
Doing good but getting lonely, missing a friendly face
Even when they're all over the place.

The girls sing, "Happy birthday, happy birthday," in the background. They're terrible. Totally off. I don't even know what to think or do, so I just stand in the doorway, laughing and smiling like a fool.

So happy birthday to you, young gun.
Happy birthday to you, son.
We can't be your family, not like the one that was.
But country songs got pickup trucks and moms and guns
And girls and jail and white people sadder than you

Who all got to say the same thing:
We can't be mom or dad—but happy birthday, son
You're with us now and we love you, you stupid bum!

Paul looks ridiculous, especially because he's working so hard to get the words in. Whatever song he took for this, he didn't match the phrasing very well. I start feeling a lot better about my own lyrics.

(Happy birthday, happy birthday
Happy birthday, happy birthday)
One-fifty plus thinks he's someone special
(Happy birthday, happy birthday
Happy birthday, happy birthday)
Well guess what, son . . .
(Happy birthday, happy birthday
Happy birthday, happy birthday)
You are.

When the song is done, they all stand there looking at me and I don't know what to do. I want to run away and I want to hug them all, but all I can actually do is shake my head and smile.

"Paul's got special skills when it comes to making things happen. He thought you needed to be cheered up," Bishop says from where he stands on the side. "Happy birthday, Alex."

He never uncrosses his arms.

I nod. "Yeah," I manage to say, but it comes out like someone's strangling me. I clear my throat.

"Well?" Paul asks.

I look at him. "It was country."

"No doubt."

"I don't like country."

"No doubt."

"It was . . ." I shrug. I'm trying to be all serious for some reason. "It was really cool, man." I turn to the others, who're still standing at the microphones. "Thanks." And now I'm tearing up because for the first time ever a bunch of people have done something really cool just for me.

"Hey." Paul grabs me by the shoulders and pulls me in. "This is the only family I've got, too." He squeezes me. "And you're already a better brother than the one I left behind."

I try to say, "You're like a brother, too," but I can't be sure it actually came out.

When Paul lets me go, Corina steps up. "Happy birthday." She hugs me.

Her smell. It's vanilla.

We press together, whole body style. She is overwhelming to me. I don't want it to ever end.

But it does and when she pulls back, I get hugs from the rest of them, too. Except for Bishop, who left when I wasn't looking.

There's cake for me in the kitchen. Damon comes in while I'm cutting it.

"Cake, man?" I offer.

He shrugs. "Sure."

I'm filled with love for everything about this place.

I'm even filled with love for him.

Back in the room, I sit down at the desk and pull a single sheet of paper from the drawer.

It's time.

I bring the pen to the paper and let what's supposed to happen happen.

Hey Alex,

This is you. Really. Please listen up, man, your stupid life depends totally on it. Can you please open your ears right now? . . .

The words come straight out. My hand operates apart from my mind. I watch myself write it. Again, it's like being a passenger. Time Zombie. My hand smears the ink as it passes again over the lines written above it in the exact way the ink was smeared in the letter I received.

This letter.

It ends just like it did when I read it:

PS. Even though you won't believe it, there are some things that happen no matter what and when they tell you that of all the ways things could have happened, this is the least bad way, it's really true.

But I think maybe now, in this place, with these people. They're good people.

I don't think they're lying.

The envelope. I watch. Passive. My hand addresses it in the same block lettering I first saw weeks ago.

My hands fold the letter, place it in the envelope.

Goodbye, Mom. Bye, Dad. "I love you." It's just a whisper, but it has my whole self behind it. Heart. Mind. Body. "I'm sorry."

Richard is in his office when I go to give it to him. He looks up from his desk and smiles when he sees me. His smile falls away when he sees the letter in my hand.

"You're sure?"

A shrug. "Yeah."

He nods, takes the letter. Then he stands and rounds the desk. He's coming to hug me. I wait for him and when he does . . .

I hug him back.

It's done.

I don't say anything to Richard as I leave his office. Out on the patio, the skies are clear for once tonight and I stop to look up. The stars are out. I stand for a while, watching them, thinking.

Feeling.

Thirty-Three

OUR TABLE IS DONE WITH ITS WORK. WE'RE MOMENTS FROM BREAKING FOR *lunch. We're sitting at the only rectangular table in the room, facing out at the rest of the room filled with kids at round tables.*

We've been in Las Vegas for two days, sequestered at the Convention Center, shuttled between here and a house somewhere outside of town. MtLA's mission and plan is nearly complete, and even though it's not anything Jordan believes, she's proud of the work, proud of the kids that created a detailed policy plan that is eligible for funding.

But that's the only good thing that's happened here, thanks to Julia.

She's been glued to Jordan the entire trip—Jordan's official Dad-approved chaperone. Jordan doesn't like Julia, doesn't respect her, despises the way Julia always looks to Dr. Halliday for permission to speak before saying things, then looks back to him when she finishes.

Doesn't like the way she sits, her back bent, shoulders in, like she's afraid of rain.

Doesn't like that Julia has managed to keep us totally separate from Will.

We look across the convention room floor, across the sea of big round tables to the one farthest from where we are. We can see the top of Will's head. He's looking at us and Jordan can't hold in the smile that knowing he's looking at her creates.

He waves. We can't wave back, but we wiggle in our seat trying to say hello. Trying to say I miss you. *Trying to say* I'm sorry.

"It's time to adjourn for lunch," Julia says, looking behind us to where Dr. Halliday is standing out of sight from the rest of the congress.

Jordan nods, doesn't smile or say anything to acknowledge Julia, and taps the mic icon on the table screen. "Ladies and gentlemen, we have reached our designated lunchtime and I move that we adjourn this highly productive and successful final session of our congress and retire to the West Ballroom, where lunch will be held." We pause, smile, look at Will. "Any seconds?"

"Second!" shouts Will from the back of the room.

We giggle. We don't mean to, but we can't help it. Hearing his voice, in person, in the same room, is the happiest sound we've heard. "Enthusiastic," we comment into the mike, pretending our giggle was about the content of the shout, not the boy who shouted it. "All in favor?"

The room erupts in an "Aye!"

"So moved." We tap the gavel icon and the sound of a mallet hitting wood comes from the coms around the hall.

We stand up, wait for Julia, who's slow to stand, and for Alex the Secret Service agent, who will lead us to the ballroom.

We walk fast, ahead of the crowd, through a hallway that's been emptied for us and into a room filled with banquet tables already set for lunch.

"This one." Julia motions to a table in the middle of the room and points at a chair for us.

We sit. "Thanks." Watch as Alex fades into the background, wait for Julia to sit down, but she doesn't.

"Darnit." She's looking at her screen. She looks up and around for Dr. Halliday, but he's nowhere to be seen. "Will you be alright on your own for a moment?"

We nod.

"I'll be right back." She scuttles off the way we came. I stretch in my chair, turn toward the door to watch people filter in.

Looking for Will.

"Water?" I'm surprised by the voice because we didn't see him approach, but when we turn, I'm even more surprised because I recognize his face immediately.

Then I realize why I know him: He's me.

I'm looking at myself through Jordan's eyes. I'm sure it's me even though I'm wearing a waiter's outfit. My hair's tied back into a ponytail. The me in the room is looking into Jordan's eyes, like he's not seeing Jordan at all, like he's seeing me up inside her mind on my perch. He's talking, saying things, but it's hard to listen because my voice sounds so strange through her ears, embarrassing, bad.

I see what she sees: a short kid whose hair is too long to be proper. MEXICAN is written in her mind, the colors bright, festive like a Cinco de Mayo sign at a chain restaurant.

Then I start to talk and everything inside Jordan freezes.

"It's your time to be Abigail," I tell her. "At the Conference in June." Then I say: "This is your sign."

And then I'm gone, walking to another table, filling water glasses.

Thirty-Four

"HEY." I'VE NEVER GONE TO RICHARD'S OFFICE WITHOUT BEING ASKED, BUT I don't know what else to do. "Can I like . . ." I wave my hand.

He looks up from what he's reading, smiles at me. "Sure, man." He points to a chair. "Come on in." When I'm in the seat, he raises his eyebrows. "What's up?"

"In my glide just now . . ." I don't even know where to begin. "I saw something I think you need to know about."

He pushes the hairs that have escaped his ponytail back behind his ear. "Did you dictate it?"

I nod. "Yeah, but . . ."

Richard smiles. "Believe me, if it's something we need to know about, we'll be notified."

I shake my head. "No, but it's—"

He shakes his head. "Alex, do you trust what we're doing here?"

I shrug, then remember how much I shrug and stop the shrug halfway through and switch to bobbing my head back and forth. "Yeah . . . but—"

"More importantly, do you trust that the Gentry know what they're doing?"

I blow out a breath. "Yeah . . ."

He smiles again. "The stuff you dictate is reviewed through

methods I cannot even begin to tell you about here and now, but you have to trust me when I tell you that they're thorough and we have yet to let something important slip through our fingers." He points at me. "Process is everything here. Trust the process."

"Yeah." I stand up slowly. "Alright."

He nods, and I turn and walk out as slowly as I stood. I stop outside his door, just for a moment, trying to come up with a new argument for telling him, but I can't. I walk back to the commons feeling alone.

Corina's sitting on the couch reading a book when I walk in. I almost say hi, but something stops me. It's getting harder to talk to her recently, so instead I kick my shoe against the floor to make noise.

She looks up at me, smiles. "Hey, Plugzer." She waves me over.

I smile back but immediately stop, because all I can see is the goofy face that Jordan saw when he looked at me. "Hey." I stop in front of her. "What's up?"

She cocks a shoulder at me, holds up her book. "Important business."

I don't recognize the book she's reading, but I think she's kidding, so I smile. "Yeah." I stand in front of her, waiting for something.

"You need something?" She's smiling, but I'm embarrassed.

I shrug, then make a decision. I sit down next to her. "I saw something really weird on my last glide." I jerk my head toward where Richard's office is. "I went to talk to Richard about it, but he wouldn't let me."

She nods. "He can't."

"Yeah." I sit forward. "I get it, but this was . . ."

She reaches out, puts her hand on my back. Her touch is firm and I can feel each and every finger. "Look, if it's really something they need to talk to you about, you'll hear from Bishop. But yeah, we see some freaky shit." She sighs. "Things are gonna get bad."

I nod. I can still see my face through Jordan's eyes.

I'm already in bed when there's a knock at the door. I look over at Paul's bed to see if he's going to say anything, but I think he's already asleep. "Yeah?" I whisper as loud as I can.

They don't hear me and knock again, so I get out of bed and open the door.

Bishop is on the other side of it. He's dressed down from the suit I usually see him wear, a pair of jeans and a polo shirt that looks like it's a size too small. "Alex," he says when he sees me. "Can I talk with you for a moment?"

I nod. "Yeah."

He stares at me for a second, waiting on something, but I don't know what it is. "Can you come with me to my office?"

I look down. I'm wearing sweats and a T-shirt. No shoes. I look back up at him. His look says I need to stop worrying about what I look like. "No problem."

He leads me through the commons to the patio and then back to the Long Hall. He doesn't turn around or make small talk as we walk, and every step makes me more nervous. By the time we get into the Long Hall, I'm nauseous. The lights inside come on when we enter. The Live-Tech wallpaper starts to glow, but before it can grab a thought, a portion of the wall to our right slides back, revealing a doorway that leads to an entry hall place with another hallway which ends at a big door across from us.

Bishop leads me to the door, opens it, ushers me inside.

The room is big, a couch and a couple of chairs face each other around a table nearer the door, but the room is dominated by a single desk which is plunked right in the middle. There are two hardback chairs facing the desk and he points me to one of them before walking around the desk to face me.

"The powers that be reviewed your last glide," he says as he sits down. "There are some questions."

I nod. I don't want to sit—too anxious—but I do anyway. "Okay."

"Had you had any previous indication that Jordan Castle was going to meet you?"

I shake my head.

"Did you see or recognize any other face or person present at the time?"

His questions feel like they're coming from a cop and the way he asks them makes it hard to think, but I close my eyes and try to picture the moment I saw myself, the room, the other tables around. It's all a blur of color and cringiness about how I look. I can't pull anything new out of my brain. "No . . ." I shake my head again. "I don't think so."

He writes something with his stylus on the desk, so I lean forward a little bit. The desk has a series of screens, low light, impossible to see or read from where I'm sitting. He's writing on one of them with his finger. "Did you give any indication that you knew you were being observed by yourself?"

I looked at me, up in my perch. The memory is strong, real.

"Yeah. I knew I was in there. I could feel me looking up at me . . ." I trail off because I don't have more words.

He taps something else on his desk and then leans back and looks at me. I feel like he's about to say something, but then I realize he's listening to something, paying no attention to me. Moments later he nods, says, "Yeah," and then refocuses on me. "Okay, you can go back to your room."

Even though he says he's done, he's not moving to get up like he wants me to leave, so I stay where I am, staring at him until he says, "You can leave now, Alex. Thank you."

I get up, slowly, and pad back out the way I came.

Paul's snoring softly when I get back to the room, so I lie down on my bed and stare at the ceiling in the dark, replaying the whole conversation. He didn't say I did anything wrong, and I know I didn't break any rules, but I can't escape the feeling that Bishop thinks I've messed things up.

It takes me a long time to fall asleep.

Thirty-Five

WE LANDED AT JOINT BASE ANDREWS LATE COMING BACK FROM VEGAS. *Jordan should be asleep, but she's not. This is our first moment alone and we're sitting on the bed behind our scrim, cross-legged with Grandma Bev's screen in front of us, waiting for a call from Will.*

We are going to tell him about The Sign.

I feel weird about this, a feeling that is strong even here on my perch in Jordan. I told her it was a sign. I knew she would think it was from God, that her prayers were answered, but it's a lie just like the ones she hates so much when she tells them.

When I say that to her, someday soon, I will be lying to her, manipulating her, and even though it's for a good reason, I feel bad about it.

But it's done and now we're going to tell Will about the busboy in Vegas. Jordan's day since lunch has been a blur of barely missed social cues and flubs, because her mind has been dominated by the busboy, what he said, who he was, how he knew.

This is her Abigail moment. This is her sign.

Even as she wonders about it, the screen lights up with a call. Jordan checks herself to make sure she's still properly put together for Will.

Voices. Urgent ones. Movement in the Central Hall. Something big is happening.

She taps the decline call button. She'll call him back.

In Jordan's mind, the movement in the hall is flashes of color—something she does with things she hears but doesn't see—and it's dizzying to a visitor perched in her brain. She's not worried—this happens sometimes. A terrorist attack, Venezuela, Iran—she just can't be caught talking to Will.

Then she hears Jack in the hallway. "Another one. Here, in Florida. There are witnesses."

I watch helplessly as Jordan drops the tablet onto her bed. "It's too late," she whispers to herself. "Too late."

She won't be Abigail. She won't be the one to reveal the truth.

The busboy was wrong. God missed the moment. David's army is on the march without her.

The voices begin to trail away, headed down the stairs on the way to the Situation Room.

She's tempted to follow them, to learn more, but she hesitates, looks at the black screen on her lap.

Whoever the busboy was, he was no messenger from God. She looks down at the tablet in front of her, wondering how secure SECRYPT really is.

He was probably just a hacker making fun of her.

No! I want to shout it to her, but I don't have a voice on my perch.

She needs to stay strong. She can't lose hope. She has a job to do. It's a requirement—my entire reason for witnessing her. She needs to change her mind. She needs to tell the world about Abaddon.

In desperation, I close my eyes and dive down.

A dive within a dive to the Jungle. I've never done it while witnessing before, but my only hope right now is that my Voice will know what to do. If I can ask her, maybe she'll have answers.

The Jungle. At first I don't recognize it because it's not loud and full of movement and color. Instead there's just a single guitar-music thread crashing loud.

I call out for my Voice, but she's not there.

It's just me and the lone guitar. I don't know what to do, but as I think things through I'm also listening to Jordan's mind and I realize something: her mind and the guitar are playing the same song. The colors flash in tune with her thoughts. The sounds mesh.

Jordan and the guitar strand are the same.

I explore the thread more closely, trying to understand. It pulses with color, thickens, thins, moves in reaction to what's happening in her mind.

But then I realize I'm wrong.

Not in reaction.

The thread changes before the mind.

The color/music on her thread is hopeless, afraid. I focus on it, feel myself drawn close to it. Up close what I'm seeing becomes more clear. The colors on her thread have meaning—the bright flashes of color and sound are strong feelings—hopelessness, fear. But there are dark spots, too, moments of uncertainty, doubt. The dark spots are like burnt-out bulbs, rests in the music. They are vacancies.

I focus on a vacancy, it grows larger in my sensations of it. I try and imagine it shifting, becoming something else, desire to follow her father.

A part of my presence in the Jungle reaches across the

small space between us, begins to bleed my urgency into the vacancy of her uncertainty.

Jordan's feelings change, just slightly—the hopelessness she feels loosens its hold.

I made them change. My excitement is contagious. I watch as it bleeds across the bridge between us, brightening her whole thread.

ABIGAIL WOULDN'T GIVE UP. ABIGAIL WOULD FOLLOW AND LISTEN.

I wish hard, like a little kid wishing for Christmas.

FOLLOW THEM. LISTEN. BE ABIGAIL.

The strand bends, shifts. The music has changed.

Jordan's mind shifts with it. I feel it.

She has a new thought. I hear it as I return to my perch: I can still be Abigail.

I just have to pee. *Jordan practices the lie as she jogs to her door and out in the hallway, slowing down for silence.* Just have to pee. *No longer a lie. She does have to pee.*

She can hear her dad on the stairs.

"Can we secure the footage? Stop it from being released?"

"Already done, sir." She doesn't recognize the other voice. Some general or another. "We have it for you to watch."

"We need a statement, sir." Carol is here. Jordan wonders whether the communications director has a house of her own.

"This is contained for now?"

The general: "We believe so, Mr. President."

"Then we maintain our position. We call it hysteria."

Jordan's heart sinks. Her father is *Nabal.*

The disappointment morphs into something else. Determination. Excitement.

The busboy was no hacker. The busboy foretold the coming world. In her mind, I appear, my hair down, the busboy clothes disappear, replaced by robes, berries, wild honey. In her mind I am a prophet of prophets. I am her Elijah.

She can still be Abigail. Jordan slips back into her room, forgetting to pee, decides she can hold it.

Back on the bed, her screen lights up. Will calling again. This time she accepts.

My job is done. I fly from my perch.

"I made her," I say before I even have a thought.

Paul looks at me. He raises his eyebrows.

I'm not supposed to talk about what I see—rules—but this feels big.

"What are you talking about?" Paul asks, and then he holds up his hand, palm toward me. "Forget it," he says, "I don't even want to know."

"Have you ever changed your target's mind?" I ask.

He shakes his head. "Not possible," he tells me.

He's wrong, I just did it. From the Jungle. Whatever it is, I have power there. I don't know how. I don't know why.

But I don't press the point with Paul.

Thirty-Six

"I CAN'T GLIDE ANYMORE," CALVIN SAYS AT DINNER. "TONIGHT'S MY LAST NIGHT."

The room had been full of noise, but it all stops when he says it. Calvin doesn't notice. He secures a few stray peas onto his fork and eats them while we all watch and wait for him to say something else.

I break the silence. "What does 'I can't glide anymore' mean? That doesn't make sense."

He shakes his head, looks down at his plate.

"There's a limit to how much witnessing we can do," Maddie says. "After a while, things get too muddy when we're gliding, and we stop being useful."

Corina asks him where he'll go.

Calvin shrugs. "I'm set up in Santa Fe. Job in a bookstore."

"That's not where you're from." And then: "They got you set up how?" I was trying to hold the question, but it spills out anyway. "What're they gonna give you?"

He doesn't seem bothered by it, though. He raises an eyebrow. "A job, man. Some cash. ID, a verifiable work history, and a brain fully scrubbed of Locusts and Gentry."

"Won't people who knew you be . . ." I trail off when he starts shaking his head.

"Nobody knows me, man. Not in Santa Fe, not in Atlanta." He's angry. "There ain't *nobody* for me out there."

I'm angry, too. At myself, though. I know his story. I know where he comes from. "Hey, man, I'm sorry. I shoulda . . ."

He smiles, but sadness is what comes through. "Naw, man. It's my bad. I just don't want to leave at all, is all."

His sadness spreads to me and I'm about to cough away the lump in my throat, but then I see that I'm not alone. Paul's got tears in his eyes. Corina's looking away at something on the wall to her side.

Maddie reaches over and puts her arms around his neck. Squeezes him. "We want you to stay, too, Calvin."

Paul steps out from his seat and comes around behind him to rub his shoulders. "You're going to make good things happen wherever you go. That's just what you do."

Calvin goes still for a moment. "Y'all gotta stop this attack, though. I don't wanna go back to real life and then get eaten because y'all screwed up."

Maddie kisses his cheek before unlatching herself and returning to her plate. Paul squeezes him once more. "We're the Justice League, man. We got this."

I look around the room. Everybody's nodding, so I nod, too.

I'm not hungry anymore.

After I clear my plate, I swallow my nerves and walk up behind Calvin. "Hey, man."

He turns around. Smiles up at me. "Alright."

"Yeah." I can't even think of words to say what I want to right now, so I just tell him: "Take care, okay?"

"I always do." He holds his hand up for me. I take it. Shake it. Don't really want to let it go.

I'm focused on Calvin, so Damon startles me when he pulls out his wallet, flips it open, and pushes it across the table to Calvin and me.

It's open to a picture of a little girl with yellow-blond hair. She's like two, smiling, dressed in a school uniform and posed against a wood picket fence with a school-picture background.

"That's your sister?" I ask him.

Damon shakes his head. His eyes are wet, and when he speaks, his voice is crackly. "Daughter. Caitlin. She's four now, I guess."

I never know what to say when somebody has a kid, so I just look at her picture for a minute.

"Since I got here, all I can think when I look at her is that I'd better not screw up or she's gonna die." He reaches for his wallet and I hand it back to him.

He glances at Calvin, then back at the picture. "Someday I want to hold this picture—or hold her—and not think about this shit." He shifts his gaze up to Calvin again, winks. "Enjoy your memory wipe, man, and don't worry. We got your back."

Everybody's quiet. Damon's staring at the picture of his daughter again. I try to make myself stay there, but it's too hard. I want to be alone. I squeeze Calvin's shoulder one last time and nod to him.

He nods back as I walk out the door.

Thirty-Seven

WE'RE ON THE BED AGAIN. IT'S LATE. JORDAN'S HEART IS BEATING FAST. *The screen is up in front of us, its camera blinking. Jordan's thought a lot about how to do this, what she needs to do to fulfill her promise to God, to Will. To be Abigail.*

She's written her speech for the Conference, drafted it and redrafted it in her personal journal until it's exactly what she wants. She's good at this, and Will has been there to help when she got stuck.

She looks down at herself. She's wearing a blouse, a muted yellow, and a white half coat over her pajama top. It feels strange, the clothes pinch in weird places where the pajama top bunches up, but it looks alright on camera.

We look down to the journal in front of us, open to the speech.

"Record," she says.

The light goes on above the screen. Jordan stares at it, smiles grimly. "Good evening. My name is Jordan Castle and I am the eldest daughter of President Vincent Castle. If you are watching this video, it is because something has happened to me and I was unable to make this announcement on live television as I have planned. I expect that if I have been stopped, it will have been by people in my father's administration, in an attempt to keep this information secret from those it most concerns: you, the people.

"Fellow citizens, the Incursions are real. People are being taken. My father and his administration know this, but they have

chosen to keep it a secret." Jordan's voice is forceful, filled with truth. She feels strong, purposeful.

For the first time in as long as she can remember, the girl that never felt okay does.

Jordan pauses, nods to accentuate what she's about to say. "If something has happened to me, and I am not able to deliver this message in person, I have faith that this version will suffice, will be enough to encourage every one of us to rise up, to force the hand of our leadership to face the threat of Abaddon head-on.

"Thank you, and may God be with you." She's ready to end the recording, but she can't be done. She hasn't mentioned the most important part.

I dive, her strand pulses, dominating the entire universe around me underneath. I find the right place, alter the notes I need to.

When I surface, she's already begun to hesitate. She smiles, widens her eyes like she has an idea.

"There's one other note I'd like you to consider. At present, little is known about the species behind the Incursions, but what we do know is this: We need to listen to the voices who are warning us about the threat. Mr. Jeffrey Sabazios should not be dismissed as a crackpot or a con man. Mr. Sabazios may just have the answers we need, but unless you force our government to act—force my father *to stand strong in the face of this threat—we may only learn that his technology can save us* after *it is far too late." She pauses, her face stone. Then: "Stop recording. Send to Will."*

It's done. Sent.

She pictures Will receiving the video, scheming ways to distribute it. She smiles.

It's good to have a partner. It makes it easier to be Abigail.

When I open my eyes, I'm feeling pretty good. I make way for Paul on the couch and when he goes down, I dictate my glide.

It's hard to focus, though. I keep thinking about Jordan, how she has someone, a person she knows, who knows her. A partner in crime.

Jordan is doing something amazing, something I'd be too scared to ever do. I'd end up embarrassing myself and everybody else, but if I let myself have a partner like she does, maybe I'd be strong like that, too.

A partner. A single face materializes in my mind.

When I finish dictating, I change out of my glide suit, then sit down to wait for him. I can barely sit still because there's something I know I've got to do.

Not an Abigail moment, but still. Calvin leaving points to the fact that we may not have that much time together. I don't want her to go without saying my piece.

Paul's barely opened his eyes when I'm out the door.

"Where are you going?"

"Got something I gotta do," I tell him. "Just go ahead with your dictation."

He squints at me through the windowpane when I close the door.

I walk fast through the hall and commons, but I slow down when I get to the dorms, suddenly scared again.

By the time I get to her door, my nerves have settled in. My chest is tight and my palms are sticky. I wipe them on my pants and force myself to breathe deep before I knock.

"Yeah?" She sounds busy.

"It's me. Alex." I'm ready to turn and run.

"Hey! Come in." She doesn't sound annoyed, which is a relief. I open the door and step through. "Leave the door open, though."

Disappointing. I guess I was hoping that she'd want some private time with me.

Corina's room is exactly like mine, except there's only one bed and instead of the other bed, there's a couch against the other wall. She's on it, leaned against one armrest with her legs tucked under her. She's reading through papers. I move closer to get a look but instead of hiding them, she holds them up so I can see them better.

She shrugs. "Glide schedules. Matching breaks for Maddie and me."

There's nothing on any of the walls, like she's only passing through.

"What's up?"

I shrug. *I need to tell you something. I need to tell you how I feel about you, that I can't think around you, that you . . . a partner. My partner* . . . It all crumbles and my mind blanks. "I . . . I just . . ."

"It's cool," she says before I finish. "Company." She reaches over her shoulder to drop the papers back on her desk. Her shirt rides up a bit, showing her stomach and her belly button. She brings her arm back and gestures at the couch for me to sit.

I sit, but I don't have anything to say.

Awkward silence.

She pushes at me with her foot. It leaves an impression on my thigh that I feel throughout my body. She doesn't pull it back all the way, leaving it just barely touching me. It's like fire. "What's up, Plugzer?"

I open my mouth to tell her about needing a partner, but it suddenly sounds ridiculous, selfish, small. She doesn't need a partner. She's solid on her own, strong without one.

What seemed so obvious in the glide chamber now feels embarrassing, something a child would say. If I open my mouth, I'm just going to make a fool of myself.

But I can't say nothing, can't keep pretending I don't have feelings about her. I've told girls I like them before—it's always been easy, but this isn't like before. Corina's older, wiser, smarter than the other girls. Than me. And I'm tongue-tied because unlike with other girls, if she says no, it'll be real, something I can't just walk off.

She's seen me up close when I wasn't together. She's seen me cry.

She's already made me stronger. She's already a partner, she just doesn't know it yet.

Say it. But when I start speaking, dumb shit comes out. "I dunno. I was bored and I wanted to come by, see what's up with you."

Corina likes that I can't hide my emotions, but hiding them is all I ever try to do.

"There's nothing up with me but schedules and romance novels," she says. My heart sinks, but then she reaches back over her shoulder for a book, which she tosses at me. "But I like having you here, so just read and don't talk while I finish up."

I look at the book. It's a ghetto romance, one of those things that girls read where there's a criminal with a good heart. Mostly, though, they're just filled with sex scenes. "You read these?"

"I read all sorts of books, so don't judge." She doesn't look up. "Anyways, sometimes a girl gets lonely."

"I don't judge." I flip the pages to find a good section to read aloud. "'His breath touched her like a hot feather. Veronica pushed into it as his mouth closed around her breast . . .'"

"Shut up," she says still not looking up.

"'Martin's tongue pushed hard against her nipple, and then his teeth—'"

"You better be done." But she's smiling.

"'Pleasure and pain coursed across her in waves, leaving her swimming . . .'"

She kicks me. "You stop that," she says, but she's laughing.

"'. . . in her own ocean of ecstasy . . .'"

"Shut. The. Hell. Up." She moves to grab the book, but I pull it over my head so she misses. She lands on top of me.

I can feel every part of her pressed against me and I have to move quickly to keep her from feeling me. Our faces are inches apart and now neither of us are laughing.

Or moving apart.

I bring myself closer. Our noses brush, and then our lips. While the moment lasts, there is nothing in my mind but Corina. Her lips are soft, but there's muscle behind them that makes her kiss firm.

Our tongues touch, and I wrap my arms around her. Pull her tight and close.

We separate a little and look at each other. The hunger in her eyes makes it a struggle for me to breathe. I move my hand from her back. I'm trembling.

"Alex," she whispers. "What are we doing?"

"I can't help it," I tell her. "I've . . ." I don't want her to know how much I've thought about this, how much I think about her, how much I . . .

"I know," she says before I finish. "Me too." She shakes her head slowly back and forth. "We'll have to be *very* quiet about this."

For a second I'm not sure I heard her right. "You really want to . . ."

She nods, leans lower. Our lips touch again, she opens her mouth slowly, her bottom lip below mine, her mouth surrounding it.

My hand is on her lower back. I slide it up slowly, feeling each notch in her spine until I'm touching the back of her neck, feeling the first hairs of her head. She pulls up slightly. "No hints. If they find out, they'll send us away."

There's a noise in the hallway and we sit ourselves back up. She grabs the papers and smooths them out.

I pick up the book. I can't read anything. It's hard to even sit.

Thirty-Eight

I'M EATING LUNCH WITH PAUL IN THE KITCHEN WHEN RICHARD WALKS IN and points at me. "Hey, man, can you come with me?"

I look at Paul, who's just taken in a huge mouthful of Cap'n Crunch. He shakes his head. He doesn't know what this is about.

Corina. I don't know how they could've found out so soon. I make myself nod at Richard, stand up and start to clear my plate, but he stops me. "Actually, leave that—Paul, can you take care if it?" He bobs his head. "Bit of a hurry."

Paul watches me as I walk over to Richard. He doesn't *officially* know about me and Corina, but I think he's probably guessed. When I get to Richard, he ushers me past him into the gym and points toward his office. "What's up?" I ask, my voice cracking.

"We need to talk," he says. He doesn't sound angry or disappointed. *Guarded.* That's the word.

"About something bad?"

He opens the door to his office, turns, and looks at me. He shakes his head. "About something different." He points at the chairs across from his desk. "Have a seat. I have to get one other person, so I'll be right back."

I'm still standing when he steps back out the door. I don't know how he found out about me and Corina so fast. I try to think of all the things I might've said or done where people might have seen me, but aside from the kiss . . .

I can't think clearly, it's all a jumble of Corina and me and glides and color and fear. However he learned, it's over. I'm getting sent away.

I sit down and wait, tapping my foot hard against the floor because I can't stop. Out of desperation I try and go deep, down to the Jungle to find my Voice, to change what's happening. It seems hopeless at first. The drain is gone.

I need the drain! I think it hard to try and make it happen. I picture it and then it's there, a storm drain, but it's secured with a thick metal grate. I can hear noise from underneath, but I'm too big to fit through the gaps.

I can't get in, but what I see when I'm down is what I expect to see. If I made the drain cover like I made the walls and the path, then I can change it. I imagine hinges for it, a padlock. Then a key to the padlock.

The lock opens and I pull the grate. It gives, moves, leaving a hole large enough for me.

I descend. The Jungle's noise is the sound of home to me right now. I follow it.

And then I'm in it. No glide room, just me, out in the open.

I'm free, and momentarily, the excitement overwhelms my worries about Richard.

The strands around me are screaming, pulsing, moving, thick ones like Corina's, smaller ones like floss, and thread spread everywhere, a mesh of life that covers everything. I focus on the strands closest to me, identify them.

I find Richard, his music like him—a predictable rhythm.

There are undertones of emotion, but they're not what I expect. There's no anger, no disappointment.

Just concern. He's worried.

I'm pretty sure closeness in the Jungle reflects closeness in our world, so I turn to the strand closest to him.

It's not Corina. It's familiar, but its noise fills me with discomfort and then I know who it is.

I have no idea what's happening here.

I surface, open my eyes, turn to face the door, ready for Richard and Damon.

Damon has no more idea why he's here than I do—I got that much from his music. He sees me and wrinkles his forehead a little bit.

"Have a seat," Richard says, pointing at the chair next to me.

"What's this *about*?" Damon asks as though it's not the first time he's asked it.

"Why's *he* here?" I add.

Richard holds up a palm to each of us as he settles into his chair. "Damon, sit down, man. Nobody's in trouble, and you'll both probably find this to be a positive development overall, so let me tell you about it."

I look at Damon out of the corner of my eye, and he's doing the same to me so it's hard for us to ignore each other. He sits.

"So, guys, this is something we've never had happen before, and it's taken some time for us to figure out how to handle it." He settles back in his chair. "A while back, Alex saw something in a glide that was, to be frank, very strange."

Vegas. It all clicks. "Why's he here, though?"

Richard nods. "I'm getting to that." He looks at Damon.

"Essentially, Alex saw himself, in Las Vegas, interacting with a glide target."

Damon squints, looks at me, then back at Richard. "What does that mean?"

"It means that Alex has to go to Las Vegas"—he points at his wrist like he's wearing a watch—"and he's got to go right now, and we cannot send him alone."

"Hell no!" I don't know which of us says it first, but we end together like we're singing.

"I don't need him," I add, talking over whatever Damon says, which I don't hear.

Richard wipes stray hair away from his face. "This isn't a discussion. We've expended a serious amount of Oracle device time and glide resources on figuring out what needs to happen, and this is how it goes. You"—he points at me—"are going to Vegas and you"—he points at Damon—"are going with him. This is the way it's been seen, so this is how it works out in the way we need it to, understand?"

I wait a moment or two before I nod.

He looks at Damon. I don't. I stare straight ahead until I hear Damon agree. "When do I leave?"

Richard smiles. "Thirty minutes. Go pack."

Thirty-Nine

WE'RE ONLY GOING TO BE GONE FOR A DAY, BUT IT TAKES ME A LONG TIME to pack because I don't know what to pack. I've never flown anywhere before and I don't know what to expect. It's April, I think, but I don't know what the weather's gonna be like in Las Vegas.

I pull my backpack out of the bottom drawer and fill it with random clothes. The photograph stuffed in the lining crinkles when I shove in my pants, and I stop for a moment to take it out and look at it.

The girl in the picture—the one who saved me from the car accident—looks happy. I'm smiling, too, but I look a little scared. The water in the background is almost white like the beach; the hills and mountains on the other side are brown. There's still nothing that looks familiar.

But I don't know what there is near Las Vegas.

When I get out to the patio, Damon's already there, waiting. He's got an actual suitcase. When he sees me he looks up, raises an eyebrow. "T'sup."

I'm going to have to spend the next day with him. I raise my chin at him and sit down on a lounge chair nearby. "You been to Vegas before?"

He looks startled by the question. He shakes his head. "Nah."

"It's pretty chill." I don't say *chill.* I don't know where that came from.

"You've been there?"

I shrug, nod. "Yeah. With my mom a while back. We drove there from LA."

He smiles. "Longer drive from Ohio."

"That where you're from?"

He nods. "Yeah. New Lebanon, actually."

"New Lebanon?" I squint at him.

"It's small, man. Between Dayton and the Indiana border."

"I'm from LA, went to Belmont High School." I immediately feel dumb because it's not like he has any idea what Belmont is.

"You play anything?"

I shake my head. "Nah." Then: "Handball, but . . ." Then: "You?"

He nods. "Football, but I played basketball and baseball, too."

I nod. I've watched him play one-on-one with Calvin. He's good enough that I wouldn't have played him if I'd been invited.

"Mr. Mata?"

I turn around. Bishop is standing at the entrance to the Long Hall. He waves me over and when I reach him, he hands me a bag. "What's this?"

"Your waiter's uniform and the ID you'll need to get into the hall."

I take the bag and open it, pull out the ID. "How will I know what to do?" I put the ID in my wallet.

He looks at me like I'm stupid. "You don't have to. You've already done it." He turns around and walks back into the Long Hall, leaving me holding the bag.

When I return, Damon looks at the bag. "What's that?" But he doesn't wait for an answer. "Never mind. I don't need to know."

Richard comes out the gym door, sees us, smiles. "Grab your gear." He points to the hallway door. "We're hitting the road."

Richard drives us back to the city, and to an airport that looks too small to be the main one. "What airline are we flying?" I ask to try and sound like I'm not completely new to this.

"Not an airline," Richard says, pulling up to a security gate. "You're flying on Jeff's plane."

I keep quiet and examine the planes around us. There are a bunch with propellers off to one side and on the other there's a scattering of private jets. Richard pulls up near a big one with six windows. There's a staircase leading up to a door, and a woman standing at the top watching us. When Richard gets out of the car, she smiles and waves. I sneak a glance at Damon. He looks as nervous as I feel, which makes me feel better.

"You ever flown before?" I ask him.

He doesn't take his eye off the plane, but nods quickly. "Once." Then: "Had to fly to Wisconsin for a Great Lakes Division tournament." He turns to look at me. "You?"

I shake my head. "Nah."

Richard's talking to the lady from the plane. She gestures to the car and laughs. Richard turns around and rolls his eyes before waving for us to get out of the car.

"You ready?" I ask Damon.

He nods. "Yeah," he says, then grabs his bag from the seat between us. "Let's go."

The lady on the plane introduces herself as Claudia. She shakes each of our hands as we walk on board. She's all smiles and chat, but I'm so distracted by the inside of the plane that it's hard to even be polite. There're couch-chairs facing each other across wooden tables. There's a bench seat along one side wall of the plane that faces the windows across from it. It doesn't even make sense until I notice the huge screen that's lifted like a shade above the windows.

"Damn." I look at Damon.

He's already looking at me. He smiles. "This is different from the last time I flew."

Claudia tells us about the fridge and snack center and that she'll be taking care of us for the duration of our flight. We both nod.

She tells us to get buckled in because we're ready to take off.

As soon as the plane starts to move, my excitement shifts and I'm suddenly nervous. It's not just me, either. Damon's looking scared. "You scared?" I ask him, hoping he'll say yes.

He shakes his head, but then there's a thump somewhere on the plane and he jumps. He laughs. "Little bit."

"Me too."

He looks at me. "Why are you scared?" He points at me. "You're guaranteed to survive—you've been seen."

He's right. I feel myself relax. "Yeah." Then: "You can relax, too. It didn't look like I'd recently survived a plane crash."

The plane takes off. The movement pushes me into my seat like I'm on a coaster at Six Flags, and then we're in the air. The plane pushes up through the clouds quickly, and then we're above them and the sun is shining bright. I smile, feeling deep relief. I didn't even realize how much I missed the sunshine. It seems like it's always cloudy in Seattle, so it's literally been months since I've seen it.

Claudia shows us how to bring down the big screen, and Damon and I spend the flight playing games. He may be better at real sports, but I absolutely own him in Madden.

The screen goes up when we start heading down toward Las Vegas, and we go back to the chairs and stare out all the windows. I point out the things I recognize—the Luxor pyramid and the Stratosphere—I tell him about going up there with my mom when I was a kid. Talking about it makes me a little bit emotional, but he doesn't say anything.

A car meets us when the plane stops, and Claudia says that it's going to take us to our residence. I'm expecting a regular hotel on the strip, but when the car finally pulls out of traffic, it's into a driveway that takes us under the front of a mall and then out the other side of it and drops us at a double-door entrance that looks way too small for the building it's attached to.

The car door is opened by a black guy in a suit and tie who greets us by name and tells us that we're in Sabazios's personal suite. He takes our bags and points us to the front desk through the double door where there's a white guy looking at us. When the desk guy sees me look at him, he smiles, gestures for us to come inside.

He gives us each a key card and points us to the elevator. I go to swipe my card but Damon beats me to it. He smiles at me.

"Dick," I say, but I'm smiling, too.

When the elevator door opens, I'm expecting a hallway, but there isn't one. It opens right into the living room of an enormous apartment.

"Jesus," Damon mutters.

I look around again. "This is all for us?"

The desk guy laughs. "Mr. Sabazios was very clear that you two should be given full access." He points at a box on the wall. "My name is Michael, and if you need anything, just press the button on the box and I'll make sure you're taken care of."

I nod, barely looking at him. The wall across from us is all windows and we're looking out at the tops of all the buildings at New York-New York and above the whole strip. The mountains in the distance are lit red with the sunset and the whole place feels like a magical kingdom. "Thanks."

"I'll let you two get settled."

When the elevator door closes, we both stand still for a moment, but then Damon jogs over to the couch and dumps his bag on it before walking around to the partial wall that separates the kitchen and dining area from the living area.

He says something, but I can't hear him. He's too far away.

I take off in the other direction and find three bedrooms, each with its own enormous bathroom. I choose the one where the bathroom has a wall of windows across from the tub because it's the coolest thing I've ever seen. I dump my backpack on the desk and flop down on the bed, which is bigger than my whole bedroom was at home.

Damon steps into the doorway a moment later. "You asshole, you took the only one with windows in the bathroom."

I laugh. "I left you the one with the hot tub, though."

"There's one with a hot tub?"

I point down the hallway. "Last one."

He nods. "Alright, then." He takes his bag down the hall, but comes back a minute later and stands there.

"What?"

He shrugs. "You tell me, bro." Then: "It wasn't my glide that landed us here."

I think about it. I actually don't know anything except that I'm supposed to be in the convention center sometime before lunch tomorrow.

I sit up. "I don't think it's until tomorrow. We're free tonight." I freeze. "We don't have any money." It's been so long since I've needed any I didn't even think about it until right now. "How are we supposed to—"

But Damon's holding up an envelope. Our names are written on it in black marker. He wags it and then dips inside and pulls out a small stack of hundred-dollar bills. "I think we're set."

I hop off the bed and go to inspect the envelope and the money. He hands it to me. "A thousand dollars. Ten hundreds. We each take five."

I nod and count off five, put them in my pocket, then rethink things and redistribute two to my sock, one to my left pocket and two to my right. Damon watches me, then does the same thing with his five.

We eat at the Hard Rock and spend hours just walking around, looking at New York, Paris, the MGM, the Monte Carlo, and the Luxor. People are everywhere. It's loud and crowded and dirty and it smells like booze and smoke and it's enthralling. Damon's focused on playing at the tables, but he's not twenty-one and neither am I. When we try at the MGM, we get booted before we can even sit because we can't show ID. The best we can do is play slots at New York, but that's only fun for a little while when I realize I've dumped $200 into them and it's only been an hour.

Eventually we head back to the apartment, but not before Damon manages to convince a guy to buy us a bottle of Jack Daniel's.

Back in the apartment, Damon makes us Jack and Cokes and we sit in the living room drinking them, staring out at the world and talking.

He hasn't seen his daughter in two years. He came to the compound because they promised him money to take care of her forever. He sends money home every week, but he can't tell them where he is or where it comes from.

The more we drink, the sadder and angrier he becomes.

I tell him about my parents, about Pete. I tell him that everybody thinks I did it, and how it makes me feel. I get angry, too.

But we're angry with the world, not with each other.

Forty

WHEN I WAKE UP, THE CLOCK ON THE BED STAND SAYS IT'S JUST AFTER nine. My head hurts a little, but my mouth tastes awful. It takes me a minute to reassemble last night, and when I do, I realize something huge.

There's nobody watching me here. I can get news from home. I can call my Tía, or Julio.

After I shower, I go to get dressed. I check out the clothes that Bishop gave me, expecting something special, but they're almost exactly like what I would wear anyways—black pants, white shirt, black shoes. I make a snap decision to wear them instead of my own clothes, just in case. Damon's still asleep, which is perfect because it means I can leave without having to explain myself.

I'll bring him back some breakfast.

Down in the lobby, I ask the guy if there's a game café somewhere nearby. He looks one up and gives me directions. He offers to get me a car, but I tell him I'm fine to walk and set off.

It's hot out, but it's not horrible. The sun is bright, the skies are clear, and there's a wind blowing through which makes everything feel better than it should. The walk takes nearly an hour, and by the time I get there, I'm sweaty and hot, but the place sells cold drinks and food. I order and get a game station for a half an hour.

I don't play any games, though. I open the browser instead.

There's nothing new about my parents. There's no new entries on the *LA Times Homicide Report.*

I check back on the email I sent to the reporter. It takes me a while to remember my password, but when I do a single new email shows up in the inbox.

It's from her.

I click on it.

> Alejandro,
>
> I am glad you reached out to me. I let Juana that you've been in touch, and she's very happy to know you're safe. I am very interested in hearing about what you saw, and where and how you've been living. Please write back and tell me what happened at your house that night, and maybe give me some details about where you've been since.
>
> I can make sure your side of the story gets told, but not until I know it.
>
> Sarah Campbell

I read the email twice and think about what to do. I don't know what I can and can't say to her. I want to tell the truth about what happened, but I don't want to compromise what we're doing at the compound, either.

> Sarah,
>
> The Locust was there when I came home. It had already killed my parents. I didn't see it at first and

then when I did, it was like I was looking at a black hole. It came after me but it wouldn't come close because I had Live-Tech. I ran away and I've been living in a safe place, doing really good things. Bad things are coming, but I'm with people working hard to make sure we're safe. Pay attention to Jeffrey Sabazios—he's going to save us all.

I'll tell you more when I can.

Alex

And then I send it even though I don't think she'll believe me.

When the inbox reappears, it's not empty like it should be, though. There's a new email there.

From: Theyllneverbelieveme@gmail.com
Subject: Keep Ur Bags Packed

Even though it's cool in the café, I feel like I'm sweating again because that email shouldn't be there. Nobody should know about this email address.

I hold my breath as I click.

Hey Plugzer,

Keep clothes in your backpack and make sure the picture stays there. Ur gonna need it when you run.

Cassandra

Oh yeah, bring your girlfriend, too. Sybil says she's important.

I read it twice because the first time it doesn't make any sense. They know my name.

Cassandra.

I reply: *Who is this?* It's hard to type it clearly because my fingers aren't working. I mess it up three times before I get it right and send it.

Then I stare at the inbox, waiting, but the clock in the corner of the screen says it's nearly noon, and I feel like I've got to get back or I might miss my moment.

"Fuck you, then." It's stupid, but saying it out loud makes me feel better about signing off.

I walk out of the café and into the sun. It's bright and it makes me squint. By the time I'm at the corner, I wish I hadn't eaten at all, because I remember what my Voice said before I got the patch.

I'm gonna have to run away again.

I buy a cheap pod and screen at the 7-Eleven across the street, and a card for a hundred minutes of talk time. I set it up as I walk and when it's ready I dial my Tía's number.

When it starts to ring I panic. I don't know what I'm going to say. I don't know what she thinks. I don't want to cry.

"Hello?"

She sounds old, like she did on TV. Weak, afraid. I open my mouth, but nothing comes out. I stop walking.

"Hello? Who is this?" Then: "Alex?" Her voice is scared, hopeful.

"Hi, Auntie." It's mostly breath.

"Alex?"

"I'm okay. I didn't kill them. I love you. It was an Incursion, like I told you. I'm safe. Everything is okay and I'm going to prove I didn't kill them so I can come home, but I can't do it right now, but I will."

She's crying. "Alex, Alex . . . you need to come home." She says it like it's the most important thing in the world. "You need to talk to the police, Alex. You need to tell them what happened, that you weren't right."

My vision goes dark when she says that. "I didn't . . ." I can't think. "It wasn't me. It wasn't me."

"I know, mijo. You weren't yourself. You need to come home."

"NO!" I'm shouting, but I don't care. "It wasn't me! I didn't *do* it. It was an alien, it was a Locust, and they're going to come for all of us if I don't help stop them. I'm saving the world and you don't even believe me." It all comes out in a tumble and I don't know what to do or say next.

We're both silent for a moment, then: "Okay, mijo. It's like you say. Come home, please? I need you here." Then: "Alex . . . please?"

I can't say anything now. My voice is gone, disappeared from me like hope. I listen for a moment longer, then hang up.

I was going to call Julio, too, but I'm not going to anymore. There's nothing to say. Nobody there will believe me until it's too late.

They won't believe me unless we fail.

I start walking back to the hotel.

I may not be able to go home, but I have another home to go to. The compound is a home. I have a family there. It's not what I had, but it's what I have now and it's good enough. Corina's there. Paul. Richard. Even Damon.

Keep clothes in your backpack. At least for now.

Run away, boy. Not yet, though.

I'm so caught up in my own hopelessness that I don't even notice how far I'm going and when I turn up toward the Strip I walk smack into a crowd of people waiting outside a service door. They're all wearing black pants and white shirts like me.

"Have your ID out and ready when the door opens," says a suited man standing on the loading dock above us. "Hand it to the agent as you walk in. Make sure the contents of your pockets are in the plastic bags being circulated. When you've had your ID checked, you will hand the bag—which will include your pod and screen, along with your wallet and any personal effects you may be carrying—to the agent standing at the interior entrance door in front of the metal detector. You will receive your bag back at the end of your shift." He pauses. "Questions?"

Nobody has any but me. I turn to the woman standing next to me. She's older, with brittle blond hair. Heavyset. "This is the catering crew, right? For the MtLA thing?"

She turns to me, looks down. "Yes." She has a thick accent. Maybe Russian or something.

"Thanks."

Somehow, without knowing, I ended up at the right place, wearing the right thing at the right time. I remember how I felt when I first looked at the bus ticket in LA and it all suddenly seems way too big for my mind to cope with.

We line up, walk inside. The agent looks at my ID, then scans it. I hold my breath until the green light blinks. "Hand your bag to the next agent," he says as he reaches for the next person's ID.

Once inside, we're given black vests, ponytail holders, and assignments. I'm a busser. They point me to the water station and set me to work filling pitchers with ice and water.

Then there's an announcement. Diners are on their way.

I grab a pitcher, stand by the water table, and watch the door.

Seeing Jordan Castle is like seeing an old friend. I want to wave, to jump up and shout so she sees me. I want to hug her and tell her that everything's going to be alright, that we're all working hard to combat Abaddon. I want to tell her that she really will help save the world, but I can't.

I won't. I know I won't because I didn't.

She sits down. Julia, Jordan's chaperone, remains standing, eyes on her screen.

She says something to Jordan and scurries away. Even as she leaves the table, I feel myself moving, walking toward Jordan from her blind side, pitcher held out.

I'm at her table now. Even though she's sitting and I'm standing, I can tell that she's tall, taller than I am, taller than I realized from the inside. This is why she thinks I'm short. "Water?" I hear myself say.

She turns, surprised, looks at me.

We stare at each other, and then I'm looking into her, trying to see if I can see myself up on my perch.

My mouth opens. I say my piece. I watch her face as I talk, and her eyes go wide.

Her color disappears.

Abaddon is real.

And then the rest of the crowd enters and I walk away without looking back. I pour a few more glasses of water, then walk back to the kitchen, through it, and back outside.

I have to leave my wallet there, but there's nothing in it of substance. Nothing that says anything about me.

Forty-One

IT'S ALREADY DARK OUT WHEN WE GET BACK TO THE COMPOUND, BUT CORINA'S waiting for us at the end of the Long Hall anyways. I'm so busy working to keep the email I got in Vegas off the psychic wallpaper that when she hugs me I almost give us away because I'm so happy to see her.

"Welcome back, guys." She leaves my hug and steps into Damon's. I can't tell what he thinks, but I make sure to step out of the hallway and onto the patio before turning around to watch them.

Paul comes out from the commons, sees me, and waves. "How was the sun?"

"Hot."

"Must've been nice," he says, then pulls me in for a hug. It's good to see him. It's good to be home. "I barely remember the sun."

"I'm glad to be back here in the great gray gloomy, anyways." The email didn't say anything about Paul.

"You sure are," he says and smiles. "I bet you're hungry, too." He tugs at my sleeve. "I'll debrief you in the kitchen."

There's somebody new at the table—a kid, younger than me and smaller. He eyes us when we come in. He looks scared and I don't like him on sight.

"Billy, this is Alex," Paul tells him. "Alex, this is Billy Williams—he just started this morning."

"Hey," I say to him before I walk over to the cat carrier. I don't want to be mean, but for some reason the kid bothers me.

"Alex is a very nice boy who is just tired from a long trip," Paul says behind me. "Pay him no mind."

I start to get mad at Paul, but I can't. He's right. It just feels weird having things be different here. It needed to stay the same.

Back at the table with a burrito, I tell Paul what I can about the trip, which isn't much. Billy watches us talk and I start to feel bad for him because I remember what it was like when I first started, so I ask him some questions.

He's from Idaho. His mom and dad died and he went into foster. He's seventeen, which surprises me because he looks twelve.

I tell him about my folks and then we talk about LA for a while because he's always wanted to go there.

By the time we go to bed I'm feeling really good about everything and the warnings from the email and my Voice feel distant and wrong, like things that I can ignore.

But I still fall asleep thinking about how my aunt sounded on the phone.

Forty-Two

IT'S MY DAY OFF. I'M ALONE IN MY ROOM, BIDING MY TIME.

People suspect that Corina and I have something *special* happening. Paul and Damon both make jokes about it, sometimes when Richard's barely out of earshot. What sucks the most, though, is that even though we're together we can't really be alone. It really can't be much of a partnership when we can't even talk, and there are only so many special secret looks we can share across a room without seeming like weirdos.

Since that afternoon when Corina and I kissed, I keep going back to my first time in the Jungle when I nearly fell *into* Corina's strand. That time, I freaked out and ran away, but ever since I broke the drain cover I haven't needed to sneak into the glide rooms to go to the Jungle, so I've been exploring. I think it may be a way for me and Corina to get some time together.

I get up and check the door, and then return to the bed. I don't know what's going to happen when we connect, so I'm nervous, but whatever happens, it won't be worse than having no contact at all.

I look at the clock on the wall. It's time. I dive.

Corina's taking my scheduled place with Paul. I've watched people witness before and I know that even if they don't hear the Jungle, they come down here when they go under. I can tell from their music.

I watch Paul's music while he and Corina are in the

chamber. Paul is easy for me to identify, because his music sounds so much like him. His rhythm is fast like Maddie's, but unlike hers, Paul's is consistent too—he never seems to get agitated or upset.

Paul sounds like the young country guitar players he likes so much.

There's a flash of color as he crosses down onto his path and travels through the Jungle. When he gets to his target, his music shrinks down until it's thin like fishing line. I can barely see it. Paul is witnessing.

I wait. Paul's thread expands again. For a brief moment between the witnessing and when he surfaces, Paul becomes huge and bright to me.

Everybody has their own theme—a recurring refrain that comes from just them. Paul's is twangy and warm. Someday I want to write down his melody and give him the sheet music to his own song. I think he'd really like that.

When he shrinks back down to normal human music I know he's woken up.

I prepare myself, wait for Corina.

Her music is the most beautiful I've heard in the Jungle. Sometimes she's like an orchestra, with music that scatters across clefs with shifting time signatures that reminds me of the free jazz stuff our teacher played us in music appreciation. Other times she's nearly silent, flashes of sound like distant thunder.

But just like everybody, there's always a part of her personal refrain playing somewhere, too. A single snatch of notes that cycles in every thread, each unique and identifiable.

Another thing I'm going to have to write down someday.

Minutes later, Corina's thread blows up as she descends into the Jungle on the way to her target. I dive into her.

Her gravity takes me, pulls me in. She grows immense as I close in, but somehow I feel like I've grown, too, like we're going to envelop each other equally.

A part of my presence bridges the gap between us, then more of me follows. Then all of me.

When we meet it's like I've landed on her breath.

I can feel her all around me. It's not like witnessing—I'm not looking through her eyes and sensing through her. It's both more than that and less than that—there's no facts or anything, it's just like I suddenly have all her possibilities in my heart.

When I witness, I'm still me and I can think about other things when I'm perched. I've still got a sense of what I want and who I am, but when I'm wrapped in Corina's music, it's like I *am* her. I understand everything. I feel her fears and I feel her hopes. It's not like knowledge—it's bigger than that.

It is deeper than knowledge. It feels like total and complete . . .

Love.

And we are together.

New music. New sounds. A mix of us, a mash-up.

A new song.

I leave myself open and feel her. She is exploring me and I am exploring her. She is knowing me in the same way that I am knowing her.

Harmony.

We disentangle. She has to witness now. I feel her go, but I still feel her with me and I know that I'm still with her, too.

It's what I hoped. More, even.

I have to float up and be me again. When I surface, I'm ready to feel like I've been cut in half, but it doesn't happen.

I can still feel her. Even out in the real world. We are connected. Partnered.

It's nearly dinnertime when I see Corina. She lowers herself slowly onto the chair next to mine on the patio. "What the *hell*?" she whispers. I can feel her fear and excitement. They make it hard for me to breathe.

Suddenly entangling without telling her ahead of time seems like a really stupid idea. "I'm sorry," I tell her, but she waves me off.

"I don't want an apology, Plugzer, I want an explanation."

An explanation is the one thing I don't have. "I found you in the Jungle."

She holds her hand up to stop me. "I *know* you," she whispers. "I went under and then there you were and I *know* you."

Fear slips back. She's blown away. I know because I can feel it.

I feel relief. She smiles, nods. "Not mad, just a little . . ." She doesn't finish.

I love you. I don't say it. I don't think it. I just feel it because it's true and it's more powerful than any other feeling I have.

She feels me feel it and I feel her feel it. I reach for her. She comes to me and we hold each other for only a short moment. Perfection.

Forty-Three

KEEP UR BAGS PACKED.

I'm standing on the patio by the wall, looking out at the view and thinking about the email from Cassandra when Corina calls to me. "I see you, Plugzer. In every single way, I see you."

I freeze. "See me what?" I walk over slowly, trying to turn my thoughts away from my fear of having to run. Now that Corina and I can communicate, we're not just in each other's hearts, we're in each other's business. Corina feels me now, knows I'm hiding something. She can feel me being more watchful than I need to be. She can feel my pangs of anxiety when thoughts about the email from Cassandra or what my Voice said bubble up.

"See you standing." She smiles up at me. "See you thinking."

Her smile makes me smile. She flops down on a couch by the fire pit and I slide down onto it next to her, our legs touching, our shoulders touching. If someone walked in they would probably think we were sitting a little too close, but right now it's worth it just to feel her heat, the resilience of her body. "What am I thinking?" I ask.

"If I knew what you were thinking all the time there wouldn't be any need to talk to you, would there?"

"You'd still talk to me."

She raises her eyebrows. "I would?"

I nod. "I'm too good-looking to ignore."

She starts to laugh, then gets serious. "I'll give you that." Her hand sneaks onto my leg and squeezes. "But I still want to know what's bothering you."

"It's . . . nothing." She stares at me. "Something that happened in Vegas."

She bunches up her face. "Someday, when this shit's all through and we're back to real life, you are going to tell me everything. You know that, right?"

Bring your girlfriend, too.

I nod. "Yeah."

She scoots away from me, turns to look at me square in the eyes. "There!" She points at me. "Right there. It's about me. I know it has something to do with me because you got dark right there when I said that." She starts to wag her finger. "I *heard* it."

I shake my head hard. "It's not about you, it's . . ." But it *is* about her, at least partly. I sigh, look at her. I think about maybe telling her everything, but I can't figure how—I wouldn't even know where to begin. "I can't tell you, but it's not about you. It's about us, this place, what's coming."

I feel her fear. It settles in over both of us like sweat.

"We're gonna be okay," I say, believing it when I say it so she'll know it's true. "You and me are going to make it through. Together." I work hard to try and fill myself with hope. "Trust me."

She looks at me for a while. Her fear melts into uncertainty, which is slowly replaced by hope. "I do trust you, Plugzer. I trust you so much it scares me."

It does scare her. I know because I'm scared, too.

Forty-Four

LAST TIME I SPENT TIME WITH JORDAN, SHE AND WILL CREATED AN EMAIL designed to be sent to reporters—and even to Jeffrey Sabazios himself—if she wasn't able to make her speech.

My glides have been getting smaller, closer together in Jordan's time as we lock in the important details we need while getting closer to her big day. When I first got Jordan as a glide target, the headphones told me what we needed her to do, but now that it's approaching, it feels bigger than big. Soon, because of Jordan, the world won't be able to ignore Incursions anymore. They won't be able to ignore Live-Tech or Sabazios, either. Jordan and me are about to save the world.

I dive under. The dark and then the Jungle. I hesitate, but I don't stop. My board takes me down the path. An off-ramp.

It feels different, though, like something's wrong, but it's too short to even become a real thought.

Darkness. Light.

Something is wrong.

No.

Everything is wrong—the colors are wrong, the sounds, the smells. There's none of Jordan's bright whites and pale colors. The smells and sounds smell and sound wrong for Jordan.

But they're not wrong. They're perfectly right. It's as normal as if I'm looking through my own eyes.

I am *looking through my own eyes.*

Panic.

Not a feeling in my host, but a feeling in me on my perch. I don't want to be here. I don't want to become a Time Zombie. I don't want to know. I try to close my eyes. I try to surface, but something is holding on to me, keeping me locked in my own mind.

"It's time. He's here," I hear my host self say.

I force myself to look, to feel, to hear, to sense what's happening around me, but my host is blocking me from his memories. I'm in a room that looks like a bedroom, but it's not here at the compound and it's not back in LA—it's somewhere new. It's light outside, but the curtains are pulled. The room is ugly. It feels dirty, like a place that's been used for too long by someone who's too tired to care anymore. I smell coffee and I can feel blankets on one side and the pressure of a mattress on another.

There's the warmth of someone's skin pressed against my back. I can feel breath on my neck.

I'm naked.

"Your timing sucks," somebody says. "Turn around." Her name is Cassandra. It's Cassandra, the girl from the picture, from the email.

We're lovers. My host starts to turn, but I don't want to look.

She's got blond hair that's streaked with red, blue, and purple, with black at the tips. Her lip is pierced, and so is her nose on both sides. Her eyes are intensely gray-blue. She's smiling.

My host, my future me, is still blocking his own mind. I can't tell anything about where I am or when. I start to fight him so I can learn more but he won't let me in.

Where's Corina?!

Don't, *he warns me.* The less you know, the better.

"Hey, Plugzer," she says coyly. She's looking my host in the eyes and I can feel him warm by her. I can feel it in his privates.

Listen to what she says, *my host says to me in our head.* She's going to save our lives. *"He's listening," I hear my host tell her.*

"Things aren't what you think they are, Plugzie." She props herself up on one elbow. "You've got to run away now. If you don't get out you're going to be put in stasis to preserve your witness memory."

My host interrupts my train of thought. "He doesn't get it, Cass—he doesn't know about the stasis chamber. He still thinks people leave."

Cassandra nods. She smiles and I think she's beautiful. I can't tell if it's me on my perch or me as a host that thinks so, and then I realize that we both do. "There's no going home, Plugzie. You'd all see right through that shit if you weren't so desperate to believe it." She makes a sad face like you do when you're telling a child the truth about Santa. "When witnesses can't glide anymore they're told they're done, but they don't go home. They get frozen so there's no chance that what they've seen won't happen. They're trapped in a permanent loop of the memories they witnessed—no sleep, no life, just memories over and over. When their last witnessed moments pass in real time . . . they're killed."

Calvin. The others I've heard about. Dead. Frozen. Letting us leave—when I think about it now—doesn't really sit right. Even with memory wipes and memory implants, it would never work. The whole thing suddenly feels like a story for children, but at the time we all just nodded our heads and said, "Yup, he went home," and forgot about it.

But if none of it's real, then Richard . . .

IT'S NOT TRUE, *I think.* BISHOP WOULDN'T DO

THAT. RICHARD WOULDN'T LET THAT HAPPEN. WE'RE TRYING TO SAVE THE WORLD.

"He still believes in the project," my host tells Cassandra. I can feel him grow sad. He's lonely even though he's in bed with Cassandra. "Keep going," he says.

"Sabazios? The Gentry? They're not the good guys," she continues. "They're trying to destroy us."

WHY WOULD THEY WANT TO DESTROY US? WE'RE HELPING THEM.

"His mind's blown. Slow down and explain."

She nods. "The Gentry *made the Locusts, Plugzie. Just like they made us." She says it like I'm dumb and won't understand. "They're the Gentry's farmers. The Locusts follow Gentry orders." She props herself up a little further. "To you and everybody else right now, it plays like Live-Tech repels the Locusts, but that's just pretend, man." She wags a finger in our face. "It's fucking kabuki theater, that's all. Live-Tech doesn't* repel *Locusts, it helps them find us—it activates like a beacon when it's attached to a person. Think about it, were there any Locusts in your life before you touched Live-Tech? Those Incursions so far . . ." She trails off, looks like she has a question.*

MY MOM AND DAD DIDN'T HAVE LIVE-TECH.

Bicycle Man, *my host replies.* You remember him—nearly hit us at the bottom of the hill. It was his Live-Tech that called it.

My host and I both remember the man at the same moment, a strange double-vision of the guy with the screen on his bike.

He did have Live-Tech, even commented on it.

Cassandra starts to talk again. "When is this for him? Like is it before Jordan . . . ?"

My host nods.

"Cool." She smiles at me up in my perch. "Those Incursions in all those foreign countries that nobody believes? You go to where any of them happened, you'll find Live-Tech nearby planted by one of Sabazios's people." She points at me. "Son, you've spent the last few months helping spread locator beacons around the world and locking in the apocalypse."

On my perch, I flash on the woman in the cage. I try to make it make sense, but it's just too much.

WHY WOULD THEY DO THAT? THAT MAKES NO SENSE.

In response, my host self's mind opens. A memory, vivid and awful. A body in a Locust cage. The same woman I saw before, but the cage is in a different place, a smaller room. There are Locusts there, three of them. They have their backs to me, focused on her.

The cage evaporates, leaving her exposed.

She tries to sit up. She struggles, but the Locusts reach out, each holding a part of her in place.

Their heads swivel in unison. Sickening full turns like the girl from *The Exorcist*. The pointed parts now point down toward the girl on the table.

The bear down on her, their razor-sharp heads penetrating the skin at her thigh, her stomach, and her chest.

She screams. It is loud and terrible, but it ends as quickly as it starts because while I watch, her body deflates like an air mattress, the skin pulling tight across the bones like a person dying from starvation. Then the bones themselves start to collapse and disappear, leaving only an empty bag of skin.

And then the skin itself begins to pull tight, to rip and separate, finally disappearing into the points of the Locusts.

When they're done there is no trace of the woman.

There is no sign of her on the table. Not even a hair.

There is nothing on the table but a design: a pentagon with gray dots and a bright red triangle.

The Live-Tech logo, same as on the compound kitchen table.

"The Locusts are going to farm *us. They're going to farm us and process us, because they're wet nurses for the Gentry," my host tells me. "The nutrition they get from us will be passed on to Gentry babies."*

Cassandra doesn't seem to know what I've just shown myself. She's shaking her head. "The Gentry want to have their babies here. I'll tell you the rest after we meet, but for now, what you need to know is that you've got to get out of the compound. Now."

But you're telling me this, and I'm here, so it's not going to happen, *I think, suddenly feeling better about my chances.*

Only because we run, *my host thinks to me.* Be prepared—Bishop is going to come for you.

It's hard to even think. All I can see is the woman, deflating.

Think! WHAT DO I DO?!

"Find your Voice. They don't know about her." Cassandra sits up a little more, leaning into my host. She's serious now, looking earnestly at me through his eyes. Her energy is powerful, and both he and I feel like we've been chosen. "She's your friend. She'll lead you to Sybil."

WHO'S SYBIL? WHAT ABOUT CORINA? *My feelings bubble up and spill out so that even my host can feel them. The fear, the worry, the desire . . .*

. . . the love.

Corina, *my host thinks back to me. His sadness is too much for me. It's too much for him, too, but he clamps down on it hard. His whole body tenses up and he bites his cheek hard to keep the feeling inside, but Cassandra notices anyway. Her eyes stop looking worried and she starts to look annoyed.*

She rolls over and faces away from us. As she moves, the blanket shifts and, briefly, I can see her nakedness, too. Her breasts are small, barely rising off her chest while she's on her back. Her stomach is flat, dimpling in at her hips, and I see a flash of her pubes before the blanket falls back, but I'm distracted by a set of thick scars that begins just above her hip and continues down her thigh. I want to ask her what happened, but I can't.

Be Abigail, *my host tells me.* You'll know the time. *And then:* When you see the Bicycle Man, run *up* the hill!

BICYCLE MAN?

You'll know.

I want to ask more, but before I can even form the thought, he tells me to get ready. *His mind fills with memories of Jordan's time packing for the Conference, becoming determined that immediately afterward she's going to tell her parents everything. I don't know if he's made it all up or if he knows for real what happened, but either way it's a lot of information, and I'm afraid I won't remember it. I want to ask questions, but instead I feel my host reach out for Cassandra and then stop and pull his arm back.*

I can feel him tremble with grief and sadness as I am pulled from my perch and get sucked back up to consciousness.

When I open my eyes, Paul is in the chair. "Took you long enough."

Even in a glide suit I feel like I can't breathe. There's too much happening in my head, too much to process. I feel like I'm going to vomit, so I sit up and put my head between my knees with my eyes closed until I can pull myself together.

"You alright?" Paul puts his hand on my shoulder.

I cough to clear my throat and shake my head. "Bad glide."

"Damn," he says, and then he sits up and reaches over for me.

I fall against him and he holds me in almost the same way Pete used to hold me when I was little. For a few seconds it feels like everything that just happened doesn't mean the end of everything.

Eventually, I pull myself back up and it all comes crashing down again.

Paul lets go, but I can tell he's worried.

I smile as best I can. "I'll be okay."

"You sure?" He raises his eyebrows at me. "You look sick."

I shrug. I'm sure I do look sick.

"Don't puke on my suit. It's bad enough being a cauliflower without having to smell like vomit."

They kill witnesses.

I want to tell him. I want to scream to him that we've got to run, but I don't. I'm too scared.

I try smiling, but I think I fail. I slide off the couch and he takes my place, watching me carefully. He doesn't say anything else and I'm grateful because I don't think I would have been able to reply.

While Paul is under, I dictate what I remember telling myself about Jordan. I try to keep my voice steady, but I'm sure that if whoever listens to these things is paying attention, they'll know I'm freaked out. Thinking about that begins to make me more freaked out, and I have to stop dictating for a minute.

The Gentry are the enemy. They control the Locusts. Live-Tech is the problem—it helps Locusts get here. I've been working to bring about the end of the world. The thoughts are too big, and trying to think them is like shoving a bowling ball into my back pocket.

The single thought that upsets me the most, the thing that I've been trying not to think or say or see or know since the trip ended has become too strong to keep down.

Corina wasn't there.

Wherever, whenever there was, is, will be, Corina will be missing and I was sad in a way that felt like she was . . .

I'm shaking. Time is short. Paul never stays down for more than twenty minutes, and it feels like it's been nearly that long. I bite my cheek and force myself to breathe deep so I can calm down and finish my dictation.

I finish at nearly the same moment that Paul comes up. He looks at me. I smile, but he's not fooled.

Forty-Five

CORINA FEELS MY FEAR. I CAN FEEL HER PRESSURING ME TO LET HER explore. I try resisting, but I can't. She reads my feelings and she knows: she knows something bad has happened.

I feel her pull back from my fear like it's a knife's blade. I can't do anything except wait for her in the commons.

Corina comes out of the glide hall into the commons with Maddie, who walks directly to the dormitories. Corina slows to a stop where I'm standing by the game tables.

They're watching. They already know.

Barely able to keep from shaking. "Chess?" I ask her. I don't play well, but it's her favorite game.

"Sure," she says, feeling my need for her to play along.

We sit at the game table and set up our pieces, but as we're about to start, movement distracts me. Corina and I look up at the same time.

Bishop is at the patio door. My chest begins to burn.

"Alex," he says. "Can you come with me, please?"

He stands at the door waiting, thickly built and sure of himself. He feels like a priest or a cop. I nod and stand up.

They're not good guys.

I try and clear the memory from my head because I'm suddenly sure he can read my mind. I force myself to think about lying to my parents, smoking weed, tagging up school property—other things that I got in trouble for that would leave me nervous.

I turn to Corina. "I'll be back in a minute." My voice is mostly breath. Our fears mix and I suddenly have to use the bathroom.

"I'll be here," she says. Her love comes in a wave that makes me both stronger and weak in the knees.

Bishop leads me out onto the patio. It's raining again. Water slides off the invisible cover in sheets.

I fall in three paces behind him. He doesn't show that he even knows that I'm there.

"Sit down, Alex," Bishop instructs when we enter his office, gesturing at the circle of furniture.

I sit down in a chair with its back to the door. He sits across from me.

"What's up?" I ask as casually as I can.

"I think you know, Alex."

I shrug. I scan the room for an escape route. There's no door besides the one we came in.

"You and Corina are in a relationship." His voice is calm, casual like it's no big deal.

I shrug.

"Richard really likes you, Alex. He doesn't have his own kids yet, but he thinks of you like one." Bishop shrugs. "He's reluctant to call you on it, but he's very disappointed." He studies me for a long moment. I meet his eyes, but it's hard to hold them. "But there's something that concerns me more."

I wait without reacting. I think about my breathing, the feel of my tongue against my teeth.

"Your work, Alex." He gestures up at the wall and the

displays change, shifting from window-images of famous places to something I don't recognize—it's not like anything I've seen before. The panel he's pointing to is just a collection of colors, lines and squiggles that move around. The colors change from red to orange and yellow. "That's what your witnessing should look like when you're visiting Jordan Castle."

"You can see when we glide? When we're down under?"

He laughs. "Of course we can. We have to know everything and we can't just trust a bunch of teenagers to behave, can we?"

"I haven't—" *They already know.* I feel the fight leave me and I slump in my chair.

He waves me off, gesturing back to the wall.

I look up at the wall—it's sort of like the image he showed me before, but this one looks like somebody puked a thousand rainbows into a bucket full of bubblestuff, then splatted it all onto a canvas. There are millions of colors and squiggles, but they're too many and too small for me to even be able to tell what they are.

"This is a capture from an unscheduled event that happened in a glide room after hours a while back." He waits, and a dozen more images like the first ones cycle through. "These events happened in your dorm room, which shouldn't even be possible." He looks at me, squints. "And yet here we are."

I look at the images and then back at him. I wait.

"Can you explain these, Alex?"

I shake my head.

"Have you been doing unscheduled work?"

I shake my head and wait.

"I don't think you understand how much this concerns me."

He looks me in the eyes and I hold his gaze. I'm not looking away before he does.

"I haven't been witnessing." My voice is stronger than I thought it would be.

"What have you been doing?"

"Nothing."

"That's not true, Alex." He pulls something from his pocket and reaches out for my hand. Something clamps down on my finger before I can pull away. It's Live-Tech, the size and shape of a sausage. I try to pull it off, but I can't. It just bites down even harder. "Don't struggle," Bishop says quietly. "Just go with it—it'll only hurt if you resist or you lie to me."

I try to shake it off, but all I get in return is excruciating pain that shoots from my hand and arm all the way through my chest and down into my feet. It's so bad that I'm afraid I'm going to mess my pants, but then the pain stops completely. "What the hell?" I shriek.

He puts his hand around mine, supporting the Live-Tech with his wrist. "I don't want to hurt you, Alex, but you can't keep secrets that would affect the success of the project. Tell me the truth and you won't have to feel the pain."

I try to shut my mind, and then the pain starts again.

It's horrific. It feels like all the skin and meat is being peeled back from my fingers and the palm of my hand. I force myself to look. The skin is still there, but I'm screaming anyway and my body is covered in sweat.

"Don't resist, Alex." His voice is soft and kindly, like a doctor talking to a child scared of needles.

My vision clouds from the pain.

"Let the truth out, Alex."

I cannot move and I cannot remove the thing from my finger. I will die from the pain.

Find your Voice, Cassandra said.

I dive, unlock the drain cover and slip down inside.

I'm in the Jungle. I can still feel the pain and I think I can even hear Bishop's voice as he asks me to "Let it out," but I can't be sure that he's said it again or if I've slowed down in time.

Bishop's strand hums in front of me, vibrating, pulsing with color. I can see him, feel him.

He's enjoying this.

I bring myself up against him, my thread against his. His music is sharp, concise, missing signs of doubt or fear. With Jordan, there are openings, places where I can push, change the texture of the thread, which makes the music change. I can erase doubts, make them bigger.

John Bishop has no openings. He has no doubts.

I try anyways:

LET ME GO.

Nothing happens. Whatever openings he has for change are too small, the notes around them too firm. And I'm too weak. The pain in my biology is too much for me to concentrate.

I try again: LET ALEX GO!

His music doesn't change. I hear him say, "Open your eyes, talk to me." The pain from my hand grows even more intense, and even the crashing noise and color of the Jungle begins to fade in me, overwhelmed by pain.

I'm going to lose. I'll either talk or I'll die.

The pain-cloud blocking out the Jungle intensifies. Things begin to grow dim. Dark.

I feel myself cresting toward the surface even though I don't want to, but then:

GRAB HIM, SCARED BOY, WRAP HIM LIKE YOU DID CORINA.

The Voice. It is loud, strong. It fills me with hope and the fog shifts, pulls back.

SHARE WITH HIM, BOY, MAKE HIM FEEL YOUR PAIN!

There's no time to argue. I shift, open myself to him instead. Immediately our gravities begin. We are crashing. We are joining.

His joy is my joy.

My pain is his pain. I feel him blanch, a stab of uncertainty. Fear interrupts his music.

He's left an opening. I pull back, refocus on his point of indecision, connect to it, use my own fear and pain to spread it until it begins to uproot the solid notes around it.

I feel him falter.

KEEP PUSHING, SCARED BOY.

I drill down further into the hole our fear created. His music is becoming a series of jangly twangs, buzzing like too-loose strings.

I spread, feel myself smothering his sound.

He grows muffled.

Then silent.

RUN AWAY, RUNAWAY BOY. IT'S TIME TO RUN AWAY!

I surface.

Bishop is on the floor at my feet, his head resting awkwardly against my foot, his whole weight propped up by a hip pushed flush against the chair where he was seated when I went under.

The Live-Tech that was on my finger is lying on the floor by his head.

I can't tell if Bishop's breathing.

He's not . . .

He might be dead.

I run.

Forty-Six

I SLAM THE DOOR BEHIND ME AND RUN DOWN THE LONG HALL TO THE COMmons. I feel for Corina—she's in her room. She's alone. She's as scared as I am.

WE NEED TO RUN.

She won't get the words, but she'll feel the urgency.

She's standing in the doorway when I get there.

"What's wrong?" Worry is written on her forehead and her heart.

She is the ultimate relief for me. I pull her close. "We need to get out of here," I whisper. "Now."

She pushes back at me, separating. "Why?"

I reach out so she can feel what I have been feeling. I watch the expression on her face as it changes from confusion to fear, and then to anger. She doesn't know exactly what happened, but she knows that it's serious, that it's urgent.

But she's not moving. "My time here's almost done . . ." She trails off. "I can't leave, Alex." She's shaking her head. "My mom . . ."

I feel her loss deep in my gut. She wants to go home. She wants to show her mom that she's different now. She wants things to be the way they should have been all along. Going home is real to her, a reason to stay.

"Nobody goes home, Corina. Not you, not Calvin, not

Marcus. Nobody." I reach out to her, let her feel me tell her the truth. "They're going to *kill* us."

She doesn't say anything. I feel her searching me, looking for something. Looking for proof. "How do you know?"

"Somebody showed me, and I'll tell you all about it after we're gone." I tug at her arm a little. "You're not going to see your mom again if you stay here." I'm trying hard to be calm, but time is running out. We've got to go. I put my hand on her arm, bring my face down into her line of sight. "The only way you see her is if you're still alive and the only way you stay alive is by coming with me now."

She hesitates, then nods. Her mind is fear.

All I want to do is hold her, but there's no time. "Grab what you need to bring," I tell her. "I've got to get something." I run to my room.

Paul's sitting at his desk. "Hey," he says when he sees me, like nothing is wrong.

"Nobody goes home, man—nobody ever leaves!" I whisper to him as I grab my backpack, still packed full of clothes. "The Gentry control the Locusts—they only *pretend* to be afraid of Live-Tech, but once it's attached to a person, it becomes a beacon and it actually shows them where to go. They're gonna kill us!" I reach out my hand to him. "You've got to come!"

He just stares at me. "Did your brain break?"

I can hear Corina coming down the hall. It's time to go. "No. I'm not insane—none of this is what it seems, man—they're going to destroy the Earth, they're going to kill us all. You've got to run away with me!"

But Paul isn't hearing me. Instead he stands up, shaking his head. I grab his arm and pull at him, but he resists, shaking me off.

"You need help, Alex," he says quietly. "Let me get Richard . . ."

But I can't let him do that. If he gets Richard, we're all going to die.

"Don't do that," I plead. "Just come with me."

But he's already looking over my shoulder, trying to find some way past me.

I have no choice. "I'm coming back for you." I say it just before I box him hard on the temple.

He falls over in a heap.

On my birthday he said I was a better brother already. Not anymore.

For a moment I can't do anything but look at him on the floor and feel sick to my stomach. If I leave him here, he's going to be killed. Panic floats up, making it hard to think. I can't leave him here. I can't leave any of them here. I've let too much family die already. No more.

"I'm gonna come back and get you," I tell him again, but he can't hear me.

I shake myself loose and feel around in the lining of my pack. The picture is still there. I sling the bag over my shoulder. Corina is standing outside my door.

She sees Paul crumpled on the floor. She looks at me.

"I didn't have a choice," I tell her, pulling her along. "I tried to warn him, but he thought I was crazy—he was going to call Richard."

I take one last look at Paul as I close the door. "We'll come back for them."

She nods like I'm wasting time. "How're we doing this?" She's calm. Efficient. No longer unsure. She's making me calmer, too.

"We walk out like it's a normal day. I don't think anybody's looking for us yet."

We walk back down the hallway together.

I pick up the pace, but Corina puts her hand on my arm to slow me down. Rushing won't help. It'll just make everybody wonder what happened.

We make it into the Long Hall without anybody wondering.

"That door," I tell her as we pass the alcove. "He took me through there and attached a Live-Tech to me that made it hurt so bad that I nearly blacked out. I dived down to the Jungle to try and find him to stop him."

"You stopped him from underneath?" She's skeptical.

I nod. "Yeah."

"How'd you get away, though?"

I shake my head. "I don't know." I look over my shoulder back at where his office is. "It's like he had a heart attack or something. When I got back up, he was on the floor and I ran."

"Is he, like . . . dead?"

Yes. "I don't know." I tell myself it's true. I didn't take his pulse. I didn't listen for breath. He could've been passed out. He could've been asleep.

Maybe I didn't actually kill him.

We reach the driveway door. We look at each other. When we open the door, we're officially outlaws.

Corina opens the door. We look out at the driveway, slick

with rain. The gray sky stretches out above the trees in a uniform low-hanging sheet.

"God this city is depressing," I mutter.

"Yeah," Corina agrees, whispering softly.

There's noise behind us. A siren. Shouts.

We're blown. "Run!"

Forty-Seven

WE'RE DOWN THE DRIVEWAY AND NEARLY TO THE STREET WHEN THE BIG gate in front of us starts to close.

Corina's lagging a couple steps behind me. "Faster!" I yell, but it's not going to help. I dive for the narrow hole between the gate and the fence, and feel the gate brush my backpack as I pull through, but now it's closed and Corina is still on the wrong side.

"Hold on," she tells me before tossing her pack over and backing up ten feet.

A bunch of men start running down the driveway toward her. "They're coming behind you!"

Instead of turning, she runs toward the gate. She jumps and gets amazing air, grabbing it above the top rail just below the spikes, then flips her left leg up and over.

"Catch me," she calls as she straddles the top between the spikes and lets herself fall to my side of the gate.

I get there just in time and she lands on me. We fall to the ground in a heap. "High jump. Track team," she explains. We can't stay there. The gate is opening again and the guys coming after us are seconds away. She's up and off me almost instantly. I'm up right after her.

We tear down the street. They're coming after us in cars and on foot and I don't know where we are or where to go.

Corina knows the area better than me and she takes the lead, running out across the street and down another. There's a park ahead of us and it looks like it has a forest in it. Corina makes a line for it and I follow close behind.

I can sense the men behind us getting closer. Corina dashes across the street and sends a passing car into a skid that nearly hits me. I slap against the fender as I jump over the back of it to warn it to watch out. By the time I'm across, Corina's already in the woods.

The followers are shouting after us. Cars are skidding to a stop and doors are slamming. Corina's left the trail and I'm falling behind. I thought I was faster than her back at the compound, but she just wasn't giving it her all.

Now that she is, I can barely keep up.

We're going through all sorts of bushes and I'm getting scraped up on my arms. My breath is becoming ragged and I can't believe how many plants there are up here. I've run through the woods in Elysian Park hundreds of times, but there, almost nothing gets in your way. Here, it's crowded with plants, and they all seem to be out to get you.

We're gaining some distance, because even though this is hard for us, it's even harder for them. They're old and wearing suits.

The woods break in front of us and there's another street, with a school on its other side.

"Hurry!" Corina shouts back at me.

I understand her plan—we're kids and we'll blend. The security team won't be able to cross onto campus without getting stopped.

We make it to the school grounds just as the first guy

behind us breaks out of the bushes. He stops short when he sees that we're in a crowd of other kids and taps his pod. Just then, one of the others comes into view. He sees us and starts across the street, but the first guy calls him back.

"C'mon." Corina yanks my arm and I turn back around. Together we walk through campus.

It's a break or lunch and there are kids everywhere. They're all white and Asian so Corina and I stand out like neon lights. "We're not exactly hidden," I mutter to her as I smile at a group of girls who are staring at us. When we pass them, I hear giggles and I imagine myself through their eyes.

She nods at two girls who're giving her the eye. "We just need to find a way off this campus without getting stopped."

There's a parking lot on the other side of the school. It's not like I've stolen a car before, but I know how to do it. I watched a bunch of videos about it when I was younger and I thought it might be useful. I'm pretty sure I can do it even without tools if I can find a gas car old enough to still have a mechanical key ignition.

I scan the lot. There's an old Honda Accord parked about halfway back.

The bell sounds and we move with the crowds as they all head toward the doors, but we peel off before we go inside and jog down to the car.

Corina keeps watch while I try to remember how to do this. In the videos, there weren't a whole bunch of people possibly looking through windows, and there weren't bad guys giving chase. Also, I could watch them again if I missed something.

Here, if I screw up, we're done. I stand next to the car with my back next to the driver's side window, trying to look casual.

"Here goes." I pull my arm forward, ready to bring my elbow back against the window as hard as I can.

"What are you doing?" Corina whispers.

"Breaking the window." I slam my elbow backward into the glass, but the window doesn't break. The pain is incredible. The videos don't show you how much it hurts to whack your elbow into something as solid as a safety-glass car window. It hurts like hell. "Oh, fuck," I say, teeth gritted against the pain. I'm not going to be able to do that again without needing my arm in a sling for a week. "Can't do it."

"Not with your bare elbow." Corina digs into her backpack for something and comes out with a folding knife. She hands it to me. "Use this."

I look at it and then at her. I don't know what she wants me to cut. "How?"

She shakes her head and pushes me aside again. She takes my place at the door and, with the knife in her hand, the handle exposed, pulls back and slams it against the window. The glass shatters into a million pieces. "Only an idiot uses his elbow," she says before stepping out of the way.

The alarm is a deafening *whoop whoop whoop*. I dive inside and reach under the dashboard for the box. It's right where the videos said it would be, so I grab the orange wire that comes out of one side and the white wire that comes out the other, and pull.

The alarm dies and I yank the housing off the base of the steering wheel so I can see the ignition system.

I take the white wire from the alarm and connect it with the orange wire and the red wire and black wire that I find under the wheel. They spark when I twist them together and I slam on the gas.

The combustion engine revs to life, loud as hell, and my chest fills with hope.

Corina's already in the passenger seat by the time I've got the door closed. As I pull away, I see school security and a bunch of students running toward us. They won't catch us unless they have a car waiting at the end of the lot.

They don't. I watch the cop radio it in from the rearview.

"Alex," Corina says, getting my attention. She points at the street in front of me. There's a black Ford Interceptor moving in to block the exit from the school.

I look around. The end of the parking lot is approaching quickly. There are security guards closing in on foot from either side of the drive and there's a school police car with its siren blaring coming up behind us.

I yank the wheel hard to the left and hit the gas. The Accord rumbles forward. It hits the curb and jumps, landing on the grass. The wheels spin for a minute when we land, throwing dirt a hundred feet behind us and I'm sure that we're going to get stuck in the mud, but we find traction, whip-tailing for a moment before getting forward motion.

It's a bumpy ride but we clear the grass and jump the curb onto the street, leaving the cop car in the lot. I jam the gas and pull out into oncoming traffic to clear the Volvo in front of me, then hang a hard left onto a busy street against the light.

"Holy shit!!" Corina yells. And then we're out and away from Seattle.

Forty-Eight

IT FEELS WEIRD DRIVING SOMETHING SO LOUD, SO WE DITCH THE CAR IN A parking lot in Tacoma. We got away, but even while we're driving, I'm growing more and more sure that our patches will allow them to find us.

Corina inventories our resources while I drive. We have about $320 in cash between us. She finds my notebook while digging through my pack. "What's this?"

I glance over from the driver's seat, and my breath catches. "Nothing." Somehow having her in my heart isn't nearly as scary as having her in my notebook.

"Can I look?" She starts to open it.

"No." It comes out harsher than I mean it to. "Not yet." I soften it. "It's personal."

She side-eyes me. "Plugzer, I have literally felt every feeling you have . . ."

I shake my head. "It's . . ." I can feel her judgment and it's making it hard for me to talk. She feels my embarrassment, too.

"Someday?" she asks.

"Yeah." I breathe out a breath I hadn't known I was holding.

We spend eighteen of our dollars at a downtown Subway. Over sandwiches I tell her what I know. I tell her about Cassandra and my self-witness, but I don't mention being in bed with her. The not-saying part is easy compared to keeping Corina's absence out of my heart where she can feel it. I tell her about the freezing and the killing, about the Gentry being here to destroy us. I tell her that the Gentry created the Locusts, about how I saw them suck the meat and bones out of a woman, and that Sabazios is going to help them unleash the Locusts on our world.

I tell her about Live-Tech being a beacon that shows the way to the Locusts after it's paired with a person, and that by helping get Live-Tech everywhere we've been locking in the apocalypse. I explain that the Locusts are just pretending to be afraid of Live-Tech so people all over the world will get it, ensuring a successful invasion.

By the time I'm finished, Corina looks defeated. She feels defeated, too, but she sounds strong when she asks me where we're going.

"We're supposed to find someone named Sybil." I try to make my voice deep and confident so she doesn't ask me any questions about who Sybil is. "She's on our side."

Corina nods. "And where are we going to find this Sybil?"

You already know where to go. I nod like I know what I'm talking about. "Can I show you something?" I pull up my backpack and reach into the lining. My fingers graze something hard and plastic—the key chain. I feel better knowing it's still with me, but I don't pull it out. Now's not the time to look at it.

I hand Corina the photo. "That's Cassandra."

She examines the picture. "That looks like you."

"It is me."

"I thought you didn't know her." She looks at me. "You said you *met* this girl, Cassandra, when you witnessed your future."

I nod. "I did. I met her for the first time today. The picture, though, I've had since before all this started." I tell her the story of how I got the picture and the trouble with the time capsule. "I'm guessing we'll get some answers once we find where this was taken."

She nods. "Yeah. That makes sense."

I look at the picture again, not at me, but at the beach, the water, the faint brown mountains that are across from it. "It could be SoCal . . ."

She looks at me and waits. "But?"

"I don't know any place in Southern California that has mountains that start so close to the shore."

She studies the picture some more. "It looks like a lake to me."

"Maybe."

She sighs and starts wadding up our trash. "We'd better find it, though."

"Corina?"

"Yeah?"

"I'm wanted for murder down there."

She turns back and studies me for a moment. "We're going to have to do something to change how you look, then."

When we're ready to go, I bring up the other thing that I've been thinking about. "We've got to lose the patches. I think they can use them to track us."

She looks grim. "Yeah. Sure. How?"

I remember how much it hurt when Damon pinched my patch and I get a little sick when I think about how much it's going to hurt if I try to take it off. "I think we just have to do it."

I lead her outside around to the back of the restaurant. "I'll go first."

I lift up my sleeve and touch my patch. I feel around the

edge for a place to get a grip. It's hard because it's fused to my skin. I find a gap. I take a deep breath, nod once at Corina, who's looking at me like I'm crazy, and pull.

The pain is blinding, but it's not as bad as what the truth-seeking Live-Tech did to me. It's the blood that I'm not expecting. It's as though the patch has created new arteries and veins and I'm suddenly bleeding like I've sliced my wrists.

"Holy hell," I whisper through the pain. I'm starting to feel weak, and my knees buckle, but I keep pulling even though I'm falling over. I close my eyes and pull harder. There's movement, but I think I'm dying. I feel the world fade and then there's a sudden explosion. The insides of my eyelids are painted white and it feels like somebody's lit a firecracker in my forehead.

Everything goes black.

Forty-Nine

"WAKE UP!

"Wake up! Wakeupwakeupwakeupwakeup.

"Patchless Alex, run away!" The Voice is in my ears. Ghostly and hollow. She's whisper-loud again like when I first heard her. She's talking over a steady rumble of guitars that leak out of the Jungle under me.

YOU'RE BACK?

"Days are still strange. I'm back up your patchless drain and in your brain."

"Wake up!" I hear it again, but it sounds different, more real. "Jesus, Alex, wake the hell up!"

I open my eyes. It's too bright at first but things fade almost immediately to gray and then the pain starts again, this time behind my eyes and I squeeze them shut.

Corina's standing over me.

"Hi," I manage. The guitars are loud inside in a way they never were before the patch. Constant noise, a gathering storm.

"The patch is gone and your drain's unplugged, Plugz, brace yourself. Patch made changes to you and the Silly Juice'll be closer than ever before."

"Jesus, man, you scared the hell out of me," she whispers. "I thought you were dead."

I shake my head. It's not clearing up. It's not getting easier to think.

"My patch is off, isn't it?"

Corina shakes her head. "It's off, but you don't wanna look."

I look. My upper arm is wrapped tight in one of my shirts, but the blood is already starting to soak through. There's something on the ground next to me. It looks like a sickly gray Pop-Tart with tentacles. It's the patch. I feel sick. I know I'm going to vomit, so I turn to the other side and manage to spray the dumpster and not Corina.

"Girl's got a patch, boy. Got to get her patch—get her patch off, boy. Snatch her patch!" I can barely hear her over the noise.

I wipe my mouth with the back of my hand. "Your turn."

My voice is hoarse.

Corina shakes her head wildly. "Nuh-uh. They can *have* me before I let you do *that*."

I shake my head. It needs to come off.

"Patch got your tongue? Girl's patch has got to go. Snatch the patch!"

"Girl's patch has got to go." I look at Corina. "I have to snatch your patch."

"Snatch her patch!"

"I'm going to," I tell the Voice. "Shut up for a minute."

"Who are you talking to?" Corina asks softly. I look at her. She's scared of me. I try and flood her with reassurance, but nothing happens. I reach for her in my mind, but there's nothing to reach for.

Without the patch, we aren't connected.

I shake my head. "The patch has to come off, Corina."

She pulls the knife from her pack, opens it. "Get back."

"Silly girl. Use knife girl. Slice the top and the patch falls off. Slice the top and off it falls. Tell her, scared boy."

I nod my head. "Corina, listen to me." I try to sound as calm as I can, but my adrenaline is pumping. I hope my Voice isn't screwing with me. "Don't pull at the patch. Just take the knife and cut across the top—not deep or anything—just a line across the top."

She looks at me and shakes her head. "How do you know that? That doesn't make any sense." She waves the knife at me. "Why would you think I'd believe you—that'll just hurt like hell and then you'll get the knife."

I shake my head back at her. "I have a voice." She looks confused. "Inside my head. It's been talking to me. It's been helping me, but the patch made it hard to hear. Now that my patch is off, I can hear her outside the Jungle again and she's telling me how to take yours off."

Corina's shaking her head. "How the hell do you expect me to believe that?" She laughs at me. "Any of it. *You're* the one who says they're going to kill us—there's no proof of *that*." She's not afraid of me now. She's disgusted.

It's written all over her face.

It's too loud in my brain for thinking. I shake my head again, one last time to try and clear the guitars. It works a little bit. They're down to a level that doesn't rattle my mind.

"Please. Just try it—if it hurts, stop." I wait for a second, but my Voice doesn't correct me or tell me I'm an idiot. I hope that means I'm right that it won't hurt.

"Uh-uh."

"If it doesn't work, then go back. Tell them I used mind

control to convince you to come with me. I won't hurt you and I won't stop you."

She starts to look nervous again, unsure.

"Keep talking, runaway. She's listening."

"The Voice is real, but I can't prove that to you unless you try this out. Corina, I love you," I tell her for the first time since we've lost our connection. It's weird because I know it's true, but it doesn't feel the same. It feels like it did before the connection, but it's half love. It's just normal human love. I feel very alone. "Please."

She looks down at her patch and then at the knife. I hold my breath while she considers it and then she nods. "If it hurts, that's it. I'll know you're crazy and I'll go back to the compound."

"Yes. Absolutely."

"Okay." But she doesn't make any moves toward her patch. "Okay."

"Okay." She starts to move the knife. She flinches when it touches the patch, and then she turns it so the blade touches the front surface at the top.

"Top edge. It's got to be the top edge."

"The top edge, not the front. Not between the patch and the skin?" I add but it's as much a question as an instruction. I don't hear anything, so I nod. "The top edge of the patch, not between the patch and the skin."

She turns the knife. She places the blade against the top edge and pushes against it. I can see the patch dimple, but she doesn't stop. She pushes harder and the knife penetrates the skin of the patch.

She stops.

She looks surprised, but not like it's hurting her. She draws the knife forward across the patch to the front edge. She moves it slowly, like she's waiting for the pain, until she reaches the front of the patch and pulls the knife up slowly.

Nothing happens at first, but then the cut edge begins to curl in and the patch starts to change color from the dark brown of her skin to the same dull red that my pod turned when I deactivated it way back when at the compound. The change happens slowly, like the color is bleeding out of it, dripping back into Corina's flesh.

When the patch is completely red, it falls off, leaving only a series of four circular scars where the blood vessels were in its place.

"Holy hell," Corina whispers. "Your voice is real."

"Yeah. My Voice is real."

She examines her patch on the ground where it fell. She seems frozen.

"Corina?"

She shudders when I speak and then looks up at me. "They're all really dead?"

"Who?"

"Calvin? Marcus? Everybody?" She's shaking. I reach for her. At first she pulls away, but then falls in against me. "They're all dead, aren't they?"

"They might still be frozen." It doesn't sound very helpful.

"And that's what's gonna happen to Paul and the rest, too?"

Flashes of Paul. Playing guitar, laughing in the kitchen. Damon and me drinking in Vegas. Maddie. But then I'm back to Paul, unconscious on the floor of the room after I dropped him. I shake my head. "No. I'm gonna get them out. I promised Paul."

She looks around at the alley we're in, the patches on the ground, the blood, my vomit on the Dumpster. "Why don't we finish rescuing us first."

I shrug, and turn to start walking.

"Alex?" Corina asks. The guitars are in my head. I can barely hear her.

"Yeah?"

"You trust this voice of yours?"

"She's been right so far."

She looks at me. "She?"

"It sounds like a girl." I shrug.

She shakes her head. "You shrug too much."

"It's just a voice." Then I shrug again. My head's too loud to do much else.

Fifty

WITHOUT CORINA IN MY MIND, I FEEL EMPTY, SMALL. JUST A BAG OF GUITARS. She's walking next to me, but she's far away. She's in another galaxy, another universe. Another body with a mind that I can't feel.

I feel lost in every way I can.

We're going to catch a Greyhound south to LA.

We buy a set of clippers at a Walmart, along with some glasses. Corina cuts my hair in the bus station bathroom. Shaves me down into a buzz cut. I try and argue with her because I like my long hair, but she says it's the best way. Then she hands me the reading glasses—the kind old people get from the rack by the pharmacy. They're thick and black and they make the world look like I'm staring at it through a fish-eye filter.

"I can't wear these."

"Do or don't, but *with* them you look like a somewhat hot schoolboy." She takes them off my face and twists her lips. "Without them you look suspiciously like . . . you." I can hardly hear what she says over the guitars.

I put the glasses back on.

Corina takes the rest of our money to buy the tickets because I can't even hear the cashier. We only have enough to get us as far south as San Francisco.

The bus is in the station already, so we get on and take seats in the front.

"What's wrong with you?" Corina asks when we sit down.

I shake my head. I don't know what she's talking about.

"You've been all up in your head—what're you thinking about?" She's just asking, but it feels like she's pressing and the guitars are so loud it's hard not to get angry.

"Nothing." I say it low, below what I can hear, because if I say it over the guitars, I'll shout it. "It's just loud."

She squints at me. "Loud? The bus is stopped. Nobody's talking."

I sigh. I want to yell, to tell her about what she doesn't know, but instead I lift my hand and point at my skull. "In here." Then: "Guitars."

"You can't tune them out?"

I try to think of something to say that isn't *no*, something to do that isn't just another shrug, but I can't. "No."

Corina takes my hand, squeezes it. She leans against me and I shift so we can be closer. "If you aren't going to be much at talking, you're gonna have to make up for it by being my pillow."

I smile. I'm all guitars in my mind, but my heart feels better.

I look down at Corina's face. In all our time together I've only touched her like this once, in her room, when we first kissed. I've barely been able to look at her without worrying that people would know.

From here I can see her hair up close—the way it curls right at the roots, dense, soft.

She still smells like vanilla.

As the bus starts moving, I close my eyes, try to tune out

the guitars by focusing on the feel of Corina against my side, her hand on my arm, her breath on my sleeve, but it's not enough. My mind is a mosh pit of noise intermixed with flashes of life from this morning when I ate breakfast and everything was fine.

Paul on the floor again. The Live-Tech torture, Bishop.

YOU THERE? I call out for her.

She is. I can feel her, but I can't hear her very well. The guitars are so much louder now than they were before the patch. It's like ripping it off tore the rest of the cover off the drain in my brain and the Jungle flooded in unchecked.

HOW DO I GET IT TO QUIET DOWN?

If there's an answer, I don't hear it.

I reach for my backpack, pull out my notebook. Corina doesn't stir when I lay it open on her lap, secured in place by her arm.

I close my eyes, ready to drown in my sea of noise, hoping to be deep under when she wakes up and reads. It's still a scary thought, but not nearly as scary as having her not know me.

Fifty-One

NO SLEEP. TIME DRAGS. THE SCENERY CHANGES FROM FLAT TO MOUNTAINS. The stops get farther apart. The guitars don't stop but they lessen, not quieter—just fewer. Corina moves to readjust next to me. I cover her with my hoodie because she seems cold.

My eyes are closed. My Voice and I are trying to hear each other through the noise. When the bus pulls out of Ashland it heads up a steep long hill into the mountains, leaving the sounds of people behind, and I'm left with just us, the people on the bus.

My heart is like a kick drum against the songs in my mind, but it's quiet enough for us to talk.

She tells me what to do.

It's not easy and it doesn't work at first, but then it does and my head is nearly quiet, the low grumble of guitars only barely audible in their new form.

Fifty-Two

IN THE MORNING, WE'RE IN CALIFORNIA. CORINA'S LOOKING AT ME WHEN I open my eyes. I smile up at her. "Hey."

"How's your head?" She puts her finger against my temple.

I blink, sit all the way up. "Fine." My notebook's not on her lap anymore. I look down and see it in my backpack. I look up at her. "You read it?"

She nods, pulls me to her. I come in under her arms as she holds me. "Thank you." When she lets me go, she furrows her brow, looks concerned. "You can hear me?"

I nod. "Yeah. I'm okay now."

"How'd you get them quiet?"

"It was like a visualization thing my Voice showed me." I think back about how it all happened. "When we got into the mountains, my head got quiet enough for my Voice to tell me what to do. She told me to reenvision the music like it's written down, like it's sheet music, and then she had me build cabinets to keep it in. Just like I reimagined my glide-path."

"And that worked?"

"Yeah. It did."

She sits up. "Wait, so you can read and write music? Not just in your head but in real life?"

I start to shrug, but I turn it into a nod when I realize she's impressed. "Yeah. I taught myself. When I was a kid."

We stay looking at each other for a moment and then she pulls me closer. When she lets me go, she asks me about the sheet music. "So you got the Jungle tamed with the sheet music—does that mean you can, like, *read* the shit?"

I think about it. "Maybe." Then: "Just a sec."

I close my eyes and find the drawer with the music in it. There aren't that many sheets right now. I pick up the stack and listen. There's a lot of quiet music, probably small animals and such, but most of the interesting music I hear nearby are sheets filled with complex notations—probably the other people on the bus.

I focus on them—they're hard to understand. They may be sheet music, but they're for the most difficult music in the world. Each page starts off with notations that look nearly familiar, like déjà vu. Those notes don't change; they're frozen music that must be the past, where things have already happened.

But each sheet also has a place where the solid notations stop, giving way to a spray of possibilities—colorful dots and squiggles that swirl. Colors come in confusing waves that crest and recede.

I listen to the songs playing nearby. My song. Corina's song. I hear myself playing. I look for the sheet that matches it. I can see the music in front of me.

Read my music.

I look down. The squiggles on the current moment in my staff are full of movement. They change in time with my sound. I listen. I watch. I think. I feel.

I begin to understand.

I look farther up the staff to where it begins to dissolve into the mass of music all around us.

I open my eyes. I am looking at Corina. She's looking the other way, out the window on the other side of the aisle.

"Corina," I say.

She turns. "You got it figured?" she asks.

"Yeah," I say. "I'm a Time Zombie right now. I already collapsed this just now when I was under."

"You sure?"

I nod. A little girl and her mother make their way slowly past us toward the back of the bus. The girl looks at me. I smile.

So does she.

I look back at Corina. "I know how to read the music."

I put the music back in the drawer and I open my eyes.

My mind is silent. There is nothing. I see what I saw. I hear myself talking.

Time Zombie.

I try and do something, anything, different from what I saw. I try to clench a fist. I try to bite my tongue.

Nothing. I'm watching the world from a formfitting glass prison until suddenly the music comes rushing back, the glass breaks, and I'm part of the world again. "The hard part is singling out the sheet music. Once I do that, I can read it."

I try and explain it all, but she shakes her head. "I'll just trust you."

She reaches out for my hand, grabs it. "Do you think that you might be able to . . . ?" She moves her head side to side and then points from me to her with her other hand. "To connect us again?" she asks finally.

My heart lifts when she asks me. I smile. "I hope so." But even as I say it, I don't think it'll happen. Things are too different now.

Fifty-Three

"IT'S TOO BAD I CAN'T PUSH THEM LIKE I USED TO," I MENTION AS WE WALK across the Golden Gate Bridge on our way into San Francisco. We've been camped out in a park near the water on the far side for a couple days, trying to spare-change enough money to get the rest of the way to LA.

"Push who?"

"My targets—I used to be able to get them to do things."

Corina stops, leans against the rail to look at me. The bridge shakes beneath us as the traffic passes. "That's not possible."

"It was for me. I just went to the Jungle from my perch and found their strand."

"Don't joke." She shakes her head, but she's smiling. "You're saying you have mind-control powers?"

I nod. "I did. I don't now."

"Did you ever make *me* do anything?"

I shake my head. "Nuh-uh."

"How do I know my kissing you that day wasn't some Jungle mumbo-jumbo mind control?"

She's not smiling anymore. She looks upset. Her music is off. "I didn't—" I reach for her. "I didn't ever do that, Corina." I'm starting to sweat.

She's still for a moment, then nods. "Alright, then."

I don't know if it's the bridge shaking or if I'm just dizzy with relief because she believes me.

She pushes herself off the rail and starts to walk again. We've gone five steps when she stops. "Back there, at the compound? How did you do it?"

I think back on it. "I just sort looked for the places where there weren't solid notes in place—places where they were having doubts or were afraid of something." I stop to try and come up with a way to explain what I did. "When I found one, all I had to do was sort of 'connect' to it and fill it with *my* thought for what should happen."

She raises her eyebrows. Skeptical. "And that worked?"

"Yeah. It did."

"Why can't you do it now?"

"I . . ." I don't finish. I start picturing the sheet music I have in my head. "Maybe I can."

Fifty-Four

WE'RE ON MARKET STREET NEAR THE BIG PARK NEXT TO CITY HALL. CORINA'S in front of me with a basket saying "Help us out" to people. I'm lying behind her, searching for good targets. It took me all morning to learn how to sort sheets and find the right ones quickly, but once I developed a method for it, it was easy.

For the last hour I've been focused on learning how to change people. It turns out it's not that different from before. When I was seeing them as strands in the Jungle, I just had to find the dark spots—the places where there was doubt and fear and there wasn't a note playing.

It took me a little time to see it—fear and doubt don't show up as blank spots on the sheet music, just as notes that are written with less force. The deeper the uncertainty, the more faintly written the note. The more faintly written the note, the easier it is for me to overwrite it, change it. Rearrange the song.

Even so, I'm finding that some people are hard to change. It's like everybody's got their own key. I can add some notes, change some others around, but I can't write things that don't fit with their overall music.

I lay behind Corina with my eyes closed while she rattles the bucket. I'm listening for people who are already keyed to give. I just write me and Corina into their generosity.

Once I figure it out, we pull in nearly three hundred dollars in the space of twenty-five minutes before a couple of cops take an interest in us. They're focused and I can't get them to go away. They're intent on harassing us. "We gotta go," I tell Corina.

"We're making good money."

"Those cops aren't gonna let us be." Then: "I can't talk to cops."

"You can't make them stop?"

"Nah, they're too focused." I stand up, reach down for her. "We've got money for the bus to LA. That's what we needed."

She shakes her head, shoves the money from the can into her pocket, and stands up without my hand. We start walking. The cops lose interest.

We're crossing up over the big open field by City Hall when I feel someone watching me. I slow and look around.

"What's up?" Corina asks, looking around herself.

I wave her off, still focused on my feeling. "Sec . . ." Then I see him.

When you see Bicycle Man, run up the hill!

A blond guy, his hair barely contained by his helmet, is drinking coffee from a paper cup, watching us from the other side of the park. Even at a distance, I recognize him. He nearly ran into me on the night the Locust killed my parents. Bicycle Man. I make myself look away like I didn't see him, didn't recognize him. I make myself smile like everything's good and start walking again, falling in right next to Corina.

"Don't act weird, but we're being followed."

She doesn't miss a step. She doesn't turn around. "Who?"

"Bicycle Man. I warned myself about him on my self-glide . . ." I trail off because I can't finish my thought out loud. Suddenly, I know the truth: He's the guy who delivered the Live-Tech. He's the guy who brought the Locust to my house. He's the guy who arranged for my parents to be killed.

"He's working with them."

She's quiet until we reach the corner. While we're waiting for the light, she looks around. "I see him." Then: "Ideas?"

"When I warned me about him?"

She looks at me: "Yeah?"

"I told myself what to do."

The light's ready to turn. "What?"

The walk sign lights up. "Run up the hill!"

We dash across the street. It's crowded in the crosswalk, so we leave the lines, running between waiting cars, getting to the far side.

"This way!" Corina shouts, pointing up the big hill to our right.

She takes off before she finishes, catching me flat-footed. I jump after her, not wanting to get separated. Bicycle Man is on the far side of the street. He's got his bike and he's starting up the hill parallel to us.

But the hill's getting steep and it's easier to run than bike. He starts to fall behind. My legs feel heavy and my lungs hurt, but we push on. Corina's still ahead of me, creating a path through the pedestrians. By the time we reach the top, he's two blocks behind us.

"There!" Corina's pointing at a hotel with a line of driverless cabs in front. We dash to the first one, tell it to drive, but it doesn't move.

"We don't have the App, Plugzer—we aren't going anywhere." She starts to get back out of the car.

I dive. The guy at the valet stand. He's an easy rewrite

and by the time I open my eyes, he's got his screen up against the tap pad.

"Thanks!" Corina says to him, closing her door.

The cab pulls into traffic.

"Where we going?" Corina asks me when she sees my eyes open.

"Back across the bridge, then I don't know."

She looks out the back window and I do, too. We both duck down suddenly. Bicycle Man is cresting the hill. "We should get out of town."

"Yeah."

She doesn't say anything for a bit, but then she looks at me. "I don't want to take more busses, so you'd better find somebody to rewrite into giving us a ride."

Fifty-Five

WE'VE BEEN IN LA FOR DAYS. NOTHING. WE'VE VISITED LAKES. WE'VE DONE what we can to avoid being seen, but every minute we stay, the chances that Bicycle Man or somebody like him finds us gets bigger, and the only thing we've learned is that Corina and I irritate each other when we're feeling hopeless.

Corina doesn't know what I'm planning. She went to get us some dinner. When she gets back, I'll know what the plan is—I'll know what's going to happen.

I won't be able to tell her because I'll be a Zombie, but at least I'll know. I lie down on the bed. I've been working on how to do this for a few days, but this is my first real attempt. I close my eyes. My music is there, top of the drawer. I pull it, examine the staff, looking far ahead, following it beyond where it splits, splits again and again, following one thread into the mist.

A week from now:

My eyes are closed. This was a bad idea. Memories are flooding in, but it's all coming in too quickly to sort. There're parts that feel familiar and then there are other parts that don't make any sense.

I open my eyes. I'm in a bathroom stall. I'm sitting on the toilet with my pants down. My head is in my hands and my legs are nearly asleep. I've been here awhile.

Corina is here, too. Somewhere. Outside. We're at a rest stop near Palm Springs. Near the windmills, past the big casino.

We got a ride here from a guy in a minivan who made room for us by asking his youngest son to sit on another kid's lap. I wouldn't have made him do it if we hadn't been desperate.

We needed to get away.

The last week comes into clearer focus:

I make a plan.

Corina and I talk it over. She wants to keep going to lakes, but I tell her it's a waste of time. I tell her about the car crash when the truck nearly hit me and how Cassandra was the one who saved me. "Maybe she's still around my old neighborhood."

Corina's sure somebody will recognize me and I'll get arrested. I point to my hair, which is now a fuzzy mess. "It looks so terrible that as long as I wear the nerd glasses, nobody'll even look at me twice except to laugh."

She comes around eventually, but she's not thrilled.

We set out the next morning. We're on the bus and then we're at Echo Park. I'm sweating bullets. Corina is walking next to me. We hold hands while we walk around the lake.

She thinks it's really pretty. The lotus flowers are just starting their first blooms, the turtles and birds are everywhere. She wants to rent a pedal boat, but I can't even think about doing that.

I'm too messed up by being this close to home.

It's like nothing's changed here at all. My family being gone hasn't brought even one part of life here to a standstill.

All the normal feels personal and it hurts.

There's no sign of Cassandra.

We go to Elysian Park. We're on the old road that runs from

Scott up toward the conference center when I hear someone familiar nearby.

It's not anybody I recognize from LA.

"Something's not right," I whisper to Corina.

"What?" She looks around. She's as nervous as me.

I don't know. We scramble down into some bushes and wait.

Minutes later, we see it.

"There!" I point back up at the road. It's not much bigger than a bumblebee, but it flies too straight for any bug. They're called dragonflies because of how they look, but nobody says that—we call them flying pigs.

She squints, then sees it. "Well, shit," Corina whispers. "Is it here for us?"

"Don't think the cops'd be using theirs to watch an empty park trail."

"Shit."

We hold still, careful to stay quiet as it flies past on the road. Moments later, Bicycle Man comes into view, walking slowly, watching the air in front of him where the flying pig's camera view is being projected.

"Fuck," I whisper without meaning to. "How's he here?"

Corina shakes her head, reaches for the scar on her arm where her patch was. "I don't know."

We go silent, holding perfectly still as he passes close to us. When he's past, we scoot deeper into the trees to hunker down until it's dark, when I move us to another place I know—a tight-knit grove of trees and bushes that has a hollow place in the middle. We called it the Den when we were kids—it's where we used to hang out. Nobody ever came here but us because it's up a steep hill that doesn't look like it has a trail.

All night long, we can hear the soft buzz of flying pigs as they circle around, looking for us. In the morning, as I'm looking for a place to go to the bathroom, I catch sight of the trail below us.

Bicycle Man's standing there, looking down the hill toward the grass.

I stay where I am and wait for him to leave, praying that Corina doesn't choose this moment to come looking for me.

He's following us, and I don't know how. He doesn't seem to be able to pinpoint us, but he's able to get a general location. It occurs to me that he might be using face-rec from public cameras, so he would have seen us coming into the park, but can't figure out exactly where we are. If that's the case, we're never going to be able to get clean away unless we stop him. I sit still, wait for him to leave, think about what to do. By the time he's gone and the air around us is quiet, it's been so long my legs have fallen asleep and my bladder feels like it's going to explode.

Corina and I come up with a plan. We wait for Bicycle Man to come back along the trail below us. I hear his music before I see him, and we brace ourselves. When he reaches the outlet of the coyote trail that leads to us, Corina makes a noise.

He stops, looks up to where we are, smiles, then starts up the hill, scrambling right past where I'm hiding.

He doesn't see me until it's too late. I kick his feet out from under him and he falls face-first into the dirt.

I bring up the concrete I've found. It's heavy, the size of a football.

I drop it on his head. It lands with a thud. His instrument jangles like broken strings and he makes a sound like a sigh, then he's quiet, his music no more than a faint reverb. We run to the road, where we meet the guy in the minivan. He was only going home to Highland Park, but I helped him want to drive us east.

On the way, I use his son's screen to send a message to the reporter:

> *Sarah,*
>
> *Tell my auntie that I love her and that she was right about Sabazios. He's working with the LOCUSTS!*
>
> *Tell everyone that Sabazios is trying to get us all to use Live-Tech because when it's connected to people it lets the Locusts know where to go.*
>
> *When everybody has it, they're going to all come at once and make us slaves and food.*
>
> *Jordan Castle is going to give a speech for MtLA where she's going to blow the cover off of everything and she's going to say that Sabazios and Live-Tech are the answer, but she's WRONG and you have to tell people. Jeffrey Sabazios is THE ENEMY!*

I don't know if she'll listen to me, but I have to try.

We ask the driver to drop us at the rest stop. It felt like a good place to get ourselves together.

To get cleaned up.

I get up off the toilet and go look for Corina. I hear her before I see her.

She's still scared. She's scared of going to jail. She's afraid of dying. She's still scared for me. I can hear it in her music.

The wind is whipping hard and my hood fills with air. I turn away from the wind, toward the mountains on the other side of the rest area.

They look familiar. They look like something I've seen before.

I turn to find Corina. I see her standing by herself near the tables. She's looking at the mountains, too.

I walk up to her. I approach her slowly so I don't scare her.

She looks at me. "There's no water."

"Not on this side," I say. I reach for her hand. She gives it to me. I lead her down to the building where the bathrooms are, where there's a map.

I point at it. I point at the big blue spot. "The Salton Sea," she reads.

I nod.

Fifty-Six

I OPEN MY EYES, STILL IN THE HOTEL ROOM IN LA. I KNOW WHAT I'M GOING to do, and the weight of it falls on me like concrete. I'm going to kill someone, and it's locked in. I can already feel my ability to make choices slip away. The formfitting glass prison descends.

Zombie Time.

Fifty-Seven

I'M STILL LOOKING AT THE REST-STOP MAP OF THE SALTON SEA WHEN I de-Zombie. The first thing I notice is the noise—the Jungle comes crashing back. To make sure, I take a deep breath, then jump up and down. I slap my face.

Corina looks at me. "What the hell are you *doing*?"

"I've been a Zombie," I tell her. "I self-witnessed back when we first got to LA."

"Why on earth would you do that?"

I don't answer for a minute because I really don't know what to say, but then: "I was scared, I guess. I wanted to know what would happen." I reach for her and pull her toward me. She comes, but she's just going along with it, which makes me feel even worse.

She pulls back and pushes me away, turns to face me. "That was idiotic!"

"No—"

"Yeah," she interrupts. "Yeah it was idiotic—you went to a future but you didn't know what future you were going to, did you? You didn't have any way of knowing that you weren't going to see a future where we die or where the Locusts and Sabazios and them get away with it." She brings her hands up in front of her. "You didn't even think of that, did you? Did you?" She claps the back of her hand with each word and it's all I can do not to flinch.

"It's not like that."

"Really?" She raises an eyebrow.

I want to argue, but I know she's right. I turn to look in another direction while I get myself under control. When I'm ready, I say, "We need to go to the Salton Sea."

I don't look to her, but from the corner of my eye I see her purse her lips and nod. "Get us a ride."

I do. A trucker who doesn't speak English. He gives us a ride and a few bucks—he doesn't have much. He also buys us lunch, which is cool. I don't really understand how I'm supposed to act around people I've rewritten. I end up saying thank you a lot.

Corina rides in silence. She just says, "I don't speak Spanish," and looks out the window.

The driver talks in Spanish and I pretend to understand more than I do because hearing him talk makes me feel closer to home than I've felt in a while. I smile some. I laugh when he laughs. But all I can think about is what a mess I've made of things.

We're on the road that runs against the east edge of the sea. I can feel the heat pushing in against the air-conditioning through the windows.

We're past the last field, the last turnoff, the last sign of civilization besides the road itself and the railroad tracks that run on the left side of it when Corina says, "Stop."

I look out her window.

It's the view from the picture.

The driver pulls over on the shoulder and we get out. He says something, waves, drives off.

It's as hot as I have ever felt it and the air smells like dead things. It's almost unbearable. Even so, the water's pretty—brilliant blue against the dead brown that's all around it.

"That way." Corina points.

I follow her down an old unpaved road that has other roads branching off it. They're spaced evenly, but there's nowhere for them to go. "What is this place?"

"How would I know?" she says. Still, she stops and looks around. "Maybe they thought people would want to live out here or something." She wrinkles her nose and wipes her forehead.

I laugh. So does she. A weight lifts.

We follow the road to the beach. Corina pulls the photo out of my pack. She studies it and then hands it to me.

In the picture, Cassandra and I are standing next to each other with our backs to the water. There are mounds of white sand all around us. I look down. I'm wearing the clothes I'm wearing now. I feel my hair. It's the same length as it is in the picture. I look up and Corina's looking at me. She's shaking her head slowly. "That's some shit."

I nod. We walk down the short hill to the beach.

The sand on the beach isn't sand, it's little tube shells. Millions of them. Billions. They're stacked two feet high in some places.

There are piles of dead fish, too, some fresh, some just skeletons. The smell makes me ill. The whole place feels as alien as the Locusts' planet I saw in the telescope. I find the place where I'm standing in the picture. I look out across the water and up at the mountains on the other side.

"Alex?" Corina says.

I turn around.

Someone's coming.

Fifty-Eight

WE STAND THERE ON THE HOT BEACH, SMELLING THE SMELL AND SWEATING. My mind is strangely still. There is no life nearby aside from us and together we sound empty like a cowboy's harmonica against a night campfire. "It's her, isn't it?" I ask Corina because I can't stand the waiting in silence.

"I expect so." She's nervous, and if it weren't so hot, I'd put my arm around her.

It feels like it takes forever for Cassandra to reach the small hill that leads down to the beach. Close up, she looks different than she did when I witnessed her—her hair is longer and it's curly, like an eighties rocker chick. She's wearing the same loose white tank top, black lace bra, and black jegging-style pants that she had in the picture. The same black Converse.

She stumbles a little bit coming down the hill. Neither of us makes any move to help her.

"Hey," she says, standing up. She looks Corina up and down and then turns to me and smiles. "You're just as cute as I knew you'd be."

I flash on an image of her from my witnessing, lifting the covers as she turned. My stomach tightens and I try to change my thoughts, but I can't. "Hey," I reply, wishing I was better at coming up with things to say.

She digs into her shirt and pulls out a little old-school camera. "Corina, right?"

"Yeah."

"I'm glad to meet you. Here," she says as she tosses the camera to Corina. Cassandra closes the distance between me and her. "Take our picture."

I feel her next to me. She's sweaty and she smells a little bad, even compared to the ground around us. Now that she's closer I can see that her shirt is dirty and so is her skin. It's been days since she's been in a shower. I look up at Corina and try to make a moment happen, but she's looking at the camera, not at me. My eye travels down to the thigh that's next to my leg. Cassandra's shirt doesn't come all the way to the waist and there's no sign of the big nasty scar I saw before.

"Okay." Corina lowers the camera. Cassandra moves over to her and I make a face, like *girl's crazy and stinky.* Corina smiles quickly and then turns to Cassandra, who's grabbing the camera from her. "Jesus—didn't anybody teach you not to grab?"

Cassandra doesn't react. She just takes the camera and holds out her hand. "The picture?"

Corina looks at her for a moment like she's thinking about beating her down, but then she sighs and slaps the wrinkled picture into Cassandra's hand.

Cassandra unfolds it and then turns to her camera. "Shit's weird," she says as she examines them both. "I can never get used to things like this. Did us getting the picture cause the picture to be taken or was the picture taken and then that caused everything else?" She pulls another sheet of paper out of her pocket and unfolds it. "Exactly the same." She looks over at me. "You got any answers, man?"

I don't even know what she's talking about. All I know is that she's holding a second picture that, from this distance, looks suspiciously like the one that I have. "That's the same picture?"

She rolls her eyes at me. "Yes, dipshit, it's the same picture. I got mine in a family photo album I found in my grandma's house—where'd you get yours?"

"Uh . . ." I stammer, which is embarrassing. "In a time capsule buried in my school's gym." I get myself together. "You didn't send it?"

She breathes out. Exasperated. "No," she says slowly. "I didn't send it."

"If you didn't send it, how'd you know to be here?" Corina asks, not bothering to keep the beef out of her voice.

"Because Sybil said to be."

"I'm supposed to find Sybil."

Cassandra looks at me. Her eyes steady. "You will." She shakes her head, shoves the pictures into her back pocket, and holds the camera up in the air like she's searching for reception, waits a minute, nods her head. "Stored in the cloud for whenever."

She brings the camera down and tucks it slowly into her bra, lifting up the fabric more than she needs to. She watches me while she does it and then winks. "C'mon," she says, turning around, "we got a lot of walking to do."

I turn to look at Corina. She won't look back at me. She waits a beat and then heads off after Cassandra, leaving me to take up the rear.

We follow her back up to the main road and turn south.

I can't see anything on the horizon—there's no town or even any buildings for as far as I can see.

I jog to catch up with Corina. "She's insane," I whisper.

Corina nods slightly.

"I don't know what's up with her."

She nods again.

"We don't have to go with her," I say. "I haven't seen this before. I'm not a Zombie here."

While I wait for Corina to say something, I pull off my hoodie and my shirt. I tie my hoodie around my waist and I turn my shirt into a turban that I put around my head.

I don't feel any less hot than I did when I was wearing them.

Corina slows a little, but then she picks up her speed again. "Yeah," she says. "Yeah, we do." And then: "We got nowhere else to go."

Fifty-Nine

CORINA AND I WALK TOGETHER BEHIND CASSANDRA. I REACH FOR HER HAND and she gives it to me. When Cassandra turns around, she sees us and she smiles. "Cute as pie, you two."

I don't think I've ever been this thirsty. I can tell from her music that Corina is feeling it as much as I do, but she's not willing to show it. No weakness from her. Not right now.

No weakness from me, either. My feet hurt like they're broken. It was stupid to take off my shirt because my shoulders are burning to a crisp.

It's getting dark by the time we reach a town. There's a mini-mart, but it looks like it's not in business anymore. Cassandra walks to it anyways and pushes the door.

The old man behind the counter is drinking from a forty-ounce bottle of Colt 45. He nods at us, but he's too busy watching the TV to pay us much mind.

"You don't have anything to eat?"

He doesn't take his eyes from the TV. "Just some waters 'n' those." He points to a display of beef jerky and snack cakes that look old enough for a museum.

"Thanks," I tell him, and follow Cassandra to the cooler, where there are water bottles. The cooler's broken, so the water's room temperature, but at least it's not a hundred and seven degrees.

Three beef jerkies, three snack cakes. Three bottles of water.

At the counter, ready to pay, I look up at the old-style wall-mounted TV screen to see what he's watching.

It's a news broadcast—one of the cable networks. There's a main anchor and a couple of windows off to the side.

One of them's got another person in it, talking, but it's the last window that stops me from doing anything. I recognize the person in it.

My heart starts to pound. It's Jordan.

She's standing at a podium with the MtLA logo behind her, set between two American flags. She's speaking and I know what she's saying because I helped her write the speech.

"Holy shit," I say to Corina. "She was my glide target." I turn to her and smile broadly. "I made this speech happen."

Corina is frozen in place. She doesn't look impressed or curious. She looks scared. Her music is quiet, uneven. "You saw this part?"

"Nah, I just did the—" But I don't get to finish the sentence because all of a sudden the little box with Jordan in it takes over the whole screen. A dark spot has appeared next to Jordan's podium, bigger than her—a shadow with nothing to cast it. It takes a moment for my eyes to focus on it, to see what it is, but even before it's clear, my stomach curls up and I want to be sick.

Locust. Jordan looks over. She's so small compared to it, delicate.

She's just a kid.

"No . . ." I don't even mean to say it. It just comes out. "No. No, this isn't . . ."

The Locust spreads its cape, revealing its arms and legs, which are almost impossible to tell from its body, but I know they're there.

"Run!" I shout it out loud.

"She don't," the counter guy says softly. "She just stands there."

I watch, as paralyzed as Jordan. She makes no move to get away from it as it moves toward her. She closes her eyes. It's hard to see what she's doing, but I know.

She's praying.

I can even read one of the words on her lips as she says it.

Abaddon.

The Locust's claw arm emerges, finds her neck. She doesn't even resist as it pulls her in toward itself, enfolding her in its cape.

"Jordan . . ." I'm nearly crying.

The camera is starting to shake and then suddenly there's movement from the left side of the screen—a guy has come up onstage. He's moving over to where the Locust has Jordan.

I know him, too, and as I watch him edge closer to where the beast has Jordan, Sabazios's plan becomes absolutely clear.

I know what's about to happen.

The guy onstage is Bicycle Man.

He's got Live-Tech.

The Locust seems to notice him approach, and instead of reaching for him, it glides back and away from him, dragging Jordan with him, only her feet visible beneath its cape.

The frame freezes and a circle appears around Bicycle Man's ear. It zooms in to show his pod. It's Live-Tech.

JEFFREY SABAZIOS'S LIVE-TECH CLAIMS TRUE? appears on the screen underneath, then fades. The screen zooms out, the action continues.

And it's clear that, just like with me, the Locust is pretending it doesn't want to be near the Live-Tech.

Everybody thinks it's afraid of it, but now that I know the truth it's hard for me to see how anybody can believe the lie.

Within moments, the Locust backs up against the wall behind the podium. The wall shimmers behind it.

It does something under its cape. Jordan's feet twitch. Her toes extend, flex in her shoes, then relax.

Blood drips down her exposed legs.

Her body drops.

The Locust backs into the wall and disappears and then Jordan's body is alone, bloody, collapsed on the ground.

She fell just like my mom did.

"Alex," Corina whispers. "We've got to go." She touches my shoulder, leaves her hand there. The sunburn under her fingers comes alive and the pain is searing, but I don't move away because I can't move at all.

"I killed her." But no one seems to hear me, so I say it again. "I killed her."

"No you didn't, Alex," Corina says. Her voice is almost too quiet for me to hear.

"I set her up." My voice is squeaky and high but I don't care, can't. "I made her do the speech. She wasn't going to, but I made her."

"You didn't kill her, Alex." Corina squeezes my shoulder, making me wince. She pushes against it, turning me to face her. "You didn't do this."

I shake my head, ready to tell her that she's wrong, but she puts up a finger, stops me.

"Sabazios made this happen, not you." Then: "Not me."

It takes me a moment. "You knew?"

She nods her head, then looks at the guy behind the counter, who's watching our conversation. "President Castle was my target. I was there when he got the news."

"That's some terrible shit," Cassandra says from behind me. "But one dead kid isn't the end of the world. The end of the world is the end of the world, and if we don't get a move on, it's gonna be here before you know it." She points at the counter guy, who's wide-eyed. "Give the guy the money."

I hand the guy the wad of ones in my hand. "Don't believe the bullshit about Live-Tech," I tell him. "It's a lie. It's how they target you—that guy on the screen wasn't saved by it, he used it to bring that Locust to her."

He doesn't say anything back. I don't ask for change.

When we leave the store, I offer Cassandra one of the beef jerkies.

"I don't eat meat," she tells me, grabbing the three snack cakes out of my hands instead.

She doesn't say thanks.

"Jesus," I mutter.

"Your friend's a piece of work," Corina says.

It's hard to focus on what's around me because my head's filled with Jordan. Not big moments, just memories. Her excitement at the prospect of waffles.

The way she thought it was funny that everybody took her dad so seriously.

How much she wanted to help.

How real she was with Will.

Will. He was there. He watched that happen in real time.

I convinced her that this was the time for her to be Abigail. We were both sure that what she was doing was right.

She thought it was God's will.

It's full dark when we pass a painted mountain. I can just make out the colors on it. It's covered with colors and designs, rising hundreds of feet off the road. I slow to look at it, but Cassandra doesn't and neither does Corina. She's too tired.

While I'm looking at it, there's a flash of light and then, a few seconds later, an explosion. It's followed by several more—big hot red round balls of fire rise off the ground in the distance. It sounds like war. "What the hell is that?!" I yell.

I can hear Corina's concern over the explosion, but it doesn't show through in her face. She's too tired.

Cassandra shrugs. "Artillery." I wait for more explanation. None comes.

I jump with every explosion. They get louder as we get closer. When Cassandra turns, the bombs are falling so close I think I can feel their wind.

Everything on this walk has been strange, but the place she takes us is like a scene from the end of the world. We're walking on a desert road across an open field, and there are fires burning all around us. I sense hundreds of people nearby, but there are no lights beside the fires. There's no cars, but I can see the outlines of camper shells.

We're walking up Fury Road, but all the insanity around me is overwhelmed by Jordan in my mind. She's everywhere and I can't escape.

Eventually, Cassandra stops in front of the nose of a yellow school bus that's rising out of the ground like a dolphin jumping from the water. It's sitting at a thirty-degree angle. Everything beyond the fifth row of seats is underground. "We're home."

Sixty

CASSANDRA FIDDLES WITH SOMETHING IN THE WHEEL WELL OF THE BUS AND moments later, the door swings open. It's a step up and my legs are so tired, I'm not even sure I can do it. Cassandra leaps up like it's not a problem. Corina and I look at each other in the dark. She rolls her eyes. I smile.

There's another generator humming nearby. I look back at the fires behind us just as another artillery shell lands on the range nearby, lighting us up like a Halloween haunted house.

"C'mon," Cassandra calls from inside. "You're letting the cold out."

I brace myself for the pain from my legs and step up inside. I turn to offer my hand to Corina. She takes it. I pull her up, and when she's in, I turn around to see where we are.

The driver's seat is where it's supposed to be and there's even a steering wheel and a gearshift, but after that, the whole thing has been hollowed out. Where the seats should be, there's a stairway that goes down. It's not fancy or even well-built, but Cassandra is already halfway down and it holds her just fine. There's light at the bottom, too, bright enough to silhouette Cassandra and cast shadows up at the surface.

Corina and I look at each other again. She shrugs. I shrug. I start down the stairs and she follows me. She's close enough behind me that I can feel her heat.

The light at the bottom of the stairs is coming from a single bare light bulb hanging from a socket attached to an extension cord. The room is hollowed out of the ground and there are boards holding up the dirt around us like an old-school mineshaft. While I'm studying it, there's an artillery burst up above. The boards rattle. Dirt and dust fall from the ceiling.

Cassandra ducks down into a tunnel that's no bigger than the frame of a car door. She crawls on her hands and knees and Corina and I follow suit. My knees are killing me and I'm dragging my backpack behind me like a stuffed toy. I can hear Corina trailing me, struggling and cursing under her breath.

Just when I think we're never going to stop crawling, the tunnel gets wide again and we're at the base of another staircase, this one going up. There's another bare bulb lighting the way. If I wasn't afraid for my life I think this would probably seem really cool, but right now it just makes me feel like I'm in the hands of amateurs. "Quite a setup," I mutter.

"You could do better?" Cassandra replies. "The bus is the only way in." She points up. "This is the safest place on the planet when it comes to keeping out Gentry and their minions."

"Can't they find us from underneath? Have some witness glide us?" Corina replies. "How is this"—she gestures at the dirt—"gonna keep them from finding us?"

Just as I'm about to pile on with Corina's question, I notice the silence. I can only hear Corina, Cassandra, and two others. The rest of the Jungle is silent . . .

"We're shielded," I tell her. "The Jungle is blocked here." I'm already beginning to feel lonely.

Corina nods slowly, still cautious.

"What jungle?" Cassandra asks.

I hate explaining the Jungle. "The noise," I start. "The loud stuff that comes up from down deep . . ." I'm sounding like a crazy person. "It's like music."

But Cassandra nods and continues up the stairs as I'm trailing off. "Oh, the Syllogos," she replies as she climbs.

"The Silly Juice?" It's what my Voice said. For the first time in forever it feels like there are answers around me, but I don't know how to ask the questions.

She stops again, turns around. *"Sil-low-joss."* She pronounces it carefully with big wide lip movement.

"What is it, though?"

She shrugs, turns back up the stairs. "It's like time and choices and stuff—it's where the Live-Tech gets access to our minds, too. Ask Sybil. She knows. She's the one who gave us the doohickey that blocks that shit so we can't be tracked in here." Then she's up out of view.

Corina and me stand at the base of the ladder for a moment. I don't know if I'm more tired from the hike and the heat or wired by the idea that I might get some answers.

I look at Corina. "We have a doohickey," she mutters. "Blocks that shit."

"The see-low-joos . . ." I whisper back to her. "Blocked that shit." For the first time since we got to LA, it feels like we're in tune.

The stairs come up inside what looks like a trailer. It's got fake wood paneling and bad carpet. There's furniture, but it's ratty and generally makes me not want to sit even though I'm totally wiped from the walk.

At first the windows look blacked out, but then I understand. The trailer's buried.

We're still underground.

We're not alone, either. The two other instruments I sensed from down below are sitting on the couch, and they aren't making it look any prettier.

They both look like gutter punks. The guy smiles up at me. "Hey," he says. "You're the picture guy."

I nod. "Yeah."

He laughs and so does the girl. "Weird. I've been looking at a picture of you looking pretty much like you do right now for nearly a year." He looks over my shoulder and his expression changes to a big round O of surprise. "Oh my God." He jumps up. "Corina?!"

I hear Corina laugh behind me. "You look like *hell*, boy!" she says as she pushes past me and hugs him in a big dancing lovefest. He swings her around, which is hard because the place is so narrow. They manage not to break anything.

When he puts her down, Corina looks at me, thrilled. "This is Sal! He was with us at the compound."

"It was before his time," Sal says. Then he sticks out his hand to me. "Salvador Pena."

I shake hands with him. "Alex Mata."

He turns to the girl who's still sitting on the couch. "This is Erica. Erica, this is Corina, and *this* is Alex Mata, the guy we've all been waiting for."

"You've been waiting for me?"

Sal smiles. "Help us, Alex Mata, you're our only hope!"

Cassandra rolls her eyes. Corina giggles.

My ears start to burn.

He holds up his hands like he's surrendering. "I don't mean anything by it, man—it's just that you're supposed to be like our Obi-Wan Kenobi." He lowers his hands and looks at my eyes. "You're supposed to be a Jedi of the Syllogos . . ."

"What are you talking about?"

Sal looks confused by my question, which doesn't help me feel better. He tries again. "Well, it's kinda like the Force from Star Wars, except it's real and you can't use it to move stuff around or make people do things."

"Except that supposedly you have such amazing access to it that you can do all sorts of stuff that the rest of us can't even imagine," Erica adds.

I don't know these people and I'm not ready to tell them that, as a matter of fact, I *can* make people do things. "Who says?"

He gestures at Cassandra. "She does." He shrugs. "But that doesn't mean as much as the other person who keeps saying it."

"Who?"

"Sybil," he says. "She says you're our best hope to save the planet."

"Don't swell his head." Cassandra ignores my question and so do the others.

I flush.

"You all need some rest," Sal says. "Erica and me bunk in the back room and Cassandra's usually on the couch here, but we got some bedrolls we can toss out on the floor for you."

I nod, not sure what else to do. "Alright . . ."

When we're settled, the lights go out and the darkness is entirely complete and there's nothing left between me and the vision of Jordan's broken body at the foot of the Locust.

Nothing between me and my time in her mind. By the time I was done gliding her, I felt more at home there than I do in my own mind. Jordan wasn't afraid to let someone know who she was, to show them what she felt.

I spent my life afraid of people seeing who I was, how I feel, and Jordan . . .

Jordan was stronger than me.

Jordan should have been the Jedi.

"Alex?" Corina is pressed up next to me even though it's hot and stuffy in here—there's no room to be separated.

"Yeah?" Even though my thoughts are making me miserable, having them interrupted irritates me.

"It really isn't your fault."

I don't respond as fast as I think she wants me to. I can feel her turning around to try and look at me, but it's too dark for her to see me crying.

She puts her arms around me. She kisses my cheek, then the other one, then my lips. "It's really not, and Jordan wouldn't want us to give up. She'd want us to finish the job. We're gonna get the assholes who're doing this to us, alright?"

I nod, my face brushing hers as I do.

When I can talk again, I tell her, "Yeah. We will." When I say it, it feels like a promise.

It takes me a long time to fall asleep because I don't know how I'm going to keep it.

Sixty-One

"I DON'T REMEMBER YOU FROM THE COMPOUND," CORINA SAYS TO ERICA over breakfast. We're eating LIFE cereal, stale, out of the box. Sal and Erica are sharing a pack of Hostess donuts. Cassandra isn't eating. She's sitting on the stairs to the tunnel, ignoring us.

"I was at the other one," Erica says.

I'm startled. "There's more than one?"

Erica nods. She points a donut at Cassandra. "I was with her."

"Who were your targets?"

Erica looks at Cassandra, who gets up off the stairs and walks to the fridge. "We witnessed witnesses," she says as she pulls out a bottle of beer.

"*You* were in *my* head?" Corina sounds ready to explode.

Cassandra shakes her head. "You weren't mine."

"Who was?" I ask, before Corina can respond.

Cassandra knocks the lid off her beer on the counter before she answers. "I had dozens, man." She tips the bottle and chases down a handful of cereal. "They go through a shit-ton of witnesses."

"There were only five of us at the compound." I'm honestly confused.

Erica points at me with her donut. "There were five of you *now*. But there have been five or so there for years. This has been going on awhile, and witnesses are only good for a few targets before they stop being useful." She takes a bite. "Gotta keep fresh meat coming or . . ."

We all ponder that for a moment. Then Corina breaks the silence. "So, the evil Gentry are about to unleash living terror on Earth and this is, like, all there is of the counter-revolution?"

Cassandra takes another swig from the bottle. "Yup." She sets her beer on the counter.

"So why do you think we got a chance at all?"

"Sybil," she says.

"You keep saying that name." Corina shakes her head. "Who's Sybil?"

"There's a rebel Gentry," Erica offers, rolling her eyes at how cryptic the other two are being. "Sybil's working with it against the rest, trying to save us."

"I was told I need to meet her," I say.

Cassandra's beer stops halfway to her mouth. "Who told you that?"

"You did." I tell her about my self-glide.

She nods when I tell her. "Yeah. I had one of those, too. Sybil arranged those for us."

"Why?" Corina doesn't even bother to try to keep the skepticism out of her voice. "Why is a Gentry trying to save us?"

"Because it wants to." Cassandra drains the rest of her beer before going on. "Sybil says this other Gentry wants us to live."

Corina asks: "Why?"

"Because it does."

Corina sets the cereal box down and shakes her head. "You're a weirdo."

Cassandra shrugs. "You don't have to take my word for it. Sybil's coming through this afternoon and you two are going to meet her."

Sixty-Two

I FOLLOW CORINA THROUGH THE TUNNEL. THE JUNGLE CRASHES IN WITH THE heat and the sunlight as soon as I start up the exit stairs, and it takes all my concentration to get it back in the music drawers. We gather outside the school-bus door.

During the daylight, the whole area looks different. There's no artillery falling—which is better—and I can see that there's actually a big hill between us and the range with a huge barbed-wire fence at the top of it.

But if coming in after dark was a nightmare, leaving during the day shows us a landscape filled with despair—shacks, busted RVs, lean-tos, and people that look just as broken as the places they live.

"What is this place?" I ask Erica as we walk.

"Slab City," she says.

It looks a lot like a homeless encampment.

"Everybody here's just trying to escape," Erica continues.

"Escape what?"

Erica smiles up at me. "Everything that's not Slab City."

We walk down the road past the painted mountain and down the long slow hill to the town with the gas station, but instead of going all the way, we stop at the railroad tracks that run through town.

"This way," Cassandra tells us, and begins to walk down the tracks.

We follow her to an abandoned train station. It looks like it hasn't seen a train for a hundred years. It's a small brick building, but the bricks are loose and there's graffiti covering it inside and out.

It doesn't seem like a meeting place. "Here?"

"Yeah." Cassandra sits down in the shade of the building and leans against the wall. "She'll be by."

I look at Corina, who looks at Sal, who nods and sits down, too.

I sit next to Corina and lean against her. Even though it's hot out, touching her feels good. She leans into me and puts her head on my shoulder and it suddenly feels like Los Angeles never happened. "I love you," I whisper in her ear.

She looks up at me and smiles. "I love you, too."

I close my eyes and listen. Everything is good.

I'm nearly asleep when I feel the ground begin to vibrate. There's a train coming. I crane my neck to look down the track. A big freight engine is moving our way. It blows its horn when the engineer sees us with our legs out near the tracks, so we pull them back and wait.

Sal puts a quarter on the track.

The train is long, with two engines in front, and it's moving so slowly that I'm sure I could hop it if I wanted to. I'm just about to say that to Corina when I catch movement in one of the cars.

Somebody's hanging off the side. He's joined by someone else. They jump off the train twenty feet down the track from us, both landing on their feet. The bigger one—a guy—jogs after the train, catching up to the car they jumped from. He reaches in and retrieves two big packs, which he hefts onto a shoulder.

He looks at us, sees Cassandra, and smiles.

"Hey, Brett," she yells.

"Hey," he replies, though I can only read his lips because the sound is drowned out by the train. He starts walking toward us. The girl jogs to catch up with him.

The train passes at the same time they reach us. Brett is white, head shaved, wearing a cabbie hat. The two of them watch the train recede into the distance before turning their attention to us.

"This is Alex," Cassandra says, pointing at me.

"Hey. I'm Brett." He extends a hand toward me and I take it. He's muscular, covered in tattoos. He turns to the woman who's standing behind him. "This is Sybil."

Up close, Sybil is strange-looking. She's small and thin, and looks older than my mom, because her face is messy with wrinkles and sunspots. She wears guys' pants and a big shirt that make her look like a little boy. Her hair is under a baseball cap that she's wearing backward.

Stranger than her face and clothes, though, is her music. Instead of being a messy tangle of notes like everybody else, Sybil reads like a single harmonic, varying only in intensity.

It's inhuman.

"Hey," I manage to say, trying hard to keep my reaction to myself. "I'm Alex."

Sybil smiles. Her teeth are perfect and straight. "Hey. Nice to meet ya." She sets her bag down and tugs open the ties, then digs around inside for a water bottle, which she opens and drinks. When she's done, she spends a minute scrutinizing me. I start to get uncomfortable. "Yeah." She reaches out for me. "Let's go talk."

"Okay, sure." I go to follow her. She catches Brett's eye and shakes her head.

"Guess I'm staying with y'all," he says, dropping his bag at his feet.

Sybil walks us across the tracks and back toward town. I have so many questions, I don't even know where to begin, so I just start asking them. "What are you? Why me?" I don't wait for answers. "Why me? What's the Jungle? What am I supposed to do?" She doesn't say anything. "What are you? Who's my Voice?" She doesn't even give any indication that she hears me.

She slows to a stop and pulls a pack of cigarettes from her pocket. It's a short pack of unfiltered Lucky Strikes, nearly completely crunched. She fishes in it for a cigarette and tweezes one out with her thumb and forefinger. It comes out bent and wrinkled, but she seems to think it's fine, since she sticks it in her mouth and lights up.

I'm getting so agitated that the sheet music is starting to fly out of the drawers, crowding my brain with sound. "Answer me!" Then I shake my head, close my eyes, and try to get it under control.

"Breathe in, Alex," she says. "You hear it like I do. The Syllogos is loud, filled with life. You can't be its master, but you can be its partner." She reaches for my arm. Her hand is cool and dry against my skin, her grip startlingly strong. "Breathe," she commands.

And as she speaks, I feel her whole self. She's not human. "What are you?"

"You know what I am," she says. "Listen. In the Syllogos."

I dive. Underneath, that single harmonic I hear is a wire-thin filament, vibrating but barely audible. I follow the thread into the distance to where it starts, and I am overwhelmed. A massive rope of life. A cacophony of jumbled notes plucked in rhythms beyond my comprehension, playing melodies I can't begin to understand.

She is Gentry. She reaches for me in the Syllogos. I don't feel fear.

Her music overwhelms me. It drowns out the rest of the Jungle along with my own scattered mind, and I surrender.

Sybil's music washes through me, filling every crack in my soul. She gives me an image: The scene I remembered on my self-witness. I watch the woman hollowed out, sucked up by Locusts again.

And then I return. I'm just me again and the Jungle is back to the sound of crashing waves coming from distant drawers.

Sybil has read me, knows me now like I knew Corina, but even more. I feel dirty, like I need to wash her out, scrub away the residue she's left on my mind.

But I'm unwashable, and completely naked to her.

"You don't work for a Gentry—you *are* Gentry."

She nods. "The Syllogos, Alex. The *Silly Juice*, as your Voice calls it. You call it the Jungle, which I like because it is like a Jungle, so tangled and full of life. It's not something that intrudes. It's not a sickness."

"I don't . . ."

"But you will." She grins. "You're not crazy—you're not flawed or broken." She shakes her head, steps up to me, puts her hand on my arm. I stare at her, waiting for her to say something that doesn't sound like it's coming from a hippie.

"The Syllogos? The sounds it makes? What you're hearing is the sound of reality. This?" She takes her hand from me and waves it at everything around us. "This place where we live is a projection—a way for us to make sense of things, but it's not *why* we're here. We're here to create the truth, and seen time is the only truth. Once something is done, there is a truth even if people may argue about it. There is a thing that happened and it happened in a particular way." She looks at me. "You've traveled back along your path. You've seen that truth, witnessed things that you could not change because they were fixed and true, and you also know what fixes things, binds them, collapses them."

"Witnessing."

She nods. "Witnessing is our reason for existing, Alex—all of us. All life. To make choices, to see and experience, to remember. We fix time in place. Time created life to transform itself from possibility to actuality. We are the stuff that tames time, binds it in place, gives it structure."

"So why do you need us as witnesses?"

She looks back at the abandoned station, then up at me before stepping up onto a rail, balancing carefully. Her voice is quiet. "There is no *us*, Alex. Just you. Corina, Cassandra, the others are here because of you. *For* you." She taps my chest with a finger. "You are the one we need."

I back away from her, stepping backward over the other rail so there's space between us. "What do you mean, me? What makes me different?"

She sighs, takes a drag. "Pete," she says through a cloud of smoke before turning to face me. "He was eight years older than you."

Hearing her say Pete's name puts me back on edge. "What does my brother have to do with anything?"

"You asked why you." She looks at her cigarette and then at me. "It has to do with your brother."

"How?" I push the breath through the word to make it loud enough to hear.

"Your mom used to tell you about how hard it was to have you, right? How there wasn't supposed to be an eight-year gap. Your mom was pregnant three times between Pete and you." She spits a fleck of tobacco off her lip. "None of them came to term, so she got help."

I dip my chin just a little so she'll know I hear what she's telling me. Out of the corner of my eye, I watch her inspect her cigarette, take another drag. "They went to a clinic where I helped create you, Alex. I *built* you at the clinic, modified your DNA to make it possible for you to be the witness I needed, and then seeded you back into your mom. The Gentry manage to enhance most of the witnesses in one way or another—fertility clinics, altered booster shots—there are a lot of ways, but you were special. All witnesses are designed for witnessing, but you . . ." She exhales more smoke and smiles at me, the tenderness and warmth from her should feel motherly, but it's wrong because it's coming from her, which just makes it feel weird and threatening. "Your genes were already ripe for witnessing, so with you I pushed the limits to see how far a human can go . . . and you are *glorious*!"

She drops her cigarette and looks past me, back at the train station where the others are. She rubs her temple. "You have no idea how powerful you are, Alex." She bends down and picks at the gravel between the railroad ties, returning with a small handful. "When you rewrite people, you change *how* they choose—you control how time is shaped and fixed, which means that you control truth itself." She smiles again. The big maternal loving smile that scares me. "I made you like this, Alex, and the other Gentry don't know what you can do. I stole you from them because I *do* know and I need you."

"Need me . . ."

"To stop things. To stop the Gentry. To save your species."

"But you are Gentry."

"Of them and against them." She kicks at the rail.

I wait for her to say more. She doesn't. I press her. "Why?"

She shrugs. Looks down toward where the others are waiting. "Love."

"Love?" She sounds dumb.

She looks up at me suddenly. "Don't discount love, Alex. Love is enough. It has been for you, and it is for me."

I look back at Corina. Then: "So what can I do? I'm just me. Tell me how to stop the Gentry."

She bends over, picks up a handful of gravel, and lets it filter through her fingers before she looks up at me. "Destroy the compound. Destroy Jeffrey Sabazios. Without the futures stored at the compound, and without Sabazios, the Gentry plan will fail."

"Destroy the futures . . ." My voice cracks, and it feels like my heart freezes mid-beat. I breathe, step back, and my hands come up like I'm going to ward her off with a spell. "You want me to kill the witnesses?"

She looks at me. Her face twists into something, maybe

sadness. "You can't save them, Alex. Their minds are the end of everything, and as long as they live, what they've seen is locked in. They need to be destroyed."

"Fuck that." I spit on the ground between us and turn to walk back to the station.

"There are choices to make," she calls out.

I turn back, study her face. She looks repulsive to me now, and I want to get away. "I am *not* killing anybody else."

She shrugs. "You'll do what you do. But if you want to finish this—if you want to be like Abigail—you'll have to do things that seem wrong to most people. Abigail disobeyed her husband. Abigail stole. Abigail betrayed. Jordan broke protocols, betrayed national security, disobeyed directions from the *president*. She wasn't afraid to do what she needed to do, Alex. She wasn't afraid."

Her talking about Jordan and Abigail is too much. They're private. They're my memories. "Fuck you." It comes out as a screech. "This isn't about fear, this is about you wanting me to kill my friends. That's not what Jordan did. That's not what Abigail did, and *you* don't get to talk to me about Jordan or Abigail."

But she just points at me. "You know that most of the future you need to stop is locked in the minds of the witnesses." She shakes her finger. "If you want to save everybody else, then they have to die."

In my mind, all I can see is the faces that she's talking about. Paul and Calvin and Maddie and Billy. Damon.

The end of the world is in their minds, but I'm not going to kill them. "No." It comes out strong, confident, and I start to feel confident because of it. "I'll find another way."

She shakes her head slowly. "The Oracle device has seen

the whole sweep of possibilities, Alex. There is no future for Earth if they live." She reaches for my arm again, but I pull away before she can grab it. "Saving them now only dooms them later . . . in a month, maybe two, they'll die and so will everyone else—die as slaves, as food for Gentry children."

"No," I say again, this time without the confidence. Then I turn and walk away.

"Alex," she calls. "Please."

I hesitate, but I don't stop walking again until I'm back at the depot.

"So?" Corina asks me when I get back.

I take a deep breath and let it out. Everybody's watching me, waiting for me to say something, but I don't want to talk. Talking means telling them what Sybil said. Kill the witnesses to save the world.

I shake my head, look at the ground.

"What'd she say?"

I look down the tracks. Sybil is still walking toward us, moving slow.

"She said some shit."

"What shit?"

If I'm going to save the world, I have to kill my friends.

I don't want to tell them that. I need help.

I dive.

WHAT DO I DO?

She comes to me quickly and clearly, my Voice rising above the Jungle, deafening:

"You've already done it, Plugz. Can't run from it, cuz you've done it."

DONE WHAT?!

"What you're gonna do, Plugzie. You've already done what you're gonna do."

Then she disappears. I wait a moment longer for her to come back, but she doesn't say anything more and I still don't know anything. I surface, refocusing on the six sets of eyes that are waiting on me to say something. I've already done what I'm going to do, she said, and there's only one thing that makes sense.

"The plan," I say finally, "is to stop Sabazios."

"How?" Corina asks.

"I'm going back to Seattle."

Sybil looks away, then down.

Cassandra watches Sybil's reaction and then turns to me. "What about the witnesses?"

"They aren't . . ." But I don't know what to say after that. I don't know how to say what she's asked me to do, and I know for a fact that I cannot do it.

"Alex?" Corina looks at me uncertainly. "What about the rest of them?"

Sybil looks at me. I look away. In my mind, I hear Jordan's thoughts about kings who weren't up to the task—too weak to do what they needed to do. I step back from them, out of the circle. I won't be a weak king. "Sybil says they need to die." But even before I finish saying it, I can hear my own music grow overwhelmed with doubt.

Erica and Sal look at Cassandra. Cassandra looks at Corina. Corina looks at Sybil. "What's he talking about, Sybil?"

Sybil shrugs and gestures at Brett, who retrieves a pack of

cigarettes from his pocket and hands her one. She holds up a finger for us to wait while she lights it and blows out a cloud. "Alex knows what to do." She examines her cigarette.

"You told him to kill all the witnesses?" Corina asks.

"He'll do what he needs to do." Then Sybil just shrugs and reaches behind herself. She pulls at the denim that covers her butt. "Whatever he does, though, you'll need something." She bends down and unties her bag, reaches in and produces a crinkly metallic envelope.

"Here," she says, handing the envelope to Corina. "Use it. Or don't."

Corina doesn't reach out for the envelope. "Just me? Why do *I* need something? What about them?"

"It's for you."

"What is it?"

"It's a patch. Wear it, or don't. Either way, if you go back to Seattle with Alex, you'll die. If you stay here, you can help."

Corina doesn't take the patch immediately. She stares at Sybil's hand instead. She looks at me, then at Sal, who nods, just slightly. She reaches out. "If I wear this, I don't die though, right?"

Sybil looks up at her. She smiles, but she looks tired. "That patch will help you live forever." Then she looks at me. "I have something for you, too, Alex. Something you'll need to do what you're going to do."

I step back from the circle as she bends down to open her bag again. She comes up with a silver foil package that looks a bit like the patch she just gave Corina. "What is it?" I ask.

"The tool you'll need." She holds it out to me. "Keep it

in the waistband of your pants, against the right hip. You'll know when it's time to use it."

I stare at it, but don't reach for it.

Cassandra grabs it from Sybil's hand and shoves it at me. "For fuck's sake, Plugzer, it's not a wedding ring, just take it."

My Voice steps in to tell me about this: *"KEEP THE GIFT, BOY. FOLLOW THOSE INSTRUCTIONS—YOU'RE GONNA NEED THEM."*

I take it from her.

We leave Sybil and Brett at the abandoned station, where they'll wait for the next freight, and walk slowly back up the hill to Slab City. Erica and Sal are in the front, Corina behind them, then Cassandra.

I'm far behind them, glad that nobody is trying to talk to me, but not about anything else.

This time as we pass the painted mountain, I stop. Corina must've have been listening to my footsteps because she stops, too. She turns around and looks at me, her face a question.

"I'll meet you back at the bus," I say. "I just need to think."

"You want company?" she asks.

"No. Not right now."

She nods. "They're asking a lot of you, Alex." She edges back toward me, slowly, carefully, like she's afraid of me. "Too much."

I shake my head. "I . . ."

She reaches for my hand. I give it to her. "If you can't do it . . ." She looks at the mountain, takes a breath. "If you can't do it, you need to know that I love you, whatever you do." Squeezes my hand. "I'm with you forever, Alex Mata, whether it's old age or Locusts or something in between that gets us."

Corina. The despair I felt in my host, whenever that will be, floods back in, collapsing me. I bend forward, landing my head on her shoulder, and she pulls me in. She's not here forever, because sometime in the future, sometime before we're old, sometime soon, it'll just be me.

Not her. Not us.

"I love you." I can't make the words sound out loud. I say it again, pull her against me. "I love you."

She pulls back just a little, kisses me. Her skin is salty from sweat, hot against my lips. "Take your time to think," she tells me, "then do what your heart and soul tell you to do, not anybody else."

"'K." I stand on the road and watch her walk fast to catch up with the others.

She looks back at me, and I wave and try and freeze the moment in time forever.

When they're gone, I walk up the short road to the painted mountain, look at the broken-down trucks and cars that've been painted to match it. There are a dozen of them scattered around the base of the mountain. There're messages on them, written in white paint against the colors, about love and Jesus. I read the ones that are easy, skip the long ones, and then head to the sign that marks the beginning of the path up the mountain.

I climb it, thinking that when I get to the top I'll be able to stop and think about what I'm supposed to do, but before I'm halfway up, I know.

I know what Abigail would do.

I know what Jordan would do.

I know what I want to do, but I don't know if I can.

I sit at the top for a little while anyway, looking out at things and feeling feelings. It's growing dark when I climb back down and I head back to the school bus, watching shadows from the mountains around us grow and take over the desert.

Sixty-Three

"YOU CAN GLIDE WITHOUT A PATCH?" SAL IS SKEPTICAL.

I shrug. "Yeah."

"And you can control people?" Erica asks.

"Yeah."

"Prove it," Cassandra says from the stairs, where she's sitting. "Show them—we'll go outside."

I shake my head. I'm sitting on the coffee table with my back to her, so she can't see me. "I can do it here. It's probably easier without all the other people around here in the background." I look for Corina, but she's in the bedroom. She's been in there since before I came back. "Okay," I say and lie back on the table, closing my eyes.

The three of them are obvious in the closed-off Jungle of the bus. There's nothing else to hide them. They're loud and clear right in front of me. Their music is on the top of the pile in the drawer. I think about what to do for a demonstration. Something too small and they won't be able to tell if it was me or not. Something to big and I could lose friends . . .

I go for juvenile. When the music is written, I open my eyes and sit up.

"So?" Sal asks.

"In just a moment, you're going to pick your nose and

eat it," I tell him. Erica looks at me and then at him. I hear Cassandra getting up off the stairs behind me.

"It isn't gonna happen," Sal tells me. He's smiling like it's a joke.

I shrug and point at his hand, which is already rising slowly to his nose.

Erica gasps. "What are you *doing*?"

Sal's hand finishes its slow approach to his nose and his finger extends up into the nostril. He's not looking at us; his eyes are focused on his own hand. He's still smiling like he was when he said it wasn't going to happen.

He pulls out a decent-sized booger, examines it on his fingertip, and then pops it in his mouth.

Erica explodes. "Holy shit!" She points at him as he's swallowing. "He did it! He did it!" She freezes, turns to me. "*You* did it."

Sal suddenly returns to life. He makes a face, gags, then runs to the kitchenette, pushing me out of his way so he can spit into the sink. "You mind-slaved me," he says between spits. "I was like, *there's no way*, and then I felt myself think, *I should pick my nose and eat it*, even though I remembered that I'd just freakin' told you all that it would never happen." He makes a face and spits again. "Augh!"

"How did you do that?" Cassandra asks. "Show me."

I try to explain.

I tell them about the music, the guitars, and how I find the sheet music. It doesn't make any sense to them.

There's movement at the bedroom door. I turn around. Corina raises her chin at me and crosses from the bedroom to the couch. She sits down next to Erica in the seat Sal left behind, not asking or anything, but nobody says a thing about it. They're all too nervous.

She closes her eyes.

I'm just about to ask her what's up, but then I can't because my head's too full.

I feel her in every sense. I smell her smells, and feel her touches. Our music is joined and momentarily we are playing the same notes, and it's louder than anything else in existence. I feel her changing my melody, my intensity. I feel myself smile.

Then I remember that I'm hungry, too, and I know what I want to eat.

My hand comes up to my face, my finger, my nose.

My mouth.

"What're you doing?" I hear Sal say it, but he's a million miles away. He's outside Corina and me.

Corina recedes. It's like a tide has gone out. I'm not underwater with her anymore, but she's left traces of herself all over me. I reach out for her and she's there. We're connected again.

"What the hell?" Erica's question brings both Corina and me back to the moment.

"I can do what he does now," Corina says. She rolls up her sleeve to show us a starfish-shaped thing on her arm. "Sybil's patch." Then: "This one's different, though. Lots of stuff I can do."

Sixty-Four

THERE'S GOT TO BE ANOTHER WAY. CORINA FEELS IT TO ME, BUT SHE ALSO feels something else. *There's no other way.* She's torn and her conflict fights in my head just like my own.

"Come with me." I feel the question as deeply as I can.

Anxiety pulses. Fear.

Then actual words: *"Sybil said I would die if I did."*

She sounds exactly like my Voice, words skywritten with clouds on the inside of my ears. My heart pounds.

"We need a plan." Cassandra can't hear the conversation between Corina and me. She doesn't know she's interrupting, but I'm annoyed anyway.

"I need to destroy the compound and kill Sabazios," I say.

"How, brainiac?" Cassandra rolls her eyes. "You're gonna go in and overpower the compound with your death grip and bad breath?"

Sal speaks up. "Getting in won't be that hard—he'll rewrite people beforehand. If he can make me pick my nose, he can get a guard to open a door and tell him where to go."

Corina brightens immediately, warm to the idea. "Sal's right—it can't be harder than making strangers give you their credit cards." Hearing her voice outside my head clutters the memory of how she sounds inside. Even with the clutter, though, I have trouble not thinking the thought that's bubbling just below the surface.

I force myself to focus on the issue at hand. We talk it through. When I get there, I dive. I find the guards and make them want to be helpful to us. Corina will work with me in the Syllogos.

Once we're inside, we'll locate Sabazios and the witnesses.

"How're you going to . . . ?" Erica doesn't finish the question. Nobody wants to finish the question.

You've already done it. "I don't know yet, but Sybil gave me this thing." I pull out the foil package and hold it up. "So I think I'll know what to do when the time comes."

"And I'll be watching over things from here to help out," Corina adds. "So he's not going to be relying just on his own brains." She taps her head. "He'll have mine, too."

"And that's going to do it? That'll be the end of it if you . . . ?" Erica sits forward. "I mean, when you're done we can all go home? It'll be safe?" There's something hidden in her words, only found in the way she says them. She doesn't think I'm coming back.

I look at Corina, who shrugs. Cassandra starts to nod her head slowly. "I think so."

"That's what Sybil said. Without the compound and without Sabazios, their plan fails."

"It makes sense," Sal says. "We were locking in Live-Tech, so without it the Locusts won't be able to invade fast enough to win."

"Especially if we get the word out."

"Word's out, dude." Cassandra waves her hand. "Watching

Jordan Castle get bug-bit on national TV pretty much did the job—people are going to be ready to fight if they need to."

"Now we just need them to get the message about Live-Tech," Corina adds. "How do we do that?"

"I have someone," I tell them. "Someone who can get the word out." I tell them about my emails with the reporter in LA.

"You're gonna need evidence," Sal says.

"I'll get some," I promise.

"So that's it, then? The plan?" Corina asks. "I stay here and glide. Alex goes there and glides. We use Sybil's thingie to do whatever it does, and then Alex grabs some evidence of some sort on his way out?" She sounds skeptical.

"Pretty much."

"And we're really going to be okay with . . ." Corina swirls her hand in the air. She's thinking about Paul, about Maddie, others I never met. "We're okay with killing them? The witnesses?"

Nobody says anything. I try to catch Sal's eye, but he looks away. So does Erica.

So does Corina.

"We're gonna have to, aren't we?" Cassandra says. "If we don't, they're all going to die in a few months anyways, along with everyone else." Even she doesn't sound as sure as her words.

Corina's still looking down, but she nods. Sal is holding Erica's hand. He's looking at her knuckles.

"I think we have to," I say eventually, hiding my doubt from everybody but Corina.

"Alex?" A word. Her voice in my head chases away everything else. Its sound is . . .

"Yeah, that makes sense." Sal blows out a breath. "But, fuck . . ."

We're all quiet for a minute, then Erica speaks up. "Somebody's got to go with Alex. He can't go under without somebody nearby to watch his back."

We all look at each other. I look at Sal. I can hear his fear. I hear Erica, more afraid of Sal going than of going herself. Then Corina's sounds grow dark and weird.

She knows who it's going to be, and she doesn't like it.

The words come through clearly, like she's speaking in my head. Like she's my Voice, with the same nearly knowable overtones: *"Jesus, not her."*

I start to shake my head, to tell her that she's wrong, but I know she's right. Cassandra is the only one who doesn't mind going. She's excited.

Again, Corina's voice in my head. Again, she sounds exactly . . .

Corina catches my eye. I'm working hard to keep myself blank, but I feel Corina notice that I'm not okay.

"Yeah," Cassandra says with a shrug. "I'll go."

I nod. I sense Sal's and Erica's relief. For the first time, I wish Corina were not in my mind. I can't let myself think with her inside.

And I cannot acknowledge what I now know for a fact: Corina and my Voice are the same. My Voice is *everywhere*, in the Syllogos.

She's untethered.

Untethered witnesses are dead witnesses.

Sixty-Five

"TALK TO ME, ALEX." I CAN'T KEEP A SECRET FROM CORINA. SHE KNOWS there's something seriously wrong and she knows it's about her. She knows I'm scared.

We're standing on the stairs that go up to the school bus exit, because it's the only place we could have privacy where I won't get overwhelmed by guitars if I get emotional. When. This is going to be emotional.

I don't say anything to her. I look away and shake my head.

Her annoyance is loud. "Don't you get quiet on me, Plugzie." She's poking around in my mind. She reaches for me, grabbing my shoulder. "What do you know that you don't want me to know?"

"I don't want to tell you." It comes out as a whisper.

"I know that. Why not?"

"Because . . ." I shrug under her grip.

"Because . . . ?"

Argh. "I figured out who my Voice is."

She looks at me and waits.

"She has a name," I say finally. "She told me not to tell you and now I think I know why."

She raises her eyebrows, waiting for me. "Well?"

I blow out a breath. "She calls herself Sly." I watch Corina's face change as I say it. I hear her grow afraid. "Are you Sly?"

She doesn't say anything, but I hear the answer.

"She's you, isn't she?" While I say the words, the implications press in on me. Something happens to her. All the ways I explained her absence in my self-witness fall apart in the face of the simple fact that Corina will become a hollow disembodied voice, untethered in the Syllogos.

Her body's going to die.

She screws up her face. "Yeah. That's what my stepdad used to call me, because my middle name's Sylvia. How is that possible? You've been hearing that voice since before I met you, and I've been here with you when you've heard it." She shakes her head. "Definitely was not me."

"I don't know how, or why, or anything." I look her in the eye, which is hard because I can feel what she feels. "I just know that when you spoke in my head in the trailer just now, I recognized your voice." I wait because I can feel her digesting it. "It's you, Corina."

"How the hell . . ." But she believes me.

She reaches for my hand. "Look, I don't know how to tell you this, but if your voice is me, then whatever untethers me up there is gonna happen no matter what because your voice is locked in—you've heard her—so there's nothing we can do to stop that from happening. But I'll tell you what."

I look up at her.

"It doesn't have to have anything to do with what's happening now. I could untether forty years from now for all we know."

I flash on my time into the bedroom with Cassandra, and I freeze, waiting for Corina to ask about what I just thought.

She doesn't.

"Maybe you're right," I say finally. I hope the relief I feel from her not understanding my memory feels like the relief I would feel if I believed her.

"I *am* right," she tells me. "I would worry more about you than me." Then: "You're going to try and rescue them, aren't you?"

I look down, but there's no sense in hiding it. "I promised Paul I'd come back for him . . ." She puts her hand on my cheek. "I've got to try."

She doesn't say anything, just strokes my eyebrow with her finger. Then: "You're going to do what you do and I love you." She squints. "But remember that this isn't about you anymore—what you do is about all of us now."

"Yeah." But I'm thinking less about the world and more about her.

"I still hear you worrying about me—you need to stop." She pushes me up against the wall. "You're the one walking into the devil's playground, and we have no proof at all that *any* of your cute self survives this shit." The words are playful, but she's not feeling it. She's feeling something else.

"I don't want to be away from you," I whisper as she presses against me.

She just shakes her head softly and brushes her lips against mine. "Me neither." She pulls herself closer to me. "Where are the others?"

We both feel them. They're absorbed in other things in the trailer.

In the time we've known each other, we can count the

collective moments we've had with privacy and safety in hours and minutes, not days. Her body is warm against mine, her breasts are outlined against my chest. I can feel her breathe.

I can feel her want. It mixes with my own into a nearly paralyzing web of need.

"I think there's something else," she says quietly, her words slow and deliberate in stark contrast to our minds, "that we need to do before you go."

The thought, the feeling, is almost too much for me. I focus on my breathing, adjusting myself away from her so the pressure doesn't lead to early disaster. "Here? Now? Are you sure?"

She's sure. I know she's sure.

We don't use words. We undress and press ourselves close together. The warmth of her skin is amazing. With eyes closed, our bodies merge as our minds and hearts are joined in the Syllogos. As I push inside her, I feel her jabs of pain, feel her wince. She feels my pleasure. I know not to move too much, too soon, for both of our sakes. We stay still, locked together. I focus on the feel of her thighs against me, the smell of her hair.

Slowly she begins to move. I do, too. We are entangled, body and mind, together and complete.

And then it's over.

It's hard for me not to ask her how it was even though I know. I was there.

We hold each other and I feel us both wishing together that we would be together tomorrow.

But tomorrow I'll be on the road.

Sixty-Six

WE TEST CORINA'S REACH WITH SOME OF THE SQUATTERS IN SLAB CITY. She has an easier time finding people in the Syllogos than I do. She's able to zero in quickly on whoever she wants. It's not music for her. She's got stacks of books like a library. She can read them and she can write them.

Cassandra says she's got books and I've got guitars because it's what we each think about. If Cassandra was connected like us, she'd probably see a liquor store.

Corina's more powerful than me. I feel better knowing that if I really screw this up, there'll be somebody else who can save the Earth. She's a better choice anyway because she's smarter.

The plan is for Corina to wait for us to get to Seattle. Once we get there, she, Erica, and Sal will leave the trailer so she can get to the Syllogos and then we'll rewrite the guards. Cassandra and me will go in and find Sabazios.

The goodbyes are awkward.

"Later, man," I say to Sal.

"Yeah." He sticks out his hand. "When this is all over, maybe I'll see you back in LA."

I smile, try not to look like I'm about to cry. "I want that more than anything, dude. My Tía still thinks I'm a murderer . . ." I take his hand and we start to shake but he pulls me in for a man hug. "Be safe," I say when we let go.

"You too."

Erica hugs me lightly, barely touching my back. I return the hug the same way. "Don't die," she tells me.

"I won't. Take care of Corina."

She nods.

"Later, boys and girls," Cassandra says as she descends the stairs.

Sal and Erica watch me and Corina, waiting to see what happens.

"Bye, Plugzer," she tries to say, but her voice isn't working. Now that I'm looking at her, I'm totally overwhelmed by our feelings. "When you're back, maybe I can meet your aunt? Your friends and stuff? Then my mom?"

"Yeah." I reach for her and she comes to me, leaning into my chest and pulling herself tight against me. "My auntie will love you." I don't know if it's true, but it's such a beautiful thought that I don't want to ever lose it.

"I love you," I whisper.

"I know," she whispers back. "I love you, too."

"I'll be back soon," I say.

She nods her head. "You will."

I reach into my pack and pull out my notebook. "Can you hold this for me?" I push it at her and she puts her hand on it. "Keep it safe?"

She smiles. Warmth. "Yeah."

But it doesn't feel like I've made my point. "I'm not leaving you."

"Just come back." She squeezes me once more and pushes back. We kiss.

"Oh, for fuck's sake, *Plugzer*, are you coming or not?"

Sixty-Seven

THE ROAD IS EASY. WE MAKE IT TO SEATTLE IN TWO DAYS WITH OUR POCKETS full of money. I use the trip to practice writing music while I'm awake. I can do it, but I end up in a sort of trance where I'm only halfway aware of what I'm doing.

Cassandra spends the trip talking endlessly.

She acts like she's all in for erasing the witnesses, but I can hear what she feels, so I know better. She's almost as conflicted as me. I don't tell her that I have other plans—that's between me and Corina.

A helpful lady gave us $17,000 and we use it to buy a car. Cassandra wants to get a used Corvette that can go zero to sixty in 2.3 seconds, make four hundred miles per charge, and has a ten-minute charge capability, but I convince her to get a Cherokee instead.

"It's bigger," I explain, "and it can off-road if we need to." I don't mention that we might need the extra room.

Cassandra drives it over the bridge from Seattle. It takes us a bit to find the right neighborhood, but when we do, we park the Jeep across the street from where Corina and me ran into the park.

It was less than a month ago, but it feels like years have passed. School is still in session at the high school where we stole the car.

"You ready?" Cassandra asks me.

"Yeah." I lean back so I can get comfortable. I need to find the guards. I can hear the noise from the students at the school; the local Jungle is filled with their jangling. The younger people are, the louder they are. I have to work at keeping them from drowning out the people I'm trying to find. It's hard because I don't know the guards. I've never met them and I've never heard them, so I search instead for Richard, hoping that I can move outward from him, reading the music of those closest to him.

I search, but I can't find him. Paul is missing, too. I find Maddie. There are instruments around her and I sort them as best I can. There are two others that are still jangly and loud, probably Billy Williams and another witness. I mute them and listen to the sounds close to them.

There are several others in the immediate area around the compound. They aren't complicated sounds—the music sounds bored, like people waiting for something to happen and thinking about things that have already happened or that will happen. I open the drawer and search for the sheet music that matches what I hear. I find it. I read the next bar:

The man is color-blind. Alan. Alan Garcia. His world is black and white but with brown and green tinges to things. Even so, I know what's red and what's green and yellow and purple. Everything is bright. I'm sitting at a bank of security monitors. Driveway, Long Hall, entry hall, pool deck, gym, kitchen, commons, witness hallway, dorm hallway. Nobody's on any of them at the moment. The kids—he doesn't know exactly what Sabazios is doing with a pack of teenagers, but he's never seen anything inappropriate—*are all in the non-monitored rooms, just like they are for much of every day.*

My back hurts. I'm hungry.

I'm bored.

The others? *I put the question in his head to see if he'll answer it.*

Sabazios's private detail is somewhere in the main house—separate team. Gordon and Nick are at their stations, Nick at the gate and Gordon at the hilltop.

I pull out of his mind and set about rewriting his tune. I do the same thing I did to the lady who gave us the seventeen grand—I write Cassandra and me into his music.

I find Nick and Gordon and do the same.

I listen for the others that Alan said were in the main house, but I can't sort them, so instead I mute all the instruments at the compound. There are things besides music here. Undertones. Notes that have been held for so long that they've faded into the background of the song. They're the sound that I imagine a witness in a frozen loop would make.

And I hear something else. Something that sounds like Sybil.

There's a Gentry here.

I surface.

"Well?" Cassandra asks, looking up from her book.

"I rewrote the guards I could find."

"Is Sabazios here?"

I hesitate a moment before I nod. The single harmonic, like Sybil. "Yeah. I'm pretty sure he is."

"Richard?"

"Couldn't find him."

"Bishop?"

"Gone." I say it quietly, like he might hear me.

"Okay." She shoves her book into her bag and tosses it onto the backseat. "You message your boo yet?"

Corina's not available. She's still inside the trailer. I can't feel her. "Not yet. She's not outside."

"So we wait." Cassandra retrieves her bag from the backseat and rummages through it. I watch her, waiting to see what she's getting. A cigarette. She lights it and cracks the window.

Annoying.

We stare out our respective windows.

"I saw something about us on my self-glide," she says finally.

My heart sinks. "Don't tell me. I don't want to know."

"Relax, *Plugzer*. I didn't see anybody die or anything, but I did see something that I've had in my head ever since."

"Don't tell me."

"We end up together, Alex."

I don't say anything because it takes everything I've got to keep from losing my temper completely. I can feel her watching me.

"You *knew*!" she says suddenly. "You already knew!" She shrieks and pushes me. "You little dog—you've been keeping secrets!"

"It's not going to happen!" I'm yelling, but I can't help it. "I love Corina, and you and me? We're *never* going to be a thing, so just forget it."

"It's seen time, Alex. That shit's fixed in stone. You and me are gonna be together someday and there's nothing either one of us can do about it." She makes bug eyes. "We're *destined* for each other."

And then Corina's there. I can feel her and she's the best feeling I've ever had. I let her flood in and my anger slips away.

"She's out." I open the door without looking at Cassandra. "Let's go."

IT'S TIME.

"Corina." Both her forms are in my mind right now, fully present, filling me and I cannot tell them apart. *"I don't want you to die."* I say it to one of them, but I don't know which one.

"SEEN TIME." Then she's quiet. Then: *"IS THE ONLY TRUTH."*

"DON'T BE SCARED, BOY. I LOVE YOU, PLUGZER," they say together, a chorus, and I know this is near the end for her.

"NO!"

"DO WHAT YOU'VE ALREADY DONE, PLUGZ. IT'S THE ONLY WAY."

And then one of them is gone and the other one's all business.

"Time to go, Plugzer," Corina thinks to me, and I know it's the live one, waiting for us to move down in Slab City.

I close the Jeep door and put Sybil's little package where she told me.

Sixty-Eight

WE JUST WALK UP TO THE GATE, MY HEAD A SWIRL OF ANXIETY, SADNESS, and nerves. It opens before we stop walking and we just continue in.

"Hey, Alex!" somebody calls from somewhere off the driveway, scaring the hell out of me.

I hunker and turn to find the Voice.

A muscleman in a guard uniform is waving at us from the doorway of a small guard shack hidden in the underbrush. Nick.

Cassandra looks at me. I give her a little shrug and rise up slowly. "Hey, Nick." I wave.

He raises his chin at us and steps back inside.

"That's just weird," Cassandra whispers.

I don't disagree.

The whole area along the side of the driveway is brilliant green and in bloom. There're more flowers than I've ever seen. It's hard to remember that we're about to do something horribly dangerous and stupid when there are such pretty things all over.

"It's really nice here," Cassandra whispers.

I nod.

The circle driveway comes into view. The car is in its usual place and I briefly wonder who the new lead witness is since Corina left.

"Where are we going?" Cassandra asks.

I slow to a stop and cast down into the Syllogos, searching for the faint sustained notes. They're close, but it's hard to tell where, because geography and the Syllogos don't match up exactly. I think they're in front of us, toward the main house, but I'm not sure.

"Sabazios first," I tell her. "I think he's—" But I'm cut short when the door to the main house swings open. Cassandra and I both tense to run.

"How can I help?" a guard calls to us. I hone in on his music. Alan Garcia.

"I need to see Sabazios," I tell him.

He hesitates. "I can't arrange that—I don't even have access."

I search his mind. He's not lying. "Then take me to the place where they take the witnesses when they're no longer useful."

"What are witnesses?" He's honestly confused.

"From the guest quarters in the back."

"The kids?" He steps out the doorway toward us.

Cassandra rolls her eyes. "Yes, the kids."

Alan's eyes look sad. He's desperate to help us.

I grab his arm. "Just open the door to the Long Hall, okay?"

"Sure," Alan replies. I can feel his relief. He's going to be helpful. He leads us to the door to the Long Hall and uses his hand to open it. "This way." He ushers us in.

"Alex, something's wrong." Corina's worry invades.

I search the Syllogos around me. I hear nothing that worries me. There's nobody excited or angry nearby. Nobody but Alan and Nick even seem to have any idea we're here.

"Everything's cool." I send back as much relaxed vibe as

I can manage, but it doesn't comfort her. Her nervousness makes me edgy.

"You first," I tell Alan. "Go fast and get the far door open onto the deck."

He nods and jogs down the hallway. Cassandra and I follow him, both working hard to keep the psychic wallpaper from decorating the hallway with our lousy happy memories. "What now?" Cassandra whispers as we get to the deck door.

"Sabazios is in Richard's office." Corina's voice is clear in my head. She's scared.

"What's wrong?" I can feel her, but she's not focused on me. Something else has her attention. Something bad. *"Corina?!"*

"Just be patient," I tell Cassandra. I listen again. All the music is calm, regular. There's nothing I can find to worry about. I look at Alan. "Open the gym doors for us."

"Corina?!" Silence. Silence and fear. She's so afraid I'm finding it hard to breathe as we walk quickly across the patio to the stairway door.

When she answers, she's so loud and present, I stumble when she starts talking. *"It's our time, scared boy . . ."* And then she's silent.

It's not alive Corina, it's my Voice.

"CORINA!!?"

No response. Just fear.

"What's wrong with you?" Cassandra asks in a low whisper.

I'm shaking. I can barely walk. "Back at the trailer," I whisper. "Something bad is happening and I can't get Corina to talk to me."

Alan opens the door for us.

"You go first," Cassandra tells him.

He shakes his head. "It'll be better for me to secure the door behind you."

She looks at me, but has no instructions. I'm barely holding it together. "Just go," I tell her. I can't stand still any longer or I'm going to vomit.

She walks into the gym.

As I'm walking past Alan onto the floor, everything changes. There's a charge of energy, something I can't control. It makes me fall onto my knees. I feel like I'm exploding inside, my organs are popping and my heart has blown up to twenty times its normal size and it's breaking my ribs with each beat.

Cassandra asks me what's wrong and I hear somebody making noise.

It's me. I'm screaming.

"RUN AWAY!" Corina's voice is so loud that it hurts my mind. The words pound against my eyes. I press my hands against them to keep them from falling out.

"CORINA!!!!" I yell it as loud as I can, inside and out.

"IT'S A TRAP SABAZIOS IS READY FOR YOU! RUN AWAY RUN AWAY!"

And then I'm being pulled under. Corina's taking me to her. I'm looking through her eyes and what I see is horrendous.

The sky is bright and it's hot. We're lying down on a blanket that's rough under our backs. There are stones underneath it that Corina no longer feels but I'm now aware of. I see the school bus above me. We're right outside the door.

We can't move because we're underneath in the Syllogos. We're watching instead. Someone is standing over us. A man.

Bicycle Man. It doesn't look like my hitting him with the rock did any damage at all.

Sal is nearby. I can see him, but he's not making any sound. Blood pools around him. He's dead. Erica is next to him. She's bleeding out. A single soft note, fading.

I try to help Corina get up, but we can't, not unless we break the connection.

LET ME GO! I tell her. YOU CAN FIGHT IF YOU LET ME GO.

"I'm scared."

YOU'VE GOT TO FIGHT! I plead, watching Bicycle Man step closer and kneel down, pulling the blade up above his head, ready to bring it down into Corina.

The blade starts its descent . . .

Then I'm back in the doorway at Sabazios's compound. Corina's with me in my head. *"Alex, I'm scared."*

Then she's gone.

I'm all alone.

There's nothing. There's no music. There's nothing at all. I can't hear Corina and I can't hear Cassandra or Alan, who's next to me. The Jungle is gone.

I'm completely cut off.

I close my eyes, reach out for Corina, but it's like I'm in an empty room. There's nothing but silence.

Someone's blocked the Syllogos.

I turn toward the door, but it's already closed. "Open the door!" I yell to Alan.

He holds out his hand to the door, but nothing happens. He looks at me apologetically.

"What the hell?" Cassandra's behind me.

"It was a trap—they're all dead."

"Who's dead?"

"Welcome back, Alex." Sabazios's voice is smooth and familiar. It's the voice of death himself.

Cassandra and I turn around together, pressed against each other for support. I feel naked without the Jungle. Empty without Corina. Naked and blind. He's standing at the door to Richard's office, looking relaxed, like there's nothing wrong in the world.

The world around me fades to a pinpoint around his face. I don't even feel the floor under my feet.

He doesn't react to my approach, but there's something in his hand. I duck, but he gets me with it. I feel it stick to my . . .

Sixty-Nine

NECK.

Everything's different. I'm not in the gym, I'm in a chair in a small room with white walls. I try to stand up, but I can't move my arms or legs. I look down and there doesn't seem to be anything wrong with them.

I'm just paralyzed.

I try to look around, but I can't even move my head. I can feel a small weight on the back of my neck, though, where Sabazios hit me with the Live-Tech thing. It must still be there.

The silence is killing me. There's nothing inside or out. The Jungle is gone. There's no noise at all. There's no hum from air-conditioning or noises from outside. There's no voices or movement from anywhere else vibrating through the floor.

My ears hurt from the silence.

I open my mouth to speak. I can't. I can breathe, but I can't use my vocal cords. I try clicking my tongue. I can't.

I cannot make any sound. I cannot hear any sound.

I cannot move.

And I cannot get the last moments of Corina's life out of my head. I see Bicycle Man over her with the knife. I see the knife go up and I know what happens next. The image starts again. Over and over. I can't stop it. I can't shake my head.

All I can do is sit still and see it.

The light in the room disappears, leaving me in blackness.

I have to pee. I try and hold it, but I can't—it just leaks out and there's nothing I can do to stop it.

The dark is dark. The silence.

Is silent.

Corina is murdered again.

The Dark.

I have screwed up in so many ways. They would all be alive if it wasn't for me.

The Earth is going to be destroyed. Because of me.

Corina is dead. Because of me.

Because of me.

Because of me.

My fault.

I should have stayed scared.

The Dark is dark.

Dark.

Silent.

Then a sudden flash of brilliant white light comes from everywhere in the room. It blinds me, and at the same time there's a noise that nearly breaks my eardrums—a single whoop from the loudest car alarm in the universe.

Then it's dark again.

Then it's quiet again.

My eyes are seeing stars.

My ears are ringing.

I can't tell dark from light and I can't tell silence from noise.

I can't tell anything. I don't know anything except that it's all my fault.

Seventy

I'VE BEEN IN HERE FOR HOURS. DAYS. THE LIGHT AND NOISE HAVE COME again and gone again more than once. A hundred times. A thousand. More than. I haven't slept.

When he begins to talk to me, I don't know for sure that he's talking or who it is. I'm not even sure that I'm hearing anything. I could be crazy.

"Why did you run?" he asks. "We're saving the Earth and you ran away."

Sabazios? "You're going to destroy the Earth." I'm not sure if I've said it aloud or not.

The lights come on. I squint against them, but they're not the bright bright lights. I open my eyes. I look down at myself and I feel sick. I'm still in the chair, but my pants are dry again, stiff. I feel like I want to vomit, but I haven't eaten or drunk anything since I've been here. I have nothing inside.

"Sabazios?" I ask. Even if it is him, even though he's the one who has destroyed everything, the one who killed Corina, my parents, Sal, Erica, probably Paul and Cassandra, too, I want to hear his voice again.

Any voice.

"Yes, Alex," he says. It's coming from everywhere, above, below, in front, behind, left, right. Surround sound. Like God. "I'm here."

"You're going to destroy the Earth," I say, but suddenly it doesn't seem like it could be true.

"Who told you that?" he asks. He sounds hurt, sad.

"It's true," I say, but I'm not so sure.

"It's not true, Alex," he says, "and if you're going to accuse me of things like that, I don't think I want to talk with you."

"No! Don't go!" I need him to talk with me. Without him, there's nothing but silence.

"I'm not going to destroy the Earth," he tells me. "Do you believe me?"

"Yes," I say. I do believe him. He's here. He's someone. I remember the rest of it, but somehow I can't seem to make it important to me. All that matters is his voice and not being alone.

"Who told you that I was going to destroy the Earth?" he asks again.

I don't remember. I try. I want to tell him. I want him to be happy with me, but I don't remember. It was a long time ago. It was before I left the compound.

"Alex?" he prompts me. "Who told you?"

And then I remember. It was me. The moment comes back. I remember being in bed with Cassandra. I remember it all. The person who told me was me, but it hasn't happened yet.

And it's a witnessed future, which means I can't die here.

I'm going to leave this room. Cassandra is alive and she's going to leave this compound. Later, a while from now, she and I will be convinced enough that the Gentry are evil that I'm going to sidetrack my own witnessing to warn myself.

"I'm trying!" I tell him. "I'm trying to remember, but I can't think. I don't know anything at all." I let the panic

I've been trying to keep under wraps come out. I don't have a plan yet, but I know I'm going to get out of this. I just need to change the situation so I can figure out what to do. "Can I have some water?"

"You can have water when you tell me, Alex," he replies.

"I don't want to tell you," I say.

"Why not?"

"Because you'll hurt him."

"Hurt who?"

"I need water."

"Tell me who, Alex."

Here goes nothing: "It was Richard!" I yell. I sell it hard.

There's a pause. Then: "Richard told you that I was going to destroy the world?"

"Yes!" I cry. "Yes—Richard told me. He came to me the day before you called me to your office when I ran. I thought for sure that you knew about it and that was why you'd called me in. I needed to get out of there before Bishop saw it with the probe. The probe—that probe is . . ."

"I don't believe you, Alex."

"It's true. It's true. If you look in my mind you can see it."

"I can't look in your mind, Alex," he whispers. "That's why I needed you in the first place. I'll have to use the probe. Are you ready for me to use the probe? It won't hurt if you just let it work."

"Can I have something to drink first? And eat? And can I get clean?"

He doesn't reply at first. Then: "Of course."

There's a noise behind me. I can't turn around to see it, but I feel something tug at my arms. They're brought behind me and I hear the metal before I feel the cuffs. There's pressure on my neck near where the Live-Tech is attached, and then a jolt of electricity through me that makes me shudder.

I can move again.

"Stand up," someone says behind me.

I do. I'm weak. Everything hurts. Everything is stiff.

"Turn around," he says.

I do. I don't recognize him. Another guard. Not Alan, Nick, or Gordon.

He shoves me through the door in front of him.

Seventy-One

THE GUARD TAKES ME DOWN A HALLWAY AND THROUGH A DOOR INTO ANOTHER corridor, where he stops. "In there."

I nod and step inside, but stop. "The cuffs?"

He steps behind me, unlocks them. I wonder if I can take him. I wonder if I can get him down and run, but I don't know where I'd go.

He closes the door behind me.

It's a small apartment. It's got a little kitchen, a bathroom, and a sleeping area. In total, it's the size of the bedroom in the trailer at Slab City, so I can barely move. There's a pile of clothes on the bed and a cat carrier in the kitchen.

Clean first. Then eat.

Seventy-Two

WHEN I'M READY, I KNOCK AND THE GUARD OPENS THE DOOR.

He leads me farther down the hallway and inside an elevator. He hasn't cuffed me again, so I debate whether to make a move or not, but I still don't know where I am.

He steps in after me and the door closes. I feel movement, but I can't tell if it's up or down. He didn't press any buttons. When the doors open, things look different.

Familiar.

We're in the Long Hall, just across from Bishop's office.

The wall across from us slides up, revealing the office door.

Sabazios is behind the desk. "Come in, please." He motions me toward one of the two leather chairs facing him. "Thanks, Jason," he says. "Please wait in the hall."

The guard nods and steps back out of the room. The door closes behind him.

"Sit?"

I do.

He sits, too, leans forward. "Do you feel better, Alex?"

I nod. It's hard to be friendly. It takes everything I have to act like I'm still as broken as I felt when I first heard his voice. A moment from Jordan's birthday party flashes in my mind: her laughing at something Melissa said, feeling empty inside.

I smile. "I do, sir. Thank you." I look him in the eye as I say it. "Mr. Sabazios?"

"Jeff, please."

"Jeff, I'm sorry I tried to hit you."

He laughs. "Don't worry about it, Alex." He sits back. "You were under a lot of stress. You thought you'd just gotten some very bad news."

"Sal? Erica? Corina? They're not really dead?"

He shakes his head, chuckling. "Nooooo. We don't kill people, Alex—we're trying to save the world. They were stunned so we could retrieve them." He gestures at the compound behind me with his chin. "They're here."

I almost believe him. I want to believe him so badly, but he's lying. I saw them: Sal, dead in a pool of blood, Erica collapsed, fading to silence. I want to reach across the desk and kill him. I want him to die. I want to end him, but instead I swallow it, grateful to be cut off from the Syllogos and therefore unreadable. I make my eyes go wide. "Really?!" I sit up, ready to stand. "When can I see them?"

He shakes his head, still smiling, but more serious now. "Hold on a moment, Alex. You'll see them as soon as our business here is done, but there are things we need to discuss." He spreads his hands on the desk in front of him. "You've made a pretty serious accusation about my friend Richard. Did you mean what you said?"

"Yes, sir. He came to me the day before we talked in here last time." I look him in the eye. "He said that he couldn't let what happened to the others happen to me and Corina and that if we didn't get out, we would be killed, either immediately if we weren't important, or we would be frozen until our futures came to pass and then we'd be killed."

His eyes go wide like he's shocked and amused while I tell him. By the time I'm done, we're both laughing a little bit because it's such a ridiculous story. "He actually said this to you?"

"Yes, sir." I think about it for a second. I shrug. "That's why I resisted the probe, I guess. I didn't want to get Richard in trouble."

He nods while I'm talking. I can't tell if we're both playing games, or if he believes me and I'm playing a game, or if he's playing a bigger game than me and stringing me along. It's confusing and exhausting. Part of me wants to say screw it, and just out the whole deal so we can get it over with.

Sabazios taps a spot on his desk. "Richard, can you join us in my office, please?"

I know I should have seen this coming, but it had honestly not occurred to me that he'd call Richard in. I cringe involuntarily, but then remember: Richard knew. He knew what was happening and said nothing, did nothing.

Nabal.

"He'll be here in a second, Alex, and we'll get to the bottom of this so you can go back to work." He sighs. "I just don't understand why Richard would do something like this."

Richard's eyes brighten when he sees me. "Alex!" He breaks into a big smile and hurries over to me. I stand up a little because it seems right and he grabs me in a big hug. "I was sure you were gone forever!" He pushes me back and looks at me like we're family.

"Yeah." Even if he's Nabal, I feel horrible. He's going to find out in about thirty seconds that I used him in a lie.

"So, Richard," Sabazios says, when we're both seated

across from him. "Alex and I have been having a conversation and your name came up."

"Really?" Richard asks, looking mildly pleased.

"Yes." He leans forward. "Richard, you recall when Alex ran away, it was shortly after he and I had met in here, and during that conversation, he overpowered poor Mr. Bishop so he could escape the compound?"

"Is Mr. Bishop okay?" I try to sound hopeful.

Sabazios smiles kindly at me. "Mr. Bishop is fine," he lies, "but he did decide to pursue a less stressful line of work after that incident." He holds up a hand when he sees my face fall a little. "Not entirely because of you, Alex—it had been a long time in coming."

Richard turns to me. "That whole thing, dude, that was completely not like you—what happened?"

I brace myself. "You happened, Richard. You know exactly why I freaked out."

He looks confused. "Excuse me?"

I roll my eyes like an eighth-grade girl.

"Did you have a conversation with Alex the day previous to that?" Sabazios asks.

He just looks more confused. "I don't . . ." He shakes his head. "Nothing out of the ordinary . . . Why?"

I look at Sabazios and he looks at me. It seems like we're both waiting for the other to lay it out. I don't think he's playing with me.

I don't know exactly what will be in store for Richard if he isn't cleared by the probe, but it won't be good, and I don't think he'll come out the other side alive.

I'm about to kill another person, after I swore I wouldn't. I feel sick.

"Are you saying you did not tell Alex that he was going to be killed if he stayed?"

Richard's eyes widen. He turns to look at me and I force myself to return his stare. "Alex?"

It's Nabal or me. "You saying I made this shit up?" I make my eyes hard. "Tell him the truth."

He shakes his head back and forth. He's scared. "Hey, man. Why—?"

"Calvin? Marcus?" I spit the names like they're poison. "You told me what happened to them—you told me that they were put in stasis if they saw something really important, until after it happened and then you all killed them. You said it was about to happen to me." I lean into it like I'm about to see red and lose it. He's still shaking his head. "Really? You don't know what I'm talking about?"

"Richard?" Sabazios asks. "Do you have anything to say?"

Richard looks up at the ceiling, and then down at the floor. He moves his foot slightly so it rests just on top of mine. I start to move it out of the way, but he presses down—not hard enough to hurt, but hard enough so that I know he's doing it on purpose. He sighs and looks back at Sabazios. "It was only a matter of time, Jeff."

It takes me a moment to process what I just heard. It takes Sabazios a moment, too. "So it's true, then?"

"It's true," Richard says. He turns to me. "I told you not to come back."

Game changed. I don't understand anything that's happening

right now, but Corina must have rewritten him before she died. I shrug and shake my head. "I told Paul I was coming back."

"Paul's in stasis," he says.

"What are you doing, Richard?" Sabazios asks, standing up from his desk.

"Richard?" I start, but he presses down hard on my foot to shut me up.

"I can't do this anymore, Jeff," Richard says. "These kids matter. Alex matters. So did Sly."

It was her! Even though she can't hear me, I think a silent thank-you to Corina. She's given me a fighting chance, but I can't take long.

Sabazios sighs. "Alright, then." He pulls a Live-Tech something from somewhere. He raises his arm to throw it at Richard.

I move before I think. I launch myself at Richard, knocking him to the floor, and the Live-Tech flies over both of us.

I scramble off Richard and reach for the small leathery thing that Sabazios threw, but I stop before I touch it. I need to find something to grab it with so it doesn't end up attached to me. Richard sees what I'm doing and tosses me something.

"Use this," he says. I grab what he's thrown.

It's his wallet. I'm momentarily confused, but then I see that it's a bifold and I can use it like tongs. I reach for the Live-Tech with the wallet, gripping it between the folds of leather, but I'm too late. Sabazios is already on top of me.

He pins me down. He's stronger than I imagined a man could be. His fingers are around my arm, pushing it down onto the ground, and I can't move it. I can't turn around to see, either, because he's keeping me still with his legs. I squirm and fight as hard as I can, but it's not enough. His other hand comes down around my neck. I feel his fingers close around my throat.

And then he's not on top of me anymore. Richard has him down on the ground nearby. I grab the Live-Tech with the wallet. I don't want to take the time to stand up, so I roll over to where they're fighting. Richard's initial attack has failed, and Sabazios is scissoring him. I slap the Live-Tech onto Sabazios's neck.

Nothing happens.

I don't wait. I get to my feet and level the hardest kick I can at the side of Sabazios's head. He moves with it and then looks back at me. His eyes are dead. He refocuses on Richard, landing a blow as hard as I've ever seen square in Richard's chest. I hear bones crack. Richard doesn't even fly backward or make a sound, he just falls into a heap.

Sabazios moves out from under him, stands, and straightens his shirt cuffs. "There's nothing you can do," he says to me. "You're not going to make it out of here alive."

I shake my head. I can't get enough spit to get words out.

There's motion behind him. It's just a small thing, but it catches my eye. Richard is alive and awake.

He's moving his hands, trying to tell me something. He's waving me back. I think he wants me to draw Sabazios away from the desk.

I step back toward the door. "I'm leaving," I tell him. "I don't die here."

"Yes. You do," he says softly.

Richard's still moving. I step farther back toward the door and Sabazios follows me, keeping the same distance. "You aren't going to get away with this." I regret it as soon as I say it. Movie lines.

Sabazios chuckles. "Of course not."

There's a noise behind him, but he doesn't turn because he's so fixated on me. Richard is at the desk. I can tell that he's in a world of hurt, because he can barely hold his hand up, but he's found something behind the desk.

And then the music floods in.

He's turned off the shield that blocks the Jungle. It knocks me for a loop, like somebody turned the stereo volume up to ten while I was sound asleep next to the speakers, but I get control of it quickly and dive in. Richard. Jason, the guard outside. Sabazios is different. He's a single filament, like Sybil. Gentry, and even though I suspected, having it confirmed makes me more afraid.

I hear some other quiet music nearby—other guards and personnel. I search for the sustained notes that I think are probably the frozen witnesses. I hear them, but I can't tell where they are. I go to Richard, dive in.

Richard's music is familiar, filled with Corina. His mind is her final gift, rewritten and molded for me. I know where the witnesses are.

And before I leave, I ask him for one last favor.

Sabazios seems oblivious to what's happened, doesn't seem to know about the Syllogos. He just nods slowly. "I'm sorry to have to do this, Alex."

"You're not sorry. You're not even a man. You're an alien, a Gentry. *You're* the one bringing the Locusts. *You* had my parents killed."

He studies me for a moment, then shrugs. "So you understand why you can't live."

Sabazios steps toward me.

"But you *created* us." I step back a little farther as he approaches. "Why destroy us?"

"We're not destroying you, we're helping you fulfill your purpose. We didn't create you so you could be an equal participant in our universe, we created you because we knew you would evolve into a sustainable source of nutrition for our offspring, the same as is true for every planet we seeded." He's still walking toward me, and I continue to angle away from him, aware of the door, aware of Richard, waiting for the right moment.

"We aren't sheep." I take another step back, toward the door.

"No, not sheep." He smiles. "You're better than sheep—you can farm your own food."

And then I'm parallel to the door, bare feet away.

I close my eyes and dive for the guard, Jason. I write myself into him. I'm now the most important thing in his life and he kicks down the door.

Sabazios is already on me when the door splinters. He looks up at the noise, which gives me time to duck under him and jab him hard in the nuts, which, it turns out, are just as sensitive on aliens as they are on people.

The guard, Jason, takes Sabazios down from above me. His advantage is over quickly, though. Sabazios is too strong.

"Go," Richard calls from the desk. "I'll lock down the room so you can get out."

I shake my head.

He shakes his head at me, which I can tell hurts him. "Don't argue. Go!"

I glance at the guard and Sabazios. Sabazios has him down. The guard is struggling, but he's losing steam.

I close my eyes.

A single sheet of music tears, then turns to dust. Jason, the guard who I rewrote to save my own life, has died.

Another one dead because of me.

I shake it off—now's not the time. I riffle through the papers searching for Sabazios.

I can't read his music. It's written so completely differently from any I've ever seen. For a terrible moment, I'm sure I've lost and that I'm going to die here on the floor of the office along with Richard, but then I hear him.

Like Sybil, Sabazios has a thin filament that runs back to an enormous rope of consciousness. Different, though, slightly smaller than hers, a Rubik's Cube of sounds and colors plucked by a hundred fingers on a dozen instruments out of tune.

I dive in blind.

The noise from Sabazios changes, grows louder, makes it hard to think.

Then there are hands on my body. Something snaking tight around my neck.

If I don't do something right now, I'm going to die, strangled by Sabazios while I watch it happen from underneath.

I'm starting to panic, beginning to die.

His unreadable sheet is still with me; I can see what's on it bubbling, changing, rearranging into ever more complicated combinations, a language all its own far from anything I could ever understand. I can't understand. I can't rewrite.

"Erase it, dead boy!" Her voice comes in slow and quiet, a barely audible shout across the crashing noise inside me.

CORINA!

But then she's gone.

My mind is clouding over. I can feel the fight leaving my body, but I focus everything I have on one idea.

Erase. Don't add to the music, don't change it, fade it. Add doubt. Add uncertainty and fear, weaken the notes, weaken them until they disappear.

His sheet. The single sustained note that connects to the massive rope. The sheet is simple, but written dark. I vision his current place on the staff, connect to it, make it a swath of emptiness, a line of nothing that separates his present from his future.

The notes resist, but his music isn't as strong as I am. It begins to fade. I spread the emptiness.

His filament empties, turns blank, silent.

His grip around my throat eases and my body begins to breathe.

I rise up.

Sabazios's body is on top of me when I surface. He's heavy, and it takes all I have to push him off of me. He's out cold, but not dead.

I sit up to look around.

"How did you do that?" Richard is propped up on an elbow near the desk. He looks bad. His music is fading and jangled. He's not going to live. I want to help him, but I don't know how and the helplessness makes it hard to even look at him.

"Erased his music." I stand up and go to the desk to look for a weapon. Before I can go to Richard I've got to deal with Sabazios.

Richard tries to say something, but he coughs instead, then moans. He tries again: "I don't understand."

There are scissors in the top drawer. I grab them. "The Gentry are here to destroy us. They made the Locusts."

Richard says something, but I don't hear it because it's swallowed in more coughs. I roll Sabazios's body onto his back and straddle him, bringing the scissors above my head. "Don't," Richard manages.

"He killed Corina, Jordan, my family. Sal and Erica." But even as I'm saying it, I can't make myself hate him like I need to if I'm going to cut his throat. The moments before Jordan's death play out in my mind. She didn't fight. She prayed, accepted, forgave.

I don't think I can kill him like this.

More than anything, I want to want to kill him, but I don't think I can.

"Paul and the rest . . ." Richard's laboring hard to talk. "Across Long Hall, other side, down beneath." More coughing, and instead of being there next to him, I'm still holding scissors over Sabazios. I don't think I can feel worse. "Think stairs and they'll appear."

I turn to look at him. He's collapsed back onto the floor. There's only small noise from him now, a fading sustain that will disappear in moments.

Then Sabazios tenses beneath me. His eyes flash open, and for an infinite instant, we're suspended. He opens his mouth. His hand comes up from the floor more quickly than I imagined possible.

But not faster than I can bring the scissors down into his throat.

Blood. Pumping blood in huge fountainous spurts. It coats

my face, my shirt, my hands, but I don't let go of the scissors. I keep them in his throat.

He swats at me, nearly knocking me free, but it's nothing like the blows I've seen him land before. He bucks, but it's weak. He hits again, but it has nothing behind it. His hand slides down my arm.

His single harmonic fades to soundlessness.

There's nothing left for me to do in here. I stand up, shaking, dizzy, and walk slowly to Richard, still holding the scissors.

He's not breathing. His sheet is missing from my drawer. I kneel next to him, unwrap his fingers from around his screen. It's locked, but I know his code. The camera is still on, still recording. I rewind it to where it begins, a few seconds after I asked him for the favor.

The video is shaky—won't ever work for solid projection—but the sound is clear.

It's all there.

"Thank you, Richard," I whisper when I stand up. "I'm sorry."

The Long Hall is empty. I look at the wall across from me and imagine stairs.

A single panel slides back to reveal a staircase that goes down into darkness. I take it on faith that I'll find my way in the dark, and head down, two stairs at a time. By the time I get to the bottom, I can't see a thing. I feel along the walls for a switch. There's a button at switch height. I press it.

A door slides open and there's a flicker of fluorescents overhead. I'm in a huge room. It seems to go on forever under the compound.

It's lined with body-shaped boxes. Coffins.

There are dozens of them. Looking at them all slows me to a stop. My hand goes to my waistband, where I re-tucked Sybil's gift when I changed into these clothes. I don't know what it does, but I'm sure that if I use it, all the people in these boxes will die.

Paul, Calvin, Damon, Cassandra. All of them.

I stand there for what feels like forever, frozen, confused.

I step over to the closest one. There's no window or anything, but I can hear who's inside. I place a hand on it and wish for it to open, but nothing happens. I examine it more closely.

There's Live-Tech leather under the metal shell. I look for a seam and find one.

I run the scissors along it and the Live-Tech turns gray. When I finish cutting the seam, the lid lifts slightly.

Cassandra's music erupts as I open the lid. She's desperate and afraid—she thinks she's drowning or dying.

I pull the lid up. There's a Live-Tech mask of some sort over her face. I cut the edge seam on that, too. It grays and falls away.

"Holy hell," she says when I get her face clear. "What the—"

"You've been frozen." I free both of her arms. "I'm getting us out of here."

She grunts as she peels back more of the material around her, sits up. "Sabazios?"

"I think I killed him."

She looks at me, takes a breath, nods, then looks at the other boxes. "Jesus."

I turn. There are twenty-seven of them, not including the one that held Cassandra. Twenty-seven. Twenty-seven kids like us.

I look back at Cassandra, who's now on her feet. I'm used to her looking like nothing's ever the matter, but that's not what I see now. She's scared. She's eyeing the coffins like I am. Then she turns to me. "What are we doing?"

I don't say anything, don't move. I close my eyes. Dive.

Corina?!

But she's not there anymore. I can sense the kids in the coffins, though, music like insects or mice, barely audible, but alive.

And then I know.

You've already done it.

"We save as many as we can." I open my eyes.

"How the hell are we gonna do that?" She stops. "You've been planning for this. That's why we got the Jeep, isn't it?" But she's not really arguing with me.

I walk the line of coffins, listening for a particular one and when I find it, I slice the Live-Tech seam and listen as the lid lifts and his music swells.

Paul watches me while I rescue him, pinned in the machine with the Live-Tech over his mouth and nose. I cut it off, pull the material from his face so he can breathe. When he breathes, his relief is deafening.

"Alex?" he says when he sits up. "What are you doing here?" And then: "Where are we? What the hell is wrong with me? You hit me—you knocked me cold. You're covered in blood!"

"Sorry, man—I didn't have a choice." I try and look apologetic, but right now I'm more worried about time than feelings. "You've been frozen."

Paul's full of questions, but I don't have time to answer them—"When we get out of here," I keep telling him.

I turn to give the scissors to Cassandra to start on another coffin, but then I hear them. People are coming. More than one. Lots. I look to Cassandra. "Company."

She looks at the row of coffins, shakes her head. "Jesus, now what?"

I look at Paul, at the other coffins, but there's no answers here.

I already know what to do. I've already done it. Corina told me, made me take the gift. I reach for the package, tearing it open. It's not a Live-Tech patch—more like regular technology, a flat piece of flexible plastic with two metal tines that fold out to become a household plug. There's a little slip of paper with it. I unfold it, read it.

It's in my handwriting. *This is what you did. Plug it in.*

I don't know what the little machine is going to do, but I suspect it won't end well for anybody in the compound if I use it.

The people are getting closer. I look back at the rows of coffins filled with frozen kids.

I want them to live. I want them all to live, but that's not what's going to happen. That's not what I'm going to have done.

Sorry . . . It's nothing more than a word, but it's all I have.

"You're going to use it?" Cassandra asks.

I hold it up to show her, start to say what it is, but I don't have any idea. *Doohickey.* The word floats up, reminds me of

Corina. "A doohickey. I need to plug it in." I scan the room for an outlet.

"There!" Cassandra points to one. "What's it going to do?"

"No idea," I tell her as I plug it in. "But we gotta go."

Paul looks around. "What the heck are you all doing? What about the others? If one of these was me, then one of them's Calvin—one of them's Marcus. Sal, too . . ." He gestures behind him. "Even Damon doesn't deserve this."

Cassandra grabs him by the shirt and tugs him toward the stairs. "We've got to go. You're gonna be special—the boy who lived."

"Who're you?" he asks.

"Later," I remind him, already easing toward the door. We don't have much more time.

He waves me off. "What about the others? The ones who aren't in here?"

I think I hear it, but I can't be sure. "We've got to leave *now*!" I growl it, grab Paul's shirt, and start moving.

We run. Up the stairs, out into the hall, where we run right into two guards.

"Dive!" Cassandra yells as they run toward us.

I do. They're easy to find, but only one is easy to shift. He's not into the idea of hurting us. I rewrite him fast, erasing and changing more than I should.

He pulls his gun, levels it at his partner, and shoots him dead. The noise is deafening in the narrow hallway, and the smoke from the gun makes the world hazy.

The psychic wallpaper shifts, is plastered with the dead man's final sight—us watching him die.

"Run!" the guard yells to us. "I've got your back."

We run. More guards find us on the driveway, but they aren't expecting to face armed resistance. Our friend shoots at them and they scatter.

"The gate!" Cassandra yells to me. It's closed and we're approaching fast, but it starts to open before I dive.

"See you soon!" Nick calls from the guard shack at the gate. He's still overwritten from when we came.

None of us bother to say thanks.

We're nearly across the street to the Cherokee when the air is sucked from around us, an enormous ear-shattering thud, pressure, then wind that throws us to the ground.

Cassandra and Paul bring themselves up to their knees at the same time I do. The ringing in my ears drowns out the guitars, but I can still hear Paul when he says:

"Oh shit."

I turn to look. The compound is an inferno.

"What did you do?" Paul whispers.

That little plug . . . I shake my head. "I . . ." I murdered them.

He stands up, turns to the compound.

I grab him. "We have to run, man—there's nothing we can do."

He shakes me off, starts walking. "They're all gonna die."

Cassandra grabs at his shirt. "They're already dead, man. We all died the day we got those letters."

"Not all of us," Paul says, still looking at the fire.

"All of us," she tells him. "Some of us just not yet."

He lets out his breath. I close my eyes, dive, fill in some faded spots on his sheet.

He turns away from the fire, smiles a little bit. "Where's the car?"

We're back in the Cherokee heading east on the highway through the mountains before anybody speaks again.

"So, now that we're away, can y'all tell me what's going on?" Paul asks.

I don't know how to answer him. My mind is crowded with music and remembrances. My family. Corina. Jordan, Richard, and the rest.

Corina. I dip down deep to listen for her. There's no trace now. If she's still in the Silly Juice, I can't find her. *CORINA!* Nothing. She saved my life.

But I heard her, after she died, underneath.

She saved me with Sabazios.

She's still *some*where. Somewhere I can find her.

"Alex?" Paul tries again.

I look at Cassandra but she's focused on the road.

I muster up the strength to speak, tell him as best I can the things he didn't know. Cassandra adds pieces, too, and between the two of us, we make sure he knows everything.

When we're done, he thinks for a moment. "You're sure?" he says.

I pull out Richard's phone, play him the video. "Yeah, man," I tell him. "I'm sure."

He doesn't respond. I can sense him in the backseat and see his reflection in the side-view mirror. When he does talk again, it's only to ask another question.

"Hey."

"Yeah?"

"So . . . it's like . . . over now?"

I look at Cassandra. She looks at me. "You sure you killed Sabazios?" she asks.

"I'm pretty sure."

"What does your Voice say?"

I shake my head, look out the window. When I can talk, I just say, "She's gone."

"Gone? Since when?"

"Since they killed her." I'm crying now, but I don't even care.

Paul puts his hand on my shoulder from the backseat, squeezes, waits.

When I can, I tell them. "It disappeared when they killed Corina." Then: "Corina was my Voice."

Epilogue

THE EXPLOSION AT SABAZIOS'S COMPOUND IS BIG NEWS. THE FIRE IS SO intense that they haven't even begun to assess the number of dead, but there are at least twelve household employees unaccounted for.

There's no mention of children.

Sabazios hasn't been seen or heard from since. He was known to be at the compound earlier in the day, so speculation is that he's dead.

It won't be speculation for long.

We're stopped at a Holiday Inn Express in Salem, Oregon. The clerk has generously offered to let us use the computer and his personal pod connector.

He also fired up the waffle maker just for us.

Paul and Cassandra are eating—they promise to bring me a waffle before finishing them all. I'm back in my email.

Sarah Campbell replied to my last one, just a short note asking me to tell her a little more about what I thought was happening.

She asked for it.

> Sarah,
>
> I wasn't lying about any of it and I can prove it now. I was at Sabazios's compound when it

> exploded and the video I attached to this email is of Sabazios confessing everything. He set up Jordan Castle. He had my parents killed. He controls the Locusts and if we don't get all the Live-Tech away from people, the Locusts will kill us all.
>
> I'll tell you more when I get to LA.
>
> Alex

When I've attached the file, I send the email. I wait, watching the screen to make sure no new email from the future shows up.

None does, which is the best sign yet that we've won.

I open a message window and dial a number from memory, but I have to try a few times because my fingers keep hitting the wrong buttons. When I told the others I'd do this back before we left the trailer, I thought it was a fantasy, but it's not.

It's real.

She answers on the third ring.

"Hello?" she asks.

"Hi, Auntie," I say. "I'm coming home."

Acknowledgments

SO, THERE ARE A TON OF PEOPLE WHO HELPED MAKE THIS THING POSSIBLE.

First and foremost are my wife, Ariadne Shaffer, and my daughter, Kizziah Singer. Not only did they offer love and support, they also endured hours-long car trips to far-flung regions of California while listening to endless lectures on tape about theoretical physics as I was working out details for the story. Not only that, but Ariadne has always been the first to read my drafts, and that's no fun at all.

Deep gratitude for my agent, Jason Anthony, at MMQ Lit. He pulled my query out of the slush pile and then spent the next six months of his life guiding me as I polished a very rough diamond into one that shined.

The same gratitude for my editor at G. P. Putnam's Sons, Arianne Lewin. She, too, saw something in my manuscript that others didn't see, and helped me make it even greater. I am forever indebted to both of them.

Also at Penguin, thank you to Amalia Frick for being so helpful, to Charis Tsevis for the brilliant cover art, to Maggie Edkins for the cover design, to Robert Farren for his copy-editing, and to the other readers, authenticity and otherwise, whose names I never learned, but whose feedback and ideas made the story better and stronger.

Further, deep appreciation to the people who read the

manuscript at various stages and had the time and willingness to offer their thoughts, encouragement, and feedback as to why it wasn't ready yet. Specifically, thanks to Ariel Pineda-Luna, Teryn Henderson, Mariana Lui, and Lacey Pizzato.

A special thank-you to my mother, Thalia Syracopoulos, for her endless belief through multiple less-than-stellar manuscripts that eventually people would see my amazing talent as clearly as she did.

And another special and especially sad thank-you to my stepfather, Dr. J. Michael Gallagher, who advised me through the psychology and pathology of early sections of this story but did not live to see it come to fruition.

To my father, Jack Singer, my stepmother, Tia Higano, my sisters, Anna and Emily—thank you for your encouragement.

To my former teachers, especially Tom Williams, Donna Dunning, Rick Nagel, and John Livingstone, and Mr. H.—half of my belief in myself I borrowed from you.

To the kind people at Stories of Echo Park and Woodcat—thank you for letting me sit for hours while I wrote this thing.

Finally, I would like to thank all of my students, both current and former, who have inspired me over the years and without whom I would likely never have set pen to paper.

If I screwed up and didn't mention you or your absolutely essential contribution to making all this happen, then email me and let me know. I am prophylactically sorry and I promise to handwrite you in on every copy I see.